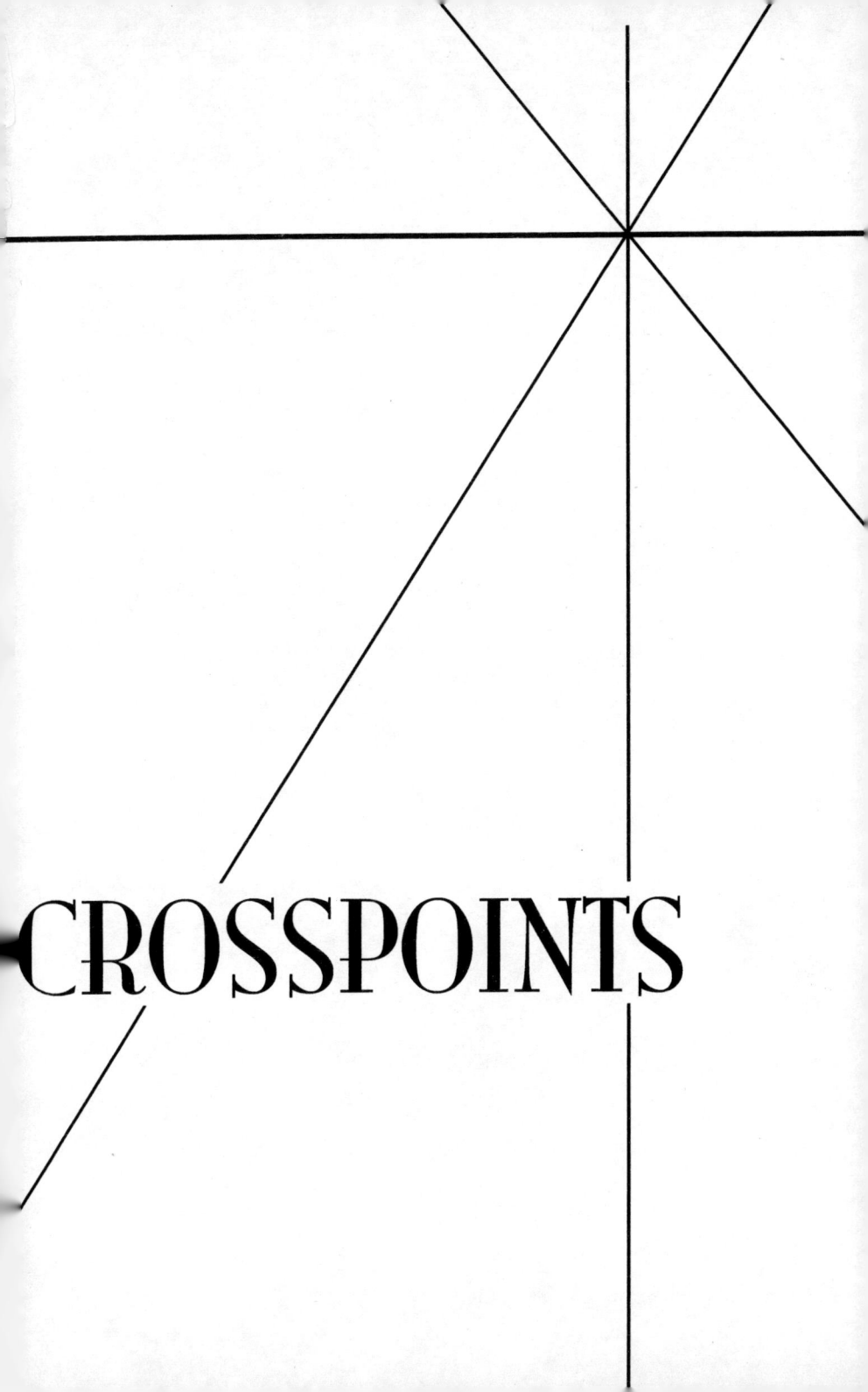

CROSSPOINTS

CROSSPOINTS

A NOVEL OF CHOICE

Alexandra York

PROMETHENA
PRESS
NEW YORK

PROMETHENA PRESS

— Bringing fire to the spirit through art —

Copyright © 2004 Alexandra York
WWW.ALEXANDRAYORK.COM

Library of Congress Number: 2003096825
ISBN :   Hardcover   1-4134-1896-1
                  Softcover   1-4134-1895-3

All rights reserved. No part of this book may be reproduced or transmitted in any form or by any means, electronic or mechanical, including photocopying, recording, or by any information storage and retrieval system, without permission in writing from the copyright owner.

This is a work of fiction. Names, characters, places and incidents either are the product of the author's imagination or are used fictitiously, and any resemblance to any actual persons, living or dead, events, or locales is entirely coincidental.

This book was printed in the United States of America.

Cover Artwork: Icara, Michael Wilkinson
                 Burned-Out Cube, James Samuels
Author Photo: Barrett Randell
Cover Design: Lisa Modica
Interior Design: Jennifer Foulk

PROMETHENA
300 East 56th Street
15th Floor - Suite M
New York, N.Y. 10022

*To Joe Bast
with warm regards for
a fellow traveler on the
road of ideas*

This novel is dedicated to
my self-created soulmates,
known and beloved
or
unknown and respected

*Alexandra York
December, 2012*

ONE

IT WAS THE STRAIGHT EDGE that had caught her eye, a sign of man's purposeful hand. Then, breaking off a large piece of sediment with her chisel, she noticed the glint of green, which meant that whatever lay buried there was made of bronze. And bronze could mean— She concentrated on keeping her hands steady while chipping away at natural faults in the rock-like encrustations, but the profusion of air bubbles rising nearly a hundred feet to the surface of the sea and the sound of her own rapid breathing in her ears told her that she was extremely tense. "Go slowly!" Just one wrong blow and she might sever an arm, or a head, or some other precious part of the trapped form she was trying to release from its watery grave. She forced herself to breathe more shallowly as the object began to take shape in her hands; she was using too much air.

A long gray creature flashed through the water behind her, but she was so intent on her find that she failed to notice it.

The piece she was working on came loose. It looked like a small box. As she rubbed sediment away from its surface, she recognized the place where a turntable had broken off— a revolving base, which over two thousand years ago had afforded an unobstructed view of a figure that had stood at its center. Then her hopes might be realized! The figure must be here, too!

Suddenly, out of the corner of one eye, she noticed a

slash of darkness, like a swiftly passing shadow. Placing the bronze slab into a basket that would carry it to the surface, and moving with great caution, she looked around.

A portion of the underwater suction pipe lay curled around her feet like a giant, sleeping eel. Today's collection of jars, amphoras and other ancient household supplies swayed with the current in several more baskets ringing the perimeter of the entire dig, all waiting to be lifted up to the boat for examination.

There it was again. And again! She heard a catch in her regulator, and for one panic-stricken moment thought it had malfunctioned. But then she realized that what she'd heard was only the sound of her own choked breath. There were more than one: the two streaks of gray were too close together to have been the same intruder passing and then returning again.

Sharks. What had brought them here? She had been diving unhindered for two months, and all fishing boats had been forbidden from the area.

She looked around for Dimitrios, but he was out of sight. Turning back to the brown hulk where she had been working, she hammered forcefully, using a larger chisel. She *had* to free the centerpiece, the figure itself. It had to be embedded here somewhere.

She was angry now. She had to have it. The oil lamps, the impressive amount of pottery, the large copper ingots and the smaller cobalt-blue glass ingots, even the bronze crest of a helmet she had unearthed only yesterday were solid finds, but this figure—this god—was her reason for the search. Her real reason for *any* search. She was seldom rewarded with an intact piece. This was bronze. It was small. It might be whole. She had to have it. Now!

Momentarily she broke through and could see it. Only the curve of a shoulder, but enough to indicate its twelve- to fifteen-inch size and its disposition in the surrounding mass. "Hurry!" Fitting the smaller chisel into a thin fissure beyond its outer measurements, she tapped it gently but decisively to release her treasure from its coral tomb. "*Don't hurry!*"

The figure fell into her hands at the same instant one of the hanging baskets slammed into her side, torpedoed by the long shadow of a shark now orbiting the dig with increasing speed.

She looked again for Dimitrios and fought against panic when she didn't see him. It was her own fault, her own damned impulsiveness. Seeing an abnormal shape sticking out from a barnacle-encrusted reef, she had been drawn away from him without even realizing it. Now, clutching her prize under one arm and gasping for air, she pressed her back into the jagged coral and held the hammer in front of her body to jab at the fish if it decided to attack. Every open water diver knows his one chance with sharks is that, although unpredictable, they are cowardly. If bumped sharply, they might give up or at least retreat for a few minutes before making another pass.

How is it possible to feel sweat inside an already saturated wetsuit? She must stop breathing so rapidly, she must, because even if she eluded her would-be killer, she wouldn't have enough air for her two decompression stops before surfacing.

Suddenly, another shadow flashed by. And then another. Three—

Dimitrios swam out from behind the rock where he had taken refuge from the sharks and squinted intently through his mask to detect any signs of her whereabouts. He couldn't stay hidden any longer. He had counted five of them. Too many. Visibility wasn't bad, but it wasn't great either. The rapid movement of the fish had stirred up the bottom, and sand swirled slowly through the water like a gently rising mist, a sensuous sight that at any other time would have captured his delight. Where *was* she? Only moments ago they had been swimming closely together, working closely together, being close . . . Fear for her safety bolted through him for the fifth time. She should never have left his side without signaling! No, he couldn't wait any longer; he'd have to search for her. If she were in danger, she would never be able to fend them off alone. He checked his pressure gauge. Approaching zero. Too close. Switching from his normal regulator to the one on the small reserve tank that he wore carrying emergency air for both of them, he breathed easier, knowing he would have at least enough air for a fight. If it were short— But even though she was smaller and consumed less air than he, her tank had to be low by now, especially if the sharks had found her and she was breathing fast. *Where are you?*

She stared in disbelief around her, pressing her body deeper into the side of the coral bed. Miraculously, she was alone.
    The sharks had abruptly vanished, even the one in the circling attack pattern. She felt her heart pounding wildly as suppressed fear ripped free and charged through her body. Her eyes stung with tears. "Think!" she ordered herself. "Go slowly." If there were three sharks in the area, there would likely be more; something unusual must be going on to draw that many at once. Her chances of attracting no others were probably slim, and the already interested one might well return. If she remained below and was attacked directly, she would benefit from the leverage and partial protection of the coral shelf at her back. But if she stayed down, she would certainly deplete the last of her air supply; she and Dimitrios were already nearing the end of their dive time when she had first spotted the bronze. Without air, she would be forced to free ascend straight to the surface without decompression stops, risking an air embolism or a potentially fatal case of the bends. Conversely, if she headed to her first decompression depth now, she would leave herself exposed to attack on all sides without much

chance for self defense; plus, she would then have to dangle like a hunk of bait on the anchor line fifteen feet beneath the surface for an additional five-minute safety stop. Which?

"Go!" If she were threatened near the surface, the crew might see it and be able to help. "Keep breathing."

Fumbling with her buoyancy compensator hose, she realized she was too shaken to push the button that would pull air from her tank into the b.c. and assist her ascent; besides, she couldn't spare even a small amount of her precious and rapidly dwindling air supply. She dropped her weights instead, but found she needed to kick her way upward anyway because of the heaviness of the bronze figure under her arm; it never occurred to her to leave it behind. Swimming upright, and turning in three-hundred-sixty-degree rotations, she rose slowly from the ocean floor, probing the depths intently for returning danger, sucking urgently on her regulator while telling herself at the same time to breathe shallowly. Her decompression stop at fifty feet seemed like an eternity. No sharks. She resumed her ascent. At last, reaching her safety stop destination, she hung on the anchor line limp and exhausted—knowing she was still vulnerable—to wait out her decompression time. If she had enough air.

She could see the bottom of the dive boat above her, but she could hear nothing. Had anyone aboard seen the sharks? And could they see her bubbles now and know that she was on her way up? She glanced at her pressure gauge. It hovered near zero. When the little air that remained in her tank ran out, she would have to surface. She reminded herself that fifteen feet wouldn't cause any trouble, *if* her decompression time were sufficient, and ... she looked down into the dark green depth beneath her, praying she wouldn't be followed. Suddenly she remembered Dimitrios. Oh god! Where *was* he?

Something solid brushed against her legs, sending waves of fear rolling through her body. Then she felt a strong arm enclosing her waist and her mouthpiece being gently removed and replaced by another. It was only when she felt the rush of air that she realized how hard her lungs had been tugging at her own regulator. She began to laugh shakily inside, her mask filling with tears, but her fingers relaxed their cramped grip on the line as she collapsed back in relief, able to rest at last within the circle of her rescuer's arm. The danger wasn't over, but she was no longer alone. She couldn't see his face, but she knew it was Dimitrios. He must have encountered the sharks, too, and followed her to the surface. She recognized the small mouthpiece as being from the reserve pack and passed it back to him. Only during her training, and then with the hope that they would never be in such dire circumstance to need it, had they shared a regulator before. Most dive masters nowadays don't even teach the procedure because of the improved technology of equipment, but ever conservative Dimitrios had insisted she learn it. Silently thanking him for that, she now let his calm strength begin to permeate her, and although she continued an alert survey of the water below, she soon fell into the reassuring rhythm of their buddy breathing as they exchanged the regulator back and forth for the short remainder of their safety stop. Dear Dimitrios.

When she handed up her exquisite find and they finally climbed aboard, she realized that the other members of their crew were shouting—shouting obscenities. Then she saw the object of their anger: a luxurious yacht, long, sleek and white, encircled by a dozen frenzied sharks as a woman on its deck heaved chunks of meat into the water, while two men fired rifles at the fish. Outraged, she started to shout at them too; actually, for one blazing instant of fury, felt like shooting them as they were shooting the sharks, but found that her desire to see the bronze figure she had risked her life for was greater.

She saw that Dumas, a visiting colleague from Crete,

had already broken away the remaining chunks of sediment and was treating the figure with chemicals to remove the rest. Dimitrios saluted her treasure with a smile and a thumbs up while he peeled off his wetsuit, then he moved immediately forward to the bow of the boat, calling angrily with a bullhorn for the yacht to come alongside.

Quickly removing her diving gear, she fell to her knees beside Dumas. He was as jubilant over her find as she was, and as they worked together, a magnificent male figure began to emerge. It was an athlete. Even the dark brown encrustations from the sea could not entirely mask the powerful, sinewy muscles of the thighs. It was easy to ignore the commotion in the background as one of the trespassers transferred from his own vessel to the dive boat. She and Dumas worked in silence. They could see the head now, lifted proudly from its powerful torso and turned to evaluate some distance or opponent. Streaks of black and green marred the lines of its face and bits of the ocean's floor still clung to its body, but nothing could obscure the confidence of the stance or the squareness of the jaw. Its expression was untroubled, but intent with purpose—

A man's voice jolted her from her scrutiny. "Please let me offer my apologies. We didn't realize there was anyone diving these waters—"

"Really? You didn't notice even *one* of the six dive markers posting the area?" She threw her head back defiantly to confront her adversary . . . and stopped, shocked into silence.

Dimitrios approached to mollify her. The danger was past, and he had already said to the intruders everything that needed to be said. "Tara, my dear, they're Americans. This is Leon Skillman, a sculptor from New York. Mr. Skillman, Tara Niforous, my associate."

Tara remained on her knees, staring up at the lean, tanned face, into the intense green eyes, and then looked back at the ancient Greek athlete in her hands. As if they had been created by the same bold hand, their strong, handsome features seemed uncannily alike.

TWO

A LARGE, BRIGHT SPOTLIGHT of a moon beamed steadily down on the Gothards' yacht. The yacht looked as unreal as the moon, like a Hollywood movie set. One could almost imagine an unseen camera, obscured by the black curtain of sky, grinding away behind the moon-spotlight and filming the opening scene: the light getting-to-know-you dialogue of Blair and Perry Gothard and their guests. As with most theatre, several layers of action and character exchange were already in play.

Leon Skillman, oblivious of the moon but touched by its magic, slumped deep into his deck chaise, one leg dangling easily over its side and one hand twirling a champagne glass. Both of his eyes were on Tara, the only hint that his mind was not as relaxed as his body. To realize that this woman could have been hurt—or even killed—because of his and Perry's shark shoot was a sobering thought, if he could think soberly at all after so much champagne. He and his hosts always downed a good deal of the stuff, but growing boredom with their six-week cruise was upping even their usual daily intake. Leon had been bored to such an extent this afternoon that all he had wanted was a diversion of some sort, and shooting sharks seemed as good as any. Now his attention was riveted on Tara. He continued to stare at her, not hearing a word Blair was saying.

"Why is it, Dimitri, that you archaeologists hoard all of those jugs and vases instead of putting more of them on the market for us poor peasants to buy?" Knowing she looked anything but a peasant in her white silk tunic, Blair Gothard laughed at her little joke and poured more Veuve Clicquot into Dimitrios's glass.

Dimitrios forced a smile. He wasn't pleased about accepting a social invitation from people careless enough to spill blood in waters clearly marked for diving. He'd politely accepted their apology and thought that gesture on his part was more than generous. But Tara had agreed to come to their boat for a drink. And Dimitrios, to his discomfort, knew why. The stunned delight on her face when she first laid eyes on Leon Skillman had been only too evident. Was it possible she could forgive this man's idiocy and the danger it had caused her?

Hoping to hide the resentment he felt toward her whole party, Dimitrios accepted a refill from Blair. What could he do now but graciously endure one cocktail hour? He sipped the drink slowly. But he couldn't let this woman patronize him by allowing her to shorten his name. That was something he permitted no one, not even Tara. "Thank you," he nodded cordially to Blair, "but, if you don't mind, I prefer to be called by my formal name, even by family and friends. I've always felt a bit uncomfortable with the diminutive."

Blair wrinkled her nose prettily. "What a 'first' you are! We've been sailing the Greek islands on and off for years, and every 'Dimitrios' I ever met was called 'Dimitri.' And I don't recall ever having come across your last name—'Kokonas'—before."

"Neither have I!" Dimitrios finally managed to suppress his annoyance and laughed with the good nature so ordinarily characteristic of his personality. His deep, inner shyness—the thing that made him feel "a bit uncomfortable" with the shortened "Dimitri"—hid itself perfectly within the musical curl of his laughter.

Blair exchanged a quick, knowing glance with her husband.

Dimitrios gave a sidelong look at Tara—she was paying attention at last—and finally, he relaxed. Well, onward and upward, he thought, they'll be out of our lives soon. "It started with my great grandmother," he slipped into his normal conversational tone, "who was called 'Kokono,' which means beautiful. Somewhere along the line, it evolved into a family surname. This is not unusual in Greece. You see, we love to surround ourselves with romantic stories, even when they're ... true—"

Dimitrios interrupted himself abruptly. The fixed smiles on the faces of Blair Gothard and her husband had finally penetrated his brain. He was known as a charismatic speaker (a reputation gained not by conscious design but simply because he loved to share his knowledge), and fake attention was a phenomenon to which he was unaccustomed. Leon Skillman, of course, had never even feigned interest; he'd been staring at Tara all along. And Tara? She wasn't listening! She really *had* come to see this ... playboy!

"But enough of my meandering," Dimitrios said quickly. Quite enough, he thought. Get this evening over with. "You asked me a serious question. Pottery! Well, even though we don't find much of it still intact, pottery can be re-assembled, rather like a puzzle. So! If we can determine the date of the pottery, we can then determine the date of the other objects found around it—"

Blair interrupted him sweetly. "*Endoxie*! You've convinced me, *Dimitrios*. If we find *any* pottery while diving off this boat, it all goes to you." Her smile remained radiantly in place. Generations of breeding had instilled impeccable manners in Blair, as impeccable as her genes, but she was caught off-guard by the sincerity of Dimitrios's explanations. The stuffed shirt thought she really wanted to know! Except for his dark brown eyes, burning with keen intellect and passion for his work, this "Dimitrios" was, indeed, a bore. Even physically, he offered precious little of interest. Blair assessed his body from habit: mid-forties and very fit. He was tall for a Greek and without a moustache (both unusual traits), but his coloring was typical and unexciting, a monochromatic study in browns. No thrill. How very insulated from the rest of the world these two people appeared to be. Well, it had been her idea to invite them aboard, or was it Leon's? Anyway, she would, as usual, ride gracefully with the tide. She turned to Tara with bright curiosity laid like a mask over her features. "And how did you, an American who arises from the Aegean like a Greek goddess, get into this sequestered business?"

Tara responded warmly to the compliment, feeling more and more that her first impression of these people must have been wrong. Blair seemed so open and charming. "Oh, archaeology isn't really a 'sequestered' business in Greece. It's more like a national preoccupation. And as far as being a woman is concerned, fully fifty percent of archaeologists here are women . . ."

Leon's lips played around the edge of his glass, his fingers caressing its smooth surface in substitute for their growing desire to trace the smooth skin of *this* woman archaeologist. The desire to touch her, to sculpt her, was as unexpected as it was compelling. He hadn't felt a desire to sculpt like this since adolescence. And now, after all these years, he felt the desire as intensely as he remembered it from his youth. It had been in his *hands*, that desire to sculpt. He hadn't understood it then, and he didn't care about it now. But it had always been in his hands. When he was young, he never felt quite responsible for his work because it was as if his hands alone were the makers. When his third-grade teacher had called his mother to school and shown her "the breast," he had stood at grim attention to accept whatever fate awaited him. Why he had formed a single breast (complete with areola and nipple) out of his bubble gum, he had no idea. It hadn't been created from any conscious will; his hands had done it. His teacher's face had been stern and accusing. But, to his utter shock, his mother had burst out laughing. "What's the problem?" she had asked his teacher. "It looks like a nicely executed sculpture of a female breast to me." Leon had not dared laugh; he was as confused as his teacher. Later that night, when his mother came into his bedroom to kiss him goodnight, she had said, "If you wanted to sculpt instead of paint, all you had to do was tell me so." The next evening beside his dinner plate, he found clay and tools for sculpting. His father said only: "Your mother tells me you like to sculpt. Well, good for you! Go to it!" Then he added, with a wink to his wife, "But how about *two* breasts next time? It's not quite fair to leave a lady lopsided, do you think?" That was all. He had sculpted in one form or another from that day forward.

Leon's eyes narrowed for a second as he sensed a slight headache coursing from his temple to his brain. His grip tightened on the glass, and he kept his fingers still for the brief moment it took for the pain to pass through. Strange. It must be from the blast of rifles all afternoon. He rolled his head to loosen his neck muscles and resumed his scrutiny of Tara, not bothering to conceal his interest. *Did* she look like a goddess? No, she was slimmer, more tense. Not with tension, but with energy. More *alive*. Inside. In fact, it was Blair who wore the Grecian tunic. Tara was dressed in a simple summer dress and sandals. But it was Tara's draped body he found himself sculpting in his mind. The folds of her coarse cotton skirt seemed softer than the silk of Blair's. So did her eyes. Gray. Innocent. A child's eyes set in a woman's face. Blair had long, blonde hair spilling down over one shoulder, goddess-like. Tara's hair was black, cut impatiently short and swept entirely back from her face as if she'd just stepped out of a shower. Yet it was Tara who raised in his memory the proud yet yielding femininity he had, as a boy, so worshipped in Greek sculpture.

Uneasy with these thoughts, he pulled his chair toward Dimitrios, and asked a question to which he knew the answer. "Why was that Greek athlete figure you found nude? Aren't all figures of Greek athletes nude, for that matter?"

Tara answered before Dimitrios could speak. "Yes. Olympian games were played in the nude in order to celebrate physical beauty as well as excellence. Or maybe the old legend is true," she smiled in mock innocence, "that during a race in Athens, one runner's shorts slipped down, causing him to trip over them before he could cross the finish line, so the competitive Athenians put the nudity law into effect before another sunrise. Anyway," Tara paused while everyone laughed at her story, "it's more comfortable, don't you think?" Her eyes were no longer soft, but glinting with amusement as she rose to Leon's bait. Who was this man with the insolent stare? She didn't need to stare back, for her first image of him was etched permanently in her mind and she had been unsettlingly aware of his presence ever since. Aware of the firm line of his jaw, of the high plane of his cheek, of the broad span of his forehead, pulled tight as if to emphasize the clear green of his eyes—eyes the color of the sea one discovered only when plunging to the depths where her athlete had been found. Bronze and flesh forged together in her mind. For a moment's respite, she glanced up at the moon, wondering why the air suddenly seemed so still. The sky hung silent and expectant above her, as if holding its breath. But her attempts at distraction were futile. All she could really think of, insanely, was swimming in the green sea of Leon Skillman's eyes. It was unnerving how those eyes kept staring at hers. She sensed the thrilling undertone of a dare.

How intriguing. A challenge, Leon thought, watching the gray of Tara's eyes soften again, and deepen in color as she gazed into the night, smiling.

Perry Gothard reclined in his chair and smoothed silver-streaked hair back over his temples with the soft palms of his well-manicured hands. What a glorious charade this was, with Leon and Blair asking all the obvious questions and poor, single-minded Dimitrios and lovely, naïve Tara answering in all seriousness. *Merde*! Except for the relatively nondescript Dimitrios, they were one group of beautiful people tonight, he thought: Tara, so unaware of her own beauty, smoky and sleek in a way that complemented rather than competed with his wife, who was her usual vision of studied perfection. And Leon, his green eyes full of humor and his body bronzed by weeks in the sun. Could there possibly be a *menage a quatre* at the bottom of the champagne bottle this evening? Perry popped another cork into the sea. No. Not possible, because the girl takes herself too seriously. Such a bloody waste when a woman does that.

"So you followed your professor from the university to the museum, did you? Find a successful man today, and you'll not only find a woman behind him, but a successful woman at that. What's the attraction, anyway? Love, position or power?"

Tara slipped her arm affectionately through Dimitrios's. "I followed *this* man because he happens to be one of the world's foremost scholars in classical Greek civilization—you must understand that the two of us *live* in fifth century B.C.—because he's my best friend and because he looks after me like a 'mother hen' and . . . Why are you laughing?"

Blair turned helplessly to her husband, still laughing. It was obvious that Dimitrios regarded his protégé in far more than a parental fashion. But, judging by the sincerity of the young woman's answer, Tara seemed to be totally unaware of the depth of her employer's feelings for her.

Perry came to the rescue. "Come on," he said to Tara. "I'll show you our little home away from home."

He led her around the deck, marveling at the sea, the night air and the moon. Tara felt early signs of a northerly wind stirring and made a mental note that extra anchors would be needed by morning to hold the dive boat securely offshore where they were working, the crossroads of the ancient world near the Cycladic island where Aphrodite was born. The site was first discovered by sponge divers at the beginning of the twentieth century; but now, with advanced diving equipment, it was possible for the area to be scientifically explored for the first time—by her. She thought of the athlete she had rescued this afternoon, and it sent a soft shudder of excitement through her body.

When they went below and reached the living quarters, Perry flipped on a radio in the sitting room and went over to the bar. "How about a 'drink' drink?"

"No thanks, I'll stay with these lovely bubbles." Tara looked around the plush, spacious room, at furnishings more elegant than one would expect to find in an extravagant home. Strange, she thought, picking up a crudely made wooden penny whistle from a glass coffee table, to accent such a setting with an object like this.

Perry pulled a new bottle from the bar's refrigerator and, popping the cork out of a porthole into the water, refreshed her glass. "Whatever you say, my mermaid." He poured himself Belvedere on the rocks.

"We, Blair and I, collect primitive and folk art, you know."

He was gesturing toward the African tribal masks on the wall; like the penny whistle, they seemed eerily out of place with the rest of the glittering room.

"No, I didn't know." Tara wished she had never come below with her host. She had only wanted to break the spell of Leon Skillman's stare, she thought, absently turning the whistle over in her hand. "And what kind of sculpture does Leon make?" she asked.

Perry glanced out the porthole. The cork lay still on the water, floating silently on a moonbeam. Maybe he wasn't the right one to chase this skirt after all. But Leon had been attempting a silent flirtation with her all evening, and she seemed to show little interest. And she *had* come down here alone with him. "Oh, Leon does important things. You know, big pieces. Heroic stuff. Shall we dance?"

He encircled Tara's waist with one arm and began nuzzling her neck as he moved her across the room in time with the music. "But Blair and I, we're just plain folks. That's why we like to patronize the primitive. You know, the unintellectual, the underdeveloped—along with important contemporary artists, of course. And what else do *you* like? Besides your ancient treasures?"

Tara withdrew herself from his embrace and headed for the stairs. "I think I'd like to rejoin the others."

As they returned to the deck, Leon noticed Perry's arm around Tara. He also noticed that Tara looked annoyed. He could see it deep in her eyes, though she didn't show it on the surface. How interesting. Intense, but controlled. "Okay," he said. "Here's our expert. Let's see if she knows the answer to this one: What was the purpose of the first life-size statues ever created?"

Tara smiled at him and then, realizing she had carried the penny whistle up from below decks, said to Perry: "Oh! This is yours." She placed it in his hand to stop him from feeling her breast as he released her to sit down again beside Dimitrios. The Perry Gothards of the world and their unimaginative ploys were not worthy of reproach. She flashed another quick smile at Leon and felt the night catch its breath again. Waiting. She tossed her head, her sense of adventure thoroughly aroused. "What purpose? Well, for what purpose is any art? Bringing an artist's inner vision into external form? Communication of ideas? Affirmation of values? Celebration of the physical world through aesthetics, the pure redemptive powers of beauty?"

"No! Much more practical!" Leon laughed deeply. "They were created at 'Tell Asmar' in ancient Mesopotamia, and they were stand-ins for the person they belonged to at the holy temple, so that constant prayers could be sent to the gods while the real person went about his daily activities. Clever, no?" Leon laughed again at Tara's shocked expression and turned to Dimitrios. "Correct, yes?"

Dimitrios hid his surprise. "Yes, precisely correct, in fact," he said as casually as possible. "The workmanship of the 'Praying Statues' you speak of was unrefined, of course, but they were extraordinary works of art." He turned to Tara. "And *you* certainly know how often early sculpture was in the form of votive offerings or death cult figures, substituting the representative for the real . . ."

Now Tara stared, long and steady, back at Leon. The representative rather than the real? Her athlete-god in bronze over one existing in the flesh? Never! *If* one could find the *real*. Who *was* this fascinating man? A lock of sand-colored hair fell over Leon's forehead, giving him an almost boyish appearance, but the set of his mouth refuted even a hint of vulnerability. She dropped her eyes to study the bubbles in her champagne. How could a man with such magnetism and such obvious intelligence have been shooting sharks for entertainment? What was he doing here, vacationing with these bored predators of pleasure? She turned to Dimitrios, who was still dismayed at her vague answer. "The 'Praying Statues,' Dimitrios! Well, of course! You know, they've been ignored for some time. Why not do a piece on them in *L'Ancienne*?"

"Why not?" Satisfied, Dimitrios turned back to the others. On that nice note they would depart this awkward evening. "Tara is an editor of a quite erudite publication that has a small but very devoted following. It's called *L'Ancienne*." Taking Tara's hand, he drew her from the couch and bowed formally to his hosts. "And now, we shall bid you goodnight. We have only a few days left at this dig, so we must resume our diving early in the morning and," he smiled thinly, "if you will refrain from attracting large numbers of sharks, we'd be most appreciative."

As they left, Perry called after them. "Tara, if you find a

female athlete tomorrow, and she's underdeveloped, bring her to me. Don't forget we collect underdeveloped art."

He popped another cork into the ocean. "Good god, she's a serious one."

"And her shy boss is in love with her," said Blair, holding out her glass.

"And I'm in love with you," Leon smirked, granting himself a long, final glimpse of Tara as the dinghy skated away over a silver ribbon of water. He emptied the remains of his glass down the front of Blair's tunic before holding it out to Perry for more.

Blair shrieked from the cold liquid. "Oh, you perfect beast! Just for that, I'm going to sleep with Perry tonight. Or," she paused seductively, "I don't know. You've both been so funny this evening, maybe I'll sleep with both of you. That is," she paused again, "unless you two would rather have it just to yourselves the Greek way?"

Leon dribbled more champagne down her dress. Part of him noticed that the headache had not disappeared completely. He could feel it embedded behind his eyes in the form of a dull pressure. He ignored it. "Are you kidding? Not for us. Perry and I are red-blooded Americans. And we go for girls, but we've learned to share."

"I beg your pardon, friend," said Perry, "but *I* am *blue*-blood."

"Well, *I'm* not prejudiced," Blair teased. "But which one of *you* is going to topple the Greek goddess off her pedestal?"

Leon and Perry each pointed a finger at the other. "You try first!" Leon laughed. "She acts like an innocent little virgin . . . and *you* specialize in virgins."

"Nope. This one's a mental virgin—trust me—and you can talk a better seduction than I can. But I'll bet she's just a tad difficult, this one."

"A bet? How long do I get?" Leon kissed champagne from Blair's chest.

"Well, okay! Let's make it a real bet. Ordinarily I'd give you two days, but she's so bloody serious and talking takes so bloody long. So, I'll give you two weeks."

"But the professor said they're returning to Athens next Thursday. That gives me only one week."

Perry pondered the thought. "So? We planned all along to take you to Athens at some point. We'll just sail up when the dive ship 'Pandora' does—we're flagging here anyway—leave the boat and crew in Piraeus, stay at the Grand Bretagne in Athens for a week or so and then sail back to the States early." He raised a teasing eyebrow to Blair. "You'll have extra time for 22-carat gold shopping! The goddess won't fall in one week, Leon, even for you."

"We'll see. And what do I get—besides the goddess—*when* I succeed?"

Inspired, Perry picked up the penny whistle from the cocktail table. "*Here's* the prize! But if you *fail*, you'll have to buy us a lasagna dinner at Mama Rosa's when we get home."

All three doubled over in laughter. Leon snatched the whistle from Perry and blew into it. "You're on! But only because I really *want* this primitive little thing."

Blair slipped out of her gown. "Well just report back to us every day how you're progressing with *your* primitive little thing, Leon darling. Splendid! We needed a 'climax' to end this cruise, anyway. But now, there's a full moon. So let's have a swim."

"Are you crazy? There were sharks out there all afternoon!"

Blair was gone.

Both men laughed, stripped off their clothes and dove in after her.

THREE

DIMITRIOS FOLLOWED TARA as she swam away from him. Again! Pulling on one of her fins to get her attention, he signaled that they should surface immediately. Astonished, Tara checked her pressure gauge and questioned him with her frowning eyes; he didn't appear to be in trouble and there was no shortage of air. Why did he want to abort this precious dive? There were so few left! But Dimitrios pointed firmly to the surface and mock-slit his throat to indicate the finality of his order.

As they clambered aboard the dive boat, the crew expressed surprise as well. What was wrong?

Dimitrios gently calmed them—he'd suffered an attack of nausea, that was all—and asked Tara to accompany him to his cabin so they could discuss their final agenda while he rested. On their way, with a slightly patronizing air, he patted the shoulder of a young female intern. "Everything's fine," he assured her. She was one of his favorite apprentices and would, one day, make a fine archaeologist; but she had developed a bad case of hero worship over the summer. This had happened three or four times before in his career, a student or a co-worker who mistook her own feelings of admiration for his knowledge and abilities as a sign of budding love. At best, he viewed their emotions as charming infatuation. Not one of them knew him well enough to begin to actually *love* him. Ever considerate, Dimitrios had devised a method that not only accomplished his goal of restoring professionalism to the working relationship but also displayed sensitivity to their fragile psychological state. Singling them out for extra attention while stressing his position of authority usually allowed him to distance himself without appearing to reject them, helping to cure their malaise. Although the attention was pleasantly flattering, he had only once succumbed to the affections of a colleague (an Italian woman), but the affair had lasted less than a year; she, too, had fallen for his position, not for him.

And then, of course, there was Tara, who *did* know him as well as he knew himself but never noticed him at all as a man. Never. Closing the door of his room, he motioned for her to sit on the couch while he took his place at the desk. And now, even though it was Dimitrios the *man* who had been terrified over losing her to the sharks, it would be Dimitrios the employer who would scold her about her increasingly irresponsible behavior. How else? He didn't have the right to speak to her in any other way.

But she was concerned for his health. Her eyes expressed worry as she waited for him to speak.

"It's nothing," he began. "I'm not sick at all. That was merely a justification to the crew for a wasted afternoon. I aborted the dive because we *must* discuss your growing habit of wandering away from me underwater. After the near miss with the sharks, I should think you would have learned your lesson, but you've continued to do it to one degree or another every day since then. This morning, you did it *twice*, and just now again. Don't you realize how you put us both in physical jeopardy, not to mention the anxiety you cause me when I can't see you? How do you think I felt that day, searching for you in the middle of shark-infested waters? We both could have lost our lives."

Tara felt a pang of contrition shoot through her. As usual, he was being so very gentle even when she was so very wrong. Somehow she felt it would be easier to accept his criticisms if he were angry; his unending patience with her always made her feel twice as badly. After all, she owed him everything. How could she misuse all he had taught her? "I'm sorry," she said. "It's not that I've forgotten about the sharks. I mean, I've never been so scared in my life as I was that day. But it *was* a highly unusual circumstance, not likely to happen again, and ... Well, once I get down there, I keep thinking that if I discovered one intact figure, there might be others. Maybe there was a whole crate full being shipped somewhere! Maybe the crate split apart during the shipwreck and there are dozens of other statues buried down there. Ever since I found the first one, it seems I'm just drawn like a magnet to every odd shape I see. I know it's no excuse, but ... What if there *is* a whole crate of them scattered about down there?"

Dimitrios smiled broadly, shaking his head. He was ever helpless before her. How could he scold that optimism? That enthusiasm! Her gray eyes were wide open and sparkling with anticipation.

"You and your gods," he sighed.

※ ※ ※

" ... and then she told me about her name, which is really *Kantara*. You thought *Kokonas* was sweet? Well, *her* name is from an obsolete Greek word that refers to the weight used to balance a scale. So she goes on to talk about the tiny scales made of pure gold sometimes found in ancient tombs that symbolize the scales used to weigh men's souls. And *then* she goes on about how in the *Iliad*, Agamemnon weighs the souls of Achilles and Hector to see which will die first—"

"I don't want to hear any more," Perry Gothard groaned.

"You have to hear it. *I* had to. And then she goes on about how her Greek father, Kostas, gave her that name so *she* would live with a light conscience and a good soul."

Leon threw his wet, naked body down on the deck of the boat. "I'm not so sure that penny whistle is worth it. I'm having to drag up every tidbit I ever learned about ancient history. She can talk about it endlessly. In fact, it's *all* she talks about."

"So what about the seduction progress?" Blair asked. "Give us some juicy details of the *action*."

"Well, we went dancing under a grape arbor on the veranda of a little taverna. The music was sexy as hell, and she moves better than a belly dancer."

"*That* sounds sexy as hell. Could it be? The serious little archaeologist?"

"So, did it put her in the mood?"

"The mood for what? She starts telling me about a place called 'Archanes' on Crete where they found what *may* be a royal tomb that *might* show evidence of human sacrifice—"

"Hardly the subject for a belly dancer in a taverna."

"I told you we were dancing under a grape arbor, which, to Tara, only reminds her of an archaeological dig. And why, you might ask? Well, ignoramus, don't you know that Archanes is famous for growing grapes? And the grapes, my friends, are as juicy as it gets."

Leon laughed and flipped over on his stomach, relishing the sun as it covered his body with an invisible blanket of warmth. What he had just said was true. But it wasn't all. He and Tara had spent three evenings and part of one afternoon together, and he had reported each time to Blair and Perry according to the conditions of the bet. But there were other things. Like the unexpected pressure of her hand enclosed in his and the soft smells from her hair as she, also unexpectedly, let him move far closer than normal for Greek-style dancing. Or the eye contact they'd shared through their dive masks when Tara took him down with her to see her dig. To watch her handle her precious artifacts was to witness her performing an act of love, and he knew that she knew that he knew it. Definitely unexpected! Yes, he had kept Tara busy discussing her work because it let him seduce her with his own knowledge of history and the words that he knew were the currency of intimacy with her. But it was during all of the pauses and delicious silences that he scored the extra points with his eyes and body language that he knew would bring her to his bed.

Perry rubbed sunscreen all over his body and gazed at the smooth, bare buttocks of his wife to see if she needed any. "For a broad pushing the far side of forty, you have one juicy little ass, my love," he mused. Blair flexed her butt muscles to acknowledge the compliment, a compliment made possible by periodic liposuction procedures that, although suspected, went unacknowledged by all. A study in golds, her long blonde hair glistened wet from a swim, and her sun-burnished skin sparkled with little crystals of salt water evaporating in the warm, dry air. She had worn a bathing suit so seldomly this trip that her bikini lines blurred into the rest of her body, leaving only a narrow band that spread like a glow between her hips. Perry leaned over and softly and wetly sucked his way across the pale pattern left from her bikini bottom. In a moment, Blair turned over with a little moan to let her husband continue on her flat, toned stomach, naked but for the fine thread of a gold chain that wrapped her waist.

"Let's have some coke," Perry murmured. He slipped a hand under her back to help her sit up on the deck. "Want to do some lines with us?" he asked Leon.

"Nope. You know I can't do it with that mellow music Blair makes us play. I need hard music to do hard drugs."

Blair and Perry went to a cupboard and did a couple of quick, short lines. Then they went below.

Lazily, Leon turned onto his back and peered at the sun through interlaced fingers. Great day! Great life! Unlimited money, fame, sex, and drugs. He had it all. And what he didn't have, he could get. He pressed both hands lightly together into a tent to shade his eyes. The bet with his hosts had turned out to be the perfect excuse for his own designs on Tara since that first evening on the boat. His hands couldn't wait to touch her.

※ ※ ※

"Isn't he magnificent?" Tara looked up into the face of the life-size bronze figure and then at Leon.

"That he is," Leon agreed. "Have they ever decided whether he's Poseidon or Zeus? He could be hurling a trident or a thunderbolt. What do *you* think?" He searched her gray eyes. There was a purity of spirit about this woman that seemed almost childlike; she exposed her inner self so naturally, without guile or sophistication. Tara's age meant that she must be experienced; she had to be in her early thirties. Well, Perry had called her a *mental* virgin, so Leon was seducing her mind. But it was time-consuming. His body was getting impatient. Her eyes were shining with interest, but... Not tonight, he decided.

"I don't care who he is, I just love to look at him." Tara was smiling back at him. Now, maybe she could get him to talk about his own sculpture. He didn't seem to want to. "Perry said you make large, heroic sculptures. Heroic, like this?"

"Larger," Leon answered, evasively.

They walked out of the National Archaeological Museum into the evening heat. It never occurred to Tara to wonder why the Gothards had decided to accompany them back to Athens at the end of the week. Leon had come with them; that was all that mattered. Getting to know the details of the man seemed necessary but almost superfluous. It was as if she knew him completely, as a sum, from the first moment she saw him. All that a man *could* be. Intelligent and confidant... but sensitive. And yes... beautiful, too. Her athlete in the flesh. Could it be true?

"Enough art. How about a nightclub?" Leon suggested.

"Since this is my first trip to Athens, you can introduce me to what's hopping Greek-style instead of tourist-style." He hailed a taxi. "Besides," he moved closer to her in the cab, "I like to watch you dance."

At a little club on the outskirts of the city, the music was almost as loud as the hard rock music he loved, but its bittersweet melodies and open lyrics of love pulsed with a complex rhythm that went beyond stimulating his senses. Deep emotions were rising in him. A singer poured her feelings into the microphone, while a pianist and bouzouki player accompanied her and joined her vocally in close harmony from time to time. It was exciting in an unfamiliar and strangely sexy way. Leon and Tara were seated at a long table with other couples, drinking wine and nibbling from bowls of fruit.

"What are all the gardenias for?" Leon asked. Greek men were purchasing paper plates spilling over with blossoms, and the room was redolent with their perfume.

"You'll see if you buy some."

He signaled a waitress and paid for an order of flowers. "What's that phrase she keeps singing at the end of every verse? 'Saga' . . . what?"

The song ended, and amid clamorous applause, the men in the audience rushed to the stage and began joyfully tossing dozens of gardenias over the performers.

Leon stood, but instead of heading for the stage, turned to Tara and showered her with his flowers.

"*Sag a Pore,*" she said with a mixture of delight and teasing in her voice, as the gardenias fell about her like a fragrant spring snow. "It means 'I love you'."

FOUR

TARA SANK DOWN on the base of a half-cleaned, life-size male figure. Leaning back against the marble, she closed her eyes. "Roman bastards," she said. "What were they doing with a fifth-century bronze figure amid all the rest of the stuff?"

"Whatever are you saying, Tara?" Dimitrios countered excitedly. "Don't you see what this means for the expedition as a whole? We can now date with certainty everything in the find. We can learn so much! A pirate ship would have been spectacular enough, but *this* date and a *Roman* ship make it a major discovery! One the whole archaeological community will notice."

"I know. I'm glad. I guess I'm just tired."

It was nearly midnight. All of their co-workers had left the museum hours before, but Tara and Dimitrios had continued working until, only moments before, they had saluted each other triumphantly.

Just before their return to Athens, one of the divers had come up with such an odd lump of encrusted metal that it had befuddled the entire crew. Even after the museum's chemists had spent days removing centuries worth of sediment, the riddle had remained unsolved.

It had been Tara, only today, who had suggested that the lump resembled a pile of unevenly stacked coins. And once they stopped viewing the find as a single object, the mystery began to unfold. The rest of the staff had stayed long enough to separate the stack, which had been fused together by the chemical action of the sea, into ten individual pieces. Coins they were, but from when and where still had to be established.

Tara and Dimitrios, alone, had spent tedious hours trying to verify their origin, knowing that when they identified the country and date of issue, they would know precisely whose ancient cargo they had retrieved from the Aegean with such stunning success.

Now they knew that their find was truly significant. The coins were Roman. They were able to fix the date at 88 B.C. During the time in history when Rome had cast her authority like a taut net over the ancient world, there had been occasional uprisings by the Greeks against their conquerors, which incited Rome to punish the rebels by sending ships to plunder the troublesome areas. But the year 88 was the year that Athens had joined other, previously rebellious cities in a major revolt against their despised rulers. And in a scenario similar to one of the famous General Sulla's loot-laden vessels two years later, this Roman ship had apparently escaped from the Greeks, gone astray on the seas, met disaster and failed to return home with its booty.

"Why are you so tired? Have you been seeing him that regularly?" Dimitrios's voice carried a sharp, harsh edge Tara had never heard before.

She sat up in surprise. "How did you know?"

Dimitrios restacked the coins into a perfect pile. They looked like one entity again. "It's quite obvious, my dear. Women who think they're in love, always *are*. Obvious, that is." With one finger, he pushed the coins back into the uneven stack in which they had been found, as if no progress had been made at all.

"Dimitrios!" Smarting from his sarcasm, Tara stood and

began to put away the dozens of books they had strewn over the worktable. "How unlike you to comment on my personal life."

"Am I not part of your personal life? Aren't we friends?" He aligned the coins into a precise pile again. He hated himself for it, but he had to know how far this senseless infatuation had gone.

"Yes, of course. But, you know what I mean, that part of my personal life."

"Haven't I known all of the men in your life since you were twenty-two years old and came to study with me?"

"Dimitrios! For heaven's sake." Tara slammed a book down on the table. "You sound as if there have been dozens. You know perfectly well that I've been in love—or thought I was in love—only twice in ten years, and one of those relationships lasted two years!"

"And both men were beautiful. Just like the sculpture you love. Just like your *gods*." Dimitrios picked up Tara's athlete and balanced him precariously atop the pedestal of coins.

"I—" Tara resumed putting away the books to hide the tears that had sprung to her eyes. Dimitrios had hurt her for the first time since she'd known him; she'd never heard these cutting tones before. "I kept hoping that the inside would match."

"Tara." His voice was gentle again, which only hurt her more. He set the athlete back on the table and tapped its head with a finger. "Did it ever occur to you that you might be in love with the heroic ideal, without applying it to the real world, real men?"

Confused, she wouldn't look at him. "Dimitrios, please. You may instruct me in all things concerning gods made of marble and bronze, but please, not about those made of flesh."

He persisted. "Tara, what do you want in a man?"

She still didn't look at him, but she answered. "The same

things any woman wants, I suppose. Confidence. Purpose. An independent mind. Intellectual ambition. An adventurous spirit. A joy of living."

Dimitrios laughed his normal laugh again, of relaxed enjoyment. "My dear Tara. To begin with, most women do not seek those particular attributes in a man. Also, isn't it strange that you never once mention on your list of requirements his physical appearance?" Seeing the sudden lift of her shoulders, he went on with a more cautious tone. "Suppose those qualities you're looking for existed in a man, and although he was extraordinary on the inside, he looked very ordinary on the outside?"

She whirled to him. "But then I might never notice him at all!"

"Yes, I know," Dimitrios said. *How well I know*, he thought. "But suppose that's because you're looking for the wrong clues? You know from your work that exteriors can be misleading."

"No," she said firmly. "This time I'm right. You heard him speak about ancient civilizations. He's even knowledgeable in my own field. We share so much!"

For one split second Dimitrios thought he would slap her face. Shared so much? With that phony? Horrified at his violent impulse, he jammed his briefcase hastily under an arm. Then, forcing himself back into control, he walked over to Tara and kissed her on the forehead in his customary manner. "Go slowly, my dear," was all he could think of to say. What else could he say? Don't go at all! Can't you see you belong to me? "*Please, Tara!*"

She looked up, startled.

He had actually spoken his inner thoughts out loud! "Don't think about the Romans, Tara," he stammered, trying to cover his outburst. "Just think about your athlete." His voice trailed after him out of the room. "Try to get some rest."

Tara slumped back down onto the base of the marble

figure as Dimitrios closed the door behind him with a soft click. It was hot. Anyone with any sense stayed on the islands during August, she thought. Why had they come back to Athens early? She knew why. The expedition had used up all of its financing for the season; now they would have to wait until next summer to continue excavating this extraordinary dig. Given the bad mood she was in, next summer seemed a hundred years away. Unbuttoning her blouse, she let it fall partially open and, slipping out of her sandals, she leaned back against the marble figure. It felt cold and unsympathetic through her thin shirt. Perspiration dripped like little tears down her face; angrily, she wiped it away. How could she have been so defensive with Dimitrios? Even to the point of actually throwing a book on the table? What had he touched in her to make her feel this way? Fear? Of what? That she might never find a man to satisfy her? Guilt? Over what? She had loved very little in her thirty-two years, and when she had, the choices had not been so unlikely, only unable to meet her needs over the long run. No. It wasn't guilt.

Fear. Yes. It *was* fear. Of what? That Leon Skillman might not be, in the end, all she thought he was? Hoped he was? Oh! How she wanted him to be! She couldn't be wrong!

But, what then, precisely, did she know about him? She knew what he *knew*, but what did he think? He had consistently avoided talking about his own work, even when she had pressed him, but there could be many reasons for that. He had not avoided lengthening the touch of their hands as they danced. He had not tried to embrace her during the two weeks she had known him, but he had danced very close with her and had not tried to hide the intensity in his eyes.

Why this worry then? Because he had been shooting sharks? Because he was friends with a shallow man like Perry Gothard? Because—she felt a truth growing in her—because he had *not* held her and kissed her, as she so desperately wanted. She pressed her shoulders back into the hardness of the marble.

But I don't ever want just *anyone*, she argued to herself. Not even as a friend. I want a value. An embodiment of my own values. Dimitrios was right about that part. You couldn't just sense those kinds of things. You couldn't let instant "chemistry" make any conclusions. You could make serious mistakes that way. And Leon's chemistry was something she'd never encountered before. He was so . . . *man*. She gazed at her bronze figure. Not a god. A *man*. For the first time in her life, she understood how tempting it could be to just let go and—Stop it! This was juvenile! "Go slowly," Dimitrios had warned.

How could she *ever* feel anger toward Dimitrios? Even for one moment? She glanced over to the table where they had worked together for so many hours. The Roman coins were stacked back together into a neat pile. Her athlete stood on the table next to them. She would never have found that bronze at all without Dimitrios's patient tutelage in marine archaeology. He had warned her to go very slowly then, especially when he began to introduce her to deep-sea diving.

"It's deceptively easy," he told her. "But, statistically, scuba diving is more hazardous than sky diving." She had smiled at him indulgently then, not believing a word.

"If someone invited you, spur of the moment, to get into a plane, fly up in the sky, put on a parachute and jump out, would you do it?" he asked.

Another smile.

"Then why jump into a whole other world, under the sea, without first learning what to expect, what to do in case of an emergency? It's only when you're secure in the knowledge that you know what you're doing that you can relax and enjoy the adventure. Go slowly."

First Dimitrios had insisted they dive for hours together in strict accordance with established dive tasks (hand in hand much of the time as "buddies") at thirty-five feet beneath the surface, and then went on to make her sit with him on the ocean's floor practicing buddy breathing, the very method that quite possibly saved both their lives the day of the sharks. And he had stayed right with her so she could see him the whole way for the most frightening part of her training: dropping all gear below and free-ascending to the surface, blowing air out of her lungs the entire time to prevent nitrogen build-up. Tara smiled, remembering. "Blow and go!" he had mouthed silently to her, forty feet under water, while his serene eyes spurred her on. As impatient as she was to pursue her delights, so was Dimitrios patient to prepare her for her explorations. Only later did he permit her to go deeper to do what *she* wanted, to revel in the spectacular wonders of the underwater world: the giant sponges, the coral richer in gold than a pirate's coffer, the angel fish leading her ever deeper as if heaven lay not above but below. And always, her ancient treasures, buried within it all.

Inevitably, his advice after a lesson: "Don't rush yourself so. Take time to find your own *controlled* rhythm." Even later, when she was an experienced diver, she would look up to catch a warning wink behind his diver's mask as she pawed into a dig, only to disturb the site and waste precious minutes of the little time they had below.

A controlled rhythm? Tara frowned; it was a weary frown born from a long history of impatience with her own impatience. Control had never been one of her attributes. She knew too well that her own natural rhythm was to jump into the deepest part of the water and dive straight down, exploring all the way, trying to see it all at once: the beauty, the wonder, the possibilities of everything in life. From the time she was small, she could remember her father's cautionary lectures too—sometimes gentle like Dimitrios's, sometimes stormy. When she was a teenager and covered herself with costume jewelry for her first date, he had, one by one, taken off each piece to demonstrate her mistake. And, true to form, he counseled her on the larger principle: "Life, too, is a little like jewelry, my headstrong one. If you are ever in doubt, *don't*. Wait until you are sure you are right before you act. Time is, most of the time, your good friend."

"What about emergencies?" she had demanded insolently.

Her father had raised one bushy eyebrow. He liked her spirit, but he didn't like her backtalk. Yet he had answered her seriously, in his still-broken English: "That is a reason you practice yourself to act slow with your head the rest of the time. Then, when the emergency comes to you, and you don't have time to think what you will do, your reflexes are sharp, and like a flyer in the sky who puts on the automatic pilot, your instrument will still do good for you."

Dimitrios had taken over her father's tutelage. "Don't form conclusions before you have amassed the facts," he had warned her about archaeology. "We don't care what the truth is, we just want to know it. Go slowly, my dear."

Tara moved uncomfortably against the cold stone, feeling chastised, but also thinking how she would rather be leaning against Leon's warm chest. She closed her eyes, remembering her head on his shoulder as they danced under that enchanting grape arbor, and she could almost smell the man-smells near his open collar. She sighed, wearily. She was doing it again. It was Leon who had the sense to "go slowly," not she. It wasn't that she'd ever jumped into bed with anyone. She had always been careful in her selection the few other times she had chosen a man. But Leon was different from anyone she had ever met. He was a dream, a god come true.

Leon stood in the doorway of the workroom watching her. Eyes closed, she was lost in thought with only a tiny frown creasing her forehead to betray her inner tension.

Tara had called him at his hotel earlier in the evening,

begging off their dinner date because she had to work late. But Leon had come to the museum anyway and hung around at a corner cafe where he could see the employees' entrance. It had to be tonight. This was his last chance, broken date or not. So he had drunk a few glasses of wine and watched several of her colleagues leave at around nine o'clock. Then he'd ordered some food. Then he'd read the paper. Then he drank a glass of Metaxa. At last, he had seen Dimitrios leave, moments ago, which should have meant that Tara would follow. When she didn't, he had entered through the workroom door. She was sitting at the foot of a half-cleaned, half-broken male figure, totally unaware of his presence.

He looked around the workroom. How out of touch these people are, he thought. Burying themselves in the ruins of the past when the whole world is rocketing toward the future with cyberspace speed. For one guilty moment he remembered a time when he, too, had been drawn to the ancient world. But that was over, long ago.

Nevertheless, Leon knew it was his knowledge of that world that had drawn Tara to him. Perry had been right. She was a challenge that required finesse. But at this moment she appeared to be as broken as the marble she leaned against. However it had happened, she was his tonight. By tomorrow morning, he would own Perry's wooden penny whistle.

He stepped into the room. Yes, she was ready. But it wasn't the open blouse or even the damp tousle of her hair that made him squelch his original idea of a walk around the Acropolis by moonlight. It was the taut lines of longing drawn around her mouth. It had taken him the full two weeks, but she was ready now. Here.

"You know . . ." Tara heard Leon's voice shatter her thoughts as if from a distance. She looked up, startled.

Leon continued, pleased at her confusion. "Blair was quite wrong, actually. You don't look like a goddess after all."

He walked past her to another marble figure of a female a few feet away, noticing that she didn't close her blouse when his back was turned. He touched the nose of the goddess playfully. "You see?" he said, teasing her. "Not really. Not here. Yours isn't as straight . . . here."

He moved his hand to the figure's hair. "Nor as long, here. Or . . ." he ran a thumb over the shoulder of the goddess and circled a bare breast, "as large, here."

Tara resisted the urge to close her blouse and then to open it further; she didn't know which she wanted to do. She felt a drop of perspiration travel between her breasts. And another slip down the small of her back. What kind of game was he playing?

Leon slid his palm over the marble hip and around in back to cup the figure's buttocks in his hand. "Or as round, here." His hand lingered. "But then, as *you* know, the Greeks didn't portray the average man, but heroic man, as athletes or in the form of gods—the human ideal. The physical perfection was only their exquisite sense of completeness, so that the outside would mirror the inside. That's all right, though," his eyes were baiting her, "I prefer real women to goddesses anyway."

Tara stood, slowly, defiantly, wanting him more than she had ever wanted anything in her life, hurling Dimitrios's advice out through a back window of her mind, her sense of combativeness rising beneath the surface of her wanting. So he was leaving it up to her. He was giving her room to accept or reject the obvious meaning of his banter. She could ignore it with a tired smile. She could laugh at his joke. Or she could meet it; she could join the game with a taunt of her own. Rising, she let a chuckle rumble low in her throat.

"You're no god, either," she said, her voice husky and warm. She traced the smooth, muscular chest of the male against which she had been leaning. Then she looked appraisingly back at Leon. "Well," she admitted, "just a little . . . here."

She dropped her hand to the marble thigh. "But not here." She pursed her lips in thought. "Well, somewhat . . . here," she decided reluctantly. "But what about here?" She fingered the figure's temple exploringly. "What about the mind? Does the inside mirror the outside? That's what I have yet to learn. 'Beloved Pan, and all ye other gods who haunt this place, give me beauty in the inward soul; and may the outward and inward man be at one'." Her eyes dared him to name the source of her quote.

She didn't feel him grab her wrist. She only felt the wrench of her shoulder and the hardness of the marble as, whispering "Phaedrus, silly," into her ear, he twisted her around and backed her into the figure's missing arms. She felt both a sinking and a rising as he pressed the length of his body against hers, the hardness of the marble god's muscles on her back and the softness of the real man's mouth on her mouth, and then on her breast. She felt that she belonged to them both in the same instant, all that the god represented and all that the man was. She felt his hand on her hip, her thigh, bruising and caressing, both, in its pressure. She felt energy escaping her and entering her, as if his hands were taking and giving to her in the same motion. She heard him say something more as they slipped to the floor, a moan of pleasure or pain, she didn't know which. But it didn't matter which, for words had lost all meaning.

And Leon, reeling through space from the shock, felt her body come alive with such an intensity of commitment—escalating his demands with incredible demands of its own—that only one thought, one unimaginable certainty went ringing through his mind: *This is the way it always should have been.*

When they lay still together, his head buried deep into her shoulder, Tara laughed softly, exultantly into his hair. There was no need to go slowly. She was right! Feeling his body shaking slightly too, she thought he was laughing as well, echoing the same silent triumph as she, a kind of inner lightness, of a battle never fought, but so easily won.

And then she felt the wetness against the skin of her breast.

She held him silently, confusion chilling her euphoria into a cold lump of doubt within her, as his tears washed all peace from her mind.

FIVE

ACCORDING TO GREEK MYTHOLOGY, the site for the ancient oracle of Apollo had been discovered when two eagles, which Zeus had released from the two ends of the world, met in the middle to determine the very "navel" of the earth.

At age six, Dimitrios had scanned the same sunscorched sky that Zeus had ruled and thrilled to trace the flight of present-day descendants of those two birds. That had been during the first summer vacation he spent with his Aunt Leda at her home in Delphi; the myth of the creation of the oracle itself had been the first his aunt had introduced to him during their daily, naptime stories.

At age seven, armed with new adventures, he had played out the battle of Apollo and the Python, slaying the fearful dragon by the sacred spring to become lord and master of the oracle.

For the next few years, the fantastic mythological characters that he and Aunt Leda read about began to fill his imagination with the only playmates who ever really captured his interest. In his world of make-believe, Hercules became a mighty friend, Poseidon a strict teacher, and Apollo himself allowed Dimitrios to guide the reins of the god's own swan-drawn chariot. Hephaestos trained his hands to make weapons from tree branches and rocks, and Eros taught him to shoot straight to the heart of a target. Left alone to entertain himself every day while his aunt and his fifteen-year-old brother, Lefteris, worked in her small handicraft shop on Delphi's main street, Dimitrios had gamboled alone, bareheaded and bare-legged, among the temple ruins at the center of the earth.

But on the eve of his tenth birthday, Aunt Leda had introduced him to the character he knew would become his favorite imaginary partner: Athena. Born in full bloom from the head of her father, Zeus, the goddess of wisdom symbolized all he could ever dream a perfect playmate should be. Not only wise, but courageous and loyal, his new companion whispered advice into his ear while, beginning with the role of Achilles, he marched off from his tent at daybreak to battle brave Hector. By noon, his protector had lent Dimitrios her warrior shield when, as Perseus, he ventured forth to decapitate the gorgon, Medusa. During a sumptuous lunch fit for the gods (an Ambrosia-packed sandwich and bottled water sweetened with Nectar delivered by Hebe, herself) Dimitrios rested on the round stage of Athena's own temple, strumming Apollo's lyre and humming in accompaniment to Athena and Apollo's twin sister, Artemis, as they danced, arrayed in garlands of flowers, amid the ruin's marble columns. He ended the glorious day by running a footrace against the swift Athena (and a setting sun) in the great stadium while wearing the wings of Hermes tied to his heels.

It was the most beautiful birthday of Dimitrios's life, the story of the goddess Athena his most cherished gift. It would be to her, first among his celestial friends from Olympia, that Dimitrios would return each summer of his childhood, and it was within the epic dimensions of her character that the young boy would fashion his own soul.

Gradually his mythical playmates took on flesh and blood to him, while the children he met in Athens during the school year faded into dull unreality. When his classmates raced around the gym chasing a soccer ball, Dimitrios sat on the sidelines mentally racing Poseidon's great steeds in chase of the highest waves in Homer's wine-dark sea. His teachers scolded the shy, sensitive boy as a lazy "do-nothing," and Dimitrios's parents expressed concern over their son's aloofness.

At eighteen, when he announced that he would become a professor, everyone was relieved, but also anxious for him because of the communication skills required. Dimitrios had never, to their knowledge, shared his thoughts with anyone. But it seemed that he had been saving his energy all his life for the subjects of his work. To his family, he continued to be an enigma. Not to Aunt Leda, of course, who had watched little Dimitrios as he charged through the archaeological site at Delphi, his dark hair streaked with copper from the sun, his bare legs heedlessly sunburned and scratched, with only the echoes of his own shouts of bravado for company. Aunt Leda never worried about her nephew's future once she saw the confident thrust of his sword, made from a tree branch, or heard him call commandingly to Athena for aid in battle.

And Dimitrios himself never worried about his tomorrows. He knew that somehow they would include those faithful images of his youth. His childhood playground of ruins became the adult arena of archaeology, and Athena set the standard for the woman of his future. It was as simple as that. It had never occurred to him that his future might not include both his chosen work and his chosen woman.

It occurred to him now.

"To the woman I shall love, I pledge the man I will become."
Dimitrios turned the rock over to read the other side: "Men created hero-gods that they might learn to be Man."
He looked up at the cracked and eroded columns of the monument next to him. He saw both the perfection and the humanity of the structure's design: the individual beauty

of each column was a conscious metaphor of man, each column six times its diameter in height because the average man's foot was one-sixth of his height. What *ideas* they had! What ideas *he* had had! Pensively, he turned the small slab of stone over and over in his hand.

He'd been nineteen when he etched those words into this piece of stone and hidden it here. He'd done it after his sophomore English Lit class had visited the Temple of Poseidon, where Lord Byron had penned his sorrowful songs. Dimitrios had visited Cape Sounion several times before that, of course, as a child with his parents and brother. But this time, he had come to visit a spirit—unlike his own to be sure; yet, on that day, Byron's ghost had inspired him to poetry too. He had returned on his motor scooter the following Saturday. And after sitting alone with his thoughts for several hours and staring, unseeing, at the graffiti that covered the monument, he had dug those words into a stone—he would never have defaced the temple—with another stone and a knife. And he had planned his future.

He was already studying the past, double majoring in Philosophy and Art History within the School of Archaeology. He knew he needed to understand both subjects from their roots in order to live out his future. It was all settled then. He would go on to do his graduate studies in Comparative Ancient Civilizations and then his doctoral work in the narrow area of Classical Greece. He would work each summer as a student assistant in one archaeological site or another, he would teach and, one day, he would lead his own expeditions.

He had planned the rest of his life that afternoon. He had also planned, that day when he was nineteen, that he would bring his woman, whenever she materialized in his life, to this spot and give the stone to her. Somehow, sitting late into dusk that day of his youth, listening to waves murmur like lovers' whispers around the rocks far below, it had seemed a romantic idea (even an important idea) to someday show his loved one what she had meant to him before he ever met her. To the woman of his dreams, he had engraved his vow into the hard and durable stone of an archaeological site. It had been so natural to dedicate himself to the one love by engraving on the other.

The stone had endured for over twenty years.

Tonight, for the first time in all those years, he found the idea childish. He held the rock in his hands, with all that it signified. But he held no woman in his arms. That part of the dream had never been realized. On other nights such as this, when he had come to visit the rock, needing for some desperate reason to know it was still there, he had wondered why there was still no woman to hold. Tonight, he wondered why he had ever held onto the dream.

He had found the woman. But, like Athena, she offered him companionship, not love. The only passion shared between them was their work.

Dimitrios walked to the edge of the cliff and looked out over a dark sea. This sea: the same sea traveled by the ancient Greeks, the first people to understand that the ideal was an approachable goal and that the joy of living was striving toward that goal. This land: home of the first civilization to value the individual, philosophy and truth, its gods the first created in heroic human images. Tara saw all of it this way too. Her Greece, like his, was not crumbling architecture, social decadence and superstitious men walking around fingering *komboli*. It was the fountainhead, the source of Western civilization itself.

All this he shared with Tara, much of which he had taught her. Some of it he had taught her to love. Could he not also teach her *whom* to love?

She had been searching ever since he met her, searching in the wrong places, for the wrong things. Now she was doing it again. How *could* Tara stand there and say to his own face how much she shared with Leon Skillman?

The American was too glib. Too clever. Too cynical. Why couldn't she see it?

Dimitrios peered down over the edge of the rocky crag. Even though hundreds of feet separated him from the water, it seemed as if he could see his image clearly there. He laughed bitterly. Hardly like Narcissus, he thought. But Leon looked the part of the god Tara was seeking. And he, Dimitrios, did not. What an irony for such a face as his to carry the name "Kokonas." For "beautiful" his face most definitely was not. Dark hair. Dark skin. Dark eyes. Not good-looking. Not bad. A face so easy not to remember. Not tall, not short. Not thin, not fat. Not . . . not . . . not . . .

Not even young. Tara had explained on the Gothards' boat that he looked after her like a "mother hen." Why did she always mistake his male protectiveness for parental concern? Perhaps he had been too subtle, too patient with her. The dozen years between them had never bothered him, and he couldn't believe the age difference would be a factor for Tara either. On the other hand, didn't it combine with the fact that, as her perpetual teacher, he held an automatic position of authority, which *could* be construed as parental? It was practically a cliché that protégés fell for their mentors; the closeness of shared values and prolonged periods of time spent together almost pre-ordained it. But not Tara. It seemed as if she'd done the exact opposite, taking an early, unexpected turn in the relationship that kept her forever by his side mentally, but on a parallel track that separated them physically. He had done everything a man could do. He had turned himself inside out for her. He had opened his mind to her. She knew him, inside, as well as he knew himself, but it was clear that she had no perception of him as a sexual being.

Yet—he peered deeper into the water—perhaps *he* was to blame. Since childhood, he had presented to everyone some kind of Platonic idea of himself, offering to others only a shadow of his true self, the self he would let no one know directly. He had never shared his inner feelings about anything with anyone, and he had never permitted anyone, including Tara, to shorten his given name to "Dimitri."

Why had he always felt it necessary to shut out other people? Even as a young boy, he had felt painfully misunderstood by everyone except Aunt Leda; he had never even dreamed that anyone else could understand him. So he stubbornly kept to himself, cherishing and protecting his private passions as too precious (and too volatile, if he admitted it) to be shared by "regular" people. That's how he had thought of them all—his parents, teachers, classmates—"regular." Well, Tara certainly wasn't "regular," but unfortunately she wasn't psychic either. *Psyche: the soul.* He had opened his mind to her, but when had he ever opened his soul to her? Now it might be too late.

Dimitrios raised his hand suddenly, angrily, far above his head, but rather than hurling the rock, he found himself clinging to it instead. In control again, he walked over to the foot of the monument and, finding its hiding place, slid the rock into the foundation. When he stood up again, he remained erect and sober for one long moment, as was his habit, in front of the ancient structure.

Locking the entrance gate behind him, he walked down the path to his car. He had planned his future here at Sounion as a boy. Now he was one of a handful of people in the world to have a key to the gate that closed the monument each evening. But it only takes a handful to preserve the art and the ideas that inspire such monuments, just a few men and women in each age to stretch their hands across time and offer the best of each civilization to the waiting hands of the next. Tara was one of those few, too. But now she might be lost to him.

As Dimitrios drove along the coast to his weekend home, he glanced down at the sea again. I'm getting sentimental, he thought, sentimental . . . and old, at forty-four. Less than a mile away, he could see his large, spotlit home standing like a lonely sentinel on top of its hill. Aunt Leda had left her entire small estate to him when she died, and he had used most of it to build this house. Dimitrios had offered half of his inheritance to Lefteris, but his brother had declined with a knowing smile. Lefteris had always understood his aunt's singular love for his shy baby brother, and since he had recently taken over their father's clothing store near Syntagma Square, he didn't really need the money. He wanted Dimitrios to have it all.

When Dimitrios had built the house fifteen years ago, it was the only one in the area; Cape Sounion had never been a fashionable place for weekend homes. But he had wanted to be within sight of the temple, the symbol of so many of his secret dreams. Now his home was surrounded by dozens of other houses, two hotels and several tavernas. His privacy was gone. But he still loved the pale cream of the stone he had personally selected, the Minoan red of the pillars and the handcrafted, red tile roof. As he drove up to the house, flanked on one side by a tennis court, he wondered absently how many games he had played there with Tara. How she loved a challenge! His gaze was pulled down along the stone wall that edged the long, winding footpath to the sea. How often had he and Tara swum away a hot summer afternoon there together?

Turning off the engine, he left the key in the ignition and slumped over the steering wheel, exhausted. From what?

Postpartum blues after a successful expedition, or the frustration of lost dreams?

He picked up the mail on his way into the house and threw it wearily on the kitchen table. Suddenly, his energies revived. There was a package from the Halldon Gallery in New York. Good! He had called the Art Dealers Association of America the very day they had returned from the islands (the moment he realized that Leon and his friends were *staying* in Athens) to find which gallery handled Skillman's work. He had requested a catalogue immediately. Now he could see for himself what kind of art this fellow made. Tara had said that Perry Gothard called it "heroic." Dimitrios doubted that Perry Gothard understood the meaning of such a term. He tore brown paper off the catalogue and flipped to the index. "Skillman, Leon." He opened the book to the designated pages eagerly and reluctantly at the same time and viewed Leon Skillman's "heroic" work.

"Thank the gods."

Later, lying in bed after a refreshing shower, he realized he could not continue to wait around worrying; he had to *do* something. He couldn't risk losing the only woman he had ever loved without a fight. He wouldn't! His failure with Tara was his own fault. He didn't even know himself when he began to fall in love—

When *had* he fallen in love with Tara?
He didn't know!

And if *he* didn't know, how by the gods could he expect *her* to know? He had always called her "dear." He had always kissed her forehead. He had always given her presents. Because his love for her had grown so naturally, had he expected her to respond to it just as naturally? Given his own age and appearance, how could he have dreamed she would ever "see" him romantically? Especially since she always appeared to be more than mildly preoccupied with the ideal image embodied in her ancient gods.

Furious with himself, Dimitrios leapt out of bed and threw open the doors to his terrace for air. It was too late for any more subtlety or patience. Tara was already taking days off from work to be with the object of her infatuation. He would have to do something radical. Dimitrios shuddered, whether from fear or excitement he didn't know. It was too risky to suddenly declare his own love for her and try to compete openly with the American. No, the only way to make Tara see clearly at this point would have to be through a back door, through some kind of reverse vision, perhaps. Could he somehow arrange for Tara to see Skillman *and his art* head on in a different venue? Yes, in the American's own glitzy—if the Gothards were any example of it—setting! Might Tara think, then, to look back to Greece, to him, with fresh eyes?

Tara had never been away from him for more than a week or two in all of her adult life, and even then she talked to him daily on the phone. Her parents had visited Athens several times, but she had never expressed a desire to return to America for even a holiday. She had been too wrapped up in her work. With effort, Dimitrios methodically pressed his thoughts forward. Manipulative machinations were not a comfortable mode for him, plus he could not permit himself to focus on the image of Tara and Leon together, or the remote possibility that Leon might turn out to be, in fact, all that Tara thought he was. He realized that she would eventually go to Leon anyway, for the simple reason that she would never stay with her marble and bronze gods if she honestly believed she had found a real one.

So he must extricate them both from the intoxicating environment of Greek sun and sea. He must create a legitimate project to demand all of her attention—thank the gods the expedition had rendered such outstanding results!—as well as give Tara a professional reason to leave Athens for a while. He knew her strongheadedness too well. Once Skillman left Greece, Tara would soon come up with her own excuse to visit America: her parents, her younger brother and sister, or, even worse, the truth—that she wanted to be with *him*. Dimitrios knew he couldn't take the chance of Tara's making her own decision to go. He would have to pre-empt her and make the choice for her.

Now, he must chance losing her for good, in order to have her at last. If he could.

He thought again of his rock. It was settled, then. He would send Tara to New York.

SIX

"KOSTAS!" MARGUERITA WHISPERED while filling a plate with rolled grape leaves. "This is the last night Kally works here, you hear me? No more. These men, they are pigs. And in front of their wives, too." In the ritual of warding off the evil eye, she pretended to spit on the floor and nodded toward the Gothards' table.

Kostas frowned and, shaking his head, went back to dicing up a huge chunk of feta cheese for the salad. He loved Marguerita (they had been married for nearly forty years), but if there was one thing he was not, it was superstitious, and he hated this habit of hers. She never actually spat, as the peasants in the old country did, but just the thought of it turned his stomach. In a moment, however, he felt a little kick on his leg and looked over at his wife. She kissed the air several times in apology until she saw him give in to her and smile, and then she jerked her head in disgust again toward the problem of their daughter.

There were nearly two dozen people sitting at the five tables pushed together for their dinner, but as usual, Kally was hovering around the head of the group, Mr. Gothard. Her face was flushed with eagerness as she listened, tittering frequently, to who-knows-what the man was saying to her. Kostas frowned again. Marguerita was right. Their daughter was too young to understand what the attention of a man like this could mean. Too innocent. He would have to stop it. He felt a moment's anger at Tara for sending these people to him in the first place. Had she changed so much? These people couldn't be her friends. Could they?

"Kally!" he called over to his daughter. "The other tables, they are waiting."

"In a minute, Papa." Kally burst out laughing. "Mr. Gothard is going to measure my hair."

Locking eyes with Kally, Perry took his knife and wiped it clean with a napkin. Then, smiling a shared secret with her, he started counting its length from the top of Kally's head, turning the knife end over end down the thickness of her long, chestnut brown hair. "Ten knives long," he chuckled, leaving his hand on Kally's buttocks for a long moment when he was finished.

"Kally!" Kostas bellowed.

She ran over to him, blushing with excitement. "Oh, Papa, what now? These people are so much fun. When they're here, it's just like being in the movies."

"Clean the tables!" Kostas ordered.

Kostas Niforous looked around his restaurant, his heavy, black brows knit together in displeasure, the good-natured friendliness now missing from his bright blue eyes. He opened a bottle of Greek wine and set it on the counter for a waiter to pick up on his way to one of the tables, just another of the many things causing his displeasure. None of these new customers used the cafeteria conveniences of his place. No more sniffing and tasting over the steam tables displaying the hearty Greek dishes prepared by Kostas and his wife Marguerita, only waiters picking up food that had been ordered by the customers from their own tables. Kostas had always kept a few menus on the tables as a courtesy to first-time patrons or tourists who might wander accidentally into his little restaurant near the theatre district on New York's West Side. But the menus were never used by his regulars, the steady, solid bulk of his business. In fact, before these last weeks, he had never employed more than two waiters, and they spent more time clearing dishes and cleaning tables than actually taking orders and delivering food. Now he had hired two more and brought in both his son and young daughter to help out on weekends. Oh, his business was booming, all right. He was making money, all right. But Kostas Niforous wasn't having any fun.

He watched his son, Nicky, carrying a tray of water glasses to the counter for filling. His neighborhood customers had filled their own glasses at that counter, where it was an occasion to say hello to other diners. It had always pleased Kostas that this idea of his had succeeded in creating traffic and congeniality. And laughter. A Greek restaurant should be a place for good times, for *glendi*. He looked at the silent jukebox filled with Greek records seldom played. His regulars kept it lively all night, and he and Marguerita often joined in the dancing. He couldn't bear to look at the coat rack spilling over with furs—Oh yes! They wore extravagant fur coats over their funny clothes—and finally, Kostas settled a glare upon Mr. and Mrs. Gothard.

When they told him they were friends of Tara's, the first night they had entered his restaurant with a bunch of friends, he had found it hard to believe. Unlike his regular poor but neat customers, they seemed either to like wearing tattered and torn clothes or else to look as if they were in mad costume for some extravagant TV show. His sixteen-year-old daughter Kally had pointed out that their "peasant" skirts were made of silk or suede. And their pants were torn on purpose! Then he had noticed their chauffeur-driven limousines waiting at the curb, and he had become utterly confounded. Why should people with so much money dress like this? Sometimes, in message tee shirts, jeans and dirty sneakers, they looked ridiculously like aging teenagers. Some of the Gothards' men friends even wore an earring or two. These people were educated. They were rich. Why should they go out of their way to look like crazy kids? He couldn't understand it.

But understand it or not, he knew he didn't like it. After

that first visit, the Gothards had begun bringing a dozen of their friends at a time. And it didn't take long for this demanding, self-absorbed crowd to drive away his neighborhood patrons entirely. Now he cooked mainly for these pretty people, who pretended to joke and act friendly with him while at the same time seeming to show him off to newly introduced friends as some sort of freak. He always felt like some big, stumbling bear in their presence. No, he didn't like this turn of events at all. But he would wait a few more weeks before doing anything about it. Then Tara would be home, and he could ask her in person.

The thought of his oldest child smoothed his forehead and crinkled his eyes instantly. He had not had a complete family gathering in his restaurant in a decade, since Tara had moved to Greece. Kostas had never admitted it to anyone, but he'd always been secretly disappointed that his firstborn had returned to the old country to live and work. He had gone to such trouble, and risked such uncertainty for their future, to take his family *away* from there— But at least she would be coming home for many weeks now. And who knew how long she would stay once she got a taste of New York again? What a day this Thanksgiving would be! He would close the restaurant to outsiders and roast a whole lamb, the way he had done as a young man in the old country. And they would combine the American holiday with Tara's Name Day celebration, as they always had when she lived at home.

Oh why? Kally tormented herself as she stacked a tray with dirty dishes. Why did her parents always step on her fun? Why couldn't they be American? Her whole family still lived upstairs above the restaurant when years ago they could have afforded to move into a better neighborhood. No American father would do otherwise. Besides that, Americans let their kids do anything they wanted. Even after living in New York for so many years, her own parents were still from the old school: do this, do that, be this, be that, don't wear stupid clothes, don't take drugs, don't drink, think before you act, get good grades, go with nice boys . . . Oh, why couldn't they leave her alone? Her entire upbringing had been one restriction after another, and it was all her father's fault.

Because he was so strict, her life had become one big sneak. Every morning at school she slicked on makeup and green or purple nail polish and then had to take it all off before returning home. She even went to the trouble of gluing little earrings on her ear lobes so everybody at school would think she had pierced ears like all the rest of the girls, and many of the boys. Papa would spot the tiny holes in her ears if she ever really had it done. And she only wanted to pierce her *ears*, forget her nose, brow or navel like so many of the others. How she hated him! And her mother was just a *peasant*. She was fat, wore dresses that looked as if they were made from leftover kitchen curtains, and she even had a big stainless steel tooth that gleamed when she smiled. Which she did a lot.

All Kally wanted was the freedom to be like the other kids in her class, to be left alone and have some fun! She sneaked a look back at Mr. Gothard and giggled when he smiled at her. He was so dignified! The silver gray frosting on his longish dark hair made him look just like a movie star, or maybe an orchestra conductor. She had noticed that his fingernails were polished with a clear enamel. Unlike anyone she had ever met, he was so refined. He even smelled of some exotic, spicy cologne.

Kostas, seeing the exchange, glowered at Perry, but Blair called gaily over to him. "Don't worry, Kostas, I won't let him bother your little *mignon*."

She turned to an ultra-thin woman with frizzed blonde hair sitting on her right. "And now, Flo. Which of Adria's paintings and which of Leon's pieces shall we give? We're donating both of Adria's *Hammer and Nail* studies, but which major works shall we include?"

Florence Halldon sipped her Greek coffee with relish; it tasted horrible, she thought. "Give Adria's *City Lights* and Leon's *Eternity*," she said easily. What did she care which of the Gothards' collection they placed in the new wing of the museum? As long as it put a gap in their collection, she could fill it with whatever she wanted. It only meant money in her pocket, and her pockets were very deep indeed.

Flo Halldon prided herself, privately, on being a gallery owner who was honest (at least with herself) about the art she sold. Some dealers were just charlatans, of course, but others actually believed, or talked themselves into believing, the double-talk of a lot of contemporary artists and critics. Flo knew better. Perhaps because she had not always lived in the world of "art." She liked money. And she had class. Once.

After her husband died, she'd decided to work and opened a stylish, quality clothing boutique on Madison Avenue. She realized very quickly, however, that many of the customers who had the money to pay high prices didn't really want either quality or style; they simply wanted what was "in." So she'd begun to carry three-hundred-dollar cotton tops with the ever-important signature of the designer in ostentatious view and dresses with various designers' initials intertwined in the fabric. That was eighteen years ago, of course, before such things became popular with the middle class and the trend still belonged to the smart set. But business had quadrupled in the first six months, once she was "discovered" by a woman browsing in the shop one afternoon. "You've changed!" the woman had cooed in delight. "Oh, how wonderful. Now you're catering to the younger set." The woman was forty-eight years old (Flo's own age at the time), but Flo didn't mind because the woman soon brought her well-heeled friends along as well.

One of those friends (who actually was younger, barely thirty then) had come in consistently and made a habit of buying one of whatever Flo had in the store in every color in which it came.

And that was how Flo had moved into the "art" world. The friend was Blair Gothard.

"Blair?" Flo hated to interrupt. Her sophisticated dinner mates were discussing which works of art to donate or loan to the museum with the enthusiasm of countrywomen assigning covered dishes at a church social.

"Listen, lovey, why don't you donate *Orange* too? Everyone could have great fun trying to guess the artist."

Blair's eyes shone. "Oh, what a smashing idea, Flo. I'll do it. Just for fun."

Flo sipped at her coffee. Poor Blair. Poor Blair's Botex-injected friends. They all tried so hard. *Orange:* the orange door. She had been re-doing the decor of the clothing shop twelve years ago, making it snappier, brighter and more up-to-date for her "young" clientele. Blair had been on one of her each-and-every-color shopping sprees and had stopped in front of a new dressing room door, which had been propped up against a mirror on the wall. The door was still just a slab of wood, no knob, no nothing; but it had just been painted. Orange. Flo had refused to hang the door until it was repainted. The painter had done a sloppy job and little globs of paint dripped randomly down the entire surface, giving it a weird, rippled texture.

"Oh, what a fabulous shade of orange," Blair had cooed. "I'd love a little bathing tank of that color."

Flo had laughed. "Isn't that some work of art? Sorry, but I won't give you the name of the painter."

That's how it had happened. Unpredictable. Crazy. True. Blair's very unsure response: "Oh, really? Do you deal in art, too? Or is this for your own collection? But how can you make a collection if you won't say who the artist is? Is this something new?"

Flo had stopped laughing. "Yeah. It sure is something

new . . ." She made up the words as she went along. "But with the rage of monograms and signatures on clothes, cars and *everywhere* these past many years, this particular artist just got sick of it. He wants to be appreciated for his work, not for who he is. But, believe me, he's going to be a very well-known no-name one of these days, that I can tell you."

Flo choked on the thick coffee. How she had managed not to choke on those words was still beyond her. It had all been a capricious and pointless jest.

But Blair had returned the next day and bought the door for $20,000. Money meant nothing to people like Blair. It was all sport: a momentary diversion, amusing dinner conversation and setting a trend.

Flo had seen magazine photos of the so-called postmodern contemporary art being produced at the "Rails." She'd visited the place the very next Sunday. An old, unused Brooklyn railroad yard, the buildings had been taken over by a growing number of artists who sought inexpensive housing, government grants and the company of each other. There, she was lucky enough to find Adria Cass, who specialized in drips and blobs on a grand ballistic scale. It was easy to move Blair on from her "no name" artist to Adria, a move that, simultaneously, put Adria's name in art headlines. With that one marketing maneuver, Flo had become an art dealer. Yes, indeed. Go with the flow, Flo. Or . . . better yet, "drip" with the "hip!"

So she lost her class. But the money she had made! She had sold to every person sitting at this table. Why not? If they didn't buy from her, they would just buy from someone else. It was all status and social glitter to them anyway. After all, they *were* the "glitterati." She ought to stop feeling guilty one of these days. Besides, by now she'd made at least five artists super famous and multiplied her clients' investments tenfold as well, including those of the Gothards. So her original fake had been more than made up for. And now *Orange* was going to hang in a museum. How hilarious!

Blair called over to Kostas again. "Kostas, darling, when is Tara arriving?" What a curious thing, Blair thought. All three of them had been sure Dimitrios Kokonas was romantically inclined toward his protégé. Strange, then, that after Leon and Tara had become a twosome, Dimitrios would send his precious one straight to New York to arrange an exhibition from their Roman ship dives with the Metropolitan Museum of Art, which meant straight to Leon.

"Tara comes home for Thanksgiving," Kostas responded laconically.

"Smashing!" Blair flashed a bright smile. Actually it *was* smashing; she'd never had an archaeologist to show off before. "She'll be here for the opening of the twentieth century wing of our own little museum. We're having a star-studded party, and you and Marguerita will come too. Say yes, Kostas."

Kostas Niforous muttered in Greek into the okra bin.

SEVEN

HELL! LEON THREW HIS BEER BOTTLE at the steel just to see some action. The bottle splintered and liquid ran down the sides of the metal, but the steel hulk remained undented and unchanged. He hadn't been trying to dent the steel, just to break the bottle. And you didn't need to purposely corrode this type of steel; it turned brown all by itself from its own rapid oxidation.

The corporation that had commissioned the piece had suggested rather timidly to Leon that something in brown, to match the corporate logo, would be appreciated. Leon always made what he felt like making, and they knew that, but what the hell, it was no big deal to select a steel that did the job for him. The Board of Directors had been delighted when he agreed.

Leon went to the refrigerator for a fresh beer. What the Board didn't know was that this steel also leached its rust all over the place, and within a short time after installation, the entire sidewalk around the entrance of the building would be stained with seeping, creeping brown crud. Great! The corporation couldn't complain; their color scheme would be completed in spades. *And* there was bound to be enough public outcry at the sidewalk mess to put his name in a headline or two. At least his work stayed intact. He thought of another artist purchased heavily by corporations as "investment" art that was beginning to fall apart all over the country. Now that *was* funny. Maybe he should try it. No, that was somebody else's joke. Gotta be original with the jokes, here. Oh yeah.

Leon picked up an arc welder and continued his work. No, the reason he needed some release was not the fault of either the metal or the corporate board. It was because he didn't seem to want to put the damn thing together. Ever since his return from Greece, he just couldn't find any enthusiasm for his work. What the source of his problem was, he didn't know and didn't care. Whatever it was, he was sore as hell about it. This sculpture had to be ready shortly after the New Year, and it was as stubborn as a bull ox. The design he had originally planned didn't seem brutal enough anymore, but he couldn't get exercised over any other shape to take its place. He knew it wouldn't make any difference to the corporation. Those guys rarely knew what they were doing when it came to art anyway (and Binky Jones sure as hell didn't know what he was doing) but all of Leon's work had always been made with a certain temperamental integrity of his own, and this piece just wasn't cooperating. Or his temperament wasn't cooperating. Or something.

Well, hey! What the hell. Leon looked at his watch and dropped the welding clamps on top of the broken bottle. It was too early to work tonight anyhow; his helpers weren't even here yet. What he needed was a good lay. What he'd needed for weeks, in fact, was a good lay. A roll-in-the-hay kind of lay. He left a note for his workers and headed out the door.

"Don't worry about it. Happens to every man at some point." Adria's voice was warm and sympathetic. Leon stared absently at Adria's huge breasts, which hung forward to rest comfortably on the ample folds of her soft stomach. She was as pink and full and ripe as a Rubens painting. That was why she had always served as the perfect narcotic for him; she was everything he disliked in a woman. She was fat, she was untidy, and she was intentionally coarse. She was also an encompassing lover and a protective friend, both of which he *did* like but wouldn't admit. Even with her crudeness, this earth mother provided him a nurturing shelter from the unacknowledged inner doubts that kept him coming to her less out of desire than out of need. Always encouraging, Adria never judged him.

Leon leaned back against the pillow and pulled the old, soiled bedspread over his groin. Depression sat on his face like a flat iron. Everything in the bedroom was distasteful to one degree or another; hairpins, an old bra and makeup were strewn over the dressing table; the mirror over it was red with the word "Cleaners" scrawled across the top in . . . lipstick? Leon pulled a wry smile. Only Adria would remind herself to go to the cleaners by messing up something else in the process.

"I can't work, either," he said, the smile fading.

"What's the matter, Baby? In love or something?"

Leon shook his head. It was the truth; he didn't know what the matter was. Adria raised both arms over her head in an idle stretch, exposing thick patches of black hair that emitted an erotic, musky smell and reminded Leon that this was one hell of a basic woman.

She was also stoned. Handing him a partially drunk glass of wine from her bedside table, she took another toke from a cigar-size marijuana "blunt" rolled in purple cigarette paper, and spoke without exhaling. "I told you you should get wrecked first. Sure you don't want some?"

Leon shook his head wearily.

"Okay, but dump the depression. A limp noodle don't mean a thing, but I can't stand depression. Forget it. I still love you, although you *are* getting a little old for me. Want me to fix some eggs?"

Leon shook his head again. He didn't seem to have an appetite for anything. Maybe he was getting older after all. Or maybe just shop-worn. He'd been sleeping with Adria on and off for over ten years now, since he was twenty, an age much more to her liking. Only last month, she had thrown a fifty-fifth birthday party for herself and invited all of her current sleeping partners to meet each other. At thirty-one, Leon was the oldest man in the room.

Well, *something* was certainly up. He hadn't been able to perform with Blair, either. During the trip home from Greece, after his first embarrassing failure with her, he'd pleaded headaches and seasickness like some simpering society bitch who wanted to steal a ride without paying her way in the only way posssible with the Gothards. Blair and Perry did expect kinky sex, together or apart, but they also were well-mannered old friends and never mentioned the subject of his impotence, pretending to understand. But the problem was that *he* didn't understand. He had not tried sex again until tonight.

Adria's eleven-year-old son, Jason, wandered into the bedroom and began to draw a mustache on his face with his mother's eyebrow pencil. The boy had never known his father. Adria's husband had been a rather successful artist who used a shotgun to blast holes in spray cans of paint, and one day when Adria was five months pregnant, he shot himself while cleaning his gun. Or so the papers reported. Jason Cass Sr. left only his name and bad dreams to his son. It was impossible for Leon to imagine what it must be like to be a child with Adria Cass as his only parent. She was wealthy, she was famous, she was sought after as an unpredictable wild card by the city's most social hostesses. Always deeply involved in politics, she filled her Brooklyn Heights townhouse with a grand assortment of people: journalists, politicians, rock stars, astrologists, TV and film industry people, socialites, models. Well, in a way, this was the world Leon moved in, too. But he never took any of it seriously. It was all a big josh to him, while Adria was a dedicated activist. Yet underneath all of her slogans and all her layers of fat, there lay a fiercely loyal friend. For that, he would always be grateful.

Jason walked over to the bed, pretended to drag on his mother's joint and returned to the mirror to draw some sideburns on his face.

Leon got up and pulled on his pants and sweater as Adria settled back into the bed for sleep. "See you," he said. He gave Jason a friendly smack on the rump.

Adria looked up and blew Leon a kiss. "Call me when surf's up again, Babydoll."

✣ ✣ ✣

The night was clear and sharp with cold (early winter was already in the air), but Leon felt energized by the briskness and decided to walk for a while. The Brooklyn Bridge stretched its multitude of light-strings between Brooklyn and Manhattan as if it were holding the two boroughs afloat. Beyond the bridge Manhattan's skyline rose, tier after tier of multi-layered lights in different shapes and heights, lifting unseen buildings so brilliantly into the sky that scattered stars became no more than a distant reflection of the city's ever-prevailing presence.

Out in the bay, one light shone bright and alone, rising from black water into black night, a reassuring beacon for all to see. Leon stopped walking and leaned against a huge suspension cable, feeling comfort at last.

"My Lady," he murmured. He had thought of her that way since the very first time he had seen the Statue of Liberty. He had been twelve years old when his mother brought him by ferry from New Jersey one Sunday afternoon to visit it. Those Sunday excursions were the high point of his week, every week. The fact that his mother was a high school art teacher made the adventures even richer, of course, and on some subliminal level Leon knew that. But his mom never made him aware of her giving him any actual instruction; she always chatted very naturally about the things they were seeing, as if she were an energetic and enthusiastic friend. Though *Liberty* had been only one of the many wonders she introduced to him, he had formed an attachment for the statue that had never left him. Now, he felt a little guilty that he could still feel so intensely about what he had learned to call "kitsch."

To his embarrassment, he still remembered every word of the Emma Lazarus poem inscribed at the statue's base. His mother had encouraged him to memorize "The New Colossus" in its entirety, and, out of habit, Leon found himself softly reciting some of the words:

> *... A mighty woman with a torch whose flame*
> *Is the imprisoned lightning and her name*
> *Mother of Exiles. From her beacon hand*
> *Glows world-wide welcome ...*

He shaped the words as if they formed an unconscious prayer to the statue, to the idea, to the country that made the idea a reality, to his mother, to his childhood, to each and all of these. But there was a despair in the tone of his voice that revealed in this rare, unguarded moment that none of his own personal prayers had ever been answered. Or ever could be. Because the only gods he had ever worshiped were those sculpted by the ancient masters.

Over time, Leon had learned that those great, historical works he revered as a child were ideals never to be reached by human beings. Why had the Greeks made it seem so possible? He hated them for it. Because he had once believed it. The indescribable awe that Leon, as a child, had felt for those works of art went far beyond the perfection of form. He had perceived what he felt only as a wordless worship, never realizing that his homage was rooted in those artists' capacity to envision human nobility as a natural state of existence.

Leon did understand, however, that what he felt for the Statue of Liberty had something to do with the fact that she exhibited, in her own way, the same calm, confident expression looking out upon the world that the Greek figures had worn, but—he resisted the thoughts even as he struggled to form them—it went even beyond that. It had to do with the fact that *Liberty* was also a woman. Even at twelve he had been certain that a work of art that held out the torch of freedom as the pride of one people to the hope of others would, by some quality of the idea itself, have to be a woman. Why, he still didn't know, but later, when he began to sculpt seriously himself, he tended to select a theme for his practice pieces that could be best realized by the subject of a woman or a girl.

When he was fourteen, after a few years of molding small animals and botanical shapes from fistfuls of clay, he had become inspired by a photo from one of his mother's art books and translated to his own medium three little girls dancing in a hand-holding circle. The finished bas-relief of the young *Three Graces* was crude, even with his mother's patient guidance, but he had captured the feeling of laughing playfulness that he had been after. Later in high school, taught officially by his mother, he had called his first mature effort *Spring Flower*. He'd paid his year-older sister, Elly, his entire allowance for a whole semester in order to get her to model for him twice a week. His goal that term was to learn drapery (the kind he'd seen as a child in the Greek and Roman sections of the Metropolitan Museum) and he had created a work that featured the draped body of a girl as the youthful blossom rising up from a bed of leaves. Elly had posed in a bathing suit covered with a piece of chiffon fabric, but what emerged as the embodiment of Spring was a nubile expression of young womanhood, nude and thinly veiled in a swirl of drapery. He had also changed the face, subtly adjusting his sister's features to match a vision he saw only in his mind. When (after staying up all night to complete it), he submitted the work as his final exam project, he didn't understand why his mother suddenly excused herself and left the classroom.

All he knew was that, in the spring, his mother had featured the small bronze in the auditorium lobby art exhibit that opened the same night as the annual school play. A good many teachers and students had resented her "favoritism," and it had been embarrassing, but she had stood by her decision. She still displayed that small figure in his childhood home—the best, and last, example of his early talent.

Leon continued across the bridge, his memory matching the night in clarity. He could see the red taillights of a few cars passing on the roadway below. They moved ahead of him, like signal lights at the crossroads of his life, each one pulling him on against his will to the next stopping point.

No. That wasn't quite true. *Spring Flower* had been neither the best nor the last of his female figures. There had been one other, no longer in existence unless it somehow remained intact at the bottom of the river.

Strange he should think of *The Promise* tonight, after so many years. Suddenly the image of Tara flashed into his mind. No! Not his mind. His hands! It was his *hands* that held her image. Held it as if he had created it. The way he had created *The Promise*. *Why*? Why should he think of them both, like this, in the same instant?

Leon stopped walking and stood perfectly still on the bridge. It was as if he could no longer do more than one thing at a time. He could walk or he could think.

Slowly but with total certainty, he began to grasp the answer to a question that had tortured him for weeks. Why had he cried that first time with Tara? Cried for the first time since his teens. Ridiculous. Embarrassing. Beyond his control to stop it. Later, he had laughed it off. To her. But he had never laughed it off to himself. Now, here, he began to make sense of it all. Tara and *The Promise*. First the crying and then his inability to have sex with his old partners? Impossible! Tara was merely the object of a bet, after all. Yet he now began to realize that from the very beginning, everything about her had reminded him of *The Promise*. All of the promise of a sixteen-year-old girl realized in a thirty-two year old woman? It was absurd, after all these years. But he knew, deep down, that it was true. He had felt sixteen when he made love with Tara for the first time in the museum workroom, that is, he felt all the newness and all the wonder. The things he had believed were real when he was sixteen, when he was with Valerie.

Valerie Charles. "Chas." One of the most popular girls in school and, without doubt, the most striking: long brown hair, a vigorous, athletic body and large violet eyes fringed with black lashes so long they looked almost unreal.

Leon, at sixteen, was still "pretty" himself, the features of his face not yet having taken on the complexities of manhood, but his body had shot up six inches that year and filled out with a masculinity beyond his age. Girls began to notice him for the first time. He loved the attention and reveled in his own sense of himself, but he was still a bit overwhelmed when Valerie approached him at a weekend softball game. She was wearing tight white shorts and an even tighter red tee shirt.

"Will *my* breasts do?" She asked, wide eyed.

Leon leaned on his bat to keep from falling over but looked straight into her teasing eyes and waited for her to go on. He refused to look at her breasts.

"I saw *Spring Flower* last year at the art show. She was pretty, but the good parts were covered up with all that draped stuff. How about doing a real nude this year?"

For the first time, he had no theme in mind, no artistic

goal, just the raw aching desire to re-create what already was: Valerie.

He decided on the sensuous medium of marble and the daring task of carving directly without a clay model. He posed Valerie on a rock, with the dim thought that he would display the finished sculpture in a pool of water with smaller stones and, perhaps, a floating flower. The working title he gave himself was *Water Nymph*. He knew he would never use it, but his mother had taught him that if he didn't have a theme or title at the beginning of a work, a name that simply captured the spirit of his intent would help him to stay on track. Somewhere in the back of his mind, his training told him that *Water Nymph* would encourage him to express the fluidity of Valerie's lyric beauty as well as retain her athleticism as a playful nymph. From then on, all that filled his mind day and night for weeks was an image, an image of real flesh and blood that became the focal point of his existence.

And Valerie *was* a playful nymph. "Like this, Leon? Is this what you want? Tell me *exactly* what you want, Leon! How about *this*? Leon?"

Stretching one long leg down the length of the rock and arching her back to thrust her full young breasts to the sun while her hair trailed into what would later be water, she seduced him so innocently that he felt guilt beneath the pounding desire that finally drove him to leave his work and bring her down from the rock into a grassy nest of love. But her eager responses were so open and willing that he soon lost all sense of nervousness and simply moved and melted into the sweetness of her body.

His love for Valerie grew in exact ratio to the progress of his sculpting. It was as if he were memorizing her live body in the frozen image emerging from the translucent white stone. His hands trembled when they touched the body in either form.

They made love lying in wildflower beds, or wet and laughing in the coolness of the stream, or against a tree: everywhere and every way they could think of. They worked, they picnicked, they played, and, some afternoons they did nothing at all, just lay on their backs gazing into the sun.

Even now, standing alone in the October cold, he remembered nothing of that spring but warmth: the warmth of her arms, the warmth of her breath and the heat she brought to his body. Had it been a warm spring? He never knew.

Leon pulled the collar of his sweater up around his chin. The night air was no longer bracing. He felt a chill run the length of his body, and the strings of lights above him glinted coldly like chips of ice, with the red lights below flashing up at him like warning signals.

He was to learn that Valerie was not his alone.

In his innocence it hadn't occurred to him to question if she were a virgin, as he was. Later, he learned there were signs, but at the time he just assumed that the wonders of what they were sharing were as intoxicatingly new to her as they were to him.

He was wrong.

When the sculpture was finished, he placed it in a shallow stretch of brook that ran alongside the grassy area where Valerie had posed on her rock and took his mother there to see it for the first time. As his teacher, she had often guided his technique on the piece in progress, of course (it was his first attempt at marble), but Leon had not let her see it at all during the final stage so he could surprise her with this dramatic presentation. The *Water Nymph* sat on her own rock, surrounded by other, natural stones at the edge of the stream as clear water moved around her. His mother had stood for a long time in silence before it. Finally, she asked, "What do you call it?"

"I still don't know," Leon had answered. "My working title is *Water Nymph*."

"It's much more than that," his mother had offered. "Much more. I would call it *The Promise*." She had never asked him about his model, and if she wondered about the circumstances under which the work was made, she had never shown it. But seeing the serenity of her smile on that day when she looked first at the completed figure and then at him, Leon sensed that she knew and was glad for him.

"Well," she put an arm around his waist as they walked from the river back to their car, "I'm sure I'm just asking for trouble from the staff, but unless somebody comes up with something very special, I'm going to have to give you the honored spot in the show again this year."

And she did. But there was no resentment this time. It was as if the work shocked everyone into silence, somehow. Not because it was a nude (that was standard media fare), but because the purity and the naturalness of the young female seemed to be a vision reaching out to them from another age. Reminiscent of some mythical mermaid coming to rest on a rock in the sunlight for a moment, the figure captivated attention even more because she expressed the immediacy of one real girl while embodying, simultaneously, the radiance of all young womanhood. But it was the face that evoked the greatest feeling. It was the kind of face people meant when they thought of an angel or a goddess . . . not an image of either, but a uniquely human face, expressing the joy of being human. Lifted into a breeze that every viewer felt rather than saw, the head flung back so that the long hair dipped into the water below, the eyes half-closed, focused on some private vision known to the nymph alone; the mouth barely parted, as if waiting for a kiss from the breeze to touch its lips with the marvelous breath of life.

At the opening night of the school play, most parents

and students simply stood before the sculpture. Very little was said, but the expression of quiet hope was visible on every face.

Then a group of varsity football players arrived.

"Hey, that's Chas."

"Isn't that Chas?"

"The face isn't right, but that body sure is Chas, right?"

"The body's not right, either. What about that big mole on her ass? He forgot the mole!"

They fell on each other, howling with laughter and the exaggerated fake boxing punches of their typical locker-room banter.

Leon stood in the corner and felt spring slip from his grasp. He had never called Valerie by that nickname; it had never seemed to suit her soft femininity.

Then she arrived and immediately ran over to the statue to laugh with the boys. "I wondered if any of you guys would recognize me," she giggled. "What a scene! What other girl can say she modeled for a real work of art by the time she was sixteen?"

She saw Leon then, and running over to him, threw her arms around him, dragged him over to the artwork, and kissed him in full view of her other admirers. She didn't notice that her kiss was not returned.

While the play was in progress, Leon excused himself from Valerie and the others, and walking alone out into the empty lobby, lifted the nude from the water and left the building. He got into his father's car and drove to the spot by the river where *The Promise* had been created. But once there, drowning his dreams hadn't been nearly as easy as he thought.

For a few long minutes, he stood at the river's edge holding the figure reverently in his hands. He watched them shake as they touched the smooth marble body for the last time, his mind grasping numbly that the female he held was far more than "a promise." She was his ideal, all he ever had imagined a woman could be.

He saw a sudden downpour of rain wash over the lush, polished surface of the stone. No sound came with the sobs wrenched from his pounding chest, only tears. She was so very . . . beautiful. And so pure, like the pristine, white stone from which she was carved. In every way, she was all that had been sacred to him. Now he held it all in his hands for the last time. He knew he must not hold any of it in his heart.

Then the courage he needed came to him in a searing flash. It came in the form of anger. But not toward Valerie. Toward himself. How could he *ever* have been so naïve? Without another second's hesitation, he threw *The Promise* into deep water. It vanished beneath the surface immediately as if it had never existed, and the tears vanished from his eyes as if they had never been shed. It was the last time Leon Skillman ever cried.

He'd never looked back. He returned to the school and watched the end of the play. He went with Valerie to the drama department's party in the gym afterward, watched her flirt with the other boys and coldly marveled at how he could ever have been so stupid and childish to believe she belonged to him, as he so completely had belonged to her. Later, his sister was going to a friend's house for an after-party party. The parents were away for the weekend, which meant there would be drinking and, probably, some drugs and, undoubtedly, some experienced girls. He decided to go along.

But before he left, he walked resolutely over to Valerie, who was dancing with another classmate, and grabbing her arm, bruised her mouth with a long, full kiss, his tongue quickly penetrating her—he knew what she liked, the bitch!—until he could feel both her breath and her body catch with desire. Then he shoved her casually back to her dance partner, slapping her smartly over the exact spot on her rear end where the mole lay. "So Long *Chas*," he called as he moved quickly away.

At the seniors' party he laughed a lot and drank a lot of beer. But he never got drunk. Kids got drunk. He was no longer a kid. He felt great! He *was* great! Before the evening was over, he had screwed two different girls in two different bathrooms.

When he and Elly returned home after midnight, his parents were still up and pacing the living room, distraught about what they assumed was the theft of Leon's sculpture. Stone-faced, he told them what he had done. His father never said a word; he just went to bed. But his mother kept him up for hours, arguing, pleading, threatening. *Where* in the river? If he didn't want his work, she would retrieve it herself. And why? Why? Leon wouldn't tell her, and he refused to explain. She went to bed in tears.

For days on end, she persisted. Every time he walked in the door, she started badgering him all over again. After a week, his father asked Leon to at least tell them *why* he had done such a destructive thing. Again, Leon refused. His mother looked as if she'd been struck, but his father had advised her that if this was a private issue with Leon, she should respect that fact and let the matter drop. Leon knew his mother's wound had stayed fresh since that day.

From that time on, he had sex with as many girls as he could find, and finding them wasn't difficult because of his remarkable good looks. It was amazing how fast they all tumbled. He got seduction down to a science; no one could resist him. After a while, he began to choose the least attractive girls he could find. His body had become anesthetized, performing perfectly without a breath of feeling, but his mind was still alive with rage, and he punished himself as mercilessly as he knew how for ever having believed that the ideal was possible, that the promise could ever be realized. After many months of whoring around, he felt a deep and satisfying change. His boyhood was over.

Leon looked back at the bridge, shaking in the cold and shaken by his memories. He had no idea how long he had been standing there. He didn't remember walking across the span at all. The bridge was from another time, he thought. As was the Statue of Liberty, as was all "ideal" sculpture. As was *The Promise*. His mother was from another time.

She had kept her silence all that summer, but when he didn't sign up for an art course his senior year, the arguments started all over. Again, his father stopped her. He seemed to understand that whatever Leon's problem was, it had nothing to do with art. He tried, once, to talk to his son Man to Man, but Leon remained stubbornly quiet, and his father didn't attempt to help him again.

In college, Leon found the artistic outlet he needed: "constructions" or "stunt" art, he called it. He was learning at last (and to his relief) that art need not aspire to be beautiful or uplifting but would better succeed by simply being different and unexpected . . . or as offensive as possible. Laughing at the idea of love and having sex with countless females had canceled (and corrected) his childhood idealism. Now he found he could also laugh at art and mindscrew everyone in the art world, too. Once one caught onto the irony of it all, the rawest and most distorted real replaced the highest and most beautiful ideal with shocking ease in every part of life. That was what the twentieth century was all about, wasn't it? And the twenty-first? Cashing in, of course.

Leon was finally, completely, happy. In life and in art. His acerbic wit and contagious good humor became a trademark for him. In college, he "created" everything from a gigantic sunbaked pretzel twisting through a Harlem housing project to a mammoth hot-air "kite" tethered to an abandoned building in the Bronx. He constructed a ladder, which led viewers to a tree house to look through a knothole at a deeply pitted "earthwork" he had dug into a hill a mile away across the Hudson River and listen to Rap music amplified through tree branches hardwired for sound. And he laughed to himself at the people, critics and public alike, who actually climbed the ladder to see his "art" and attend to the bruising lyrics that turned the grotesque charade into a multi-media event. Only one secret thorn pricked his carefully constructed persona from time to time. Through it all, even after Robert Van Varen in one of the most prominent art magazines had given him lavish coverage as a spirited, young talent, he sometimes disgusted himself by being drawn to an occasional course in Classical Greek or Renaissance art. He sneaked off to these classes in shame, hoping no one would notice, especially himself. During the sporadic visits he made to his parents' home, he sometimes wasted hours reading some art history book from his mother's library; he told himself that the reading avoided conversation, and he no longer had anything to discuss with his parents.

His mother said nothing when his new "constructions" were accepted at Flo Halldon's chic new, ahead-of-the-crowd Chelsea branch of her well-established Madison Avenue gallery; Robert Van Varen had introduced him to Adria Cass who, in turn, promoted his work to Flo Halldon. It had been Flo who had introduced him to the Gothards. His mother also had said nothing when he'd quit college in the middle of his junior year and went to live at the "Rails," alone at first and then for a while with Adria. And she said nothing when he switched suddenly from his "stunt constructions" to the work he had become famous for: the huge, steel and iron shapes with the rough, corroded surfaces that destroyed any hint of the metals' natural beauty or sensuousness. She had broken her silence only once by asking him why he called one particular piece, the bronze one the Gothards were loaning to the museum, *Eternity*. "Because matter lasts," he had answered. He never told his mother of the one, private concession he made to her in his abstract work: he never signed his pieces with the name "Skillman," only with his initials, "L.S." He did it out of his old, automatic love for her—she was still his mother, after all—but refused to tell her about the concession as punishment for her having filled his mind with her outdated views about "beauty" when he was too young to know better.

Leon hadn't seen much of his mother over these past years. She still taught art at his old high school in New Jersey. He'd gone to a couple of concerts with his father, but never again could he spend real time with a mother whose silent condemnation hung like acrid air between them. But tonight, suddenly, he felt an overwhelming desire to visit home. In the next instant, he remembered having seen copies of a certain journal in her study: *L'Ancienne*.

A tiny voice at the back of his mind warned him that he should not see his mother now, especially in the aftermath of so many childhood memories. The same voice told him that he also should not see Tara when she came to New York, because he now knew that, despite his frivolous intentions, Tara had touched something very deep and fragile yet still alive in him that he assumed had been permanently buried. He brought his hands up in amazement before his eyes, remembering that from the day he met her, his *hands* had wanted to sculpt her in a way he hadn't worked in his entire adult life. From the outset, Tara had caused him to tread on the edge of a razor blade; he was dangerously off balance when he was with her, vulnerably close to being the self he had abandoned to become an image he'd invented. He shouldn't see her again.

But other impulses urged him forward—the same automatic life-preserving impulses a suicide victim feels when, certain he has succeeded and is already dead, he sees life-lines he never knew existed just within his reach. One of these lifelines—his mother—lay just across the Hudson River. And the other? An image of Tara flashed into his hands again.

Leon skipped down the stairs of the nearest subway entrance, noticing neither the cold nor the lightness of his steps.

EIGHT

THE HOUSE WAS DARK, but Leon knew where to find the key to the kitchen door: it was wedged, as it had always been, between the cracks in the neglected cement stoop. This convenient hiding place was undoubtedly the reason his father had never fixed the porch.

He let himself in quietly; his parents always retired early, and it was well past midnight. A low light burned in the kitchen, a remnant of the days when his mother had left it on for middle-of-the-night refrigerator raids. It was a welcome sight. The kitchen itself was spotless and cheery. Just like his parents, Leon thought ruefully, to be concerned about the inside with no thought at all to exteriors.

The house was a modest one, but it exuded a warm dignity. In the living room, seascapes painted by his mother were hung among other works, and although Leon's artistic sensibility had expanded far beyond their pretty simplicity, he still felt a certain sense of peace when he noticed one of them.

The den was the largest room in the house, and unlike the kitchen, it was not spotless; it was a jumble. Books spilled from the shelves and some were left open and scattered on his mother's worktable; old phonograph records and cassettes and new CDs were mixed at random with videotapes and DVDs. Piano music was piled everywhere except on the piano, which was crowded with family snapshots from the time Leon and his sister were young. His mother's easel and palette table occupied one corner, surrounded by a large bay window.

Being excessively neat and orderly himself, Leon never understood how his parents functioned in such a room, but it had always been this way. His most vivid childhood memories of this house were of his mother reading here in the evening, or painting on weekends, while his father played the piano. He had often tried to join them with his homework but couldn't concentrate because of the music, which never seemed to bother his mother.

Looking around the den, Leon realized for the first time that his parents probably had a good marriage. This room, so full of both of them, must be as intimate for them as the bedroom above him where they now slept. The ingredients for a good marriage had never crossed his mind before, but at this moment, looking about him, he felt in some wordless way that he was seeing them. Pleased for some reason with that feeling, he went to the liquor cabinet and poured himself a Gentleman Jack. Then he began looking through a stack of magazines that were piled up on the floor.

Soon he found a dozen or so issues of *L'Ancienne*; evidently his mother saved only those of special interest to her. Glancing at his mother's easel, he paused to see her work in progress. He froze. She was painting his *Spring Flower*. He looked scornfully at the image he had created at fifteen. How trite, he thought.

He followed the line of vision from her painting to his draped nude, sitting on a plant stand by the window. It had been arranged so that real leaves from a green plant fell from the statue's base, as if in continuation of its bronze foliage, trailing it to the floor. He stared back at the canvas. The medium of oils and his mother's characteristic choice of a vibrant palette brought his subject alive in a new way. She was not copying his work, but using it as a model and recreating its theme according to her own purpose. What an odd thing to do!

Opening one of the journals, he scanned the list of editors. There seemed to be one each from England, Israel, Italy, America and Greece. "Athens: Kantara Niforous." Tara, in my bed, he thought. What he had felt with her! Joy, certainty, power. Even a sense of play. Making love seemed so natural to her. She held back nothing. And yet within that ability to be playful, she communicated to him a feeling of profound seriousness. What he felt afterward: uplifted, clean. The way he hadn't felt since Valerie. He remembered a night many months ago with Blair when, after sex, she had turned to him wistfully and said, "Remember the fire, not the ashes."

With Tara, there were no ashes. It was as if her fire burned him to a state of purity where there was nothing left of his body afterward but a radiant glow from the flame. He hadn't seen her for two months, but he felt an awakening in his groin for the first time since he left Greece. He *had* to see her again, couldn't wait to see her again, to hold her again.

He flipped through several of the magazines and found two articles she'd written. He also noticed one by Dimitrios Kokonas (a long one), where his mother had scribbled notes at various points along its margins.

He began to read one of Tara's articles. It was about the different marbles used in ancient Greek architecture and sculpture, and it explained the difference between Parian and Pentelic marble, contrasting their uses and describing the way they weathered: one in deep grooves and the other in random pitting. He dropped the magazine to the floor. Who in hell cared?

Scanning the next article, Leon remembered Tara's intense excitement over finding the small bronze athlete on the day he'd met her. Here she elaborated on the rarity of the small figures, pointing out that in ancient times most of them had been melted down for weaponry.

He got up from the couch and headed for the kitchen,

reading as he went, needing some escape from the trivia of it all. How could someone who was so alive in bed bury herself in such dead subjects? He made himself a sandwich and poured a glass of milk, reading in snatches as he ate.

> *It was in the human nude that ancient Greek artists discovered a beautiful and versatile form through which to express a supreme state of spiritual ecstasy, striking the perfect balance between consciousness and existence—mind and matter integrated together in perfect harmony.*

Leon flopped back down on the couch, skipping to the end of the article:

> *The earliest male nudes in Greek art were traditionally known as "Apollos." The god of justice [sol justitiae], he was also called the god of light because, to the Greeks, justice could be served only when facts were judged by the light of reason. Who else but a Homeric hero [Ajax] would cry for more light, even if it were but light to die in? To the greatest of the ancient Greek thinkers, nothing could be more exciting than that which was real and true to its nature, and to be human was the most exciting thing of all—*

Leon closed the journal slowly. In the few weeks he had spent with her, he had known that Tara was intelligent, that she was lovely, that she was devoted to her work and that he wanted sex with her. Now, he began to wonder for the first time why she wanted *him*. What had she responded to in him that impelled her to give herself so freely? Or did she respond this freely to others? No, he thought, she had rejected Perry from the start. So was it just his good looks? No, her article stated very clearly that it was body *and* mind that made Greek nudes unique. But he had already guessed that. He already possessed the body, that's why he had seduced her with words. He had, in fact, adjusted his whole personality to tumble her and win the bet. He thought of the bronze athlete. Was it the idealization that she responded to, the larger-than-life quality of that kind of art? Then why her obsession with Greek art? Renaissance art was larger than life too. Why Apollo and not David?

Tara had prompted him again and again to talk of his own sculpture. During that short span of time, he had been able to evade her inquiries easily enough with opaque answers. He had never planned to see her much beyond winning the bet anyway; in little less than two more weeks after he was awarded his penny whistle, he and the Gothards had sailed home as planned. But now she was coming to New York, and he realized how much he wanted to see her, to pick up with her where they'd left off. But once she arrived, she was bound to insist on seeing his work. A shiver of dread coursed through him. It was the same subliminal warning signal that made him avoid any real description of his work in Greece.

Leon looked at his watch calendar. Tara would be arriving in New York in a couple of weeks, just before Thanksgiving. So he had plenty of time to figure out how he would approach her again. Well, hell! He'd think of a way. He always did.

Rummaging again through the journals, he found the article by Dimitrios Kokonas: "Classical Greek Art: A State of Mind." Tara might not be romantically interested in her employer but, as Blair had observed, he was clearly enamored of her. Given Tara's predilection for gods, the man hardly seemed a force to be reckoned with. In any case, he was a total bore, and Leon knew he couldn't tolerate reading any more accolades to Greece tonight. In fact, in today's living-on-the-edge, terrorist-riddled, war-torn world, this whole publication was irrelevant except to archaeologists, historians and his mother. Artists of the moment had to feed their public whatever they could digest in one quick swallow, whatever was current, amusing, disturbing, and immediately relevant to—or distracting from—their own lives.

So! He would get back to work on his own "relevant" commission tomorrow. Enough self-indulgence, mooning over Tara as if he actually *were* sixteen again. But he would have to jar her loose from her static fixations on antiquity somehow, or she really might not be able to deal with his work or his fast-track life in New York. He thought of Dimitrios, whose tastes and views were even more petrified than Tara's. It was as if Dimitrios was to Tara what Leon's mother had been to him. Stultifying. He thought of Tara's clear gray eyes, so honest and direct. He'd have to choreograph *this* love affair very carefully— God, his mother!

Struck suddenly by the full impact of where he was, Leon jumped up. What in hell had he been thinking? He had to get out of here! He could *not* risk seeing his mother. What would she think? What would she ask? Whatever had possessed him to come here?

Helene Skillman stood at the top of the stairs, listening. Noise from the kitchen had awakened her well over a half-hour ago. She had started downstairs just in time to see—her son!—pass the staircase in a flash on his way to the den. Shocked beyond thinking, she had crept back up the stairs out of sight and remained frozen on the top landing, feeling a mixture of tenderness and pain. The clock in the hall read two-thirty.

He came so seldomly, and then only when some family occasion made it awkward not to appear. Yet here he was, in the middle of the night. Her mind was in turmoil, hoping, yet afraid to hope. Even as the years passed, she had never permitted herself to believe she had lost him completely. She had lived on the kind of hope only a mother can harbor that her son would, someday, outgrow his rebellion and return to himself. After the horrible incident in high school, Leonard had convinced her that continuing to pursue the subject would only drive Leon farther away. So they had waited patiently together, praying that their once-remarkable child would survive his self-destructive path and resurface at some point when his mysterious rage and bitterness had subsided. It never did. He was over thirty. Maybe the boy she'd loved so dearly was totally lost by now. The man, she didn't know.

Helene held her body to the wall to keep herself from moving down the stairs. What was he doing? It was quiet now. Perhaps he was sleeping on the couch. If she went down, she might not be able to resist smoothing away the sandy lock of hair that always fell over his forehead while he slept. And if she permitted herself that small gesture of love, she might kiss the forehead as well. Then he surely would leave quickly, regardless of what had driven him here.

Why *had* he come home after so long?

Helene stole down the stairs. There was no sound in the house except the ticking of the old Grandfather clock. She peeked into the den. He was gone! She looked wildly about the room. Then she noticed that her reading pile had been disturbed. Going quickly through the magazines, she saw that all of her copies of *L'Ancienne* were together on top. Nothing else was out of place. Her mind reeled. Why had he come? Why had he gone? Why would he be reading *L'Ancienne*? Confusion and pained love spread through her as the memories flooded in.

Spring Flower came into blurred focus. The day he brought it to school, when she had seen it completely finished for the first time, she had managed to hold back her tears of joy until she reached the teachers' lounge. Loving, elated, and intensely proud of him, she knew that Leon's talent was truly none of Leonard's and her doing. This was his achievement alone. She had taught him technique, but seeing the depth of his romantic spirit and the profound emotional commitment imbued in *Spring Flower*, Helene had known she could teach him very little more. Even if he was unaware of it, she understood that her son had already surpassed her in many ways, and that he would have to strike out on his own and find other, better teachers to guide his singular talent. There, alone in the windowless bathroom of the teachers' lounge, she had felt her most satisfying moment of motherhood; the bare walls had seemed bathed in sunlight.

Looking at the exquisite female figure in the same room where her son had returned tonight, for whatever reason, made Helene feel the joy of that day again for one warm moment. Then it was immediately clouded over by other images: Leon's present work, those cold, hard, metal hulks that had brought him his fame. Suddenly, a surge of anger at the offense to his youth and to her own values drove her back from the door. Leon had come and gone in the night. But why?

NINE

A LIGHT SNOW SWIRLED between the buildings before settling restlessly on the sidewalk. The energy Tara felt crackling like electricity throughout New York seemed to find its way even into the white flurry, making this, too, pulse with its spirit. Snow didn't fall in New York; it skipped down the wind and vibrated on the streets.

Alive. Whatever challenges had ever in the past or would ever in the future test it, the soul of this great city was eternally alive. Because its spirit was indomitable. She couldn't recall experiencing such a sense of self-generated energy anywhere else in the world, from the moment she stepped off the plane three hours ago to now, as she wound her way through throngs of hurrying people. She was a day early. No one knew yet that she had arrived, not her family, and not Leon. On an impulse she couldn't quite identify, she'd checked her bags at the East Side Terminal and ventured out unannounced and unattended to greet her favorite city. New York! Even as a child, she'd felt that only special people belonged here: people determined to rise through life like the tall buildings in which they lived. Was it really possible she had stayed away for ten years? All of her adult life, she realized.

Then she remembered why she had left. College over, it had been time for graduate school. The men she was meeting in New York were mostly career-driven and shallow, obsessed with money and sex, or sex and sports. Her interest in Greek history, in Greece itself, offered a logical environment in which to pursue her education with greater depth. Meeting Dimitrios had been key, for it had confirmed her desire to go into archaeology. She had felt reassured, somehow, by spending her time surrounded by gods of reliable character, albeit of marble and bronze; at least, if they had their heads on at all, they had them on straight. Aside from a few important exceptions, most of the men she had met in Athens were even cruder when it came to women than the men she had met in New York.

Feeling cold, suddenly, Tara realized that her feet were wet. She ought to stop into the next shoe store to buy a pair of waterproof boots. She'd never needed them for the few days of snow each year in Athens.

Never needed much of anything outside her work, actually, not even her family. Had she missed them? Loved them, yes. But missed them? Not really. Except for a sporadic social life, she had cloistered herself like a nun inside the museum where Dimitrios reigned as high priest. It was all that she had wanted.

Now, wandering past the sparkling store windows in New York, the routine of her life in Greece seemed dull. How was that possible? The feeling had come to her instantly, even as she departed the plane; it was as if she were stepping from one era into another, as if she had been aboard a time machine.

Thanksgiving was still two weeks away, but the stores were already beginning to decorate for Christmas. Tiny lights linked the street lamps above the sidewalks, marking some of the most luxurious shopping avenues in the world with the merry colors of a child's holiday. Many of the stores carried out the theme with artificial snow, stars and the red-apple cheeks of dozens of Santa Clauses; some windows were pure magic with animation and music. Others called it vulgar commercialism but, to Tara, the custom had always seemed joyous and perfectly logical: bursting with exuberance for all things, New York just couldn't wait to get on with the festivities.

Turning up Madison Avenue and looking into a shoe store window, she felt her mind boggle at the choices. There was another shoe store next door and a third across the street, and all the department stores carried boots too. How did one *shop* here? She burst out laughing at the impossible abundance of this city. A smartly dressed woman standing next to her glanced over and joined her with a congenial smile. And they say New Yorkers are unfriendly, Tara thought. If she had stood alone on a busy street in Athens and laughed aloud, people would have looked at her as if she were mad.

She bought brown boots made of leather as supple as silk. It seemed impossible that such elegance could be waterproof as well, but the young salesman assured her that they were. "Boy, did you need these," he laughed, "your feet are soaked!" Standing before the mirror, marveling at their style and comfort, she inspected her old, blue winter coat. She had owned it since college, and it had hung in her closet for years, barely used. She looked around at the other women in the store and then back at the mirror. Well! She *had* been out of touch!

Completely in the mood for Christmas now, she walked over to Bloomingdale's. Today, all presents were going to be for her. She began her purchases with a gray wrap coat and a fur hat— "I have sold a lot of hats, my dear, but I have never seen blue fox look so stunning on anyone. It intensifies the gray of your eyes." Tara spun through the crowded aisles, drunk with delight, if not intoxicated by all the squirts of perfume she accepted from too many smiling sample-sprayers. Money was no object; she hadn't spent any in years. A soft gray sweater-dress belted in the same soft leather as her boots— "Not everyone can wear a dress like this, you know. You have to be slim." But while in the dressing room, she noted with astonishment that she also needed underwear. It was as if each new thing she bought seemed to illuminate the necessity for something else she had been neglecting.

In the lingerie department, she remembered Leon. The array of choices was dazzling, but now she felt highly directional in her selections. Creamy satins slipped over her skin with his hands in mind. She had never been so aware of the sleekness of her own body. Perhaps she *had* removed herself from real life and, as Dimitrios had warned, from real men. The saleswoman was saying something to her about washable chameusse, but she wasn't listening.

On the way out of the store, a new purse over one shoulder to leave her hands free for the many shopping bags full of her new wardrobe, she caught her image in a cosmetics counter mirror. Her face looked unfinished somehow. In Greece, there had never seemed to be any reason for makeup, but now, especially with these clothes— "I have a new mauve eyeshadow that will really bring out those gray eyes," the young clerk said.

What next? The lace of her slip clung to her knees as she stepped back into a snowy breeze. The cashmere of her dress wrapped her body in the most sensuous warmth she had ever known; wisps of fur blew against her face with gentle touches. No, she thought. No, Leon. Not yet. But a soft shiver ran through her body.

She hopped into a cab and gave the driver the address of the only place of worship she had ever known.

Out of old habit (her father had always cautioned her to note the names of both the cab company and the driver when she got into a cab) she looked at the cabby's name on the license card. "Konstantine Niforous," it read. She gasped. "That's my name, too!" she burst out.

He looked at her through the rearview mirror, at her attire and the shopping bags that labeled her a rich passenger from the East Side. "Oh, yeah?" he said with a thick accent. "And when did *you* see the old country last?"

"This morning," Tara answered in Greek, laughing as his expression of contempt began to break into one of incredulous delight.

"You're kidding?"

"No, I'm not," she laughed again, shaking her head at the silliness of it all. "And you won't believe this, but my father's name is 'Kostas Niforous'."

"You're kidding!" he spoke in Greek now. "You mean the guy who owns that little cafeteria on the West Side? That's your papa?" Flipping off the meter, Konstantine Niforous slowed the cab to a crawl and shot fast questions at her through the rear view mirror. Did she know the island of Paros, where he was born? Yes, that's where the great marble was quarried for ancient Greek sculpture. Her father had lived there at one time too. Yes, he knew that, but they weren't related as far as they knew; common Greek names were common. Was that little taverna with the vine-arbored terrace still near the Acropolis in Athens, in Plaka? Yes, she and Dimitrios lunched there often. Was the wine still undrinkable? Yes, but we drink it anyway. In the country at sunset, can you still hear the bells of the goats returning home? Yes—

Tara couldn't finish the sentence because of a strange tightening in her throat. Visions of sunsplashed hills, rising columns and Dimitrios's smile choked off words for one, brief instant . . . and then she was laughing and talking with the cabby again.

"Only in New York!" he chuckled with pleasure, "could you get off a plane from Greece and land in the cab of a Greek!"

"Only in New York," she repeated.

When they were within a few blocks of her destination, she leaned over and asked the driver to stop. "This is where I used to get off the bus as a child," she explained.

"I'm gonna eat at your papa's place *tonight!*" he called after her.

The snow had stopped, but enough of it remained on the ground to bring the peace of the countryside to Central Park. There used to be a bench . . . there. An old bum used to sit on it. He'd been there every time she had passed by. One day, she had seen him eating Chinese food out of a white cardboard container and drinking from a bottle of Johnny Walker.

The bum was no longer there. Not even the bench was there. In its place was a long, dull mass of metal with a pebbly, rough-hammered texture. Obviously a work of abstract art, it, ironically, it was being used just like the bench that had preceded it. Several listless people in heavy overcoats sat in collective solitude on what had to be a very uncomfortable surface. They looked like old crows, their only company the pigeons that occasionally vied with them for space on their sitting slab. How funny! It was as if the City had replaced a bench with a "Bench." Only in New York.

Other ungainly constructions loomed here and there in front of the apartment buildings across the street on Fifth Avenue. Had they been there a decade ago? Tara couldn't help but think of the magnificent art that had graced public spaces throughout the ages: heroes, gods, warriors, or even idols, placed in public view to remind passersby of great achievements, great people, great hope, or, at least, great power. Greatness. Of what use to *people* were these ugly, misshapen masses of material?

Then the great Met was before her.

She looked up at the massive building, its fountains rising majestically on either side of the entrance, and experienced anew the excitement of her youth. She had come here to the Metropolitan Museum of Art for the first time with her school class when she was ten, and had never stopped coming back regularly to visit her "friends" until she came to say good-bye when she was twenty-two. Other little girls she knew went to church every week. Her fiercely independent father didn't believe in organized religion, so as a child, Tara never knew what those buildings were all about, but she did know that when people talked about their churches or their synagogues, they seemed to feel something like what she had always felt here. With an air of easy familiarity mixed with her old awe, she passed through the sacred portals.

Checking her coat and shopping bags, she mounted the grand interior staircase as if she had been here yesterday—and with the same anticipation. She always felt that she was ascending to a higher world via those stairs, a place where lofty images and ideas sang with color and movement, a world of beauty and hope and promise. In art, somehow, even suffering and defeat seemed to illuminate their opposites of joy and triumph. Breathless, she headed for her special rooms only to find that everything had been rearranged, which oddly enchanted her. She had always loved treasure hunts; wasn't that the basis of her work? Finding her favorites, one by one, she tried but couldn't remember exactly when she'd begun to think of these several works of art as her "friends," but she did remember the day she'd brought her father to meet them. She was eleven and already completely at home in this huge place. Every Thursday after school and before her ballet class three blocks away, she had come here. Twice a year, her father would pick her up from school and come with her to the lesson to see how she was progressing. One day she had begged him to accompany her to the museum as well. He hadn't wanted to go.

"Listen, Charis" (his pet name for her), "I want you to know all these fine things from the whole world, that is why we come to America. But I . . . your mama and me, we are simple people. We know only Greek things."

She'd insisted, and they had missed her dance class altogether that day. Her father had stood silently before each of her favorites for a long time. Once, he had reached over and, putting his hand on her hair, drew her to him and pressed her head into the side of his big stomach. "I do not know if these are good art, my Charis, but these are, I think, beautiful 'friends,' like you call them."

Then they had passed through a room re-created with historical furniture, and there she had lost him. Having been a carpenter in Greece, he became totally absorbed in the workmanship of seventeenth- and eighteenth-century European furniture: inlay, gilding, carving. They had remained in those rooms until the museum closed. Her father had never returned; he felt too uncomfortable in such a place, he said. But sometimes on a Thursday morning when she left for school, he would say with a little wink, "Say hello to *my* friends, too."

Today she was seeing these beloved childhood treasures even before she saw him. A pang of guilt shot through her, but it vanished instantly, along with all other conscious thought for the next two hours, once she became involved with what she had come to see. *Salome* grinned insolently out at her as she always had: the exotic colors, the sweeping yet intricate brush strokes, the bold composition, all working harmoniously together to express frank passion without apology; the female with the parrot lay nude and nubile, as candid about her nakedness as ever, the artist's palette subtly intensifying the very real and very beautiful vulnerability of the moment; the warrior returning in triumph on the prow of his ship, standing eternally in brilliant colors and blinding light and—Tara felt the triumph swamped by pain—Icarus fallen, the magnificent hero defeated by his own audacity. Then pain lifted into tribute: *What audacity*!

In the rooms filled with Greek and Roman sculpture, she looked with seasoned eyes, remembering herself fondly as a child and how it had upset her so to see men and women with their heads and arms cut off.

Then she found herself standing in front of the marble sculpture of a group of richly modeled figures in flight, from what, it didn't matter. There was urgency in the work, but no fear. The woman carried an infant in her arms, protecting it under her shawl. The man's cape swirled up and around, enclosing all three figures and completing a courageous human moment with a daring abstract design. The man looked ahead, leading his family to safety. The woman looked to the man...

The doorman at Leon's building hesitated. Not that it was uncommon for a woman to visit Mr. Skillman, but it was only three o'clock in the afternoon; he would still be sleeping and wouldn't want to be disturbed. On the other hand, the woman was obviously "class," and she said she was a friend from Greece and wanted to surprise Mr. Skillman. Plus, she had pressed a five-dollar bill into his white-gloved hand. He let her in with the promise not to ring up.

Tara slipped her address book back into her purse and stepped across the sumptuous lobby and into the elevator. Even in her dazed condition, she noticed the intricate Art Deco designs of stainless steel, copper and brass. What a beautiful building Leon lived in! The operator smiled at her flushed cheeks. "Getting chilly out there, ma'am?"

Walking down the corridor, she thought how impulsive this was. What if he wasn't home? No, the doorman would have told her. What if someone else was with him? She pushed the doorbell.

No answer. She waited, then rang again. *He wasn't home*! Good! She had almost made a fool of herself. She turned to leave.

The door opened.

In the instant before she was in his arms, she saw that he was clad only in a towel, that his hair was tousled and that his eyes were full of sleep.

In that same second of stillness, Leon struggled to wake fully and comprehend the reality of her presence.

Then neither of them knew anything but the locking of

their bodies, the melting of their mouths.

Somewhere on the periphery of her mind, Tara noticed her new lingerie fall to the floor . . .

. . . and somewhere in the recesses of his, Leon registered the full meaning of the woman who had materialized outside his door.

He claimed her with a hunger—yet with a new, awed tenderness—Tara had not imagined was possible in a man. She had not planned it this way, but she knew it was right. It was as if they needed to confirm their togetherness before they acknowledged each other again separately. She felt his teeth graze a shoulder as their bodies merged and moved together as one. *Not a god. A man.*

Leon pinned her arms to the floor and, then, with each quickening moment and looking straight into her eyes—as if awake for the first time in years and looking into his future through her eyes—he conquered the errors of his mistaken past.

It *is* possible . . . it *is* possible . . . it *is* . . .

Wrapped toga-like in a dark blue sheet, Tara wandered about Leon's apartment while he prepared a meal in the kitchen. The antique furniture was superb in quality and workmanship. From many different historical periods, it had the common denominator of excellence in design and attention to detail. The room itself was architecturally commanding. "It never occurred to me that an artist would live in a penthouse on Park Avenue," she called out to him. "I thought you all lived in some enclave down in the Village or somewhere."

"That was over a half-century ago, my love . . ." she heard back from the kitchen. "Although I take plenty of razzing for living this far uptown and on the East Side. I wanted to be away from the art crowd and still be able to see my two favorite buildings from my own place."

Tara glanced out the window. New York's midtown skyline wasn't as arresting as it used to be. She remembered, as a teenager, staying up late to watch old movies on television just to get a glimpse of New York as it had been before she was born. In those movies, the skyline had made her think of a dramatic signature made by an impatient hand. Now, the dominance of monoliths made it look crude, their squared-off shapes drawn by a child struggling with the new skill of handwriting. But she knew which buildings he meant. In the midst of them all, the Chrysler Building and the Empire State soared up to provide the skyline's stunning focal points.

She dropped down onto an embroidered floor pillow and traced the pattern of an oriental rug. In all this careful collection, even to the view, there was not a drop of art in the room. Why? The walls were hung with etched mirrors and hand-blown glass sconces; bronze urns and porcelain vases sat on various tables, but neither a painting nor a piece of sculpture could be found. Not one.

Now she had *two* disturbing questions: why had he cried the first time they made love? And why would an artist live without art?

She rose and headed deliberately for the library. Here she could get to know him better than by his choice of furnishings. But something turned her attention from the book-lined walls. Lying on Leon's desk, pushed to one side by a group of papers, was a copy of *L'Ancienne*. She opened it to a turned-down page and saw with astonishment that the article marked was written by Dimitrios; Leon had made several notes in the margins. The second thing that caught her attention was a wood penny whistle, identical to the one she had seen on the Gothard's boat. She picked up both items and walked back to the kitchen.

"Organic eggs, Vermont bacon, fried Brooklyn bagels, and Krug for breakfast," he announced. "Okay with you?"

"Breakfast?" She watched Leon set the dining room table: hand-painted china, cut crystal, antique silver flatware. The man had impeccable taste.

"I usually sleep until around four in the afternoon," he answered, "and then go out around seven or eight for the evening. I get to my studio in Brooklyn around one or two in the morning and work until eight or nine. Then I come home to sleep. I've been on this schedule for years." He noticed the copy of *L'Ancienne* in her hand. "You *are* self-centered," he teased. "Couldn't you find anything else of interest in my library?"

"There's an article in here by Dimitrios that I've been thinking of condensing for a digest publication. Do you mind if I borrow it? I also see that you made some notes in the margins. I'd like to look at them too, actually, if I can make out your scribbling."

"Oh. Sure." Leon poured champagne. "Well, I often do that," he lied. "Helps me think." Even though he hadn't read the article yet, he could imagine the astuteness of his mother's remarks. His hand stopped in mid-air as he noticed the object in her other hand.

Tara held up the penny whistle. "And this! Don't the Gothards have one just like it?" She laughed. "Or did you pilfer it as a memento of your trip with them?"

He stared dumbly at her hands, his mind frozen. She held a senseless lie in one hand and a cruel joke in the other.

Tara put the whistle to her lips and began to dance around the dining room, slowly unwinding herself out of the bed sheet with each step, her eyes inviting.

Leon felt as if his brain were beginning to crack, an ice block breaking up under a series of successive blows to its surface. He closed his eyes. Let it all blow apart and blow me to Hell with it, he thought.

"Leon! What's the matter?" She was beside him, both toga and penny whistle falling to the floor in her panic. "Leon, speak to me! What is it?"

His arms crushed the breath from her.

"Tara." It was all he could say.

"I'm here." She pressed her body into his as if to infuse him with her energy, she kissed his face to clear it of its anguish—the source of which she could not fathom—and she smoothed his hair and whispered sounds of comfort into his ear. The crying in Greece, it was repeating itself. This time without the tears.

Leon felt his hands moving over Tara's back, clinging desperately to the curves of her hips, as his mouth sought the sounds of comfort coming from hers. How could this have happened, what had started out as a mindless bet? How could he ever have imagined he would come to feel so deeply for her? How could he ever have dreamed that he would . . . love her? Could it be true that he, Leon Skillman the great cynic, was actually falling in *love* for the first time in his adult life?

He lifted Tara into his arms as if she were made of fragile glass and carried her to the living room, where they slipped as one onto the floor pillows, she wrapping her body around him as gently as a dressing to a wound—to soothe him, to heal him, to draw the pain from within him and make him whole again.

Late in the evening, lying awake, Leon leaned on an elbow and watched Tara sleep next to him in his bed. Once again, she had not pressed him to share his inner torment with her in words. But he had not laughed it off this time. And he hadn't lied. He had said only that it had nothing to do with her. That much he owed her. And everything more, in fact. How could he explain now, without losing her, that what had started out as a joke had become authentic for him? How could he explain his crying in Greece and his anguish tonight? He wasn't sure he understood it himself.

The city lights cut through an open sliver of drapery, causing the blue sheets to accentuate the outline of Tara's face and give an opalescent quality to the texture of her skin. A pale shade of pink lay on her cheeks. He studied the fragile detail of her closed eyelashes. The stark blackness of her hair in contrast with the pale delicacy of her features made him wish he were a painter. The inner purity of this woman, the freshness, the life.

So his youthful ideal of a woman *was* possible. It was here. It was his. But what was he to do now? How could he keep Tara when he had lied and cheated every inch of the way so far to get her?

TEN

"NO MORE!"

The moment the Gothards and their crowd left, Kostas locked the restaurant door for the night and glared at his daughter Kally. "No more!" he bellowed again. "Your mother said 'no more' weeks ago, still I give you a chance to stop your nonsense and behave like a lady. But you go on making a fool of yourself over this Mr. Gothard, and all you do is laugh at your foolish self."

Kally glared back at him, her bright blue eyes the mirror image of his own stubbornness. "I am *not* making a fool of myself. I am merely having *fun*, something you would know nothing about."

Kostas turned to his wife. "You see how she talks back to her papa? You see what kind of daughter we are growing here? She smokes in secret in the bathroom—" He nodded knowingly at Kally's shocked expression, "Oh, yes, your mama and me, we know, but we try to let you, yourself, find how foolish that is. But *this*! Throwing yourself around like a— Why you can act like that in front of a man?"

"I am *acting* like nothing in front of anybody. I am being myself and I am *trying* to have a little fun in a place you run like an army sergeant."

"Oh, you think it is like the army to have your mother dance from the kitchen with a pot of *bamyes* in her hands? You think it is the army to laugh and drink with my customers?"

"You don't do that with your *American* customers," Kally pouted.

"Not true! I have good times with many American customers. But I do not share *glendi* with people who treat my restaurant like a sideshow place or a married man who makes handpasses with my daughter of sixteen. And for you? Now! You must stop and decide with your head what to do. No matter what you *feel*, you must ask what is *right*! Is it right to work in a restaurant, mine or anybody's, and play with customers? You get paid for your job. Just 'crosspoints' like this—"

Here we go with the "crosspoints." Kally's brother Nicky smiled indulgently as he cleaned tables for the night. It wasn't until he was twelve that he realized his father meant "*crossroads*"—"crosspoints" being a mixture of "crossroads" and "turning points"—but when Nicky shouted the error at him during an argument, his father hadn't cared; it would always be "cross*points*" to him. Nicky chuckled to himself; maybe "crosspoint" was actually more precise after all.

"All your life," his father was talking patiently now, instructing Kally as if he had never said it before, "you will come to times when the thing you choose will affect the rest of your life." Nicky heard the words more from memory than in actuality; they were always pretty much the same.

"It may not seem like important things. It will not be like 'should I marry to this boy or not?' More like 'should I cheat on just this little exam?' or," Kostas looked sternly at his daughter, "should I sneak anything from Papa and Mama like, maybe, smoking in the bathroom? Every little thing you decide will affect your future because the *way* you make habits for yourself will affect the future. You understand?"

"Oh, Papa!" Kally sounded bored. "I only want to have some fun like other kids."

Kostas's voice rose again. "Why? Why you want to be like other kids? Why you don't want to be like yourself?

Listen, school is not to teach you to be like everybody else. It is to teach you to *think* for yourself."

"How would *you* know what school is for?" Kally snapped.

"The world can be a kind of school . . ." Kostas paused, "a harder kind." Nicky heard the hurt in his father's voice. "Your mama and I come here so our children will grow up in America, in freedom and with good schools, with opportunity."

Nicky scowled at Kally, hoping to warn her off. She saw him but stubbornly refused to follow his silent suggestion. Sometimes it seemed to Nicky as if his sister were consciously trying to enrage their father, as if she hoped to pay him back for some enormous wrong he had done her. All of Kostas's children knew in some unspoken way that their father felt inferior to educated people. Kally had been the only one to ever hurt him with that knowledge. Nicky didn't understand Kally any better than his parents did. At this moment he only wished she would settle down, so his father could finish and they could eat dinner.

"When I was half your age and Soviet Union came to my village, that was 'crosspoint' for me. We weren't even Russian, but they made my father who was a good carpenter go to feeding pigs on a farm. Crosspoint. What should *I* do? I see everybody do the first thing coming to their mind. Some ran, some obeyed, some fought, some bent like the weak branch of a tree. I did not know what is a good thing to do either, so I try to think, at least, what is *not* good things to do. It is not good *not* to be free. It is not good to be a coward and let others order you around with guns. It is not good to fight when you know you will lose. By myself, seven years old, I hid on a fishing boat to escape to Turkey first—"

"Crosspoint." Tara repeated the word silently to herself as she stood outside the restaurant door, about to open it but stopped by the roar of that word. Papa and his "crosspoints." She had forgotten all about his lectures over the years. She might have known that he would never forget. And, it appeared, her young sister did not want to listen. Tara had loved Papa's stories about his life before she was born. He had come a long way the hard way, and she admired him. And loved him for everything he had become. If he hadn't escaped on that fishing boat and made his way back to Greece, Kally would never have existed at all, let alone with "opportunity" in America. Tara waited patiently at the door; it would embarrass everyone if she walked in now. The lecture was almost over anyway; the "opportunity" part was next, and it was usually last. She knew the sequence well. Why didn't Kally listen? Papa's voice was no longer angry; it was clearly full of worried love for his rebellious young daughter.

"Yes! I finally get to Paros, where I know I have an uncle, and I find him. He beat me every day, yes, but at least he is a relative. I work as carpenter for him and also take tourists on the mules, two hours each way from my town, to the marble quarries where the ancients got their stone for the statues. I grow up on mules with wood dust in my hair. When I was Nicky's age, on one of those trips to the quarry, I meet your mama getting water at her village well." Kostas looked over at Marguerita, who was stacking plates from the dishwasher. "She was thinner then," he teased, enjoying his tale.

"Crosspoint. We are in love but we cannot marry. She is youngest, and two older sisters have to marry first. It is a stupid tradition, but does Marguerita hurt and embarrass her family? We wait, *then* we marry.

"Your mama becomes with a baby. It will be Tara. Crosspoint. Do we let our child grow up in this backward place? We know nobody nowhere, but we know there is opportunity in America. Maybe not for us, but so? We are poor already. But our child, and our children which will be you and Nicky, you all will go to school and learn how to use that opportunity—"

Kostas stopped and swallowed.

Nicky could see tears in his mother's eyes as she turned quickly back to her work.

"Crosspoints!" Kostas roared the word with gusto. "How *my* life would be different if I take a different road at each crosspoint! When you were small, it was a crosspoint to spank you or not. I felt like it, and you know it is true, but I never did it. Because feelings are not the way to decide what is right or not right. Listen to your feelings, yes. You can learn much about your inside self by listening to your feelings, but in order to take action, you must *think* about what to do. If your head decides it is not good, believe me, in a little while your heart will agree, and you will be glad you did not race into things. It is my job, as your father, to teach you these things. And now, Kallisti, my little baby, *you* are going to be becoming woman. Your mama was a mama not much older than you. But you must decide what kind of woman you will be. Whatever you want I will want for you. But I cannot have you running around acting like a—"

"A *what*?" Kally screamed. "You never say what you mean! What word do you mean? Tramp? Slut? Whore? See? I learned those words in *school*! And school also teaches me that you—and all old foreigners like you who came to the great America so their children could have *opportunity*—are from another world, not just another country. *I* am an American, and we don't need all this heavy thinking at every 'crosspoint,' because any and all roads are okay. *Whatever* we want is okay. And what I want is to have some *fun*!"

"And what is fun? Anything that gives you giggles? You have to decide even what is fun!" Kostas grabbed the mop from Nicky and whipped the floor furiously. "Why are you refusing? Look at Tara. She *decided* her life. Her work is fun to her, living in Greece is fun to her. And now she's coming home to us for some time. Maybe you could learn a little about how to be a lady from her."

"Oh, Tara again!" Kally snatched her coat from the rack, crying and screaming at the same time. "It's always Tara this and Tara that. The perfect child!"

"Tara was never perfect. She's impulsive! She had to be taught to slow down and *think* at the crosspoints, too. One time when we went to the seashore, she got so excited she ran right into the water with nothing on! She took off her clothes and forgot to put her bathing suit on—"

"Tara!"

They all said it at once, Kally backing up in shock because she had flung open the door and run smack into her sister, who was waiting to enter. Nicky, who grabbed the mop as his father dropped it. Marguerita, who stood rooted to her spot behind the steam tables. And Kostos.

"And *where* have *you* been?" he bellowed. "Oh, yes! I *know* you come to New York but do *not* come home to your family. Oh, yes! Konstantine, the taxi driver, tells me. I did not even dare tell your mama, she should worry so about you. Well? What do you say to your papa? Eh? Eh?"

"Kostas?" Marguerita's voice was choked with emotion. "It's Tara, Kostas—"

"*I* know it's Tara, woman! What I *want* to know is— Kantara! Charis! My baby! My darling girl! Tara!"

Kostas crushed his daughter to his big chest. "Marguerita! Kally! Nicky! It's *Tara*! She's *home*!"

"Well? What are we waiting for?" Kostas demanded, his blue eyes bright. "Here is our whole family together again! The customers are gone for the night! Hurry up! Put out the dinner!" He bear-hugged his daughter again, pushing his broadly smiling wife and his other children away from their group embrace and taking her back all to himself.

Then his exuberant tone dropped to a stern growl. "And

where *have* you been, Miss Kantara, firstborn child of mine who came to New York yesterday?"

Nicky quickly handed his father a bottle of Greek wine, as Marguerita and Kally started laying huge platters of steaming food on a table. "Let's celebrate, Papa! Besides, you've already given one lecture tonight, and Tara's heard it a million times anyway when she was young."

Kostas opened his mouth in shock at his son's audacity, but before he could reprimand Nicky, Kally, throwing off her anger, danced over to her father with glasses in her hands. "And wine for Nicky and me, too, Papa! We *all* are celebrating, aren't we? 'The whole family together,' right? Besides," she giggled dangerously on the edge of insolence, even *I* don't have to hear the 'Crosspoint' spiel twice in one night, do I?"

Marguerita stopped spooning soup and looked up, worried at her husband's reaction to such daring from their children.

Nicky offered Kostas the wine screw and spoke to him quietly and firmly. "Tara is an adult, now, Papa."

Kostas glared at him and then at Kally. "You are *right*!" He stomped his foot on the floor, adding an emphatic exclamation point to his words and, shaking his head in wonder at all three of his children, grabbed the tool from Nicky and began furiously to open the wine. "Well?" He glowered at Kally, but a slow smile began to creep over his face as he handed her a half-full glass. "We were talking about dancing, weren't we? So turn on the music, and let's *dance*!"

ELEVEN

THE TINY BALLERINA turned perfect pirouettes on one pink, porcelain toe to the tinkling sound of Tchaikovsky. The dancer's tutu spun in perfect circles of stiff, blue net and her glazed hair, pulled into a perfect pony-tail with a pink ribbon, shone in lacquered black under the glow of a bedside lamp, edged in the same blue net. Across the bottom of the little music box, in not-so-perfect letters, the name "Charis" had been handpainted in red nail enamel.

Tara, lying in her childhood bed for the first time in a decade, watched the dancing doll and felt engulfed in the familiar comfort of her father's home; a place full of laughter and music (and restrictions), yet filled, as well, with enormous caring, and a certain gruff tenderness. On her eighth Name Day Papa had given her the music box along with a check for her first month's ballet lessons. "Charis," he had called her long before that holiday. "Grace" or "charm," it meant in Greek.

Looking about the sparsely furnished room, Tara wondered how her father had ever been able to afford dance classes for her, and piano lessons for Kally, and art instruction for Nicky. So ignorant of the arts himself that he felt awkward in a museum, he had made sure that each of his children was introduced to some part of that foreign world of which he knew nothing but valued in some unspoken way. It was his heritage and his responsibility to them, he always said, from his birthland of Greece to his chosen land of America.

Kally had played the piano tonight after dinner with a poise beyond her years. What an arresting young woman she was going to be, Tara thought. And a firebrand, too, if the commotion she'd heard going on inside the restaurant was any example. She felt a small tinge of regret that she really didn't know her sister and brother at all. After years of inability to conceive another child to follow their first, Kostas and Marguerita had finally given up hope of a large family; then, within three years, both Nicky and Kally had been born. With Tara nearly a teenager, it was like a second family for her parents, but Tara remembered with acute fondness that although her mother had become preoccupied with her new babies, Kostas had always remained sensitive to his firstborn's needs: attentive to her activities and adamant about her "crosspoints" education.

Tara stared at the ballerina, her throat tight. Nothing had changed. Even during tonight's festive dinner together, after the kisses and news exchanges were over, her father had still managed to grill her about her first night in New York. The Greek cab driver had actually gone to eat at the restaurant within hours after meeting her, so she had little choice but to tell her family about Leon right away.

Except—she looked around the room—everything had changed. Her parents were older; strange she had never noticed it during their trips to Athens. Nicky and Kally were nearly grown; Nicky was already a young man. And she? She lived in another world, one as unfamiliar to her family as their world was to her now.

The tinkling sound stopped abruptly, and she turned, startled, to see her ballerina still poised on one pink toe, but perfectly motionless. Childhood seemed very far away. And Greece seemed far away too. Dimitrios's face was only a memory.

She pushed herself out of bed and spread papers from her briefcase over the top of the dresser, staring blankly at photos from the undersea exploration. For the first time, her athlete looked not like a god but like an artifact. Somehow, all of the objects, news-breaking treasures a couple of months ago, seemed lifeless here. What had emerged from the sea as living testaments now appeared to her as historical objects.

She climbed back into bed. It was cold. Her Mediterranean blood couldn't adjust to the winter temperature. She snuggled deep into the warmth of flannel sheets. She was glad she had come home when she did to be reminded of Papa's special word. Now she could recall freshly the many nights of her childhood, when she lay in this very bed mulling over the "crosspoints" of her own life: school decisions, career choices, even hairstyles and clothes. Nothing had ever been too unimportant to approach consciously, as her father had taught her, with only one goal in mind: what is the best thing to do? And why?

She thought of the warmth of Leon's bed, the warmth of his body curled around hers and the warmth of his breath in sleep. She also thought of his troubling behavior, twice now. What it meant, she didn't know, but the intensity of it certainly made her uneasy. They would have to confront it together sooner or later. Did she love him? Did he love her? If she was already making love with him, this should not be a question, she realized. Everything was happening between them too fast. From the beginning she seemed to have had no power to resist him. But wasn't that feeling of powerlessness part of what she liked? Leon was the only man she had ever met who possessed the full power to wipe out hers.

Her father's aura permeated the room. In an instant, she jumped out of bed, ran to her briefcase for pen and pad and, with the eagerness of her childhood, leaped back into the warm nest of covers. Remembering a "crosspoint" exercise her father had taught her when she was still nine or ten, she also remembered that she had loved it then and used it often throughout her teens. But it had never occurred to her that she could apply "crosspoint" principles to the selection of a man. It would never have occurred to her now except that the proximity of Leon's bed and that of her childhood upbringing were so very close. Even though the idea seemed rather silly, it was also compelling. All right, she thought, feeling her sense of adventure rising. Try it! Put it down in black and white. She printed his name across the top of a page: "LEON SKILLMAN." Then, she drew a vertical line down the center and headed each column: "PRO" and "CON."

The "PRO" side was easy, and her emotions had no trouble corroborating the list. "INTELLIGENT," "WORLDLY," "EDUCATED," "STYLISTICALLY FASCINATING," "SUCCESSFUL," "KNOWLEDGEABLE IN THE ARTS AND IN MY OWN FIELD," "ARTIST," "SEXUALLY . . ." She hesitated, searching for a word. "THRILLING?" "EXHILARATING?" "HUNGRY?" She'd learned to put down any word that came to mind because she could analyze the list later, but now she couldn't seem to settle even on the first word. Something was wrong. "FULFILLING?" "NOT QUITE FULFILLING?" "POIGNANT?" "GLORIOUS?" Silly words. Making love with Leon was the most thrilling she had ever known. But there was a quality in *his* lovemaking that seemed touched with pain. Too much hunger? Too great a need? There was something desperate about his pleasure. She moved her pen to the "CON" side of the line. "TWO DISTRAUGHT EPISODES AFTER LOVE," "PERRY GOTHARD FOR FRIEND," "SHOOTING SHARKS," "WILL NOT TALK OF OWN ART," "NO ART IN HOME," "HUMOR . . ." Stuck again. "SLICK," she decided. Remembering his apartment, she went back to the "PRO" side: "TASTE MAGNIFICENT." Then across the top of the page in huge letters, she wrote "ART?"

She sat back and chewed on the pen, her conscious mind

racing now, her emotions refusing to listen, a frown creasing her brow with one vertical line as if marking the division of an internal "PRO" and "CON," her body watching the battle and waiting like a sentinel to serve the winner.

"Not enough information," her father would say when she got bogged down like this. "Ask different questions." She looked again at the "CON" listing. These were *actions*, not *attributes*. She needed to know the "whys" behind the actions.

She remembered Dimitrios's article and bounded out of bed again to read the notes in the margins. Maybe they would reveal some of Leon's secrets.

Opening the journal, she heard low sounds coming from her parents' bedroom. Unable to resist, she crept to her door and listened. They were laughing—chuckling, sort of. She sprang back from the door in shock. Her parents were making love! At their age!

Of course, at their age, she chided herself, climbing back into bed. Wonderful! she decided. She found the article and began to read.

"Classical Greek Art: A State of Mind," by Dimitrios Kokonas.

She looked back at the door. Did Dimitrios, too, have a love life with women? Of course, with women. But *what* women? What *woman*? She cast her question over the years. Surely her mentor must have had romantic relationships, but whom had she seen him with regularly? As far as attending important museum or cultural events, they had always gone together, even when she'd been involved with another man. Dimitrios took her to dinner often, even dancing, but always after work; these weren't *dates,* just a continuation of their workday; of course work in Athens didn't end until seven or eight in the evening. But had she never run into him alone with a woman at any restaurant, for example? Her recollection seemed to picture him in small groups, with other colleagues, or colleagues and their wives. The rest of the time, it seemed that he and she had been together. Whenever Dimitrios had a party, she was always the hostess. And whenever their friends had one, she and Dimitrios naturally went together. Actually, that's probably why neither one of them had much time to date. They made their own "couple"; both of them had been so committed to their common work for so many years, there hadn't been room in either of their lives for many other people. Work was their life.

But it did seem disconcerting to imagine Dimitrios in love with some woman she'd never met, in the same way it had just been initially disturbing to think of her parents making love as two separate people. Like them, Dimitrios was an anchor in her life; it had actually never occurred to her to wonder if he had a personal life of his own.

And it suddenly seemed odd, now that she thought about it, that she had never wondered about him this way. As Dimitrios said, he had known *her* lovers, meaning the two with whom she'd had affairs in Greece: Marc, the dynamic young American who had come to Athens for a summer fling after having just passed the Boston Bar but found a more serious pursuit in her; although exciting and promising, she'd lost interest within six months, once she learned that he loved not justice but the joust. And later, Jean-Claude, the fine arts photographer who she truly thought was the one and only mature love of her life because at thirty he seemed to be an older and deeper version of her beautiful, youthful Michael but with more intellect and ambition. It had taken a two-year liaison with the dashing Frenchman for her to reluctantly admit that his subject matter was not what motivated him; he just loved to take pictures and happened to work for a publisher of art books. It was photography for its own sake that he loved, which was fine, just not deep enough for her in the long run.

And before these, of course (and after these forever in her heart) there would always remain Michael, the one love Dimitrios never met. Though others called him "Mike," he was her *Michael*, her first love and her first lover. Michael, whose masculine essence she still carried within her in the form of a permanent and precious mark on her feminine soul.

Half dozing, now, Tara lazed deeper into the comforting cocoon of sheets and drifted into a hazily sensuous awareness of lying in the same bed where, when she first met him in junior high school at age twelve, she dreamed of romance. In the same bed where, when they finally became lovers during their first year of college, she had returned home to dreamless and peaceful sleep after having spent hours in his bed . . . in his loving arms.

Michael, who set the first romantic standard for her because he was the first male in her life to love her who was not in some regard unsure around her. Michael (her blond Adonis), who exuded the confidence and virility of a Viking, who laughed at her spirited challenges rather than running away or caving under, as did the rest of her many suitors. Michael, who passed every test she devised because he refused to be tested.

When she was thirteen and read *Romeo and Juliet* for the first time, she'd wept with empathy at the virgin's orchard scene:

> *Spread thy close curtain, love-performing night,*
> *That runaway's eyes may wink, and Romeo*
> *Leap to these arms untalk'd of and unseen!*
> *Lovers can see to do their amorous rites*
> *By their own beauties; or, if love be blind,*
> *It best agrees with night. Come, civil night,*
> *Thou sober-suited matron, all in black,*
> *And learn me how to lose a winning match*

"And learn me how to lose a winning match . . ." Let me challenge, and let me *lose*. Within Juliet's own thirteen-year-old cries to the wilderness, Tara for the first time vaguely and poignantly recognized her own feminine yearnings. And in all her youth, Mike Westland *was* her only match as a man. She loved him passionately and almost completely (she would always love him), but even at the time, she sensed he would never be enough for her. Although she slept exclusively with him, she dated others constantly, doing things with them in areas where he had no interest: the ballet, the opera, jazz concerts, and poetry readings. With him, she canoed, water skied, ice-skated, picnicked and mostly just *loved*, learning from him the sounds of her own body and the capaciousness of her own heart. She loved his love of himself, his love of life and his love of her, but when she left New York, she left him behind with the rest of her youth, as she always knew deep down she would someday do, because he failed her ultimate challenge by never matching the zeal of her mind. But she had loved him, and more: she had loved loving.

Languidly, Tara attempted to rouse herself from sweet reverie by winding the key in the music box until it was tight and watching absently as the ballerina whirled around again on one tiny point. But there was a soft, wistful smile on her face as Michael's pale blue eyes faded back into the past.

A journal lay open on her lap. She stared at it dumbly for a moment, thinking she had nodded off into a delicious dream, and then remembered Dimitrios's article, forgetting entirely her earlier wonderings about him. Shaking herself into semi-alertness, she began to read it:

> *We have only ruins, yet we cling to them as if to our own sanity, for ancient Greece was the fountainhead of Western civilization. Yet, there is still that missing link between the more primitive, previous cultures and the great, life-loving Greeks who produced the first philosophers. Evidence continues to point to the pre-Greek culture of the Minoans. Their art—in contrast to that of their Egyptian contemporaries, whose every moment of life was dedicated to the enshrinement of death—focused on life:*

> *plants, animals, and especially humans in sportive activity. Somersaulting over the horns and back of a bull was serious business, but vase paintings depict a playful spirit that projects confidence in human abilities to succeed. Men who are afraid of life do not play—*

In the margin, Tara read Leon's note: Affirmative art/orderly universe.

Oh, yes! She breathed softly.

> *We see that, in fact, there simply was no "West" until the Greeks and that from their seminal era on, East and West were premised on opposite states of mind.*

In the margin, Tara read: If human life is the standard, humanistic art necessary for spiritual connection?

Good god! she marveled, fully awake now. What must Leon's art be like? Eagerly, she began to scan the article, looking for more margin notes.

> *... harmony. This is precisely why we find physical fitness given equal emphasis with scholarship and spiritual fulfillment in Classical Greek culture.*
>
> *The Greeks invented the Olympian Games to take pleasure in the beauty and excellence of their bodies as well as their minds. Balance and order in everything. And the joy of it all!*

Tara smiled at Dimitrios's "joy of it." Leon felt the same way! There was a huge exclamation point in the margin. Leon should hear Dimitrios give the speech in person. Whenever he talked of ancient Greek values, his own love for the subject became contagious. She felt close to Greece again. And even closer to Leon.

> *This does not mean that the Greeks were unaware of*

> pain. Their tragedies are the most tragic of all. But they also excelled at comedy. The whole of life, as the whole of man, was the Greek concern. They severed man in only one regard. From fear. Greek figures stand alone. Man free, unafraid and unashamed. Man and Woman with feet firmly on this earth. Note that the 'Winged Victory' is from a late period; the temple on the Acropolis was built to the 'Wingless Victory'. Victory on earth!

Tara felt her throat constrict. The intensity of the man! She read Leon's notes in the margin: "Human form, now, nudes distorted and ugly. Beauty? Define art/beauty in terms of man's psychological/spiritual needs." So Leon must sculpt nudes! She read on:

> In studying these great works of art, there is much to contemplate, much to cling to for our sanity in an increasingly insane world—

But new, unsettling thoughts crept into her mind now. What made her presume that Leon sculpted nudes? She hadn't, in fact, a clue about his work. Perhaps she *had* responded only to his personal chemistry? Failing all advice, she had not "gone slowly" at all with him. In this room, with all its cherished memories, she felt more like a silly schoolgirl, infatuated and foolish, than she ever had when she was young.

Yet Leon had written these life-affirming margin notes long before he knew her. And they had talked endlessly for many evenings together; they did share important values; he did match her mind; and he certainly matched—

There was a soft knock at the door.

Tara slipped out of bed, and grabbing her robe, threw it around her shoulders.

"I saw your light—"

It was Nicky with a cup of tea for her. Setting the tray

on the dresser, she embraced him. "My brother." *Who is a painter now,* she thought. What will *his* work be like?

TWELVE

NICKY BANGED A BROOM HANDLE on the steam pipe in the corner of Dorina's studio. Bastard superintendent! he thought. The guy actually turned off the heat when he knew Dorina and he weren't there. Every time one of them came in, they had to bang on the pipe so he would restore it. It was freezing in the studio, and it wasn't good for their paintings to have to endure such extreme changes in temperature. Bastard!

Nicky put a kettle of water on the hotplate and carefully scooped some tealeaves into Dorina's fine china pot. He took two antique cups and saucers from the cupboard and set them cautiously on a lacquered tray. He would just as soon have used earthenware mugs, but it was Dorina's studio, and everything she owned, it seemed, was fragile. Except her soul, Nicky thought affectionately; that was made of steel. Waiting for the water to boil, he stood opposite his work in progress, intent on examining it, but found himself pondering his older sister instead.

Tara said she would meet him at the studio around four, when she finished her afternoon conference at the museum. But it was already four-twenty, and Nicky worried that soon there wouldn't be enough natural light for her to see anything. Tara certainly seemed eager to view his paintings. What would she think? Did he really care what she thought? She was his sister, but he hardly knew her. I like her, though, he thought happily. If I just met her, at a party let's say, and she wasn't my sister, I'd like her immediately. She has such a natural candor and generosity, but at the same time she holds her opinions very dear. Like Papa, he thought. Tara is like Papa. Kally does everything she can do *not* to be like Papa. Where do I fit in? He moved the angle of the easel so that the light (what was left of it) would wash the canvas directly through the window and then, deliberately, set an alabaster carving on an end table where Tara couldn't miss seeing it. He was haunted by the possibility that his sister might share an artistic dichotomy similar to his own. Could it be? At least Dorina called what he had a "dichotomy."

When Tara had told their father on her first night home that she was "seeing" Leon Skillman, all Papa knew about Skillman was that he was a man who had kept his daughter overnight. But Nicky had been floored. He knew Skillman's sculpture, of course; anyone who had ever leafed through an art magazine did. But it seemed impossible that a woman whose life's work was the preservation and study of Greek history could be involved in any way with Leon Skillman, who was considered to be the only living minimalist to powerfully carry on the American tradition of viscerally confrontational abstract art. Dorina had more than once cited his work as the contemporary epitome of nihilistic art. Conversely, Nicky's college professors regarded Skillman as the last "fair-haired boy" of the avant-garde. All of them agreed, of course, that there *was* no avant-garde left in today's pluralistic, postmodern art world because there was nothing left to rebel against, but even though minimalism as a movement had been a dead duck for years, they all thought of Leon Skillman as one of the last great revolutionaries. Newspapers chronicled his every move, and photos of him with prominent socialites were all over the place. One current fashion magazine even featured him with a group of edgy young models in a six-page spread. He was a "hot" artist to the point of being as much a "star" in the art world as any rock personality was in the music world; he was rich, and he continued to be successful at everything he touched. Nicky shook his head in wonder. He just couldn't seem to picture Leon Skillman and Tara together.

He poured water for tea. Where *was* she? Suddenly he felt more annoyance at her than was called for. This Skillman and Tara business was only adding to the frustration he already felt about his art.

All his annoyance vanished in the next moment, however, when Tara burst into the room and without even kissing him "hello," walked straight to a painting. "I'm sorry," she panted. "I can give you three good reasons why I'm late, or you can save us both time and just forgive me. It was unavoidable."

Nicky grinned; his whole face grinned. "You're forgiven." She accepted tea and stood looking at the painting without taking off her coat. Gradually, a smile warmed her face. Nicky tensed; was it the painting or the tea? Damn it! At last, without a word, she set her cup down and turned to the two companion paintings hanging, finished, on a wall. She looked at them for a long time. Then she sat down on a chair and began to cry.

"Oh! You don't have to like them!" Nicky was on his knees beside her. "You don't have to!"

Tara wiped her face with the napkin she had crumpled into her fist. Staring at her brother in horror, she covered his face with kisses. "Don't have to *like* them?" She laughed and wept again, her face wetting his face with new tears. "Don't have to *like* them? *You dear sweet fool*! I *love* them! Oh, Nicky, my little brother, I feel such a loss at not knowing you better! You've made me so proud to be your sister, and I don't even know you!"

He took the napkin from her hand and, like a big brother, dried her tears, one by one, until he was sure he could trust his voice. Finally, he managed a low, "You know me."

Standing again in front of the paintings, she asked, "How is it that you paint these places? You've spent your life in a city with neon lights and garbage cans lining the streets. Have you ever been to these places?"

"Well, Tara, of course I've been to the sea. You know, Papa does get us away once in a while. But I spent several weeks over the past couple of summers with my teacher, Dorina, when she goes on her annual 'immersions,' as she calls them, into nature."

"Oh, Nicky, I've never *seen* such purples and oranges and turquoises . . . bold yet blending. Your passionate palette reminds me a little of Turner's, but I love the way you capture *both* the wild and the willful. I'll never be able to look at the sea again without these paintings leading my vision." She gazed at the pictures in amazement, commenting quietly, almost to herself. "Endless in serenity and peace. But so alive. Oh! The energy! Singing with vitality. The world, from whatever vantage point, affirmative and reassuring. But exciting! Beauty. Renewing beauty. Redemptive beauty."

"Thank you." Nicky felt stinging in his own eyes now, but Dorina had taught him to stand very still and say a simple "Thank you" whenever some one-in-a-hundred person said all that could be said . . . or verged on that which never could be said.

Tara went from one painting to the next, viewing each from a variety of distances and angles. "The perspectives are absolutely unique. Some of the picture planes are so shallow, I don't know how you managed to separate them and keep the perspective. And the impasto! You are daring! I've never seen anything quite like these declamatory gestures with a brush before. It's obvious you don't build up the paint but lay each gesture on in one passionate stroke. Very . . . well, yes, 'daring'! What do you do if the gesture is wrong?"

"Scrape and do it again, fresh, until it's right."

Tara inclined her head in a small bow. "What do you call this series?"

"*Sea Spells*."

All three works were large. In each painting the point of view was from a different man-made object. Tara felt she was seeing the sea from a different perspective, literally and figuratively, in each one. In the first, Nicky had painted the half-round of a balcony into the foreground. She felt as if she were standing on that balcony at twilight. Naked. It had to be naked, after a shower, perhaps, clean and fresh and at peace with her day, herself and the world. The colors were deep and dramatic, the lighting bold for twilight, drawing her to the majesty, that sense of being charmed by mysteries.

In the second painting, the partial presence of an umbrella and a brightly colored beach ball drew her attention to the warm texture of the sand and the playful roll of the surf, then cast her eye out to the brilliance of a shining sea. The aesthetic values of the work were absolutely mesmerizing on their own, the deeper themes profoundly moving: the merging—the harmony!—of the man-made and the metaphysical. Her skin tingled from the anticipation of falling under still another "spell." In the one unfinished canvas, the point of view was from the bow of a sailboat, one part of the sail catching a breeze and catching her breath at the same time, a moment of time arrested, a portion of time stopped. Humanity and nature; the eternal and the temporal. "*Sea Spells*! Yes! Nicky, there are so many levels."

"Thanks," Nicky said. "I'm learning, I think. My favorite aspects of other artists' work have kept me moving on to deeper levels of appreciation. Sort of like peeling layer after layer off an onion," he laughed at his awkward metaphor. "Anyhow, I just keep going as far as I know how. I think about these things, you know, when I'm looking at other works or writing a paper or working at the museum or something. But when I paint, after my goal is set, I just paint. I try to work according to a quote by Corot that Dorina told me: 'Never lose sight of that first impression by which you were moved.' So sometimes I think I paint these scenes because while I'm creating them, I can live in them, in that feeling of 'the first impression.' There's a lot I don't understand."

"On the contrary, you understand so much. Working at what museum, Nicky?"

"I work part-time at the Brooklyn Museum in the art and music division. And when I can, I help out at the telephone and e-mail reference department. That's my favorite work. The things I learn! It's just fascinating."

"I thought you waited tables for Papa as your part-time job."

"I do, but that's my second part-time job. I do that because Papa needs me. The other, I really love."

"What about money?"

"Oh, I get paid both places."

"What do you do in your spare time?" Tara joked.

Now she looked around for the first time at Dorina Swing's studio. Strangely, the first thing she thought of was Dimitrios's article: *Balance and Order*. Even more, the studio itself, in some elusive way, reminded her of Dimitrios's home overlooking the sea. Dorina's place was a one-room art studio in a shabby building on the West Side of New York with overflowing trashcans lining the street. Dimitrios's home was large and stark and dramatically perched with an open view of endless space over an endless ocean. It was the attention to detail, Tara realized. Nothing here or at Cape Sounion was accidental. She noted an antique shawl thrown casually over the end of a petit-point settee and the tapes of concert music and jazz stacked neatly, but clearly used, in a sheer fabric-lined cupboard. There was paint on the bare wood floor (it was a working studio) but the windows were spotless. A partially filled wine rack sat atop a small cabinet; the glass cupboard doors above it were lined with white lace. "How old is Dorina?" she asked. She knew Dimitrios would like this place. He crossed her mind often in this way, ever since she'd arrived in New York. Well, after all, she told herself, she spent nearly all of her waking time with him in Greece. Wasn't it only normal to feel as if she were missing an arm or something without him nearby?

"Dorina's fifty this year. I'm taking her to dinner at Papa's to celebrate," Nicky was saying.

Tara wandered past smoky purple mountainscapes shrouded in heavy atmosphere and deep mystery, and male nudes shrouded in nothing but their own pride. Something about the drawings made her stop. "Dorina seems to be an interesting woman," she mused to Nicky.

"She is. And she's a tyrant of a teacher. She also disagrees violently with my professors at school."

"How so?"

"Oh, a million things. Dorina and my professors even disagree about what art *is*. Dorina's big on form serving content, and my other teachers say that *process* is all. Dorina says art should be objective; they say subjective is superior. It goes on and on."

"Subjective *versus* objective? It sounds like Plato *versus* Aristotle all over again," Tara mused.

"Still." Nicky corrected. "*Still*. The argument has never been settled."

"Perhaps it never will be. Are you trying to sell your work yet, or is it too soon?"

"I've sold one painting." Nicky turned on a light and held a slide against the bulb for her to see.

A dozen birds shot like the point of an arrow across a red sunrise. Tara saw stunning colors and she saw birds, but what she experienced was the freedom and the joy of flight. From a slide! "Nicky! Really! Where did you sell this?"

"At a very little-known art gallery called A IS A GALLERY. And for very little money, I might add."

Tara looked around the room "And does Dorina make her living by selling her art or by teaching?"

"Neither. She sells her stuff at A IS A GALLERY, too, but she makes her living as an art restorer." Feeling disappointed that the day was gone and she hadn't even noticed it, he lifted the alabaster piece from the table and placed it under the light. "What about this?"

"What about it?" Tara asked, not understanding.

"I did this, too." He could see the confusion in her eyes as she stared at the piece.

"You sculpt, too?" she asked warily. "It's so different from the rest of your work."

"Well, Dorina says it's so different that it's in a different category altogether. But I'll tell you something. This alabaster *will sell*, quickly, and it takes a fraction of the time it takes to make any one of my paintings. And I *am* taught in my college courses that the construction of a piece alone should occupy my attention, not any deeper meaning or even a subject. Well, this alabaster piece has no subject and it has no content. It's all aesthetics. It's just a shape, a form, something to please the eye and give tactile pleasure. It pleases me to make it, too. Dorina says this is decorative art, that it speaks on a sensory, perceptual level, which is fine, but . . . well, what do you think?"

"I don't know." Tara gazed thoughtfully at the gray spiral. It was nearly two feet tall and sensuously smooth: a gray, smooth spiral. That was all. "It's very lyrical." she ventured. "I know very little about contemporary art. That's odd, isn't it? You're living, so you're 'contemporary,' but I somehow don't imagine your paintings would be considered *contemporary* in the current art world, would they? Well, I don't know, really, about any of this. But your spiral is beautiful—the harmony of design and the way it flows—so I suppose something that's primarily pleasing to the senses can be valid in the same way all good design and decor is valid."

"Now you're into a question of what's 'good' and 'bad' design and decor. Now you're into a question of aesthetics. Not so simple, is it?"

Tara looked soberly at her brother, whom she had grown to love enormously in the span of this one precious hour. "What a deep person you are," she said, her wonder and respect blending into a flat statement of fact.

"No." Nicky washed their cups carefully in the sink, then dried them and put them away in the lace-windowed cabinet. "I'm just me. Papa taught me to ask 'why.' That's all I'm doing. It doesn't matter to me what the truth is. I just want to understand it, and express it my own way."

Where had she heard that statement before? She watched how her brother handled another person's property. He was so sensitive—Dimitrios, of course. It was Dimitrios who always said it didn't matter what the truth was, and that the proper search for it was as important as the truth itself. Perhaps *Leon* could help, she thought suddenly. Of course! Leon's work *sold*, and although she hadn't seen it yet herself, Perry Gothard had called it "heroic." What a perfect thing, to introduce Nicky to Leon. Clearly, this Dorina person and Nicky's professors were the only voices he heard about art. And Leon wasn't a teacher of art. He was a working artist, out there in the real world, both creating and selling. "Had you ever heard of Leon Skillman before I mentioned him the other night?" she asked.

"Of course." Nicky grabbed his jacket and turned out the light. "He's very well known."

"What do you think of his work?"

Nicky looked astonished. "What do *you* think of it is a better question."

They walked down the five flights of stairs. "I haven't seen it yet. I've only been in town for a few days, remember?"

"Well . . ." They joined the mass of people on the street, pushing home after work like an evening tide.

"Well *what*?" Tara asked, linking arms with her brother.

"Well, I think you'd better see Leon Skillman's work for yourself," Nicky said.

THIRTEEN

Taking refuge from the conversation of Blair and her cohorts surging inside the museum, Kronan Hagen stepped onto the balcony that jutted out like a parapet over a small garden to smoke a cigarette; he felt suddenly light, instantly suspended in both space and time. Yet, inner worries haunted him. *I filled this new wing, he thought uneasily. It has been my responsibility. But there has been no way to do it responsibly.* His eyes rested on the curvature of a bronze thigh and traveled upward to the round (and ripe) buttocks of a large female figure in the center of the garden. He felt a stirring in his groin and hurried his glance up the arched back of the sculpture to arms reaching yet further upward. Bronze vines swirled downward from the figure's open hands to mingle with real foliage on the ground, while living vines climbed upward again, clinging to a tree and climaxing in an exotic burst of multi-colored orchids. Kronan felt guilt blur the edges of sensuality, and then both were mercifully rescued by Blair Gothard's voice calling him back into the room with a question.

His employer drew him close to her so that the photographer could get a shot of both of them conversing. "What was that quote you used from the Bible that got all of your contributors to come forth with such generous gifts for that church project of yours?"

Kronan concentrated on keeping his expression expressionless. "It was Deuteronomy 15:11," he answered. "For the poor shall never cease out of the land; therefore, I command thee, saying, thou shalt open thine hand wide unto thy brother . . ."

"Ah, yes." Blair radiated a smile into the camera. "You would be amazed to know how much money Kronan has raised for his church," she confided to the others. "Anyway, I'm going to use the same theme for my Christmas party in Palm Beach. Kronan is so clever! He doesn't ask for money, but for *things*, which can be translated back into money." Blair beamed at the thought. The camera clicked away. "And it works to the advantage of the donors, too, because by contributing appreciated property—securities, real estate, jewelry, cars—rather than cash, they get big tax benefits."

"It would be even more advantageous if the funds went to a public or a university museum," Denise Sommers cut in sharply.

"Unfortunately," Blair sweetened her tone (Van Varen had warned her that the Sommers girl was with the Arts Council), "my mother is against redistribution of money by the government for any reason, and she's especially against government support of the arts because she considers it a form of censorship. So," she shook her head to clue Van that this was not for publication, "although I've helped Kronan acquire the *art* for this new wing, my mother has to approve the architecture and the funding. And she will accept no government money. So," she shrugged apologetically, "private we remain."

The critic Robert Van Varen turned to Kronan, trying to help. He had been around long enough to know that whenever Blair's mother was brought into a conversation, the conversation died. "And what do *you* think of the architecture, Kronan? Do you think a museum building should be one of the objects viewers come to see? As we speak, you're one of fifty or so other American museums renovating or 'new winging' themselves into zillion-dollar signature buildings with brand-name architects. How did you choose?"

"As Blair said, her mother chose. And you know Margaret couldn't care less what anyone else is doing, so although highly respected, Daniela Fredson is decidedly *not* 'brand-name'." answered Kronan. "But most of those other museums have B-grade collections, so their new buildings, if they're crazy enough, can become draws in and of themselves to help increase the gate. We've got what's considered to be an A+ collection, which attracts viewers on its own, so *this* building shows off by *not* showing off. For myself, I not only appreciate the understated architecture, which *refrains* from distracting from the art by being a perfect balance between form and function, but I also love it because it's a conservator's dream." He wanted to add that he'd give anything if the art from this collection and that of the main museum could be reversed so that the *real* treasures could be so well housed, but "Van" was taking notes, so he continued carefully. "The temperature and the humidity are computer-controlled. This entire enormous glass expanse is subtly screened in order to protect the art from damaging sunlight, and filters in the ceiling further remove any traces of ultraviolet radiation. Plus, air pollution removal devices are installed throughout the building; they're so sensitive that if a woman uses hairspray in the ladies' room, I'm not sure if any of it will reach her hair before it's sucked up into the system."

Van ignored Kronan's lame attempt at humor and stepped out onto the parapet. "This strange little garden seems both out of place and absolutely perfect at the same time. What's it doing here?"

"My mother's contribution," Blair interjected. "She abhors most of the art we've chosen for the new wing and insisted on adding a little 'respite,' as she calls it, for any like-minded visitors."

"What's that suit of armor doing in the corner? It's like

some spirit voyeur gazing out from another century at the female nude."

"You may recall that my grandfather—not my father—started the steel production business. It was Grandfather's hobby of collecting armor that began the original atrium museum—my grandmother's way of getting all that stuff out of the main section of the house, I imagine. Don't include the garden in the story, Van," she warned. "You know my mother won't abide the mention of her private projects in print. Let's just think of it as a charming peek into the art world of the past from the art world of the present, and a beautiful *hortus conclusus* full of nature's wonders among the wonders of man. How's that for vagueness?"

"The flowers and foliage do provide a haven though," Van mused. "Even for one who *does* appreciate the art in here." He turned back to Kronan, pen poised again. "Twentieth-century and contemporary art aren't your field, Kronan, I know."

And don't *I* know, Kronan managed not to say; he concentrated on Van's question.

"So how did you select the art contained here?"

Kronan smiled at the diplomacy of the query. "Mostly, I tried to imagine what, a hundred years from now, will be representative of this era in the continuing history of art. I also gave considerable weight to public awareness of the artists. You know, with economic pressures the way they are and all the competition from the big blockbuster museum exhibitions, we need to attract the largest-volume attendance we can. So the art is sometimes, regrettably, not as important as the prominence of the artists." Kronan changed the subject abruptly; he was answering more than he had been asked. "I also considered relative positioning, size, scale, color, texture, things of that sort," he concluded.

Adria Cass drew the photographer over to one of her huge paintings, which took up nearly a quarter of an entire wall. "But Kronan, Baby, spectacle *is* art. That's what brings 'volume attendance' to any museum. Look! What I've created is a new object, a new entity, never before existing on earth." She stood in front of the painting to let the photographer get a good shot. "It's spectacular. *And* it's magic! I just blank out my mind and trust the astral hand that guides my hand. *That's* what keeps the work hot. It throws viewers off balance and stimulates a visceral sensation cuz they can't comprehend it with their brains. I mean that literally. It excites the senses in a way that's both physically titillating and mystically profound." She looked up at the mammoth canvas and glanced over to make sure Van was taking notes. "This one I did with tiny balloons. I filled hundreds of them with different colors of paint and stuck them up all over the canvas. Then I threw darts into the balloons and the paint spurted or dripped any way its Karma dictated it should spurt or drip. I got the idea from my late husband, for sure, but the result is something that could never have been created by human intention or design. Certainly not by reason. Viewers can project whatever meaning they like into it, or they can just let the configurations work on them physiologically to elicit any visual or gut reaction they might. It never happens the same way twice. *That's* innovative! That's what's exciting about art. But," she laughed uproariously, " I'm pretty old fashioned. If I were really 'with it' today, I'd piss or spit or shit on the whole canvas before I called it finished. What do ya think pals?"

Kronan forced himself to look at Adria's painting and concentrated on keeping his face blank. He couldn't bear to look at Adria herself. She was a mess. And her painting was a mess, a sticky mess of swirling, bleeding colors; it looked like the battlefield of a war going on in some poor psychotic's demented brain. This society is truly sick, he thought sadly. It has no beauty, it has no morals, it has no values. And it has no art. God is not dead, people are. If men are sick in spirit, he wondered, does it help to hold up before them the face of death, or to remind them of the radiance of life?

Adria struck a pose in front of another canvas, hugging Van with one arm and Denise Sommers with the other. "Van gave this one a rave and Denny financed it," she was saying as the photographer flashed away. She turned to Denise. "Remember, Denny, it was part of that grant I got eight years ago when you were still interning."

"Why do you call it *City Lights*?" Blair asked. "I don't know why I never asked you before. I've owned it for five years."

Adria chortled. Kronan concentrated on hiding his disgust.

"It was Flo's idea," Adria explained. "My name for it was 'Screwing,' but Flo thought it was too explicit for Madison Avenue."

Blair looked uncertain. "Screwing?" Then she brightened with understanding. "Oh! Is it a sequel to my *Hammer and Nail* series?"

Adria bubbled over again. Kronan thought he would be ill if he had to listen to her much longer. "Not bad," she said, "but, no, it was just cuz that's how it was created. Leon and I got ahold of some special paint you can cover all over yourself without suffocating; so we got wrecked, rolled in our chosen colors and then screwed on the canvas to become a dual channel through which the cosmic vibes could leave their pattern. As you can see, it was true. We didn't suffocate. Leon's white, brown and gold, like sculpture, and I'm black and blue, symbolizing the depression of our age, plus all the rest of the colors symbolizing the art of painting. So it's conceptually multi-media. See?"

"Good grief! That's strictly off the record, Van! On government money! With all the continuing controversy over NEA grants and obscenity in art in general! We don't want to give those fanatics in or out of Congress more ammunition!"

"Oh, what's the difference how it was created, Denny?" Adria turned serious. "It's the result that counts. Look how that ground glass I tossed onto the wet paint glitters. That's what made Flo think of *City Lights*." She turned to Van. "Too bad Leon couldn't be here. He'd give you a perfect blurb or two about that painting, for sure." She pointed to a section of the canvas. "In fact, I think that sharp smudge right there is a print of Leon's gorgeous tight ass."

Denise stood back and surveyed the painting. "Interesting. The composition *is* interesting. And the colors, they're so wonderfully incongruous. It does have an electric ... emotional excitement, first the surging and then the collapsing shapes. And the glass does give it a provocative, aggressive surface." She looked back to Adria. "But you know, friend, you and Leon have really become 'establishment.' Most young artists coming up today are way beyond insider games *or* pure aesthetics. They're focused on a very intense dialogue about compelling social-political issues." She faced the photographer so he could get a shot of her gesturing. "They make their art with activist intention and global commitment, not impulse."

"Don't believe everything you hear," Adria snorted.

"Well, whatever the intent," Van interrupted, "a lot of artists of all persuasions are getting big career boosts from all the zoning boards that require art in public spaces within private buildings and mandatory outdoor art for others. Even New York's deteriorating public schools full of illiterate kids who can't add have an art budget that must be fulfilled."

"You bet," Denise agreed. "Art should be for the people. It should be available for all people of all ages to enjoy, not just a select, rich few." She raised an eyebrow at Adria. "And your last commission, that huge amoeba-like mural for South Bronx High School brought you $187,000, I believe."

"I have a question for you." Silent in his work all afternoon, the photographer spoke up. "Van said you're with the Arts Council, right?" Denise nodded. "Well, what about all the taxpayers who have no say about the kind of art their taxes support, or about which artists will get their money? What if some taxpayers don't have any interest in art at all or even know the word 'aesthetics'?"

Denise looked surprised. "It's in the *public* interest," she said flatly.

"Ri-gh-t," drawled the photographer. "Smile right into this taxpayer's camera, Ms. Sommers."

"Now, just a minute. We already said that the money for this museum is all voluntarily donated," Blair said, anxious to smooth a thorny moment. "Although the way my mother gets people to 'volunteer' goes beyond good manners. She uses the 'flinch' test, you know." Seeing she had diverted everyone's attention, she hurried on. "If a contributor offers a sum without flinching, she asks him for how many years he plans to give that *annual* sum. Then she just keeps going until she sees him *flinch*." She turned to Kronan. "But I like *your* scheme better. Besides, I go by the rule of 'thirds'. I count on getting one-third from the ten largest gifts, the next third from the next one hundred gifts, and the last third from all the rest. I got my first two-thirds from people I've dined with all my life. The last third will come from the guests at a media event we're giving down at the house in Palm Beach, the last third being people who want to see the first two-thirds and be seen by them at the same time." She hugged herself with delight. "Oh, it's going to be such fun! I'm going to have *real snow* spread all over the property. The press won't be able to resist! I'll undo you, Kronan." She looked for some response from him; even in his advancing years, he was so damned attractive—tall and patrician—why did he have to be so cold and religious? Seeing not a glimmer that he heard her at all, she sidled up to him and whispered so that everyone could hear. "Well Kronan, don't you care if I *undo* you?" She winked and kissed the air.

Kronan smiled; he was used to Blair's flirting. "As Ingres once said," he whispered back, "'They say I am not of this century. If I don't like my century, artwise, must I belong to it?'"

"May I quote that?" Van asked.

"I don't think so." Kronan fought his weariness, afraid it might show at last. "Margaret Harrington Crane's views on art may be more in common with mine than with her daughter's, but she is committed to this new wing because it makes Blair happy, so I wouldn't say a thing against it, no matter how far I am from understanding it myself. Many museums, now, are headed by administrators who admit no knowledge of things artistic. In a way, I've just joined their ranks, that's all. I'm better off than most, actually. At least I can walk back over the bridge and feel quite at home in the old wing. All of that is also off the record, by the way."

Blair handed Van a large envelope. "All of this is *for* the record, the nuts and bolts information about the art and the building. You did say this was going to be a cover story, didn't you?" she pleaded. Seeing Van's slanted smile, she tucked her arm in his and walked him down the stairs. "Van, don't tease me, I'm serious. Look, I'm even prepared to bribe you. Go treat Denny and Adria to dinner and charge it to me." Struck by a sudden connection, she turned to Denise. "Sommers? You're not related to *Senator* Sommers, are you?"

"Sort of," Denny grinned impishly. "I'm his daughter."

"Oh," Blair breathed, and then brightly, "well, you must fly down to Palm Beach with us. Van, you *must* bring her." She turned to Adria, "You're coming, aren't you?"

Adria laughed, causing Kronan to step back onto the balcony. "You just said it's going to be a media event, and you're asking me if I'm coming?"

※ ※ ※

Kronan found himself standing at dead center of the enclosed skyway that would take him back to the building that had been known for sixty-odd years by visitors from all over the world as "The Harrington Museum." Most people simply called it "The Harrington," their tone of voice alone adding "the special," "the wonderful," "the unique." Some New Yorkers (not forgetting they are supposed to be possessive of everything quintessentially New York) spoke of it as "*Our* Harrington." Kronan knew that the public's affection stemmed from its having once been a family home; the place had never lost the warmth of a quieter, more gracious time. In a few weeks, "The Harrington" would be known as the "Old Wing." He was beginning to call it that himself.

The bridge had been constructed at enormous cost in order to connect the old and new wings of the museum so that visitors could cross over in inclement weather. But that function was the least of its achievements. Aesthetically, the architectural motifs of the original nineteenth-century mansion were ingeniously repeated in various forms of the span's design until it became like so many links that, at some indiscernible point, merged them with the equally distinctive but soaring architecture of the modern new wing on the opposite side. Thank God Margaret had chosen the architect. If that decision had been left to Blair, she surely would have hired one of the brassy, brand-name breed of deconstructionists that Van was referring to, whose buildings drew crowds because they looked as if they were exploding or falling down or zipping around like a roller coaster. Like most contemporary art, architecture was becoming an entertainment. Feeling grateful affection toward Blair's mother, as he always did, Kronan walked the rest of the way across the bridge, studying the elegant design as it drew him toward the spirit of the old wing and the art it contained. His expectations began to rise. Then he turned and walked back to the new wing, studying the subtle changes in reverse until—he still couldn't pinpoint the transition mark—he felt drawn toward the spirit of the new wing with the same rising expectation. Brilliant!

But given the art in the New Wing— Suddenly, Kronan decided that starting right now he would cross from one building to the other at street level. He would feel better actually crossing the physical divide that split the spirits of the two art collections as absolutely as the spirits which had created them were split. The bridge proclaimed that these two aesthetics could live peaceably together. Perhaps they could. God worked His wonders in mysterious ways. But not for him.

He headed for the stairs of the new wing and, exiting the building, strolled briskly across the street to the mansion where he opened the door to *his* world and felt instantly at home. Home. Here at the museum he had headed for twenty-seven years, his only real home. Except for the church, of course; and there, if he were truthful, he felt at home only folded to his knees in penance. Why did Blair have to mention his charity work? It was discomfiting enough to answer questions about art he detested, with Adria Cass there in his face every minute. Did he have to be reminded of his infinite guilt as well?

It had not been the infinity it seemed, of course, only a little over a decade, but . . . His daughter was now twenty-four years old. Yet, he never seemed able to erase from his memory the image of her budding breasts, her smooth skin and her parted lips. For twelve years he had done all that his preacher had said he should do to atone for his sin. No one but he even *knew* of his sin, not his daughter, not his wife. And yet—

Kronan dragged his guilt like a cross through the foyer. God knew. God always knew *everything*.

Reverend Garren had been kind and understanding

when, after months of private agony, Kronan had finally taken a trip back to his Wisconsin hometown seeking advice from his childhood preacher. No one at his Park Avenue church would have remotely understood what was torturing him, not even the minister. No one in New York's sophisticated religious community would; cosmopolitan places of worship were more social institutions than religious ones. Kronan didn't know a single soul who took the Bible literally, not even his own wife, so how could any of them understand even if they wanted to? His adopted church was so progressive that they sponsored jazz concerts on Sunday afternoons and, once in a while, had allowed some "performance artists" to try out new, rather off-color material within its sacred walls.

He knew that, over the years, he had departed in many ways from his fundamentalist religious roots because he had become comfortable with big city life. He had also come to understand that orthodoxy itself was often harmful. As a world-traveler—and especially as a New Yorker!—he had seen first hand how fanatic religious sects were tearing the world asunder. As a religious man, he respected all religions, but as an educated man, he found it impossible not to shrink in horror as religious zealots—madmen!—terrorized not only governments but also innocent tourists, business people, even artists and writers and little children, all in the name of their God. Ethnic cleansing and Holy Wars. It was all barbaric beyond belief. Even in New York's normal daily life where certain passive sects did no harm, Kronan found himself cringe whenever passing by members of old-world adherents. What saddened Kronan most about these insular groups was their bringing children into the world and warping their little minds while they were too young to resist the oppressive indoctrination.

Irene Jones, his assistant, startled him by peeking out from his office. "How did it go?" she asked with real concern, knowing her employer resisted prolonged visits to the new wing. Seeing Kronan's weary eyes, she shook her head in sympathy. "I'm sorry. By the way, I made an appointment for the restorer, Dorina Swing, to come over at ten tomorrow to examine *Lady at Her Toilette*. Okay?"

"Fine, thanks." Kronan turned down a corridor that would lead him to the badly deteriorating painting, his mind back on Reverend Garren.

Old Reverend Garren, now in his late eighties, was an American, of course, and the enlightened American clergy would never think of imposing outward signs of piety like restrictive dress or codified demeanor on practitioners. The responsible religions today were entirely different from the old schools, their leaders culturally realistic, personally compassionate and concerned only with the souls of their flock. There was no powerful clergy to translate for God in the church where the Hagen family worshiped. There was no need, for God had spoken directly to His people through His Savior Son and the apostles. Only God's Word was Law. If the truly religious family structure is preserved, then the Devil cannot make his way into the thoughts and deeds of individuals, for if the *mind* is pure, then evil deeds *cannot* be performed. Reverend Garren had taught Kronan well about the penalties of breaking The Law, even when Kronan was still so young he couldn't quite understand the concept of Sin, especially what was meant by the sin of lust.

One visit to his hometown was all it had taken to show Kronan the right way back to his spiritual home. He had gone in turmoil, but Reverend Garren had explained that the whole incident was, in fact, a blessing, an unequalled opportunity, given to him by God, to be reborn. Cosmopolitan life had corrupted Kronan; here was his chance to return to the literal God of his own pure childhood.

Reverend Garren had been patient and loving. He had explained what it meant to be "born again," how by turning to God in repentance and inviting God, by faith, back into his life, he could become a new person. He had shown him the very words in the Bible, in 2nd Corinthians:

"Therefore, if any man be in Christ, he is a new creature: old things are passed away; behold, all things are become new." He had encouraged Kronan to go to God in his heart in the simple act of complete faith and trust that God would forgive him and accept him again as one of His own.

Kronan had never dared ask Reverend Garren how he would know whether or not God had forgiven him and accepted him back as reborn. In the privacy of his own heart, he had gone endlessly to God and begged for forgiveness. Yet, his guilt had never left him. Perhaps God had forgiven him and he just didn't know it, but in the innermost recesses of his being, he feared that even a merciful God would never forgive a man who could commit that kind of a monstrous sin. *His own daughter*. His stomach turned in revulsion toward his soiled soul.

Passing through a fully furnished drawing room, Kronan tried to change the direction of his depressing thoughts by embracing with his glance the work he so loved. The new wing's rooms are too stark, he muttered to himself, too impersonal, like the art. There's something so warm about a personal collection, one that's been "collected" rather than *calculated*. A museum should be a sanctuary, not a department store! A sanctuary for household gods in the same way the church is a sanctuary for the one, true living God who created us that we might create for Him . . . *if* we are worthy.

Kronan couldn't escape himself, today, it seemed. *No one* could resist the ultimate Judgment that is always meted out in the center of the soul, he thought with weary satisfaction. No matter that everyone else may think highly of us; in the secret chambers of our minds we all must live with our private demons, locked and hidden from the world but not from ourselves. No one ever really knows anyone else, he mused in abject wonder. We are born alone, we die alone and, really, as much as we desperately try to share them, all of life's glories and terrors, in the end, are experienced alone.

He came to the painting in the mansion's master bedroom and cursed the life he felt beginning to pulse again in his groin, wondering how he could be so demoralized and aroused at the same time. It must have been that damnable nude in Margaret's garden that had begun his juices. Curse the Devil in his body! How could he ever believe that he was reborn if he couldn't control these attacks of physical need?

He began a close inspection of the largest crack in the canvas that just last week had not only advanced a full inch but had widened considerably. He pushed his mind to think that the humidity control of the two wings should be reversed; the artificial heat from the old mansion's antiquated system drove moisture from the air, and dryness was the greatest threat to these treasures.

Irene's head popped around the corner. "I'm leaving now. See you in the morning. Hope the 'Lady' isn't too bad off. I know she's one of your favorites."

He mumbled a "goodnight" without taking his eyes from the painting. The force inside him was growing, and he fought silently against its reaching the surface of his consciousness. He mentally listed the things he would have to discuss with Dorina in the morning and noted the discoloration creeping into the flesh tones of the innocent young woman. All young, all sensual: qualities expressed in art more perfectly than they could ever be expressed in life. A sensuality contained only in youth, youth so unaware of its appeal, and, therefore, so appealing: forbidden fruit in the Garden of Eden that turned the Garden into a forest of Hell.

The image of his daughter when she was twelve intermingled with the painted image he was examining. She had been ill with the flu; he had stopped by her room on his way to bed to check on her; in her sleep, she had thrown off the covers; her nightgown had crept up above her chest;

a pale glow of perspiration lay over her entire body; her firm little breasts lifted and dropped from her labored breathing—

He had never touched her; she never awoke, nor ever knew he was there. But he had made love to his daughter in his mind that night. He had never masturbated in his whole life, even when he felt the Devil's urge, because he knew even as a young boy that *that* was a sin sending you straight to Hell, no penance allowed. And he hadn't really *done* the foul act on that loathsome night; the feeling of lust had overwhelmed him so suddenly and so completely that he had merely slipped silently to his knees beside the bed and released his uncontrollable desire into a handkerchief. It was over in seconds. It felt like an accident. But he knew better. The Devil had entered his soul. Because he had permitted it! He had committed incest with his own child.

He and his wife had a sparse but reasonably satisfying relationship; they were married; therefore, sex was sanctioned, however reluctantly. He had been brought up from earliest memory to understand that sex was a necessary evil. Well, he had married. He had procreated (he and his wife had two sons besides their daughter), but he had always harbored, since adolescence, the secret fear that he actually wanted sex for the *pleasure* of it. And God had punished him for the desire of pleasure. Ever since the night of his daughter, he had rarely turned to his wife in bed. When he had, he had never again experienced pleasure, only release.

To this day, he didn't know what had made him do such a terrible thing with his daughter those many years ago. But he had done it. And God, no matter how much repenting He had heard from Kronan since that time, had seen him do it and had punished him ever since.

Kronan searched the room for another nude; he was no longer seeing *Lady at Her Toilette*. There was a nude from the Middle Ages somewhere in this room, a small statuette? He couldn't remember, but any elongated, stomach-protruding Northern European Christian nude would suffice to cool his mounting heat, any early Christian nude cowering from the knowledge of her nakedness, from her sin. But he could not always resist the Greek nudes and especially not Renaissance nudes like *Lady at Her Toilette*, nudes devoid of even the *concept* of sin, all innocent and pure.

He found himself heading for another room, knowing it was too late; he was out of control again. It didn't happen often now, perhaps once or twice a year. What was it that had made him lose control today? The anxiety of a press interview about art that he hated emotionally and didn't understand intellectually, combined with the sudden arousal he felt from Margaret Crane's garden sculpture? Was it like the anxiety over his daughter's health and her sexual vulnerability? No, the days of rationalization were long gone. It was incest, now transferred harmlessly to art, but nearly as evil. He followed the route in a blind trance—past the Indian dancer of the eighth century, electrifying in her passive eroticism; there was no shame in her bearing—until he stood, at last, before Vanderlyn's *Ariadne* ... sleeping, vulnerable beneath a tree, so innocent she could not yet love or desire but could inspire such desire. It was a curse.

He followed his familiar path, languid except for the one, hard devil that demanded payment. Safe in the private bathroom adjoining his office and under the command of his own hand, he exorcised both body and soul of the demon that possessed him.

FOURTEEN

"I WANT TO GO someplace *high*," Denny demanded. "The rich bitch is paying for dinner."

"Good dining is not necessarily expensive," Van explained, noticing how the lights from passing cars caught the red hues of Denny's hair and made it glimmer. The last time he had seen this young woman she wore braces on her teeth. Now she was twenty-eight and, although taller and thinner than his usual taste, she was delicious. What spunk, confronting Blair like that. Had Blair actually invited this little stingbee into the Palm Beach bonnet? Unconsciously, he straightened his shoulders and tucked in his stomach.

"I mean high *up*," she said.

All three of them were walking down Fifth Avenue, not even scouting for a cab during rush hour. "Most high-*height* places are for tourists, and since you're a New Yorker now, let's go someplace with its good food feet on the ground." Van slipped an arm through Denny's. He could smell her perfume, which at first appeared to be a floral scent, but as he drew closer, he caught the odor of erotic, earthy undertones. Well! Her choice of fragrance went perfectly with her lace Victorian dress, demur by itself but which was hiked short by a belt and brass buckle at her hips and finished off with leather boots that reached over her knees to accent her trim thighs, all wrapped in a velvet cape that flipped open just often enough as she walked to be thoroughly tantalizing.

"Don't you call Blair names." Adria clamped an arm around Denny's shoulder. "She puts Beluga on my toast points and when she says 'snow' in Palm Beach, it don't mean just the cold stuff."

"Palm Beach mansions, private museums! These people are living in the dark ages." Denny's snort was entirely to Van's liking.

"But what about the fact that the public can visit their private museums and enjoy the art, too?" He was baiting her.

"They shouldn't charge admission." Denny pulled a thick booklet from her briefcase and handed it to Adria. "Here. Take this down to the Rails and pass it around. It's the new set of application guidelines for New York's Arts Council grants."

Van intercepted the book and leafed through it. "'All applicants are urged to challenge themselves by transcending disciplinary constraints. Especially welcome are programs/projects that are risk-taking, experimental in nature or that stress process over product,'" he read. "What on earth does it mean to 'transcend disciplinary constraints'?" He was teasing her.

"It means to break the boundaries, do your own thing, anything goes, no holds barred." Denny beamed. "It's fantastic!"

"You're fantastic!" Adria kissed her on the cheek.

Do your own thing? They recycle forty-year-old platitudes as automatically as they recycle paper, this generation, Van thought. He passed the book to Adria. "Let's eat!"

Rounding a corner, he settled them quickly into the *au moment* "Barralito's," where he knew Blair had an account and whose cigar bar was exempt from the aggressive, new smoking bans. He'd noticed that Denny seemed to smoke rather heavily and didn't think she could make it through dinner without lighting up. He ordered a bottle of Corton Charlemagne and a raw seafood tier and slid closer to Denny along the banquette. She had materialized in his office this morning without even a phone call, announced that she had moved from Connecticut to New York and invited him to lunch. Intrigued by her boldness, he had let her pay for their $160 meal and then taken her to the new wing.

Denny lit a cigarette and continued her monologue. "Look! Innovation has been and still is all that counts in the big art world. Confronting and breaking convention. Iconoclasm. If you don't bash and trash the status quo first, you can't weaken the more deeply rooted traditions, which have to be destroyed before any real social progress can be made. Luckily, in today's precarious political and corporate climate, it's easier than ever before to aesthetically prepare Americans, whatever their professed persuasion, for a truly global government overseeing a truly New World Order. If an artist is doing any of that, and their work has no commercial market, they should be subsidized by every enlightened government, including ours. Period. It's an investment in the future."

Van inhaled the cigarette smoke, mixing sexily with her perfume. He had indulged in neither a cigarette nor a woman in six months. Now he was crazy for both! Deliberately ignoring her typical, politically correct verbiage, he leaned forward to get them off that tiresome track. "What if the artist's work is just no good?" he mused. "What about 'quality'?"

"*All* art is good if it expresses its own time and impacts society," Denny said fiercely.

Van studied her closely, imagining how her long red hair would look spread out on a pillow. She was near his own daughter in age, too young for him to be imagining her hair spread out on a pillow. But to feel that vitality of youth again, to partake of that energy—

"How long have you been a critic?" Denny's cigarette punctured the air and his thoughts at the same time.

"Fifteen years," he answered almost apologetically. "And an art history professor before that. But those credentials haven't mattered for years. It's the dealers who wield the influence."

"Well, what do *you* mean by 'quality'? No one on the planet ever defines it. All I ever hear is, 'just look long enough and you'll see.'"

"My wife has said that for years."

"How *is* Maggie?" Adria asked.

"We're getting divorced."

"Why?"

"I don't know. The kids are up and gone. There's nothing new. I'm too old. She's too tired."

"How old are you?"

"Fifty-two."

"You're right, at least you're too old for *me*." Adria laughed. "You're almost as old as I am!"

"Not too old for me." Van's daydream came true when, slithering close to him, Denny's hips connected with his. "I like older men," she said. "If my father weren't my father, I'd want to sleep with him. You were his frat brother, right?"

"Right." Van covered his astonishment by waving at the waiter. "Another bottle."

With one of her black polish-chipped fingernails, Adria peeled the label off the empty wine bottle. "Did you know Flo made me do some paintings that were reproduced as wine bottle labels? She sold the original canvases for big bucks, and the wine sold like mad, too. I don't know why. I wouldn't have washed my feet in the stuff."

"Big bucks! Is that all anybody thinks of?" Denny demanded. "Screw the dealers and the art-star world. There are serious idea-oriented artists out there who can't make a living!"

"Who says they can't? I'm serious and I'm filthy rich. Contrary to what you may think—get your hand off Van's thigh, Baby, he thinks he's too old for you—all of my work is about ideas, the mind, a cosmic intelligence. See? I don't assume that the mind is as aspect or a function of an individual brain, or that it necessarily contains processes or thoughts. My paintings all express different forms of the same idea, in fact, and that idea is the denial of all human ideas. Get it? My work is living proof that you can have what they like to call *cerebral art* that contains *no ideas at all*. Look long enough and you'll see it. And the 'quality' too, my little chickadee." Adria stood and kissed them both on both cheeks. "Bye-bye. I can't stay for the main course. I leave you to your Karma, kids."

Van sighed in relief as Adria's scarf departed. Now they could relax together.

"Let's go to my apartment," Denny said, returning her hand to his thigh.

Van took her hand in both of his to cover his shock. "I can't," he mumbled. *I'm beat*, he wanted to say.

"Why can't you?"

"One, I can't watch you smoke another cigarette without having one. I quit six months ago. Two, we haven't had our meal. Three, I have to be in the house by eleven o'clock during the divorce proceedings or my wife can claim abandonment. Four, I live an hour-and-a-half train ride away."

"You aren't serious?" With this, Denny grabbed his hand and her cape and led him briskly out of the restaurant into the sunset.

Stunned, Van recovered enough to mumble Blair's name to the maitre d' before the door closed behind them.

Denny hailed a cruising stretch limo. "Well, let's hurry. We'll have to make this a quickie."

She meant what she said. Once in the car, she guided

his hand under her dress and inside her thong panties, tongue kissing him so aggressively that all he could think of was that he'd never be able to perform once they got to her apartment. He needn't have worried, though, because he found her energy flowing into him with such force that by the time she had him pressed up against the wall in her hallway and felt her unbuckling his belt, he was more than ready for her. Until she reached into her handbag and pulled out a little package wrapped in red. My God! Did they *travel* with them, this younger generation?

"Here." She tossed him the package. "Better put on your dancing shoes. Safe sex and all that. Meet you on the couch."

Inside, Van pulled himself together while she went to the kitchen for two bottles of Corona *sans* lime, but nearly lost it again when he saw her throw a match into the wood ready-laid in the fireplace. It entered his mind that if a *man* behaved the way Denny had for the past hour, he could be charged with sexual harassment.

What was he dreaming of? He should have known that a bed and a pillow would be too tame and that she would want to be on top. When her ride was over, and he lay exhausted, she sat up, glistening gloriously with sweat and, still straddling him, lit two cigarettes.

"*Now*," she said, smiling happily, guzzling her beer. "Let's talk about quality."

✻ ✻ ✻

"Where to now, Mrs. Gothard?"

Blair checked her watch as she got into the car. It was seven-thirty. She had left Van and the others over an hour ago and had at least another half-hour to kill before going home to dress for tonight's dinner party. No, an hour to kill; she'd already showered, steamed and had a massage at the club. Her nails didn't need touching up, and since she was wearing a sequined turban to dinner, she didn't need to stop in and have her hair done. It was too late to drop into her favorite clothing boutique or jewelry *boite* to browse, but it was too early to go home with nothing in particular to do except pretend to oversee the preparation of dinner and that, she knew, would upset the cook. There was that book she had promised her friend Heidi she would read, but did she really have to? It was a bother when people you knew became editors or designers or whatever engaged them at the moment and they expected you to read their latest releases, wear their latest creations—

William sat, waiting patiently, in the driver's seat of the limousine. He slipped a Beethoven tape out of the cassette player and replaced it with Telemann, whose music always seemed to give Mrs. Gothard a lift. And himself, too. Thank heaven she had better musical taste than her husband. She often sat like this, deciding which of the many important things on her agenda needed her attention. Her schedule was always so amazingly full; the poor woman never seemed to take time to relax. But her position demanded a busy calendar; even beauty appointments were important to someone as socially prominent as Mrs. Gothard. An attractive appearance was expected of a woman of her stature.

And attractive she was. William gazed at her through the rearview mirror. She was snuggled back into the seat in a fluffy white fur coat. William always appreciated his employer's beauty (silently, of course) but he liked her best in this particular coat. When she had the fur hood up over her head, she looked like some fragile blonde angel girl, so different from the sophisticated, world-traveled woman she was. What a relief she was from his previous employer, the strawhaired, twenty-three-year-old "performance artist." The way that tough little cookie dressed, and the things that had gone on in the back seat of that car! She'd never even bothered to close the curtains. On the other hand, what did he expect from an "artist" who fornicated with inanimate objects on the stage to the "music" of a hardcore band before diving headlong into a mosh pit full of screaming, writhing youths from the burgs? Although overpaid, he had quit the job after only two months.

"William, take me to Flo Halldon's, will you please?"

Blair settled farther back into the seat and made mental notes, which would, later on, become dinner chat. It was to be one of her small weekly gatherings of thirteen, her favorite number for intimate, sit-down dinners. All of her guests had already contributed to the new wing, so there was nothing to be done there. The big holiday charity balls were coming up. Why wasn't she looking forward to them the way she'd always done? Was she getting bored just because they were so predictable?

Palm Beach will be unpredictable, she thought happily. Real snow. She must remember to have a half-dozen horses and a few sleighs trucked down from New Jersey. Mother won't like the whole idea, she warned herself. Too showy. She smiled. Why is it that one generation of wealth "shows," while another decides it shouldn't?

All the guests would be new money and they'd love a show. With so many from California and Texas, they should absolutely outdo each other in outrageous gift giving. And why not outdo each other? Blair thought. What fun it would be to be *nouveau riche*. The thrill of getting everything for the first time. Sometimes being born rich is a bore.

"Here we are, Mrs. Gothard." William rubbed a smudge off the door with his sleeve. The mauve of the car's finish started to deepen and shimmer as the city began to blink to evening life. William was tall and blond and dignified. Must have some Scandinavian blood, like Kronan, Blair thought. She wondered lazily if he was as sexless and aloof as Kronan Hagen, whom she had been trying to tease into bed since she was in her twenties. A substitute?

Flo had already shut down the back gallery. Her paperwork done, she was ready to go home, or to stop there and get ready for an important dinner party at the Wilson's, to be exact. If you wanted a blue-chip gallery, you had to dine with blue-chip collectors. Seeing Blair hang her coat in the private closet, Flo went to the refrigerator under her desk and produced a bottle of Saratoga Water; her clients were well beyond San Pelegrino. Glory! What one had to do to keep up!

"Don't you look radiant and relaxed!" She poured the water into two hand-cut glasses and slipped a tiny linen coaster over each base.

Blair took the drink and began to wander around the main room. "I had a massage at the club late this afternoon. Sometimes I find it nicer there than having Annya come to the house."

Flo eyed her client carefully. Was this a "one-in-every-color" mood from the old dress-shop scene? By the aimlessness of Blair's path, it looked as if it might be. There was a sale brewing here, she could feel it in her rib. Which piece should it be? Heaven knew, she would have to lead Blair; the woman would never find anything by herself.

Blair was musing. "Van came over to the new wing this afternoon for a photo story. Denise Sommers of the Arts Council was with him, daughter of Theron Sommers, you know, and she was talking about this new twenty-first-century 'dialogue' that's going on between artists."

Flo turned on the lights in the back room again and began restacking some paintings in the corner. Ah, the proverbial "dialogue," she mused to herself, the same tired term dragged up by every generation for the past hundred years as if it was something new. Come on, little Blair, come to Mama, she hummed without words, half listening to Blair's patter.

"So do you have anybody really new and outrageous that you're keeping hidden away like you did *Orange*? I'd like to see something really new and exciting on my walls; half of the city house is empty from our loans and gifts to the new wing. So why couldn't I have a 'dialogue' on my walls? I could display a conversation from Paleolithic yesterday to space-travel tomorrow. Kronan would love it. Not the *Tower* of Babel, but the *Townhouse* of Babel." Blair stopped wandering. "Well, do you have anybody new and novel?"

Flo restacked the stacked paintings in the corner, noisily dragging one huge rectangle to the front. "You know how hard that is? To find something new, *authentically new*, like *Orange*, is like finding a swan in a swamp." She refilled their glasses and tapped her long fake fingernails lightly on top of the stack, hoping to draw Blair's attention to it. Little Blair had to find it all by herself. "Originality doesn't exist today because *everyone*, not just the art world, is buying into the 'fifteen minutes of fame.' And *everything* is still hype, hype and more hype. And hype has no staying power. That's why you buy art from me. No? Like when you used to buy clothing from me. *My* name guarantees the quality of the goods because, unlike so many other dealers over the past few years of art-buying fall-off, I still have a continuing track record for investment winners: goods that won't go out of style before they 'go the distance' financially. Yes?"

Blair pulled open a file drawer. "Maybe if I could peek at your slides?"

Flo closed the drawer with a firm smile and guided Blair away from the cabinet back toward the stacks.

"I could go 'direct,' you know," Blair grimaced. "Lots of people do, nowadays."

"That you could." Flo turned the backlights off again and headed for the main gallery. "I'm sure William knows the way to the Rails."

Blair trailed behind her like a scolded child. "But you let me go to Leon's studio *direct*."

"That's because I can't exhibit Leon's stuff. It's too large. Besides, you pay my commission just the same, don't you?"

"Yes, but . . . well, Flo, honestly, you're talking about art as if it's a commodity like soybeans or pork bellies. I know you don't deal in art only because of the money. You've always been fair."

Flo shrugged. Turning out all of the lights, she pulled Blair's coat out of the closet. "Being fair doesn't mean I don't like money," she countered. "Of course I do. I can't let your lynx hang next to linoleum, can I?" She fished her own mink out of the closet. "But . . . so . . ." Okay, one last try! "You're right. I don't do it *all* for the money."

"Ah," Blair breathed. "Then why? Flo, we've been friends for a long time. Why?"

"Because . . ." Flo narrowed her eyes at Blair. Maybe this sale was going to require just an itsy bitsy more than the usual breezy jargon; Blair's meandering did seem a little more tipsy than usual. She added a tiny edge to the tone of her voice, but she was a pro; the edge was very slight, just sharp enough to poke Blair out of her apathy. "I already told you," she began. "I create *stars*. I know one art dealer who says he sells 'art history.' Some dealers even sell *art*! Others sell . . . well, whatever it is they sell. But *I* sell *art stars*. Think of it. Some artists today make as much money as movie actors or sports figures or rock singers. So I promote the artist first, the art second. That's why Adria, that noisome cow, and Leon, that sexy hunk, are so sought after, *and* independently wealthy I might add, thanks to me. They lead colorful lives and they have charismatic personalities. That's why they've both been guests at the Whitehouse and I haven't. They're *stars*. And *I* make sure they stay lit. You know from your museum exhibits that you have to keep the stars bright not only in the art buyers' eyes but also in the *public eye* so they don't burn out." Flo laughed contemptuously. "And who is the public? Not even wannabe connoisseurs! The public doesn't want to learn anything. Or think at all. They only want to gorge on what's sensational. They want glitz. Americans are *star struck*, and they couldn't care less whether the star is a madman, a murderer or a messiah."

"Well, if you think so little of a culture that worships

stars," Blair interrupted with some annoyance, "why do you say you're in the art business to create *art* stars?"

"Because I like the money!" Flo laughed again, gave up, and put her arm around Blair's shoulder. "Come on, you've made me late. Now you've got to let William drop me off on your way home. Come on, I was just trying to get your mind off your 'dialogue.'" Tomorrow is another day, she thought.

"But it *is* a good idea, Flo. On my walls first, then after we get good media coverage and massage the concept for a couple of years by adding startling new work to keep critics interested and dinner conversation popping, I'll donate it all to the new wing and transport the whole dialogue there. Maybe if it all hangs together long enough, it will *say* something—" Blair's gloved hand stopped hers just as Flo was about to pull the iron gates closed across the storefront. "Wait! There *was* somebody new. In the back room. Back against the stacks. I remember it now. Very precise and very symmetrical, like lots of little boxes being born out of one big box, like a painted collage. So stark and so intensely rude. Who is that?"

"Oh, that's not for *sale!*" Flo sang the words. Well, well, well. At last. I'm not losing my touch after all; Blair is just awfully slow today. "That's mine. I'm just waiting to get it to the framers. It's a little girl I found over in Hoboken. You know, a lot of them can't even afford to live at the Rails or downtown anymore. It's all become so gentrified, seems only doctors, lawyers and hairdressers live there now." Flo let herself back into the shop, smiling like a cat (I'll be damned if I'll get the bubble water back out, she thought) until she was standing stoically beside Blair and her new "find." If Blair hadn't been in such a daze when she came in, she would have seen it right away. The game began.

"Now, Blair, I told you it's not for sale. I don't think this kid's *star* material. I just like her work, personally, that's all. This is mine."

"Not for long, it isn't. *Yours?* Like *Orange?*" Blair felt herself come alive for the first time all day. She didn't know whether or not she liked the painting; what she did like was the momentary sense of purpose, the thrill of a challenge, the crazier the better. With her pocketbook, she rarely lost challenges, but she enjoyed them just the same because the outcome was unpredictable. One couldn't always be sure. And she did like Flo. Flo was hard, but she was honest. "Now, how much? Remember, the artist is from Hoboken! I'll have to hang it as an example of a foreign language on my dialogue wall!" She tittered at her little joke.

It always works with New Yorkers, Flo was thinking. Someone from the Midwest would simply accept "That's not for sale," and move on to another item. And Texans were a different breed altogether. Once, when she had tried it with a woman from Dallas, she'd stalked out of the gallery, flinging back: "Well! Cartier *will* take my money. They sell what *is* for sale!" But New Yorkers, bless them, love to get something that can't be got.

"Flo, for heaven's sake, you can have visitation rights! How much?" Blair's eyes were shining with mischief.

"With or without framing?" Flo asked. She went to pour more mineral water, already rehearsing how she would parlay this sale at tonight's dinner. There were to be at least thirty guests. Yes, indeedy. She'd sell two more of this "little girl" before the evening was over.

FIFTEEN

FRESH AIR! DIMITRIOS walked out onto the terrace for a taste of it. A strong breeze from the sea whipped a chill into the morning, but the sun was bright and he welcomed the invigorating sense of space and freedom that his country home always gave him after a week in his Athens apartment, surrounded by concrete, car fumes and the clack of city sounds. Here, on these weekends near Sounion, there was no sound at all but the wind; he was too far up on the escarpment jutting out over the ocean to hear the surf, even during a storm. The only asset of his city place was that he could view the Acropolis from his living room; especially at night, it was one of the most soul-stirring sights in the world.

He looked down at the dolphins worked into the pebble mosaic of the patio's flooring and felt the thrill of discovery charge his mind back into action. He had copied this dolphin motif from the Cretan palace of Knossos. Now, unexpectedly, Knossos was very much again on his mind. If it were true that the palace had been a necropolis and not a royal and religious living and administrative center, as was previously thought, it would radically change all accepted theories concerning the ancient Minoan culture of Crete. It would tie the culture much more closely to Egypt and leave open, once again, the missing link between the dark, death-oriented cultures of the East and the glorious life-serving achievements of later, Classical Athens. And yet, provocative evidence had been there from the start for anyone with eyes to see. The iconography of that age dictated birds, flowers, fish and especially dolphins to accompany the souls of the dead into the hereafter. With his foot, Dimitrios traced the back of a dolphin outlined in smooth, white pebbles against the blue background of slate. Even blue had been the color of mourning.

He went back into the house and sat down to the letter he had begun to Tara. "Think of it!" he wrote in his impatient longhand.

The facts are there! Fragile gypsum as flooring and staircases in the lower rooms and limestone or slate in areas of either traffic or exposure; that could not have been accidental. Eggshell ceramics could never have withstood actual use by living human beings. They might have been votive objects, as we always assumed, or they could have been meant for use by the dead, by spirits. Paintings of women baring their breasts—the hallmark of grief in both Egyptian and Hebrew mourning rituals—surrounded by snakes: we call them snake goddesses or priestesses when we all know that snakes were standard in the belief that the dead returned in the form of reptiles to take food offerings from the tombs. I've read Herodotus dozens of times! How could I have missed the obvious similarities when he described Egyptian labyrinths where he could visit the upper rooms but was barred from descending to the identical lower rooms because they were for the dead? If this new theory is substantiated, then the competitive games that I have called the "invention of play" in my lectures were held in honor of the dead! The bull leaping was not a sport, but a ritual of sacrifice, a death drama that, to this day, finds its last remnants in the tragedy of modern Spanish bullfights. Well, I could go on and on, Tara, even to the preponderance of rose engravings that we call benevolent signs of a life-loving people. We all know that the rose was the sacred flower of Aphrodite strewn over graves in both Greece and Italy and found, even today, on the gravestones of the Turks and Israelis. We may just have been blind rather than critical students of history. We absorbed the conclusions of those who had gone before us when we should have tested them at every turn by looking with fresh eyes at the ruins. I of all people! Worse, if those conclusions are false, I have passed them on to others.

I've spent the last three days with this German geologist who has been all but laughed out of the archaeological community, which takes their turn-of-the-century conclusions as givens, and I tell you, he may have a point.

Do you remember the report published by the American Archaeology Group in Texas, which confirmed that the ash from the eruption of 1500 BC carried over eastern Crete and more than halfway to Egypt? I have written to the head of the Oceanography Department who led the diving team to see if he wants to join us in another exploration of the area. The slow erosion of the land after the Roman period on the East Coast of Crete makes an underwater exploration there a real possibility. Remember that Homer cited ninety to a hundred Cretan cities. Some of them are bound to be diggable and may corroborate or dispel this theory. We must go with the AAG because they have the diving subs necessary to go as deep as we may have to descend to find what we're after and keep us at constant pressure for the entire time. Plus they have robots and laser cameras for the dangerous, preliminary "look see." The geologist wants to go with us, along with Dumas, of course, who hasn't had anything really exciting down in Crete since he found possible evidence of human sacrifice at Archanes. So I'm working out a three-country team. Aristide, bless him, will help finance us again. It could be one of the most important ventures of the century. And I've decided to let you publish the results rather than I. It's time—

Dimitrios heard the mailbox snap open, threw down his pen and went, anxiously, for the mail. Tara had been gone for almost two weeks. There must be a letter here, today. Good! There *was*.

He scanned the first two pages: her family reunion, her young brother and how impressed she was with him, New

York and how alive and beautiful it still was, the restaurant she had been to with Leon and Blair and Perry, they had missed him— I'll bet, Dimitrios thought, noting that there had been four of them. But what of her and Leon alone? Finally, on page four, her work:

> *The progress on the exhibit is going well. I get along well with the exhibit coordinator, Pierre Auguste, and he seems genuinely excited about the artifacts we'll be bringing over. There are some problems, though. One is that this museum is over-organized. They exhibit specimen beside specimen—glass next to glass next to silver or bronze—not always displaying the items with any faithfulness to the stratifications and locations where they were found. This won't matter to viewers who are historically ignorant, but it will frustrate any serious observer. The museum, although cognizant of the importance of the artifacts themselves, seems to view a public exhibit as an entertainment rather than an offering for historical contemplation. I feel that the exhibit should, above all, be accurate. I hate to cry for help as I know you placed great confidence in me to let me mount this exhibit alone, but if you can spare the time, I do think you should come and view the situation. It's such an important exhibit, it just kills me not to do it properly.*

Dimitrios scanned the rest of the letter. He smiled. She had finally got a chance to look over the *State of Mind* article again and thought the subject well distilled for the layman and a candidate for condensation. "Kudos" from "your editor." He frowned; wait till she reads his letter about Crete.

> *Leon Skillman had the journal. I still have not seen his art yet—my brother knows of him—as Leon insists that I wait until the opening of the new wing of Blair's museum to view it for the first time, so I can see it in a proper setting. I'm dying to see it, of course, but the drama of waiting a few weeks for this gala*

opening is worth the impatience. Everything is so stimulating here. My adventures are not unearthing the old but discovering the new. It's refreshing, for a change.

Dimitrios walked pensively back to his desk and looked down at the letter he would have mailed to Tara in the afternoon. What a fool I am, he thought. Once again, I'm appealing to her through the common love of our work. Leon Skillman appeals to her as a man. As a man should appeal to a woman. He entices her with surprises, creates *drama*. He approaches her romantically. He's the outside; I'm the inside. What a bizarre situation! I make the same mistakes over and over. Why can't I show her that I love *her*, not just her love of our work? Why can't I let her see me as a real, living, breathing man?

He walked into his bedroom and opened a velvet box containing her Name Day gift. He had planned to mail it to her along with the letter. *Mail it?* You must be delirious; he scolded himself, his anger growing. How could you be such a fool? He looked at the gold armlet. He'd commissioned the piece from an old craftsman who recreated museum pieces exactly, even using ancient methods of construction and the nearly lost technique of filigree. Dimitrios had given Tara several rather important pieces of jewelry over the years on her Name Day. This twenty-two-carat gold triple circle spiraled into the figure of Poseidon riding up out of a wave. She would wear it, as did the ancient women of Athens, on the upper part of her arm. It was the perfect companion piece to the earrings and ring he had already given her. Well, these are certainly romantic gifts, he thought, soothing himself somewhat. But how had he given them? One in the middle of a big party with colleagues standing all around, and the other at the end of a workday over dinner in a crowded restaurant. And Tara had misread all his gifts, perceived them all as thoughtful but predictable expressions of their shared love for all things Classical Greek. Skillman took her for moonlit walks by the sea. No misreading the motives in that!

"You deserve to lose her," he muttered aloud to himself. "You thought you were so daring and brave to send her away. Then you compete for her by *mail*. Oh, the Greeks should have created another character in their Olympian family. The god of Fools. 'Dimitrios' would be his name."

He placed the armlet back in its box, went to his desk, and tore up the letter to Tara.

Did I expect her to do it all by herself? In *his* setting? Blasted clever! He's even managed for her not to see his *art* right away! I can't believe it! I *counted* on its being as bad as it is and her seeing it! Now, I *have* to go there and give her this present in person.

But to go to America and see her without the protective covering of work would be to approach her even more naked than if I shed all my clothes. Well, isn't that what I want to do? And to make her want to shed hers, too? Idiot! Did I really think, even if she saw through Skillman, that she would come running back to me as a *lover*? And even if I go now for her Name Day, won't she still think I've come to her because of the "cry for help" in her letter? Every problem I must solve, I have created. I've complained for years that I "missed her at every turn." Yes! I missed her because *I* missed her. Because I didn't put forth the effort.

He stared down at the tessellated dolphins, reminded again of ancient Minoa. Legend held that a Minotaur, half-man, half-bull, lived at the center of the labyrinth of King Minos, who ruled the Minoan capital two generations before the Trojan War. Every seven years, the Minotaur required seven Athenian youths and seven virgins as a sacrifice to him. Theseus, an Athenian hero of royal blood, finally killed the beast and, with the help of the king's daughter, escaped the Minotaur's labyrinth, thus saving not only his own life but those of future youths who would have lost theirs to the creature. He also won the hand of the king's daughter in marriage.

I am my own beast, Dimitrios thought. I have constructed my own labyrinth and I wait passively in the center of it for *her* to find *me*. I sacrifice days and years, one by one, and I sacrifice my own love, because I *wait* for her rather than fight for her. Now I must find the way out of my labyrinth and expose my deepest self to the woman I love. I have only this last chance.

Dimitrios lifted a determined face to the cutting wind and measured the ancient challenges of Homer's tempestuous sea. The temple of Poseidon gleamed in the sunlight; a brilliant sky was divided sharply and clearly into narrow blue stripes by the white marble columns of the monument. You don't have to be a hero, he thought with sudden confidence. Just a man.

It was settled, then. He would go to New York.

SIXTEEN

HELENE SKILLMAN STOOD at the door and watched her son and Tara pull out of the driveway in Leon's long, gray sportscar. When the car disappeared around the corner, she turned into her husband's arms for support. "That's why he was reading the magazines. Oh Leonard! She's everything I would have ever dreamed for him, utterly beautiful, inside and out. They are a stunning couple."

"I know," Leonard said quietly, his hand smoothing her back. "Maybe he'll come through after all. Bringing Tara here was a big step for Leon. She must be very important to him, and," he pressed his lips gently into his wife's hair, "maybe we're not as *unimportant* to him as we thought."

Tara leaned her head back against the car seat in utter contentment and watched rows of evergreens speed by as they drove back to New York; each tree drooped gracefully under a weight of whiteness. The city's snow had melted immediately, but here in the country it was still clean and bright and beautiful. The late afternoon sun warmed her cheek as it slanted its last rays directly upon them. A warm, sunny, snowy winter day, she thought lazily. Who would have thought that one could drive a convertible with the top down in November and still be comfortable?

It was her first real day off since arriving in New York just over two weeks ago. Overwhelmed with meetings, luncheons and dinners with museum people, she'd barely had time to meet Leon for a quick drink, let alone spend a long, open-ended day like this. But the afternoon with his parents had been easy and natural. Leon's mother, in particular, had shown such affection for her son and such loving pride in his work as she pointed out his childhood pieces for Tara to admire: the numerous small animals he had done even before reaching his teens and a little dancing girl relief that was so innocent and sweet; plus, of course, the exquisitely draped female nude that Helene Skillman was now using as a model for a painting of her own. Seeing those boyish efforts in his art made Tara feel that, in certain ways, it was as if she had known Leon for years. She glanced over at his hands on the steering wheel, a sculptor's hands. Her man's hands now.

Then she noticed the stern set of Leon's jaw and a cold remoteness icing over his sea green eyes. At this moment, those eyes made her think of a frozen lake. Suddenly uncomfortable, she felt as if she didn't know him at all. Had something happened between him and his parents that she hadn't seen? His father had played magnificent piano for her, and the brunch his mother had given them had been simple but obviously prepared for "company." There was no doubt in Tara's mind that both Helene and Leonard Skillman loved their son deeply.

"Your mother's seascapes are lovely," she ventured with a smile toward Leon's unfathomable rigidness. "My brother Nicky is in the process of finishing a seascape trilogy. Did I tell you?" Leon nodded stiffly. She had told him. "And your *father*!" She raked her fingers through her hair, letting the wind whip it into a tousled mass. "It's so hard to imagine that a chemical engineer could play the piano on a concert level. Did he ever consider music as a career?"

Leon kept his eyes on the road. "Yes."

"What made him decide on chemical engineering?"

"A wife and two children."

"I see." Tara sat up straight and watched the white line

on the road race to meet them and then vanish under the wheels as if the car were erasing the line as it sped over it. "Have you ever heard of Dorina Swing? She's Nicky's art teacher, and she's an artist in her own right, and does art restoring as well, I understand."

"No."

"Have you ever heard of an art gallery by the name of A IS A?"

"No."

"Leon, is anything wrong?"

"No."

Tara leaned her head back against the seat again. Turn the subject to something positive, she thought. It was getting dark now. Perhaps she should just be quiet.

"I love *Spring Flower*," she blurted out involuntarily. "If you were capable of that at fifteen years old, I can't *wait* to see what you're doing now. I knew from the notes that you made in the margins of Dimitrios's article that you must do nudes—it just had to be—but this *Spring Flower*, it's breathtaking!"

"Would it matter to you if I didn't sculpt nudes anymore?" Leon interrupted, his tone as frozen as his eyes. Was it the right move to have taken her to meet his parents? He'd known she would like them. Just as he'd known she would admire *Spring Flower*. That's why he'd called home and invited himself over. But he also knew that these calculated movements of "leading her carefully" were constructing a highly censored view of himself that conflicted with . . . other views of himself. He couldn't keep certain things under wraps forever. But timing was everything. This particular choreography was very tricky, this ballet of seduction. Because it was real. Strange. When it had been a simple bet, he'd operated with confident ease. Now that he knew how much she meant to him, he felt awkward, unsure.

Tara felt as if she had been slapped. "No, of course not," she said softly. "It's just that, I guess . . . well, anyway," she watched him carefully out of the corner of an eye, "it *is* frustrating to wait until the museum opening to see your 'grown-up' work. I know you've explained about the scale of the pieces and how they have to be seen in an appropriate setting. But you can imagine how madly curious I am about it. You've left one of the most important pieces of the puzzle of getting to know you entirely out of the picture. I mean, it's not as if we're casual friends, Leon."

"What about sleeping with me? Isn't that a big *piece* of the puzzle?" There was no humor in his eyes.

Tara didn't answer; she didn't think his joke was funny either. They crossed over the bridge into Manhattan. Damn him! She was getting angry now. If there was a reason for this moodiness, she had a right to know it; if there wasn't a reason, he had no right to behave this way. Trying to calm herself down, she concentrated on the span of lights strung above them on the bridge.

"My brother Nicky is having some problems with several art issues," she tried, desperate to get them both back on an even keel; the day was too precious to lose like this. "He's a very confused nineteen-year-old right now, but he's also incredibly talented, and I don't want his confusions to influence his work. Would you be willing to talk to him or even, perhaps, introduce him to your agent so he could have the value of her expertise as well? He needs some fresh advice, I think."

"Of course I'll talk to him. He'll be at the Thanksgiving dinner?"

"Yes." She breathed a sigh of relief. Was he softening?

"By the way," Leon said tonelessly, "it wasn't necessary for you to invite my parents to that celebration."

"Oh!" She was taken aback again. "I'm sorry. Don't you think they'll want to come?"

"Probably." He pulled off the West Side Drive, ran three red lights and drove the car into a garage in what looked like a seedy part of the largely gentrified section of Chelsea. "The restaurant's just around the corner," he said, preoccupied. Act Two coming up. Careful.

"But this is a *thrift shop*!" she exclaimed, crossing the shabby entranceway.

"That it is." Leon led her through the store to an unmarked door at the rear and opened it to let her enter first.

If he hadn't been close behind, she would have backed right out again. Except for strobe lights splintering the darkness with fragmentary illumination, the entire room was pitch black. Loud, jumbled sounds seemed to come from nowhere and everywhere at the same time. As her eyes and ears became accustomed to the sound shock, she was able to identify a piano with a woman playing loud progressive jazz, bubbles of conversation bursting into laughter, ice cubes tinkling against glass like the futile attempt of an orchestral triangle trying to be heard, and the blast of a trumpet that seemed to spurt in and out of the other sounds at random. Then a black face loomed before her, friendly and smiling. "When's your birthday, darlin'?" It was a wandering horn player; his whole body moved in time with the beat of the piano as he waited for her answer.

"November 27th," she answered, not knowing what else to say.

"A *firebird*!" he shouted to the others in the room. "We've got ourselves a real firebird!" Crooking one arm through hers, he danced her around the room, blowing long, strident notes until Leon, laughing at last, disengaged her and led her to another door at the back of the room. She let herself be guided.

The door closed behind them. Silence.

The dining room was candlelit, the tables set with crystal and yellow roses. One entire wall of glass looked out upon an enclosed garden gloriously abloom with exotic flowers of every color. A copper waterfall spilled silently into a pool glinting with golden koi jewelfish, and strains of a recorded string quartet wrapped the room in nineteenth-century grace and order. Tara felt her coat being removed and a chair pushed beneath her by a waiter in a tuxedo. She stared at the garden and then she stared at Leon.

He sat across from her, ordered Gray Goose, Krug and osetra caviar and then told the waiter to inform the chef that he was there with someone very special and he would leave dinner to the chef's choice. "Now," he said, feeling relief spread over him as the waiter nodded his head to confirm that everything was ready as planned, "Tell me about this Thanksgiving dinner where I am to be skewered by this formidable father of yours."

Tara had noted that there were no more than a dozen tables in the entire restaurant and that only three of them were occupied, but it was still early in the evening. She decided not to ask any questions; whatever was causing Leon's cold preoccupation would have to come out sooner or later. If he was playing games, she would not play. She would simply wait. "The music at Thanksgiving will be very different from what we just heard," she said, not masking the irony she felt. "We have a jukebox filled with Greek records. My relatives will dance to the music, they'll drink a lot of wine and eat a lot of food that my father will prepare with great pleasure. They'll all talk about the 'old' country and politics there. Never here. No matter what anti-American feelings might be in Greece itself these days, nothing America could do would be wrong in their immigrant eyes. They'll ask your parents about your family background, but they won't care about your art. They'll try to find out how much money you have. They'll ply me with presents because we'll be celebrating my Name Day as well as Thanksgiving. They'll all tell me that I'm getting too old to be single and that I should settle down and get married, and they'll all look at you when they say it. There may be an argument or two over family slights that are twenty years old. Kally will play the piano—I'm finally too old to be ordered to dance any more—and my father will offer a toast. A typical American Thanksgiving Day celebration by Greek Americans."

Leon turned pensive again, staring out the window into the garden with a concentration that made her think he must be counting the petals on the flowers. She felt her anger begin to flare again. Had he heard a word she said? They were both eating without tasting and talking without meaning.

"Why do you celebrate your Name Day? You told me your father wasn't religious, and a 'Name Day' means you celebrate the day of the saint you were named after, right?"

"That's correct. Kally and Nicky have birthdays because they were born over here. Since I was born in Greece, my father didn't want to embarrass my mother's family, so I was named Kantara Anne and we celebrate the Saint's day of Anne. It's early in December, so it's the closest Saint's day to my birth date. The Greeks make a big fuss over a person's Name Day, but to us it's like any birthday, and since mine is so close to Thanksgiving, we've always celebrated them together."

"I see. Well, now that I understand it," he motioned to the waiter, who returned with an enormous box wrapped in white paper and a red satin ribbon, "Happy birthday." He pulled an empty chair next to Tara so she could set the package down to open it. His eyes were clear again! Anger, surprise, confusion and delight all collided within her; suddenly, she wanted to cry. If this was the lovely end of this lovely day, why had he withdrawn, cold and pensive?

"Thanksgiving is two days away and my Name Day is a day after that," she said, forcing a smile.

"That's all right, we'll celebrate it now." He was coming alive again. "We don't want your whole family to know how much money I have, do we?"

She untied the ribbon and took her time unwrapping

the paper. Then, lifting the top of the box, she did cry.

The first thing that hit her was the fragrance. She lifted the gardenia and held it to her nose, remembering the nightclub in Athens where Leon had showered her with a dozen of them. She didn't dare trust her hands to lift the mound of fur that had been the flower's nesting place. Leon rose and, gathering the moon-blue clouds of fur up from the box, coaxed her to stand as he slipped the blue fox cape around her shoulders; it fell in drifts to the floor. "You had to have something to match your hat, don't you think?" he teased her, feeling better now that he had her reaction. "Now, dry your tears. Fur can stand snow, but not rain."

"But I'll never be able to wear it in Greece!" was all she could think of to stammer.

"I know," he said, smiling his old smile at last and wrapping his arms around the wrap of the coat. "How about a dance?"

He led her back through the door, where the strident music was still in loud swing. She could distinguish a long bar in one corner, some couples sitting on stools at high tables drinking and talking over the music and others moving disjointedly in strobe lights over the dance floor. Leon gathered her into his arms, and the other customers stopped drinking, talking and dancing to stare at the blanket of fur moving slowly about the dance floor, totally out of rhythm with the frenetic trumpet and piano duet. Subtly, the musicians adapted the music to Leon's dancing, and Tara lifted her head from his shoulder to see smiles coming from every direction. When their dance was over, the music blared again and the other customers took over the floor in a kind of wild dance frenzy that seemed to obliterate the moments before.

Leon led her to a table, then returned with a full champagne bottle in one hand and two glasses and the gardenia in the other. "Let's go," he said. "And, by the way, there's something else for you in the pocket of the coat."

She pulled out a slip of paper with some writing on it, but in the darkness it was impossible to read the message. She burst out laughing. "What on earth are you *doing*, Leon Skillman? You're driving me crazy!"

"What's the matter? Don't you like your present? What's the matter, can't you read?" He caught his breath. Act Three coming up.

"No, I can't read! It's too dark and the lights are too jumpy. And you know it."

"Oh! Well, then, I'll read it for you," he shouted above the din. He snapped the paper from her hand and, without looking at it, read into her eyes: "WILL YOU COME AND LIVE WITH ME? I LOVE YOU."

They lay together, covered only by the fox cape, on the couch in Leon's living room and looked out at the night skyline of the city.

"I'm glad they're still lighting the tops of the most distinctive buildings," Leon commented unguardedly. "Allegiance to beauty is always in some way an act of defiance against barbarism." The show, for tonight, was over. Now he could stop acting, stop worrying and just be himself for a change. The remainder of the evening would be for real.

"Oh yes, Leon. The boring boxes fade away when the beauties are brought into focus." Tara turned her head away from the view and rested her cheek against his bare chest, remembering the similar, affirmative margin notes about beauty that he had made alongside Dimitrios's article.

"Will you stay?" Leon's voice was low.

"I don't know. It's a big question."

"Do you love me?"

"Another big question. How do you know that *you* love *me*?"

"Because I want you with me, to be part of me . . . part of my life. I can't think of breathing without you . . . now." It was the truth.

"Is that love?"

"To me it is. I can't experience myself with anyone else in the same way I do with you. I need you for that, and I love you for making that possible." Another truth.

"Is that why you cried?"

"Yes. You made me know that what I dreamed of as a boy is possible for me as a man." All of this was true. She had to understand these truths before she came to know other truths about him.

"Is that what you were dreaming of when you sculpted *Spring Flower?*

"Yes."

"Must I really wait until the opening to see your work? It's so strange that you don't want me to, Leon."

He listened to a solitary horn blasting away from the street far below. Someone's car was penned in and the horn was blaring out in anger. "Why is my art so important to you? You know everything you need to know to love or not to love . . ." he let his words trail off into shallow silence. Either the owner of the offending car had moved his vehicle, or the penned-in person had given up. "My art is the way I make my living. Nothing more."

"Every person chooses how they make their living," Tara persisted, "even if they *fail* to choose. You can choose by omission, you know. But making art isn't like being a stockbroker. Art is such an active, expressive choice. Your art is important to me because I can't know you fully until I see it." She slid her hand under the fur, totally forgiving his earlier coldness.

Leon's worries came back.

SEVENTEEN

"*H*RONIA POLLA!"
"*Hronia Polla!* "*Hronia Polla!*"

"Thank you, Uncle Basilious. Thank you Aunt Anastasia and Uncle Thrasy. Thank you for coming. It's so—" Tara's throat constricted; the present moment of greeting her relatives and her childhood memories of them collided within her to choke the words, "*good* to see you." She swallowed, and then smiled. "Efharisto." She hugged all three at once, but found them, all four, gathered roughly into her father's huge embrace.

"Come, come. You are late. *Mezethakia* has been set out since four o'clock. It is already four-thirty. Wine for you? Or Ouzo? Speak to me. Drink. Eat. It is *glendi*! How do you like this grown-up Tara, my beautiful daughter?" Kostas drew Kally into his group hug. "The young, baby daughter—my *Kallisti*, she serves her name well—is 'perfectly' beautiful, too!" Then laughing and dancing the entire tangle of arms and legs over to Nicky: "The son is not beautiful, but he is bright. Marguerita!" Marguerita came shuffling out of the kitchen beaming a wide smile and dabbing perspiration from her forehead with a dishtowel. Kostas spun her into the group circle, his blue eyes dancing in time with his feet, until each person finally dropped out of the group into a chair with happy exhaustion. Kostas sprawled onto a couch, wiped his face with Marguerita's towel and surveyed the room, his eyes brimming. "My family! Together. For the first time in ten years!"

"Ouzo! Nicholas! Pour!" Kostas jumped up and rearranged everyone's chair so that family was quickly mixed with guests. "An American birthday game," he chuckled, "musical chairs . . ." and turned to Leon, Leon's parents, the restaurant's two regular waiters and their families plus Dorina, Nicky's art teacher. "Ouzo or wine for you my friends . . . and my daughter's friends? Drink, eat, it is *glendi*! Ouzo or wine?" He landed back on the couch, satisfied.

Basilious rose and pulled two bottles out of the shopping bag he had brought. "Or home-made *Mavrodaphne?*"

Marguerita grabbed one of the bottles and headed back to the kitchen. "*Mavrodaphne*, for the Mama! Kally, bring a pretty glass to the kitchen and help a little, eh?"

Tara sat on the arm of Leon's chair, sipping ouzo and nibbling from one of the many trays of appetizers. Leon smiled up at her, shaking his head in wonder. "I didn't understand a word, but it seems everybody sort of likes one another."

The phone rang and Kostas bounded off the sofa to answer it.

"*Mavrodaphne* is a rather sweet, fruity wine that Greeks make in their own homes," Tara explained. "*Mezethakia*, 'appetizers' in English, means 'to whet the appetite'." She dipped some bread, "*psomi*," into a salmon-colored dip, "*tarama*—fish roe, Greek caviar—"and fed it to Leon. "Ah, yes," he remembered. "We had this at that taverna with the grape arbor, didn't we? But what was that word your aunt and uncles said to you when they first came in?"

"*Hronia Polla* translates to 'many years.' It's always given in greeting to the person whose Name Day is being celebrated."

Tara filled two plates from the trays and handed them to Leon's parents: "*Yiaourti Skordalia*—yogurt, cucumbers, garlic—another dip for your *psomi. Tiropetes*—philo and feta cheese triangles; *Spanakopetes*—spinach and cheese pies; *Dolmadakia*—rolled grape leaves; *Keftaidakia*—meat balls."

"Where's the *Loukanika*?"

"Oh, you're right," Tara turned to her Uncle Thrasy. "I forgot to put them out. They're still in the kitchen."

"I'll get them, and help your Mama, too." Anastasia hurried to the kitchen.

"*Loukanika*," Tara went on, "is Greek sausage. We love to eat, you see. *Glendi* means 'good times,' a zest for good living, good wine and good food."

"*Glendi*, yes, but always remembering that life must be the balance of work and play. That is the Greek understanding," Kostas lectured, coming back into the room. "On the phone was Dimitrios."

"Dimitrios? Calling from Athens?" Tara got up to go to the phone.

"Never mind! You can speak to him in the person in twenty minutes. He just now arrived and called from his hotel to tell you he's in town. He didn't even know it was Thanksgiving—of course, who thinks of 'Thanksgiving' in Greece?—but I told him we were having celebrations for Thanksgiving and your Name Day combined and gave the invitation to come over. So he can tell you he's in town himself. *Endoxie*! Now we can show a Greek that we Greek-Americans still know how to cook!"

Leon suspended a spinach pie in midair. Why the hell was Dimitrios in America? Just to further mess up his plans?

Tara pressed her hands together thankfully. "Bless him! I knew he'd come to help me with the exhibit."

Helene Skillman held up her glass for more ouzo. "I love it," she exclaimed, "it's like drinking licorice candy."

"Careful, mother," Leon warned. "It packs a wallop."

"Who does the cooking, Kostas?" Helene asked. "You or Marguerita?"

"Both of us." Kostas raised both hands and clasped them

together in a gesture of championship. "Our recipes are handed down generation to generation. The cookbooks Americans have for Greek cooking are never what we do. You must *watch* your mother and your grandfather. That is the only way to learn all the little things a person forgets to write into a paper recipe. There is always something extra that can never go into words or measures." He shrugged. "But not one of my children ever had interest to watch. Not one can do more than heat up frozen pizza pies in the oven. Marguerita and I still hope that when our children have children," he glanced pointedly at Leon and Tara, "some *grandchildren* will want to watch and carry on the tradition. Otherwise, in our family, it is lost."

Leonard Skillman scooped *Tarama* onto his bread. "It's not lost on me. This is delicious. Thank you for sharing this day with us, Kostas."

"When my daughter and your son share nights together, it is time for the parents to share days," Kostas said. He was scowling, and the crowd stiffened at his bald statement. Then his eyes were merry again. "Let's have music," he said. "One thing you must know is that a Greek feast day goes on forever. But we can't eat all night long, so we break it up with music and dance and stories. And because we... Because we are *ecumenical*," Kostas stopped and, raising both bushy eyebrows pointedly, surveyed the room to see the impression his big word had made. It was good; everyone was staring at him. Emitting a satisfied growl, he went on. "Yes, we are *ecumenical*! So! We mix up a Greek Name Day with an American birthday and national holiday. Tara even gets to open presents, if she is good girl. We used to make her dance—" he glowered daringly at Tara, but she shook her head vehemently, "so now we make Kally take the whole show. Kally! Come! Play for us!"

Kally rushed out of the kitchen, her cheeks flushed from the heat of the skewered lamb she had been basting. "At least it's cooler out here," she exclaimed. "Okay, Papa. I'll play. But only if I get to have some ouzo afterward." *Please, Papa,* her eyes asked silently.

"A deal is made! Now play. And no mistakes. We have company!" Kostas smothered Kally with a kiss, filled a small glass and set it on top of the piano. He turned to the others. "I should charge you admission to hear this talented child. What do we hear? Greek or classical?"

"Both." Leonard Skillman answered.

"But classical first," Dorina added.

Tara's glance floated over the room with the music: from the burnished brown of Kally's long hair to the bleached brown of the old upright piano, from the shine in her father's eyes to the dull linoleum flooring, from the pale sparkle of resina wine to the pale, scrubbed paint of the walls. She could smell both the tea rose of Dorina's perfume and the lemon and oregano from the kitchen. Leonard Skillman's hands, she noted, were slender and fine, her father's large and workworn. Her uncles, listening to the music, sat so still they looked like old photographs of themselves.

Leon, watching her, took her hand and brought it silently to his lips.

"No mistakes," Kally repeated quietly to herself. She finished the piece with an intricate arpeggio and then crescendoed into another and finished it just as perfectly for good measure. "There!" She turned, blushing with achievement, and clapped her own hands back at the applause. Her father was standing and pounding his big hands together, a broad smile splitting his face with pride. "What did I tell you? What about that talent?" he was shouting above the din. "That is *my daughter!*"

Leonard Skillman approached the piano and whispered into Kally's ear. She nodded, turned back to the keyboard, and began another piece. Standing behind her, Leonard leaned over her back and, encircling both her arms with one hand each at the far ends of bass and treble, played a counterpoint to her melody. Marguerita and Anastasia hurried out from the kitchen to listen while Kostas remained stunned with pleasure in the center of the room. When it was over, Leonard handed Kally the glass of ouzo. "You're right," he said nodding to Kostas. "She *is* talented."

"She certainly is!" The voice echoed from the hallway. "Why didn't you tell me you had a star in your family, Tara?"

"Dimitrios!" Tara ran to him and hugged him happily while pulling him into the room. "Oh, I'm so glad to see you! Why didn't you tell me you were coming?"

"I wanted to surprise you."

Well, you have, Leon thought. He walked over to shake hands and help with introductions.

Kally traced Leon's steps with her eyes as he moved through the room chatting effortlessly with everyone. So at ease. Just like Mr. Gothard, she thought; he always knows exactly what to do. Papa would have just let poor Mr. Kokonas find his own way to both people and food. She sneaked a glance at Leon's father, seated again on a sofa with his wife; they were so refined! *Why* couldn't I have American parents like them? she pouted. She watched her own mother waddle back to the kitchen, *in her house slippers!* Kally drained her glass and looked pleadingly at Nicky for some more. Oh! She stuck her tongue out at him. He was as strict as her father! When it was her turn to shake hands with Mr. Kokonas, she reeled with surprise as *Leon* took her hand and kissed it. Just like in the movies! "Your piano playing was lovely, Kally," he said. The words rang in her ears like a melody.

Anastasia and Marguerita came hurrying out of the kitchen bearing platters of potatoes and vegetables and a huge pot of *bamyes* in tomato sauce, Marguerita's okra specialty. Perspiration glistened on Marguerita's forehead. "Kostas, carve the lamb. Everything else is hot and ready. Tara and Kally, get the salad and the soup. Hurry! Kostas, the lamb!"

"Not until everybody *sees* it first," Kostas insisted. Motioning for the others to follow, he led them all to see his masterpiece: a whole lamb roasted on a spit over the open fireplace in the restaurant's huge kitchen. "I have not done it whole, the old way, for many years," he announced solemnly. "Now, sit down. Eat! Everybody sit to your soup right away so the rest will still be hot."

"The *avgolemono* is superb, Marguerita." Dimitrios tasted the lemon soup with relish. "Homemade soup is a special treat to someone who usually eats in restaurants."

"Sit down and eat!" Kostas bellowed as his two waiters jumped up to help him bring the lamb from the kitchen. "Today, you are guests and friends, not employees. Everyone here can help themselves. It is all family."

Marguerita and Kostas let Leonard Skillman pry recipes out of them. "You must beat the eggs first and then slowly beat in the lemon juice till you have a sauce, and *then* beat in the hot chicken broth . . ."

Tara turned to Dorina Swing. The woman's controlled grace had intrigued her all evening. Dorina joined in conversation only when she had something to say; she was clearly enjoying the food and drink and had listened attentively, not just politely, to Kally's playing. She was a small woman, but her quiet confidence gave her otherwise plain appearance a certain inner radiance, like fine silver that gains luster with time as its patina enriches and deepens its beauty. They had all settled at one end of the table together: she, Leon, Dorina, Dimitrios, Nicky and Leon's mother. The rest of the family and Leon's father were deep in cooking conversation at the opposite end. Dimitrios was talking to Tara's Uncle Basilious, who had also been born in Greece.

"I'm happy to meet you, Dorina," Tara began. "I've seen Nicky's work and I can't tell you how impressed I am at the depth and intensity of his paintings. You're quite a teacher."

Dorina smiled affectionately at Nicky. "I am impressed, too," she said. "But I take credit only for teaching Nicky the techniques of our craft. Nicky himself has gone far beyond my expectations in the areas that cannot be taught: maturity of content and individual style."

Listening, Helene Skillman thought of a time when she could have said the same of Leon.

"I suppose *you* mean *objective* content—" Leon interrupted. Hey! It was an automatic response. Part of his calling card in the art world was controversy.

"Yes, I do," Dorina sipped delicately at her soup, "but I suppose you disagree, Leon."

"A whole century disagrees." Leon flashed a disarming smile. Roll with it, he thought. It's a chance to give Tara an inkling of what's in store. "But for myself, *I* make art that sells. I don't care about art theories."

Nicky's eyes brightened with excitement. "What about art as process? For a school project, I did an abstract alabaster piece that was just process. It was fun."

Leon rolled his eyes. "*All* art is 'process,' and always has been. Anyway, that's old news. Today, the operative word in the art world is *politics*."

"Art is politics? Plato said *that* over two-thousand years ago!" Uncle Basilious stormed. "Dorina speaks in the vein of Aristotle. And Aristotle was right!"

Nicky nodded to Tara. "See what I mean?"

Tara was staring, stunned, at Leon. He couldn't mean he didn't care about his work!

Dorina smiled at Dimitrios. "Which, professor? Plato or Aristotle?"

Dimitrios demurred. "Not a subject conducive to digestion, I'm afraid."

"You're right," Dorina said. "None of this is dinner talk. Wouldn't you all like to come up to my studio over the weekend and see Nicky's work? We could talk more then. I would like it." She seemed to be looking particularly at Dimitrios.

Tara sensed his discomfort as Dimitrios smiled back at Dorina. While they discussed the details of Dorina's invitation Tara decided she had to test Leon. It wasn't possible he didn't *care*. "Leon! In the margin of Dimitrios's article in *L'Ancienne*, you cared enough about 'theory' to make a note about the connection between art and beauty. So what did you mean?"

Helene Skillman's head shot up in a spasm of shock.

Leon cut carefully into his meat. Would his mother cover for him?

"I was only struck by the observation," he began, watching his mother out of the corner of one eye, "that throughout most of history, man has created art, but only artists in certain eras in certain places have gravitated toward beauty. It was just a thought . . ." Dismissively, he trailed off.

"It was an important thought, however." Helene Skillman addressed her son with what it seemed to Tara an awkward tenderness. "Could you have been thinking that beauty in *art* depends upon values in *life*? And that if valueless things are thought to share equal status with those of true, lasting value, then the power of *all* values can be diminished, and the concept of beauty itself lose any standard of assessment?"

"That's why I don't like this so-called postmodern art," Uncle Basilious broke in. Tara and Nicky exchanged a glance. Wherever he started, Uncle Basilious would end with Aristotle; they knew that much from years of experience. "What does it even mean, *post*modern? The term contradicts itself. And so much of that stuff is so *ugly*." Basilious made a face, "I don't think a lot of it is even art anymore. It's entertainment, or an amusement, or an investment, or an offense. When art loses meaning, life loses meaning. As Aristotle . . ."

Tara looked with great affection at the lines in her uncle's old face. They were like underscorings of the written word, the living underscorings of a lived life, written by him, all the way. The lines of his forehead all led upward and curved at the temples into question marks; the lines around his mouth all lifted upward into optimism;

the lines around his eyes all burst upward into laughter. It was a face of questions tempered by optimism, of intense curiosity, all culminating into the burning black intelligence of two inquisitive and penetrating eyes. Tara had known from childhood that no one could lie to those eyes, and she knew, too, that they would never lie to anyone.

Kostas raised his voice from the other end of the table. "Not 'Aristotle' again. We've all heard the story of your statue a hundred times."

Uncle Basilious was not really anyone's uncle, but a first cousin of Kostas. About Kostas's own age, Basilious had left his partner in Athens and expanded their small cargo shipping company to New York. With the additional American base, they had both become multi-millionaires fairly quickly. Yet even though his partner still lived there, Basilious had not returned to Greece for many years. Because of the incident with this statue.

Basilious grimaced and prodded another piece of lamb from the platter. "Not enough garlic, Kostas!" Then he turned to the others.

"You see, I was born in the same place where Aristotle was born: Stagirus. Ergo: Aristotle was the pride of my province. Well, after I came to America and made my fortune, what do you think I did for that little place in Greece? I'll tell you! I paid sixty thousand dollars to commission a full-figure sculpture of Aristotle, and that was sixty thousand dollars twenty years ago! Then I sent this beautiful gift back home to stand in the central square of my little village. It was my tribute to that man, and to his ideas *and* to the town. Anyway . . ." Tara, Kally and Nicky began to remove dishes from the table. "Would you believe that the politicians and the church fathers—the church was also in the same square—got together and after only eight months of letting my statue stand there—a tribute to the only achievement that burg ever managed, to be the birthplace of Aristotle—they took down my statue and put it in the basement of the church. Can you imagine? The greatest of all Greek philosophers, the champion of *reason*, in a church! I have never set foot in Greece since that day. Aristotle's Greece is long, long gone. And if that isn't sad enough, I now see the last of his great ideas destroyed every day right here in America, along with *beauty*. America! The country born out of Aristotle's philosophy but not willing to live by it. Maybe Leon, here, is right that art, today, is politics. Because, today, *everything* is politics. When philosophy dies, brute power-plays are all that's left—"

"Oh! Turkish coffee! I love it! Helene Skillman reached for the tiny cup Kally offered.

"*What?*" Basilious's face burned red, all lines raced upward in incredulity. "*Turkish* coffee?"

Helene glanced around the table for help.

"This is *Kafes. Coffee. Greek* coffee. It does not matter that our preparation of it was first introduced to Greece by those barbarian Turks who invaded our country—"

Tara quickly slid some change into the jukebox, knowing that the pulsing folk music of their homeland would call them all to the center of the room. Everyone, especially she, needed to remember that this day was a celebration. All conflicts and all confusions we're out of place today. "Uncle Basilious, will you dance with me?" Tara swayed her body and clapped her hands to the beating rhythm of the song and, true to form, her father took charge. After the men removed their suit jackets and rolled up their shirtsleeves, he hauled his handkerchief out of a pocket, and giving one end to Basilious, began a group dance that wiped all controversial thoughts from the minds of everyone present. Within minutes, the table was empty, and Greeks, Americans, and those who knew no country except themselves danced to the music of Life. Tara looked at Dimitrios, here with her on this happy occasion, and recalled the words from his article: "To the joy of it!"

Suddenly aware of the elegance and fluidity of his movements, it dawned on her that although she had danced this ethnic style with him hundreds of times in Greece, he appeared quite different here in this foreign setting amid, well, "foreigners." The power of his grace seemed to come so easily from fathoms deep within him, from his profound understanding of the art of all dance in general, but especially the one informing his own heritage. Aside from her much older father and Basilious, the others in the room were enjoying a perfectly spontaneous physical response to the unique rhythms inherent in Greek music, but they could have no idea whatsoever about the spiritual depths to be approached through such bodily expression. Although done in groups (and misconstrued because of it) Greek dancing was primarily an individual experience. What she witnessed now was Dimitrios dancing with his own soul, connecting and celebrating physically with the animating source of all that he was, all he had become as a person and as a man. All this passed unconsciously through her mind as quickly and naturally as her breath passed through her body, mesmerized as she was for this one split second in time by the utter rarity of her mentor and dearest friend, by his dignity, by his understanding of the *seriousness* of the joy of it all, mind, body and soul. He reminded her at this moment of a torero, slim and taut and singularly focused upon the underlying purpose guiding his every step and gesture, as if the key to the sublime lay in the act of integration: gathering knowledge, skill, discipline, style and beauty into one expression of the whole, expressing an ultimate intention whose drama evolved into the summation of some metaphysical fundamental of life: in the case of the torero, a dance defying death, in the case of Dimitrios, a dance embracing life.

Inspired and deeply moved by the sight of Dimitrios's total commitment to joy, she danced over to Leon and gave herself over to the music too, resolutely dismissing any earlier uneasiness she had felt toward him. It was her birthday, after all. "How do you like *this* music and dance?" she teased. "That place you took me to last night reminded me of primitive mating dances."

Leon, watching her flowing and uninhibited undulations, remembered his description to the Gothards of Tara's sexy "belly dancing" in Greece. What a crass description for such exquisite movements; it was hard to believe he'd ever thought such a thought, let alone uttered it.

Tara raised both arms and, clicking her fingers, swung away from him and, taking Dimitrios's hand while still holding on to Leon's, danced between them, smiling up at both. "This music is to the joy of it. The joy of life."

Quickly, Leon pulled her back from Dimitrios and began to waltz out-of-time against the music's strong beat. Holding her close, he whirled her around the room. "And *this*?" he whispered into her ear.

Marguerita, on her way to the kitchen to return the huge *bamyes* pot, stopped and, with one arm around the pot and one arm around Leon, continued the dance with him. "Kally!" she shouted. "Come take this pot!"

Kally skipped to their side and slipped under Leon's free arm. "No!" she shouted above the din. "You take the pot. I'll take Leon!"

Marguerita released Leon and headed for the kitchen, her ample hips still swaying to the music.

Leon eased Kally away from his body and held her hand, Greek style, to dance back to the circle, but she clasped her free hand around his neck and, pressing close to him, guided him to the far side of the room.

Amazed, Leon felt her small breasts against his chest as she lengthened her body against his and moved sensually to a rhythm of her own. He glanced down at her half-closed eyes. What the—? Then he felt her snatched from his arms and watched her vanish through the kitchen door, propelled by the rage of her brother. Amused at the adolescence of both of them, he looked around the room; no one seemed to have noticed the exchange.

Nicky pushed Kally through the kitchen, past his mother and into the storage room. Marguerita was busy filling platters with cakes and cookies.

"What do you think you're doing?" Nicky hissed through clenched teeth. "Leon belongs to Tara! And even if he didn't, that's no way to behave!"

"Every woman for herself!" Kally retorted, wrenching free from her brother's hold. She laughed into his face, "I *like* mating dances!" and started to bump and grind like a striptease showgirl.

The blow wasn't as hard as it seemed. Nicky only slapped her cheek, but Kally felt his words sear her very soul.

"You tramp!"

Through blinding tears, she watched her brother disappear back out the door. Kally sat down on a crate of canned tomatoes, her eyes blurred with resentment, her nails digging into the wood.

Nicky stormed back into the dining room and tried to calm himself by taking one of his father's hands and one of Dorina's in the dance. He let the music wash the anger from his body. Then, suddenly swamped by a different emotion, he found himself with both arms around Kostas, spiraling into a passionate bear hug that spun them around and around until they fell into a chair as one. Gasping for breath, his father called out, "Basilious, you take this son of mine. He is too much for me!"

Basilious grabbed Nicky's hand, and Kostas reached for a glass of wine, wiping his brow and grinning with pleasure. He lifted his glass in a toast to the room. "Happy Thanksgiving," he growled. "Today we give thanks *to me*, for bringing my family to *America*!"

Dorina linked her arm with Dimitrios's, smiling evenly into his dark eyes. "You will come to tea?" she asked.

"Of course."

"Fine." She removed a hairpin from the coils that framed her oval face and Dimitrios watched, stunned, as thick, honey-colored hair tumbled to her waist. A few silver strands shone through the gold.

Nicky, now connected to Uncle Basilious by a handkerchief, stared at Dorina's undulating hips and the long mass of hair brushing to and fro over them, accentuating the movement even more. He had never seen this stern woman with her hair loose. She looked young and expectant. Tara was sitting on Leon's knee in a corner chair; they were talking quietly. Kally had come back into the room and poured herself more ouzo. Nicky decided not to notice.

"Dessert!" Marguerita came bustling out of the kitchen with a platter and stopped to sip wine from Anastasia's glass on the way. "Come! Eat! Dessert!"

"More? It's getting late. We ought to be heading for home," Helene said. But she and Leonard went eagerly back to the table to view the new delights.

Marguerita pointed to each variety: "*Baklava,* honey cake; *Galatoboureko,* custard cake; *Kourabiedes,* with almonds and walnuts—"

"Like air in the mouth," Kostas interrupted, coming to the table to take over. "*Koulourakia,* sesame cookies. *Fenikia,* honey-dipped cookies; *Ravani*—"

"*And,*" Uncle Basilious came out of the kitchen bearing a pink cake with lighted candles, "an American birthday cake on an American holiday for Tara, an American girl!"

Is she? Leon and Dimitrios asked the same question silently, independently, simultaneously.

Kally sat sullenly on the piano bench gulping her drink. No one had noticed when she took the second glass. No one except Nicky. He had said nothing, only turned away from her. An *American* girl? she sulked. *I* am the only American girl in the room!

They all sang "Happy Birthday," and Marguerita and Nicky brought gifts to the table. Tara opened her presents while everyone else ate cakes.

When she came to the package from her parents, Kostas

and Marguerita stopped eating. "It was hand-woven by my mother," Marguerita advised her. "It was the wedding gift to us from your grandmother," Kostas added. "We were saving it for your wedding, but this is such a special birthday with all of us together and you home for the first time in so long, here it is now."

Tara lifted the blanket from its box and wrapped it around her shoulders like a shawl, hugging herself in the warmth of family, history, and friends. The soft, magenta-dyed wool was edged in a gold, Greek "key" pattern.

"Look at the corners of the key, Marguerita urged. "They are perfect, every one."

Tara looked around the table, her throat tight. "*You* are perfect. Every one."

"Wait," Kostas broke the moment, embarrassed, "you don't wrap yourself in that when you have Leon's gift! Tara, go get it and show to the others."

When she returned, displaying the blue fox cape to "Oohs" and "Aahs," Dimitrios heard himself wondering aloud, "But when would you wear it at home in Greece?" He blushed deeply.

She *is* at home!" Kostas bellowed. "Maybe," he locked eyes with Leon, "to stay?"

Helene Skillman slipped a hand into her husband's for support. Anger thundered across her eyes. First the lie about the margin notes and, now, a bribe? But Tara could be just the force needed to pull Leon back to life, she thought.

Dorina watched Dimitrios watching Tara, heard his statement, and saw the wounded look on his face. Sudden knowledge spread through her like an ache. She had been instantly, powerfully, drawn to the depths of this man. She twisted her hair into a long rope and, winding it around her head, fastened it back into place with the single pin. "Will you walk me home, Dimitrios?" she asked. "It's dark, and it makes me nervous to walk alone."

Nicky dragged his *Baklava* through more honey, not looking up. Dorina had never been nervous in her life.

At the door, Dimitrios helped Dorina into her coat, glad to have a reason to leave early so it wouldn't seem he was hanging around Tara with Leon there. Amid handshakes and "goodnights," he whispered to Tara: "I brought your Name Day gift with me to New York. Could we celebrate tomorrow night, just the two of us? Will you let me take you to dinner?" Thank the gods he'd decided to bring his own present in person. That coat! He leaned over to kiss her on the forehead, as usual, then changed his mind. He might not be very adept at it yet, but he had to start competing sometime. Now! Lifting Tara's chin firmly with his hand, he kissed her lightly on the lips.

"Yes, of course," she said. "I'm so glad you're here." Tara hugged him happily. "Goodnight, Dorina. See you in a couple of days."

As the door closed behind Dimitrios and Dorina, Tara's hand went involuntarily to her lips, her brain half-registering Dimitrios's kiss, her mouth half-tasting the sweetness of his breath. Then she turned and went back to her guests.

Leonard Skillman shook hands around the room. "We must go, too. We have a drive to get home." He turned to Tara and Leon and spread his arms wide to embrace them both.

"Don't go! Have some more sweets. We will go on for hours!" Kostas insisted.

Tara, still surrounded by the aura of blue fox, walked with Leon's parents into the foyer. "Thank you for coming," she smiled. "Thank you for having such a wonderful son." Impulsively, she leaned over and kissed Helene on the cheek, her eyes warm with affection.

Helene turned and faced her squarely. "Tara, what made you say that the margin notes in *L'Ancienne* were Leon's? Did he tell you that?"

Tara was brought up short; the question was so far afield.

"Well, yes. Well, not exactly. I found the journal on his desk and just assumed the notes were his. Why?"

"When you assumed it, did Leon correct you? Have you ever seen Leon's handwriting?"

What questions! "Well," Tara thought back. "When I mentioned the notes, Leon said he often took notes while reading, that it helped him think. And," she thought of the paper in the pocket of the fur cape; she hadn't been able to read it because of the dark and the strobe lights, and Leon had tossed the paper away after he read it to her. "No, we've never written to each other. Why do you ask these questions? I don't understand."

Helene's green eyes, a softer, bluer shade of Leon's, were sympathetic but set with decision. "I apologize for telling you this here and now, but there is no good place or time. The notes in the margin of the *L'Ancienne* article are *mine*, not Leon's. The thoughts and ideas are mine, not his. You have said that my son has asked you to wait to see his art until the Harrington opening. I strongly suggest you see it as soon as possible. Perhaps it won't matter to you what kind of art he produces, but it matters very much to me. Whatever Leon is, he is still a Skillman. And Skillmans don't lie. I *do* wish you a Happy Birthday and," she let Leonard help her ever so gently into her coat, "I also hope *very* much that Leon's future will be with you. But I cannot permit my son to make me a party to deception. I'm sorry! Goodnight, Tara."

Tara stared after her. What? Who *was* Leon? Now, she would have to find out immediately.

EIGHTEEN

"FOR TONIGHT. I'LL pick you up at 8. D."

That's all the note said. Tara opened the package accompanying the note and, in a daze of wonderment, slipped a gown over her head and fastened the gold shoulder clasp. She could feel the weight of the clasp, but the gown was of such a light fabric that it seemed weightless; nothing more than two triangles of silk sewn together at the sides, the entire garment was held on by the single jewel. She stared at herself in the full-length mirror. Where could Dimitrios be taking her in *this*? In colors of dusk—no longer blue, but not yet gray—the silk shimmered to the floor hinting purple hues of evening, draping the supple curves of her body in misty shadows while clinging here and there to define her outline and leaving one shoulder and both arms bare. She reached for her earrings with the unconscious hope that they would make her feel more dressed, but the tiny gold scales—to weigh men's souls—that Dimitrios had given her for her thirtieth Name Day made her appear even more fragile and vulnerable. She added another of his gifts, a large gold conch shell, to her finger. Except for her short, straight hair, she looked to herself as if she were some ancient image about to step out of the mirror from fifth-century Athens. The clasp of the gown matched the deep gold of both ring and earrings, and the three gifts, given over a period of ten years, looked as if they were created at the same time as a single thought:

an image in the mind of a man for whom nothing was accidental. Dimitrios.

Tara smiled at the woman in the mirror. Nice! She'd wear this gown to the Gothards' Christmas party in Palm Beach and save the new one she had chosen on her first day in New York for the opening of Blair's new museum wing.

Then a frown spoiled the image in the mirror. Something told her that Leon wouldn't like the idea of her wearing an evening gown given to her by another man, even an old friend like Dimitrios, to the party. Well, too bad. She didn't like a lot of what Leon was doing these days either. She moved to the dressing table to finish her makeup.

Blair had not been at home when she'd telephoned this afternoon. The butler said that the Gothards were still in Florida where they'd gone for Thanksgiving; they would return Monday morning, meaning that Tara couldn't see whatever of Leon's art was already installed in the new wing until Tuesday at the earliest. She'd called the Halldon Gallery as well, as a potential customer, but was informed that since Leon's works were too large to be shown in the gallery, she would have to visit his Brooklyn studio if she wanted to see them. That she definitely did *not* want to do, since by now she knew she had to see his sculpture for the first time without him.

She told herself again not to let Helene Skillman's warning about Leon's work make her rehearse trouble. Leon was asking her to wait and see it in a proper viewing environment. What could be the worst that the Leon Skillman she knew could create, anyway? She thought of *Spring Flower*, and she thought of his apartment. Then she thought of his lies. The notes in the margin weren't his. Why would he lie to her? And he'd talked about art so strangely on Thanksgiving, not at all the way he'd talked about it in Athens. He had seemed so flip.

Telling herself to postpone her concerns for the rest of the evening, she slipped into gold sandals and went to the closet to get her fur cape. Once it was around her, she knew she couldn't wear it. The fur complemented the gown beautifully, but something about wearing them together bothered her in a way she couldn't quite identify. Different eras, she decided. Pulling the blanket made by her grandmother from the foot of the bed, she folded it into a triangle and draped it over her shoulders just as the doorbell rang.

She turned back to the full-length mirror. The blanket-shawl, with a softness and lightness that only hand weaving could achieve, added deep, subtle shades of magenta to the folds of the gown. It, too, looked beautiful with Dimitrios's gift but erased the modern image created by the fur cape. She looked out curiously at herself again from the mirror, a woman, once more, from ancient Athens.

"Which are you?" she asked herself silently. Then she consciously replaced her frown with a smile and, slipping her evening bag under an arm, went to greet Dimitrios.

Tall and elegant. Her first impression of him, dressed impeccably in Black Tie and standing with her father in the living room, was that he seemed taller than usual. Tall and very elegant.

"Tara! You look beautiful!" Kostas exclaimed.

"You *are* beautiful," Dimitrios smiled as he led her down the stairs and out the door.

"What?" Tara stopped short on the sidewalk. "What is this?"

"Your carriage, Mademoiselle." Dimitrios opened the door of the hansom cab and extended a hand to help her in. "Thank goodness the snow you wrote me about has gone. It's actually rather balmy tonight."

Tara stepped into the carriage and felt a fur throw being settled over her lap. "It's always like this in November," she said in a daze, "You never know what the weather will be from one day to the next. Dimitrios! What are you doing? Where are we going like this?" She was laughing now.

Dimitrios opened a bottle of Dom Perignon, thinking how much he loved to hear her laugh, and signaled the driver to start, his dark eyes alive with pleasure. "*I* am celebrating your Name Day and *we* are going to dinner, but," he handed her a glass, "first we're going for a ride through Central Park."

Tara watched the horse wind his way up Eighth Avenue to 59th Street traffic as if cars were his natural companions until, as if drawing them into shadows of the past, they entered the secluded world of the park. There, the steady clip-clop of hooves became the only sound she could hear. She turned to Dimitrios, sitting close beside her, and reached under the carriage blanket to squeeze his hand. "It's magical."

Dimitrios raised his glass in a silent toast. This wasn't nearly as uncomfortable as he had supposed. He was beginning to enjoy his romantic scenario.

The snow of a week ago, long gone on the city streets, lay in white patches here and there on the slopes of the low hills. Tara pointed to tiers of lights rising beyond the bare branches of trees from buildings that were felt rather than seen, sentinels edging the park on all sides, spotlighting and sheltering it at the same time.

"What? Music, too?" She pulled her gaze from the wall of lights and looked around.

Dimitrios leaned forward. "I hear it." He poured her more champagne and smiled at the anticipation widening her eyes. Tara's childlike curiosity and love of adventure had never left her as an adult; those qualities had always enchanted him. "I wish I could say that I'd planned it." He told the driver to follow the sound.

Moments later, they pulled up across from a delightful street scene. Two young ballet dancers—a girl and a boy, both apparently in their late teens—moved effortlessly across the empty stage of the bandshell that was used in summer for outdoor concerts. At one corner of the stage, a violin player spurred them onward with a sprightly tune, his violin case open on the ground to invite contributions. A dozen or so spectators sat on rocks or leaned against trees, watching the trio.

"In November?" Dimitrios marveled.

"Only in New York," Tara said.

Dimitrios pulled the carriage robe closer around her. "Warm enough?"

Tara nodded. "They're beautiful. I love the way they look, and I love the way they make me feel."

"I know." Dimitrios reached into his pocket and gave the driver a handful of change for the violin case. "You would. Sculpture in motion."

When they had finished the last of the champagne, Tara turned to him. "We need to discuss the glass casing for the pieces to be displayed in the exhibit—"

Dimitrios put a finger over her lips to silence her. "Shhh. No business tonight. We're celebrating."

The building, a soaring architectural sculpture of gray granite and black glass, spiraled slowly and sensually upward from its base like rising smoke, narrowing in ascent into a gleaming spire: a silver bayonet that, penetrating through low-hanging clouds, embedded itself in the night. Or did it just keep rising? Tara wondered, looking up at it while Dimitrios paid the carriage driver. Like hope, ever upward.

"It was designed by Daniela Fredson, and built by an import-export friend of your Uncle Basilious's," Dimitrios explained as the black glass elevator let them rise with the building. "The top floor is a private club."

Thick carpet swallowed their footsteps at the entrance to the restaurant. They continued down a passageway that narrowed into an ice tunnel of faceted black glass on both walls and ceiling, as if cut by hand out of one crystalline block. The dining room at its end was simply a circle of windows suspended over the city, a sparkling spaceship hovering for a moment in the sky. Couples moved over a granite dance floor that was polished into a black mirror, which gave the effect of doubling their numbers. A quartet of musicians in black tuxedos filled the room with an exquisite serenade.

Tara took Dimitrios's arm as the maitre d' led them down another ice tunnel to their table. "*More* than magical," she whispered.

"There are only four of these secluded rooms in the restaurant," the maitre d' was saying. "Mr. Alexandros said you were to have one or he would have my head." He bowed. "Enjoy your dinner."

Tara found herself seated in a glass alcove behind a black granite table in a small silver velvet booth for two, illuminated only by soft candlelight. Dimitrios and she were alone, floating through space in a crystal bauble. She looked down and thrilled at the lights of New York spread at her feet.

A waiter appeared, and she heard Dimitrios ordering champagne as if nothing out of the ordinary were happening.

Indicating the view with a wave of his hand, he said, "'Dear to us ever is the banquette and the harp and the dance and the changes of raiment and'—we'll skip Homer's warm bath for now—'*no desire* for sleep.'" She watched him reach into his jacket pocket and set a velvet box on the table. "Happy Name Day, my Athenian lady."

Tara looked from the package to the city lights to Dimitrios's eyes and back to the view. Her throat tight, she said nothing.

Impatiently, he waited. Was the drama too much? Was the separate room too private? Why didn't she say something? The waiter reappeared, poured champagne and left them alone again. Strains of an old-fashioned waltz drifted into their alcove from the main dining room.

Dimitrios raised his glass to her and drank, still not daring to breathe until she reacted. Tara sipped her drink, not able to take her eyes from his, her throat still constricted, preventing speech. *He is as at ease here as he is amid the ruins of Athens,* she thought. *He is a timeless man.*

"Aren't you going to open your present?"

Dimitrios watched her eyes begin to fill with tears.

Then, to his delight, she burst out laughing and threw both arms around his neck, kissing his cheek. "What have you done, you wonderful, crazy man? You can never tease me about my gods again after trying to make me over into a fifth-century woman. Whatever made you plan such an evening? This isn't even a special birthday! You really *are* mad! Are you intoxicated with New York or just intoxicated?"

Catching himself leaning too close, Dimitrios picked up the package and handed it to her. "Open your present," he ordered quickly, afraid that given another moment he would say too much. What he wanted to say was, "I'm intoxicated with *you*."

"But I thought the gown was my present, with the clasp that matches my other jewelry. Oh! I never even thanked you. *I* was so intoxicated by the carriage ride and the park and this place. Where did you find this gown? Not in Athens!"

"I had it made, and it's only a backdrop for your present. Now open it before I take it back."

She opened the box and lifted the armlet from its satin lining. The tears began again, and spilled this time.

Dimitrios handed her a handkerchief. "What's all this teary business? Here, you'll spoil your makeup, which I like very much, by the way." He dropped his hand quickly into his lap, having noticed it was shaking slightly. "I meant to make you happy, not to make you cry."

Tara dabbed at her face and handed him the triple spiral of gold, her eyes still bright and brimming. "You have, my dear friend. It's just that you *are* so very, very dear to me. Thank you. Now I understand the gown. Will you help me put it on?"

He clasped the bracelet to the upper part of her arm and pressed his fingers to her bare shoulder for a moment, doubt clouding his eyes. She stood to see her reflection in the tabletop.

Friend, he thought uneasily. She was smiling down at him, eyes sparkling, full of warmth and affection for him, her *friend.* Was this her way of letting him know? Was she telling him that she could only care for him as a friend?

He touched the button for the waiter. "Shall I order for both of us?"

Tara nodded, staring again at her reflection in the table. "And more champagne, please." The armlet made her feel very close to Dimitrios in a strange way ... as if she were owned somehow. Suddenly ill at ease, she walked to the window and looked out, wondering why, in fact, she *had* reacted to his gift with tears. And Leon's gift, too. Why crying at these happy moments? But she had cried over Nicky's art, too, so it just must be an overflowing of affection.

Dimitrios joined her and, putting a hand on the back of her neck, rubbed gently. "What's the matter, Tara?"

"I was just thinking of this birthday: this armlet and Leon's fur."

"You won't need the fur in Greece."

"Leon has asked me to stay here with him."

"As I am asking you to come home." *To me,* he wanted to add, but didn't. Was she telling him about Leon to warn him that she truly wasn't available? Dimitrios looked carefully at Tara's face as she gazed pensively out over the city; he could find no veil of hidden meaning there. Go slowly but not too subtly, he warned himself for the tenth time this evening. He turned to get their drinks and break the mood.

They stood looking out over New York, sipping silently

for a long moment. "It *is* an intoxicating city," he whispered. For a moment he was aware that he really had no experience in openness at all. He had never even had a sister or a close friend; his intimate experience with women was painfully limited, let alone his experience with love. Tara could not be the Athena of his childhood, able to divine his feelings. No woman could. It was up to him to make himself known. But how?

Thankfully, their dinner arrived before his inner awkwardness could assume outward form. Tara dove into the meal with characteristic enthusiasm; Dimitrios tasted her enjoyment more than his own. Although utterly refined in all she did, Tara always seemed to exude a sensuality within her every action, devoting herself completely to whatever occupied her attention at the time. She wasn't eating dinner, she was eating life. Tara. Kantara." He sighed contentedly. Even her name brought him pleasure.

"Dimitrios, maybe we should discuss this exhibit—"

He put a finger over her lips, shaking his head with a firm smile. "No business, remember? I really mean it, Tara. Tonight is just for pleasure."

"Yes, but that's silly. Neither of us likes small talk and, besides, I need to speak to you before you meet with the museum people on Monday."

"Who says I'm meeting with them?"

"Isn't that why you're here?"

"Not at all. I told you I came to celebrate your Name Day with you. I haven't missed one in ten years. I'm leaving to go back on Sunday night. Come, let's dance."

Tara giggled. She was beginning to feel giddy. "All the way from Athens to celebrate a birthday? You *are* extravagant!"

"And *you* have had too much champagne." Excellent. Too much talk and too much drink. He was doing wonderfully!

Tara felt Dimitrios's breath in her hair as he guided her smoothly over the dance floor. He was a good dancer, whether Greek style, wearing a cotton shirt in a taverna, or in this sophisticated setting, elegant in Black Tie. She leaned her head back to look at him, realizing that, in fact, they had never danced like this before, in evening clothes with candlelight. She became suddenly aware of his hand, firm around her waist, and remembered the strength of his grip holding her safe during their decompression time the day she found her bronze athlete. She felt her breasts pressing lightly against his chest. Momentarily confused, she felt oddly aware of her every movement, of every part of her body . . . of every part of his. It must be the gown, she thought hazily. I would never have chosen it for myself, it's too revealing; it makes me too aware of myself as a woman. Then why did he have it made for me? No, it's not the gown; the gown was made so the armlet would look right. It must be the champagne.

"Why did you have this gown made for me?" she asked, moving closer to him again, feeling reckless somehow, as if they were dancing precariously on a narrow ridge and she held the power to keep them there or tip them over the edge.

Dimitrios slid his hand from her waist to the nape of her neck. "I had it made because I wanted to see you in it," he said, his voice low.

The music stopped. Tara stood back from him, trying to understand something she couldn't quite grasp by asking a question she'd never asked.

"Dimitrios, why have you never married?"

He clapped politely as the musicians began another piece. "Because you never asked me," he answered, looking straight at her, his eyes smiling but serious. "Shall we dance?" He swept her again into his arms and began circling the dance floor.

"No. I think I'd better have some coffee." Feeling dizzy, she slipped out of his arms and headed back to their dining alcove. "I think I must have had too much champagne." *What am I feeling? What is he feeling? I've gone to dinner with him hundreds of times. He's given me beautiful presents before.* "Oh, look, it's beginning to rain." She took her espresso to the window and sipped at it, feeling better, more in control again. "I'm learning that marine archaeology is not yet very highly esteemed," she said, moving back to safe ground. *Why did she feel so shaky? Dimitrios seemed so strange. So distracted. Or distracting. Or something. She really couldn't drink like this. She wasn't feeling like herself at all.*

"As success comes, esteem will come. It's still a field in its infancy. People need time to see how underwater explorations are contributing to our understanding of ship building in classical times and how it's offering new hypotheses about trading patterns in the ancient world. When you're discussing it, try to get others to see the value of a sea wreck as a sudden catastrophe. Explain that if we find a ship and contents that have not already been looted the way land explorations have, we can view everything in its original state as it was then, a stopped moment in time—" Dimitrios clamped his mouth shut. *Here we go again. Every time I get us onto a romantic basis, one of us ruins it.*

Tara laughed. "Do you remember when we recovered the remains of that fourth-century Greek merchant ship and found *ten thousand* perfectly-preserved almonds?"

It was pouring when they reached the street. "You stay here," Dimitrios said, and pushed through the revolving door. "I'll get a cab. If the temperature drops, this will be snow again. Who would want to live with these unpredictable seasons?" He ran to the curb, immediately soaked from head to toe. At last, he saw a cab going in the opposite direction and ran across the avenue to hail it. He started to get in and have the driver make a U-turn to collect Tara, but looked up to see her skipping down the steps of the building, laughing and waving for him to wait there.

He ran back across the street to help her. "Why did you do this? There's no reason for both of us to get drenched!"

"Why not?" she laughed, not noticing that her rain-soaked gown clung to her body like a second skin. She did notice it with a start, however, when Dimitrios put his arm around her in the cab to warm her. *Idiot!* she thought to herself. "It's a good thing you got fine silk," she said, forcing a laugh, "otherwise, this gown would be ruined." She pulled her grandmother's wet blanket close over her pert nipples and a moment later she was laughing easily again. "What a birthday!"

"Not quite a perfect ending to a perfect evening," Dimitrios observed wryly, smoothing wet hair away from her face.

"Absolutely perfect," Tara countered. "Baptized on my thirty-third birthday, first with champagne and then with rain, where's the fire?"

In my love for you, he thought silently. *Were you warmed by that fire at all tonight?*

"Wait! I'll walk you in." He leapt out after her as the cab stopped. She was running ahead of him again in the pouring rain.

Finally, they stood together in the hallway of Kostas's building, breathless, laughing at each other and dripping water all over the floor.

"You're coming to Dorina's tomorrow?" Tara panted, trying to catch her breath.

"If you are. Shall I pick you up?"

"No, I'm coming with Nicky. I'll see you there." She reached a hand up to his right cheek and kissed the left. "Thank you, Dimitrios, for the most beautiful Name Day celebration of my life."

He lifted her chin with a finger and kissed her softly

but firmly on the mouth. "Thank *you*," he said, "for being born. See you tomorrow." He was out the door.

Tara's hand went to her lips. Feeling a strange sinking feeling and a sudden weakness in her legs, she leaned against the wall behind her for support. Absolutely too much champagne, she thought shakily. Both of us.

Dimitrios sat back in the taxi savoring the scent of her perfume and the soft warmth of her lips still lingering on his. His arms ached to hold her again. To hold her forever. He hadn't done too well this evening, he knew. It had been too jumbled, romantic one moment and business the next. And he shouldn't have let her drink so much, she wasn't used to it. It was a beginning, though. Wasn't it? He looked out through the rain at the city lights blurring his vision. Leon Skillman lived in one of those buildings.

"You can't have her," he said aloud, his voice low and level, his eyes wet and dark as the night. "I will not let you have her."

NINETEEN

NICKY BANGED ON THE PIPE for heat and began wiping slush from the floor of the studio with a rag. He called over to Tara, who was putting a kettle of water on the hot plate for morning tea. "We'd better take off our boots. Paint on the floor, Dorina loves, slop, she hates."

And Leon Skillman's art, she hates, he thought excitedly. He would never have thought it possible to have Dorina Swing and Leon Skillman in the same room for long. Leon, the darling of the freewheeling contemporary art world, and Dorina, one of a small group of living artists in America to carry the techniques of fine painting from master to pupil in an unbroken line from the Renaissance. Dorina's teacher's teacher had studied with Gerome, who studied with Delarouche, who studied with David, who established a direct line through Raphael to Leonardo and Michelangelo. From artist to pupil, again and again to, now, himself.

Nicky banged on the pipe again and began to unpack a bag filled with breads, fruits and cheeses. Leon is rich, Nicky thought, and he is successful and following no one and nothing but his own impulses. What an explosive morning this is going to be!

"What is it, exactly, that you want from this get-together, Nicky?" Tara stood pondering Dorina's nude drawings. The males reminded her somewhat of her Greek athlete, yet they expressed something more. She would have to ask

Dimitrios about them. The two female nudes had not been on the wall during her first visit.

"Because it's obvious Dorina's invited us all here for your benefit," she went on. "I got the impression at Thanksgiving that except for your interests, she'd rather not talk to Leon at all, for some reason."

"Well, you haven't seen Leon's work yet, and that puts you at a disadvantage, but Leon's work is, well . . . totally twentieth-century. And who knows yet about the twenty-first? But Dorina is advancing—not repeating, she will stress to you—the traditions of many past centuries. So they're on different wave lengths altogether."

Tara gazed distractedly out the window. It had been such a strange evening with Dimitrios. Wonderful, but strange. She shouldn't have drunk so much. He seemed so different here in New York, somehow, than he did at home in Athens. Last night's rain had turned again to light snow, and it lay in stretches like a fragile white carpet over sidewalks not yet muddied by Saturday shoppers. "What do you mean, exactly, by 'twentieth-century,' Nicky? You sound as if it's a label rather than a time period."

"Well, in many ways it is, I guess. Actually," he had a thought, "maybe this is a good thing for you. After today, you'll be better prepared to understand Leon's work when you do get around to seeing it. His kind of art takes some acclimation to appreciate. You know," he continued cautiously, "your work does keep you pretty buried in the past."

Tara remained quiet for a moment, thinking that she would be seeing Leon's art sooner than anyone, including Leon, imagined. She smiled at her sweet brother and slipped an arm around his shoulder. "You mean if I come into the bright light of the twenty-first century too quickly, I might hurt my eyes?"

✼ ✼ ✼

Leon shuffled sloppily through the snow, never noticing the delicate netting of silver that iced the trees, edging the solid whiteness of the park's meadow like intricate lace trimming on a fine linen handkerchief. His eyes turned only inward, toward a recurrent, internal brooding. This visit, this confrontation, was his own fault. Why had he challenged Dorina the other night, anyway? It was as if some tightly harnessed part of him had broken loose to defy her, Tara and his mother, all in the same instant.

Well hell! So what? He'd just turn this non-event to his advantage. Hey! He was used to that. He'd probably have to be a lot less cocky than usual because Dorina's was bound to be rigid turf. No point pulling any punches though. She'd see right through that. Yet, he needed to maintain a certain respectful demeanor in front of Tara. No sarcasm, then. *That* would be novel. No way there could be problems. For years he'd had manipulated interviews with the press adroitly enough. Then add all the speaking engagements, lectures at universities, dealings with curators, collectors, dealers— Hell! He'd done it all! But Dorina Swing was likely to be a tough tiger. Fighting for a cub at that. Well, they didn't matter a whit. Neither did their art. What mattered was that this morning actually offered a great, unexpected opportunity to open some doors in Tara's mind about his own work. "Okay, you asked for it, guy! Go for it!" He said the words aloud this time to make sure he heard himself.

His boots left tire tracks in the snow. He didn't see them. Whatever her art looked like, Dorina seemed as outdated as his mother. Amazing. Just when you thought all the old relics from the past were dead and gone, up pops another one. He kicked a thick chunk of ice in his path and sent it spinning through space like a Waterford football. Suddenly he felt braced by the cold air and the challenge ahead. Great morning! Great morning for icon bashing!

❋ ❋ ❋

A snowball hit his shoulder. Dimitrios whirled, then smiled in recognition.

"How do you like our weather?" Dorina skipped up beside him, a wool ski cap pulled down over her ears. She smiled into his eyes.

"It's changeable," Dimitrios confessed, thinking of last night's drenched and drunken ending to his carefully planned evening.

"Well, whose side are you on today?"

"Actually, I prefer to bring my own side."

"And Tara?"

Dimitrios held the door of Dorina's building open and stomped his feet to rid his shoes of snow. "I don't honestly know," he answered, wishing for the tenth time that he did.

"I hope she's on my side. She could be a big influence on Nicky." Dorina led the way silently up the five flights of stairs, acutely aware of just how important today could be in her fight for Nicky's future. If only she'd had someone to fight for *her* when she was his age. Nicky's professors were nothing new in art education; they were mere copies of her own generation's college art teachers, the same teachers who had tried to make her a clone, too. How embarrassed they had made her feel about her love of drawing, and of *beauty*.

Because she had grown up in a small town in Minnesota, because her father was a tradesman and her mother a housewife, and because she had moved from that very sheltered world to go to school in the big city environment of Chicago, her professors had been able, early on, to shake her confidence in her drawing abilities. Throughout childhood, those abilities had inspired her; other kids couldn't do at all what she had always been able to do without thinking, even when she was a very little girl of four or five. At home, she had been appreciated; her natural talents were constantly in demand for everything from school play programs and sports posters to high school newspapers and yearbooks. She reveled in any project that allowed her to do all she ever wanted to do anyway: make beautiful pictures. The only drawing instruction she ever received was from the wife of a furniture store owner, and then only during summer vacations and always interrupted whenever a customer came into the store. In college, her drawing abilities were simply ignored. She was taught very specifically that "her" kind of art was "over." Devastated that she had been born too late, she switched to art history for her degree and became an apprentice to an art restorer in order to help pay for her education. Both disciplines kept her in contact with the art she continued to love but saw no reason to pursue as a practicing artist. After graduation and her move to Minneapolis to work, if a small fire in an art atelier hadn't created a need for a restorer and introduced her to the art teacher who owned the loft, she would have given up *making* art forever.

But what about Nicky? Was what she'd found to be right for herself really best for Nicky as well? If he turned to abstraction, he could probably make a living with his art, something she had never been able to do even after regaining her confidence and pursuing a career as an active painter. Nicky's alabaster piece was pleasing enough to look at. And he could always make his serious art for pleasure.

But he won't. As she and Dimitrios neared the top of the last flight of stairs, Dorina felt her usual calm composure turning to stubbornness. If Nicky jumped into the economic sea, his representational work would undoubtedly sink as a result. She couldn't let that go under without a fight. To sanction Nicky's wasting his skills on abstract work would be to consign him forever to play over and over only a few notes of a vast repertoire. No, not Nicky.

Dorina took a deep breath outside the door of her studio. "Well, here we are. May the best man win!" Only when her hand was turning the knob, did she notice the worried expression on Dimitrios's face.

"I meant Leon and *me*." She smiled, without humor, and opened the door.

※ ※ ※

Leon was prepared for anything, but not for pain. It hit him immediately, with the impact of a body blow.

He fought for control, fought to keep his face expressionless. *What?*

He forced himself to move from painting to painting until his inner turmoil culminated into a rapidly beating pulse tormenting his temples. He was glad for that, and for the throbbing pressure behind his eyes as well. These kept him from breaking down altogether.

Why? Why should this work *hurt* him so? Yet, he couldn't stop looking.

Nicky's seascapes: the eternal and the temporal harmoniously juxtaposed. The compositions! The colors! The exuberance! Dorina's mountainscapes, profound hymns to the awesomeness of the physical world, her eye sure and mature: purples hovering in a luminous mist of mystery over mountains conceived in the clarity of a sun-washed dawn. Shapes sensuous and undulating, drawing the eye farther and farther into the hidden recesses of their primordial beginnings with a rhythm pulsing from passion held in check, a passion straining to break loose from the rhythm but held in thrilling control by the sheer brilliance of her technical skills. A complex study in aerial perspective that was perfection, her hand so subtle that, although every mark mattered, one was unaware of any texture to the atmosphere at all, merely an invisible breeze that passed over the surface of the canvas, every line poetic. The lighting was so bold that it held one range of mountains in a spotlight of beauty so arresting that one knew with certainty, no, one *felt* with certainty, that the universe itself was harmonious and... No, Dorina's landscapes went far beyond the magnificent beauty and tranquility of the Hudson River School because, although expansive like theirs, hers were full of movement, bursting with energy, seeming to celebrate earthly rather than spiritual grandeur. This woman was a mad romantic! Leon's turbulent emotional reactions raced on, but his brain felt tight, in a vise. It was as if her mountains, rather than being passive wonders of creation, were the act of creation itself, each one rising gloriously to its summit, almost certainly a metaphor for *human* potential, for the challenges and joys of human achievement, of the ability to climb from one personal summit to another. Dorina was too humanistic *not* to have meant that metaphor.

Enough! He studied the drawings stoically, wondering how his tumultuous inner state and the sweat accumulating beneath his shirt could go unnoticed by the others. Dorina's drawings were rendered in fine, sharp pencil requiring great judgment and control. He couldn't look at them for long. The forms were too close to sculptural forms. Against his will, his hands—*Damn his hands!*—began to see them in solid form. He walked carefully back to Nicky's work, still fighting for control. "These won't sell, you know," he said to Dorina, his voice as icy as the green chips that were his eyes. He stood again before the seascapes, his emotions frozen, finally, into safety. "They're too 'one on one.' And they're too beautiful for contemporary tastes. They won't get media blitz, and you know it," he added in accusation.

Tara thought she would faint. How could anything in life be "too beautiful?" Leon had mentioned "beauty" several times lately, but there seemed to be no consistency in what he said or wrote.

"Nicky's work has already sold," Dorina said quietly.

"For how much?"

Nicky showed Leon the slide of his birds. "This sold for eight hundred dollars. Of course, it's not very big," he added tentatively.

Now, Leon felt a different kind of shock, the automatic shock of indignation. He distracted himself by looking out the window.

Why should he feel indignant for the boy? He barely knew him! And why should being here cause so much physical pain? It was the same sort of helpless pain that had made him cry immediately after making love with Tara for the first time. Piercing and deep.

He fixed a cold eye on Dorina. "Is a life of eight-hundred-dollar sales what you want for him? Or even eight-thousand? Given the time it takes to finish one of these things, Nicky could never support himself with his art. And you know it," he repeated.

Dorina touched the alabaster. "Is *this* all you want from *him*?"

Leon shrugged. "I don't make the rules. I just play by them. Look. You and I both know that Realism never died out completely and it's even had a bit of a comeback in the past many years, but most of it doesn't sell *big* like the work of dead artists from past centuries because this kind of art *made today* just isn't relevant in *today's* worldly-worn-out world. Even when it's well done, most of it is banal. Pretty pictures. End of story."

Dorina kept her voice even. "Relevant to whom?"

Nicky passed cups around the room, his brain reeling. Leon hadn't said a single concrete thing about his paintings, just that they wouldn't sell, that they weren't relevant. He swallowed his tea with difficulty. "What do *you* think is relevant, Leon?" he asked, keeping his hands clasped tight around his cup. "Besides selling, that is."

"Fair enough!" Dorina placed a large drawing pad made of newsprint on her easel. "Let's do it right." She grabbed a piece of charcoal and poised it over the pad. "Okay, Leon. What *is* relevant in art today? Let's be systematic."

"Oh, come on," Leon groaned to Tara.

"Do it for Nicky's sake," Tara whispered.

"I'll do it for *you*," he whispered back. He walked up to the easel, took the charcoal from Dorina's hand and wrote, AESTHETICS. "That's all that's been relevant for nearly a century, the *process* of art *as* art. But," he kept his tone from turning sardonic, "even *that's* not relevant, nor remotely radical anymore. It's a commonplace, universally accepted and established. Anyone who doesn't understand this is simply ignorant and out of touch with twentieth-century and contemporary art. Even in representational art, most of what's successful uses subject matter only as abstract form. And if it *does* have content, it's making statements on politics or the environment or some form of social criticism or collective angst. Content art that's relevant today is, in one way or another, activist art. It's not a personal celebration of life like Nicky's, here or," he locked eyes with Dorina, "like yours. It's meant to change the way *others* view the world."

Dimitrios wandered over to Dorina's drawings, feeling the need to let Tara see his indifference to Leon's "relevant" opinions. "I'm going to bow out on this subject in favor of these magnificent nudes," he said.

Tara turned to Leon. "Wait a minute, speaking of nudes! Is the art you make today so different than when you were younger? *Your* nude, *Spring Flower*, is a lot more than just aesthetics. It's profoundly humanistic. It expresses deep philosophical value judgments that go way beyond existential, cultural issues."

"*Spring Flower*?" Dorina looked astonished. "A nude? Representational art by Leon?"

"It's just so lovely." Tara couldn't help smiling at Leon. Maybe his current work had a more modern feeling, but how different could it really be? "In fact, it has a lot of the spirit of your drawings, Dorina. It's a young female rising up out of a bed of flowers at the moment of new womanhood, as if she were one of the blossoms themselves—"

Leon cut her off. "It was very literal, and very immature," he said, squelching the subject.

Dorina stared at Leon with unabashed interest. "You mean at one time *you* made not only representational art, but idealized art?"

"I was very young."

"How interesting," Dorina said softly. She gave Leon a long, silent appraisal and went to the hotplate to pour more tea.

Tara fingered the alabaster piece. "How did you ever get the idea to make this in the first place, Nicky? I love the feel of it, but it's so different from your serious work."

"First of all," Nicky dragged a piece of bread across some cheese and began to nibble on it, "a whole lot of people, including my other teachers, wouldn't consider that alabaster piece non-serious. But anyway, you know how Papa whittles out of wood and has made some nice things for around the house? Well, I like their shapes and surfaces. Then some kids at school were working in alabaster, and I found I like working with it, too. Between watching Papa and watching them, I got the urge to make this piece. I want to do something in wood next."

Dorina pulled up a stool and blew on her tea. "All right, Leon. Let's consider your argument for Nicky's benefit. Because the only thing 'relevant' to me about abstraction is that it interests Nicky. Okay. Abstract art *is* aesthetics. We agree on that. I'm not saying that abstract art is invalid—at its best it can be well designed and even beautiful—only that it's not a compelling form for an artist with highly developed technical skills because the form itself is so limited. Which, of course, brings us to one of the reasons for the dominance of the abstract aesthetic and the near loss of twenty-five hundred years of Western-heritage art techniques. They've hardly even been *taught* for the last three or four generations. So many contemporary artists of all persuasions, abstract *or* representational, don't really know how to draw, for example."

Leon turned over a fresh sheet of paper on the flip chart and began to sketch rapidly. "It can be tremendously interesting to concentrate on one element at a time in order to make it stand alone," he said. "As a sculptor I deal in shape. Form. Volume. And space. The theme of the piece *is* its shape and the interplay of space and light in and around that shape. So the art engages the senses and not the mind," he glanced up at Tara and then returned to the pad as he talked, "so what?" He danced across the room and looked back, seriously regarding Tara for a long moment. Then he winked at Nicky and sat back down to draw with supreme concentration.

Dorina watched him, fascinated. "So, it would be like asking me to drive my car at one-mile-an-hour for the rest of my life, *that's* what. Because art has the ability to please the senses, stimulate the emotions *and* challenge the mind. All! It can be appreciated physiologically, psychologically and philosophically as an *integrated experience.* By focusing only on the parts, as you advocate, what have you done to art as a whole? Even if it were of help, which I seriously doubt, to take it apart and lay it in pieces all over the place like a child does with the workings of a clock, the question now is: who is left with any ability to put the pieces back together so that the clock will serve its function again to tell time?"

Leon set the pad up on an empty easel. "There! That should refute your theory about lack of drawing ability!" His green eyes rested for a moment on the sketch he had made of Tara's head and then they teased the room with silent laughter.

Dorina stared without amusement at the excellence of Leon's technique and his astonishing flair. Amid her shock and disbelief that *Leon Skillman* could possess such ability, she remembered Tara's description of *Spring Flower*. Then, overwhelmed by a great sadness, she thought to herself that among all of the treasons possible to commit in this world, Leon Skillman had committed the greatest. She couldn't think of a thing to say.

Nicky stared at the drawing, at the arabesque of line, at the sensual rhythm and at the astounding likeness to his sister, simultaneously seeing in his mind the huge, lifeless shapes of Leon's that squatted, dead or defiant, here and there throughout the country. He tried to think about the comparison, but he also had to concentrate on keeping his mouth shut. All he wanted to do, out of some impetus he couldn't define, was shout "NO!" Then, coming quickly to Leon's defense, the unspeakable-in-this-studio words "Why not? It's his choice!" pushed out the "No." He was left speechless.

Dimitrios stared at the drawing from a distance, wishing that what he saw didn't exist. It had all of the spontaneity and power he might expect in a quick sketch from a master hand, but he had never imagined in his darkest nightmare that Leon's was a master hand. Besides, the drawing was finished in a detailed fashion he had rarely encountered in a sketch. Even worse, Leon had captured far more than a direct likeness of Tara. In those few lines, he had deftly expressed her inner spirit, her directness, her openness. The thought he couldn't permit himself was all he was conscious of now: What if Tara had seen the inner Leon all along? Because *this* man, if he *was* the inner Leon, was a far more serious threat than he had believed.

Tara ran over to the sketch. "It looks just like me!" she marveled. Thank god! she thought, her emotions soaring in relief.

"I'm pretty rusty," Leon grinned. He looked at Dorina with an amused smirk. She continued to regard his sketch.

The silence became awkward for everyone but Leon.

Finally, he laughed out loud. "You see, Dorina, I make the art I make because I want to."

"Yes," she answered slowly. "I see. What I wonder is why you want to."

"How nice," Dimitrios said dryly, knowing he had to change the subject. "But, speaking of drawings, Dorina, I'd like to discuss yours for a moment. Do you mind?"

Dorina pulled her stool over and sat next to him.

"But what about our discussion?" Nicky asked anxiously. "We've hardly *begun* it!"

Dorina shot a smile over her shoulder, a smile that surprising herself, included Leon. It was impossible to dislike him completely now. "Don't worry. I imagine Leon and I will both be around to finish it with you, but Dimitrios is leaving soon, so let me be self-centered for a moment and hear what he has to say."

"What I have to say is that I think you have brilliantly succeeded in projecting the quintessential twenty-*first*-century nude! These images merge the real with the ideal just as the Greeks did, but yours are completely contemporary in their *awareness* of their own individualism. They're *full* of their own independence. Especially the females. Educated and exercised, both. So modern, yet utterly timeless. Very exciting, Dorina. Have you drawings of double nudes, as well?"

Dorina nodded her thanks, warm and winning, and edged her stool closer to him. "No. By putting both man and woman in the same drawing, I'd automatically introduce the issue of sexual identity into my theme. Here, I'm exploring *human* identity, the individual as an undivided *self*. It would be much better expressed in sculpture, but," she shrugged with a quick glance at Leon, "I don't sculpt."

Completely at ease now, his eyes agleam with triumph, Leon stared smugly out the window as he dried the cups Nicky had washed. He knew he had won the day with his sketch.

Tara sat in front of Nicky's paintings, her thoughts cast out to sea, wondering if she would ever see Greece again. *My brother needs me. Leon says he loves me. And even though he's such a mystery, I feel love for him; I've been drawn to him like a magnet from the moment I met him. I certainly love New York. The future of the world, therefore the future of art is here in America. Even Dimitrios says so.* She glanced over to him and Dorina, a frown creasing her brow. *It's so bold, the way she flirts with him,* she thought, unaccountably annoyed. *Dimitrios seemed captivated.*

"Would you permit me to purchase two of these?" Dimitrios asked, his dark eyes smoldering with passion. "You've done an incredible thing here. I don't want to live another day without seeing these figures, having them in my home."

Dorina sat very still. "Thank you, Dimitrios. Of course, you may purchase whatever you like." *I would love to be in a position to give you one,* she was thinking.

"Tara!" Dimitrios called over to her. "Come and look at these drawings! You will *love* these male nudes."

Dorina stiffened.

Tara gestured to the female nudes instead. "I know. I realized what you were saying when I first saw them, but I couldn't pinpoint it then. It's the females that I find more powerful, though. They're so American. Just what you said, Dimitrios. But more: It's woman, truly free in every way. Proud, intelligent and . . . *sovereign*! That's it! Not just her physical or legal or moral sovereignty, but her *human* sovereignty." She slipped an arm through Dimitrios's and leaned her head against his shoulder. "You know, so many things about being here, including these drawings and Nicky's situation, make me wonder if you and I are too buried in antiquity. There's so much to the here and now."

"There's much in both civilizations," Dimitrios smiled, glad of her head on his shoulder, but disturbed by the words. Even though he told her he came to New York for her birthday, he was certain she expected him to go with her to the museum tomorrow to deal with the exhibit. But if he did that, it would undercut the drama of his trip, taken for the sole purpose of celebrating personally with her. How he wanted to stay! Yet for his journey to be effective romantically, he would have to say goodbye today. When? How? He'd take her home, tell her along the way; they could discuss the museum problems over the phone later if she actually needed his help; he really had come just to be with her. Then leave her wondering at her door. With or without a kiss this time? No, too much. It was settled. That's what he'd do. Quick goodbye. No kiss. Well, maybe— No, no kiss.

Leon watched them intently. It troubled him to see Tara's head on Dimitrios's shoulder. Well hey! What the hell! They were close friends. And if Dimitrios hadn't interested Tara before this, nothing was likely to happen now that Leon himself was in the picture. His first, painful reactions to the work in this room were forgotten. He had accomplished his goal; his sketch had overpowered Dorina's polemics. Tara was on his side, he was sure of it. He took the drawing pad from the easel and handed it to Nicky. "Why don't you hang on to this? We can finish the discussion another time, and," he lowered his voice so that only Nicky could hear, "I think if we work together, we just might be able to get your sister to stay here with us. What do you think?"

Nicky stared open-mouthed from Dimitrios and Tara, who were still discussing the drawings, to Dorina, who was putting dishes away. "I think I don't understand anything that went on here today," he said slowly.

TWENTY

THE TINTED WINDOW of the limousine felt cool to her forehead as Blair leaned against it and stared idly out at the people hurrying along Park Avenue. She could see them, but they couldn't see her. What could be so important in their lives to make them rush around so? She was always busy, but never rushed. She fingered a large jeweled collar that lay in her lap. It was precisely as she had designed it. Set with hundreds of golden topaz stones, it fanned out from the neckpiece in a sunburst fashion that would reach nearly to her shoulders. Unseen clasps were hidden beneath the platinum backing, clasps to which any of her variously colored gowns could be attached. She was having seven gowns made, one in each color of the rainbow, from which she could select at whim to wear with the collar; this clever move would give her seven photo mentions in *The New York Post, Town & Country, Vanity Fair* and *New York Magazine* at the very least. She had decided to wear the white gown to her Palm Beach party for the new wing, since it would be so close to Christmas. The topaz stones matched her blonde hair and, she knew, would add a golden sparkle to her brown eyes. She would wear no other jewelry except a simple, gold wedding band. But her nails would be painted gold, and she would wear on her ring finger one artificial, eighteen-carat gold fingernail with diamonds set in it to form the initial "B." She was having the heels of white silk sandals studded with topaz stones as well.

A new, feathery snow had fallen over the weekend, but traffic had already turned it to brown slush on the city streets. Blair thought of the fresh snow that would be spread over her Palm Beach lawn for the party. They'd said forty-five truckloads of Vermont machine-made snow would be required because she needed the stuff to be thick enough to last for three hours. She was starting the event while it was still daylight, so the TV crews and newspaper photographers could get sun-scintillating shots of the snow and the horsedrawn sleighs that would bring celebrities to the door. After that, it didn't matter if the snow melted. Once the guests became involved with the whirl of the party, they'd forget the white stuff outside in favor of the white stuff inside. Too bad she couldn't offer some more exotic *au moment* drugs, but her mother—

She reviewed the guest list in her mind. Most people were coming from Los Angeles, Dallas and D.C. But New York would be represented too. Tara was coming (among the glamour folk, an archaeologist would be amusing) and Leon, of course. Tara had certainly taken that man over! Leon had not slept with Blair since Greece. She and Perry hadn't even been able to tease him into a threesome. Adria was coming. Denise Sommers was coming. Lord help us! Mother will hate it, but the art crowd will fall all over her; she *is*, in her own predictable way, a cute little Joker to spice up the big deck. Van would bring her. Maggie hadn't been invited; why throw Van's meandering in her face? And without Van, Maggie wasn't important anyway. Well, Kronan would head up the show, and hundreds more from business, society and the art world would play their little parts. She had almost considered inviting Tara's parents, just for the novelty, but her private jet was already full, and she knew Kostas probably couldn't afford to fly himself and his wife on a commercial airline just for a party and that he'd be too proud to accept gratis tickets. She'd invite them to the New Year's opening of the new wing in New York, though; that would be jolting to the solid set. Flo, of course, was coming as well.

Blair leaned forward suddenly, her eyes sparkling. "William, take me to the Rails, that little artists' neighborhood in Brooklyn down underneath the Manhattan Bridge overpass."

What an idea! She would just show little Miss Flo that she didn't need her at all, after that snide little lecture of hers on art stars. Why hadn't she thought of this before? She could create her own art stars! She could create her own "dialogue" without any help from anyone. If a former dress shop owner could "create" Leon and Adria and now discover a new, unknown artist way out in Hoboken, then the owner of an art museum should certainly be able to find something exciting in one of New York's recognized art neighborhoods!

Blair chuckled at her own impulsiveness as the car turned onto the East River Drive. What fun when a crazy idea popped up like this. Like when she had on the spur-of-the-moment invited Theron Sommers's daughter to Palm Beach. Of course, once Perry met her, he'd surely have her in bed by the end of the party. Oh well, she'd probably be in bed with someone else. Well, *who* was coming to Palm Beach wasn't important. What came with them to be donated to the new wing, *that* was important.

"Let me off here, but follow me," she instructed William. It was exhilarating! The neighborhood was so sleazy! The first gallery she entered displayed huge comic-book-like paintings hanging from chains attached to the ceiling. Each picture shouted neon colors and showed grossly enlarged genitalia (some of them even cross-switched!) on men and women who were all famous movie stars. Blair knew several of the actors personally. She shook her head, amused. There was Tiffany Tate with a great big erect penis. It was hilarious. But she certainly couldn't buy these! Or, maybe she should! It might just be so bizarre that her friends would get a kick out of seeing themselves with oversized or opposite sex organs, and *she* could create an art star out of an artist who painted film stars. Still... maybe not.

She picked up a guide to other galleries in the area and, after an apologetic smile to the clerk, she left.

The next gallery offered the work of a young woman who had, according to the owner of the place, already won several awards. She specialized in watercolor smears painted on huge fragments of wallpaper that had been crumpled up and then flattened out again. And then crumpled up again. Blair found herself up to her knees in crushed wads of paper scattered all over the floor. In order to look at a work, she had to flatten each one out on a huge library-type table in the center of the room. That's how you were supposed to show them in your own home, the man said, like instant Rorschach tests. Blair looked uncertain.

Her eyes darted about the room as a feeling of restlessness began to flutter in her stomach. The restlessness increased, gallery by gallery. Perhaps discovering new art was a little more complicated than she realized. These were all rather original ideas, actually, and some were fun, like the sex pictures. But were they something that could really catch the eye of the commercial art market? After all, art had to be an investment as well as an amusement. Perry insisted on it. The sex things might work though. There was that on-going Off-Broadway play called "Pussy and Peter: A Dialogue"; it was still such a hit you couldn't get tickets unless you knew someone. There it was again! Another *dialogue*. If they could do it, she could do it.

The next gallery offered painted "found objects" that seemed sort of silly to Blair—painted cassette cases, old vending machine condom packages, scratched mirrors—but who knew? Many museums included found-object art in their collections. There was probably a profound social statement in each of these that she just wasn't seeing. Flo could explain the metaphor contained in each object. That's what Flo was so good at.

Restlessness turned to real anxiety when she entered the last gallery on her map. The walls were covered with "*Twenty-thousand*" (that's what the sign said) individual, hand painted matches. The match stems glowed with neon colors applied with—what? A toothpick? The match heads were all unused. All Blair could think of was lighting one of them! One was all it would take to send the whole place up in flames. Oh, Lord help us! What a smashing blast! Nihilism for its own sake did have its appeal. And, in its own way, just undoing the already done: there was a certain creativity in that, wasn't there?

She flashed an ever-escalating, nervous glance out the window. Her limousine was parked at the curb. Immensely tempted to light a match but equally panicked by the temptation, she bolted for the car so fast William didn't have time to get out and open the door for her. Once inside, she took the jeweled collar back out of its satin pouch and furiously fingered the stones to give her hands something to do because they were trembling so badly. Gratefully, she felt the car turn and head back to Manhattan. "Where I belong," Blair thought, while again pressing her forehead against the cool window of the car. She was removed again, and safe, from the demands of the world. And from her wild imagination. "Forget the art, forget Flo," she repeated to herself like a litany. But deep inside, she felt her respect for Flo rise, her need for her intensify. How did the woman *choose* the art she would represent? It really was a bit overwhelming.

As usual, William admired his employer through the rear view mirror. She was wearing his favorite coat, the one that surrounded her face with fluffy white fur when she brought the hood up around her head. She had seemed in a hurry when she returned to the car, but it never occurred to him to wonder why she had not yet given him directions. She would let him know when she was ready to make the next stop. He would simply make his way back to midtown so that wherever the next stop was, it wouldn't be far.

What a mass of humanity, Blair thought, passing the massive post-WWII housing projects along the FDR Drive, feeling gradual relief from the diversion of the mesmerizing jewels in her lap.

She thought of her phone conversation with Tara last night. Tara's historical work meant everything to her. Yet she seemed so eager to learn about new things. When she had asked Blair for a private preview of the new wing today, Tara had seemed genuinely interested in learning about the twentieth-century art it contained. She didn't seem at all embarrassed that she knew next to nothing about contemporary art.

Well, I'm not *embarrassed*, either, Blair hastened to think, blocking out the recurring flashes of the confusing art images she had just seen. These things actually just cause boredom in me. That's why they make me feel so unsettled. If only life had more genuine surprises. I mean, wadded up sheets of watercolored wallpaper? After the first shock, predictable.

Blair remembered being bored while she was still a child, and even sometimes a little afraid, somehow, that although every wish was fulfilled immediately, she was *missing* something. Everything always seemed the same to her. Her life seemed so *prescribed*.

All except for horseback riding, of course. That, she had always loved. Because animals weren't *entirely* predictable. A horse could be well trained, but you never knew for sure if it would respond just perfectly enough to carry you in a leap over a wall, or if it would round a corner without slipping. The sense of risk, the sense of challenge and control—of power—she felt while riding was unmatched in any other part of her life.

Later, when she was older, even sex with the most unlikely of people was a bore compared to horseback riding. She shook her head, smiling to herself and humming a little.

One time in Newport, when she'd been on summer vacation from college, she had even had sex with a lobster fisherman. She'd been free diving for seaweed for a clambake and decided to steal a couple of lobsters from one of the pots bobbing on the surface of the water, just for fun. When the fisherman saw her and motored angrily toward her in his big boat, she had thrown him back his lobsters and her bathing suit at the same time. Even now, as she remembered it, she could almost feel his big, rough hands squeezing her small pink nipples as if it were yesterday, not twenty-five years ago. Perry had loved hearing about that lobster fisherman.

She had met Perry that very summer, at her younger sister's coming-out party. Two years older than Blair, he was attending school in Switzerland and told her straight off that nothing but skiing interested him, not even sex. In an instant, Blair had found herself interested in him. "Bunny" Harrington Crane (Blair was still called "Bunny" by certain of her old friends) had never met a man of any age who was not interested in having sex, especially with her. Her name, her looks, her money had always assured attention. She had experienced her first sexual encounter when she was fourteen. What else was there to do, anyway, to secretly defy one's mother? Especially a genuinely gracious and loving mother, who believed that being born into money brought with it the responsibility of deserving inherited wealth by living an exemplary life of high moral and ethical conduct. Excessive drugs and alcohol seemed too middleclass forms of rebellion, and she was allowed to do just about anything else she felt like. Wild sexual flings became the one dissonant note she could strike (unsuspected by her ever-attentive parents, which was the kick of it) upon the harmony of her otherwise orchestrated existence. Long before college, she had tried sex with (among others) a homosexual, an African diplomat, a Muslim warlord's son, a prince and a former President's son, not to mention a couple of older women.

By the end of her sister's party, Blair had interested Perry enough to have sex with her. She could never have guessed, that night, that they would one day be married. He had merely been another improvisation, another unpredictability to bring under her control. In fact, Perry had turned out to be, in the end, all too easily controlled. After she learned, to her delight, that his stated lack of interest in sex had only been a ploy to get her into bed, she had always led the way in their relationship. But it had impressed her at the time that he had the guts to surprise her.

She glanced at William's hands on the wheel of the car. They were large, and a little red. Like the lobster fisherman, William was probably big *everywhere*. No need to paint an enlarged sex organ on him, she mused.

Blair shifted restlessly in her seat again and fingered the gemstones again in agitation. Then she smiled and bit her lower lip, a child's mischievous smile at the thought of a new prank. Forget sex organs as art. Forget twenty thousand matches as art. She had a better idea. She'd light a real fire with a real man. She looked at her watch. So she'd be a little late meeting Tara at the museum.

She instructed William to take her to the Queens side of the Fifty-ninth Street Bridge. "I think there's a covered market under the bridge there," she said. Then she pressed the button that would close the curtains between her and her driver and leave her in privacy.

William turned at the next corner, careful not to swerve the car too sharply and jar his passenger, and headed east. To Brooklyn, and now Queens? And under two different bridges? What an unusual itinerary! Didn't she mean the market-restaurant complex under the bridge on the *Manhattan* side? Well, he'd find out soon enough. He slipped a Mozart concerto into the CD player and regulated the volume. The clear voice of a flute floated through a theme shaped by a single harp, the flute's song rising and falling as if forming spirals of sound in and around the melody line. Not too loud, not too soft. Mrs. Gothard was very particular. He drove up the entrance ramp to the lower level of the bridge.

Blair felt the rush of excitement, of challenge. Her voice was bright over the intercom. "When you reach the other side, turn right and down under the bridge." She glanced out the window, her inner rhythm keeping time with the spinning wheels of the car as they clicked over the iron grid.

When they had crossed over to Queens and turned into a spot down an alley and well hidden from ordinary traffic, she spoke again. "All right, William. That's good. Now turn off the engine and come back here, please. I need you for something."

Seeing no covered market or anything else, really, except the empty boat ramp he had driven down to get near the East River, William looked around, confused, but he switched the ignition off, got out of the car and opened the rear door.

His hand tightened on the handle.

Slowly, he moved back to the front of the car and, adjusting the ignition key, he removed the Mozart tape and inserted one from Mr. Gothard's collection. Loud, disjointed sounds blared through the car's stereo system. Then he returned to the back seat.

He felt his body go weak, and then strong again.

Blair Gothard sat sprawled back into a corner of her seat, one leg raised, her foot resting on the bar, her red boots still on. The boots were all she wore. Except for a topaz-jeweled collar that shot a sunburst of glittering arrows to the tips of her breasts, and the white, furry coat, thrown open, its hood framing her feverish eyes.

    He got in.

TWENTY-ONE

COLD, CRISP AND CLEAR. A good day to learn the truth, Tara thought, as she and Kronan Hagen stood on the enclosed skywalk that led to the new wing of the Harrington Museum. Kronan seemed sensitive to the bridge's purpose and acclaimed the architect's brilliant design. He was a gracious man, Tara felt. When the Gothards' chauffeur had phoned from the car saying Blair would be late, Kronan had offered with unconcealed pride to conduct Tara through the old wing himself.

To Tara, Blair's background seemed straight out of a novel. It was incredible to think how certain people could grow up with such an abundance of opportunities. Blair's steel magnate great-grandfather must have been some man to meet. Kronan said that Leland Holmes Harrington was reputed to have spent ten million dollars a year on art. The wealth of treasures in the original mansion confirmed that estimation, and in his day, that was a serious expenditure. But beyond that, Tara would never have expected to encounter such a diversity of significant work in an individual collection. Aside from the impressive paintings and sculpture, Harrington had amassed the largest private collection of Renaissance bronzes in existence, as well as stunning examples of portrait miniatures and jewelry. It was this last preoccupation, Kronan had explained, that had made Harrington such an eccentric character. His habit of keeping his left hand in a pocket caused many people to conclude that he was handicapped. But the man was simply forever fingering some new find—a priceless, tiny brooch or an ancient, carved stone, perhaps—a pastime that led, eventually, to this unique jewelry collection. Within a few hundred objects, he had succeeded in representing fifty centuries of design, from early Egyptian amulets through Greece to the Renaissance and beyond.

Tara had already noticed Blair's unusual flair for jewelry; now she understood. How could one *not* have such a flair, growing up surrounded by such examples? Harrington's son and Blair's grandfather had focused on the armor. He had contributed his own mark to the mansion by turning the skylit center courtyard into a myriad of intricate winding pathways that were like a garden walking tour of superb armor making. The outstanding examples were clearly presented not as objects of curiosity, but as extraordinary works of superb craftsmanship and feats of functional design.

Because of the garden, according to Kronan, Blair's mother had gravitated to a love of horticulture, and it was she who had raised and enclosed the courtyard into a four-story aviary, complete with an exotic assortment of specimen trees, flora and rare bird species. So Blair (a generation of art collecting having been skipped) had been able to follow her own proclivities without any pressures of taste. It would be interesting to see how Blair bore out her legacy in the new wing. The sole reason for Tara's visit, however, was to view only a *few* pieces of Blair's collection: Leon's work.

She looked out the floor-to-ceiling windows of the sky-walk and saw Central Park a half-block away. Today she was going to really take a good open-minded look at what had "sold" in the art world of her own century. Because Leon's work was part of *that* evolving heritage. She heard Dimitrios's words: "We don't care what the truth is, we just want to know it." Why, then, did she also feel she had to be *brave* to do this thing? Because she cared what the truth was this time, she admitted. For all her self-lecturing, deep down she wanted the truth to be what *she* wanted it to be.

A solitary object at the end of the street, where Fifth Avenue meets the park, caught her eye. She lay a hand on Kronen's arm to interrupt his monologue. "Isn't that abstract sculpture in the same place where there used to be a bench? I remember an old bum there."

"Oh, yes," Kronan nodded. "Ironically, as you see, the 'sculpture'—for which the City paid $400,000—is serving the same purpose." A single figure huddled, motionless, on one end of the artwork.

"$400,000? You're kidding! Is that the kind of art in the new wing?"

"Come see for yourself. Blair should be along any moment," Kronan said. "I can't imagine what's making her late, she's usually so prompt. The new wing is her brainchild, not mine, but I can try to get you started. We have many different kinds of art over there." He sounded as if "over there" were another continent, not another building across the street.

Kronan had been right about the design. Tara felt her apprehension turn to anticipation as they approached the entrance to "Blair's brainchild." The design *was* astounding. By the time they reached the end, the ever more economical lines and increasingly integrated ornament subtly coiled into a spiral staircase down which one seemed to glide rather than descend by steps to the ground level entrance of the museum. Unlike the old wing, where art of various periods were mixed together, Kronan believed that modernist, abstract and contemporary art should be viewed in chronological order; therefore, all visitors would start the exhibit at the same point, whether they entered the building via the bridge or at street level.

Directly in front of the stairs they had just descended, and extending to the lobby entrance door, lay an imposing arrangement of flat, distorted shapes made of corroded metal "tiles" over which one either had to walk or, with great difficulty, sidestep along a narrow, cracked (or corroded?) asphalt path at its edge. Tara hesitated.

"You can walk on it," Kronan offered.

"Is it a work of art?" she asked.

"So they say. A corporation donated it, largely to get rid of it, I think. It caused such a furor at their Sixth Avenue headquarters that it made the newspapers. The artist placed it, as he has here, directly in the path of the main entrance to the building. Everyone knew it was a work of art, so nobody felt comfortable walking over it even though the artist said they could. But they didn't want to go around it to get to work every day either. Some employees did end up walking over it, but not without getting angry every time at having to confront the thing. Some used another entrance that allowed them to avoid it altogether. Some even went to City Hall to protest because it had been installed on a public sidewalk. Now we have it here. Who knows how museum visitors will react to it? You can't ignore the blessed thing."

Tara walked gingerly across the center of the—what? Why would an artist want people to *walk* on his art? She looked back to the two-story lightwell. The spiral stairs they had just descended curved through space like a smooth white marble slide as the sun's rays slipped down like water made of light before spilling out into the lobby in one glorious splash. Now *that*, Tara thought, remembering Nicky's spiral and the discussion in Dorina's studio, is inspired, abstract art!

The main staircase constructed of pale granite, clear glass and gleaming steel spread open like a set of enormous wings at the other end of the lobby, beckoning the visitor to soar up to the first floor to . . . what art treasures?

Kronan was explaining that there were no escalators in the building. The architect had conceived the interior space to create not only a positive visual environment but also to choreograph a time experience. She wanted to stimulate a feeling of anticipation because she felt that art was a personal experience and that the building itself should serve to prepare all visitors emotionally for a singular experience by encouraging each to follow designated paths but at their own pace.

A clinking sound caused Tara to look up at the ceiling of the lobby. A large mobile, moved by the museum's subtle ventilation system, swung in a lazy circle beneath a prism skylight. Its many, dangling parts were painted in bright primary colors and looked to Tara as if it belonged in the nursery of some giant baby. Whimsical and charming, but is it really fine art she asked herself? Or a form of amusing entertainment?

The winged staircase called to them, and she and Kronan began their ascent to the main collection. Once again, she sensed her expectations rise as she mounted the grand sweep of stairs. The architect had succeeded. Forgetting for the moment her specific purpose, Tara found she couldn't wait to see the entire exhibit. But the world she now entered appeared to be not a vision of the future, or even the present. It was, instead, a strange reincarnation of the past. Primitive worlds. Against her will, she felt the wave of anticipation ebbing away, its undercurrent pulling at her buoyant mood in warning of deep waters to come. She willed herself to tread lightly, to view the work as objectively as possible.

"This opening section is full of the first 'masters' of the early modernist movement," Kronan was informing her. "Here is a record of the birth of twentieth-century art after Impressionism."

"But," Tara kept her voice impersonal, "these are very reminiscent of African primitives." The tribal masks that had leered down from the walls of the Gothards' boat were recalled in her memory. Am I missing something? she wondered. Where is the originality in this art? Real primitive art made by genuinely primitive peoples had such power, such integrity, because it had served such life and death purposes. This all seemed so derivative, hence so shallow. "Could you tell me why this art is important?" she asked Kronan. "I visited the MOMA several times with a class when I was in high school, and, of course, these images are commonplace by now, but I'm afraid that most of this kind of art just doesn't speak to me, so I've never really taken the time to look seriously at it before. I can't begin to know what to think of it."

Kronan drew her over to one section of the room. "I'm afraid I don't understand it very well myself. They say that these paintings in particular," he gestured at a wall, "are the most important in the twentieth century because they created a whole new way of seeing, from many points of view at once. They say that this cubism has influenced all art since."

"A new way of seeing in our century, perhaps, but the Egyptians depicted the same idea with simultaneous, multiple images in their low-relief sculpture thousands of years ago. For the purpose, I might add, of aiding perception, not fracturing it. The Etruscans did it too. And look at this sculpture." Tara gestured. "This reminds me very much of early Cycladic art from the second millennium B.C." She next walked over to a fantastical painting with delightful, story-book-type characters seemingly afloat in the air. "And this is very like the ceramic paintings from the island of Skyros four-hundred years ago, with different themes, of course. But the style's the same. Oh, now I remember, he's the same artist who painted those huge hanging things that never quite seemed to belong in the front of the Metropolitan Opera House."

Spying a gigantic piece of sculpture in the corridor outside an archway, she remembered her mission and moved resolutely to it. Since she didn't know what she was searching for, she had to examine every piece of sculpture until she found one of Leon's. No, it couldn't be this: African and Oriental images merged to create a hybrid creature twisted into an external sign of internal pain. It was very forceful, but the *malevolence*! She stooped to read the label plate attached to the base of the work. The plate flashed an unknown name up at her; she breathed again.

Kronan was chuckling softly as he came up behind her. Touching her elbow, he guided her down the hallway. "You're very refreshing," he said shaking his head in disbelief. "I have never met another person who so succinctly said what she thought while saying she didn't know what to think."

Tara smiled up at him. This was the most "human" museum director she had ever met. So unpretentious. Remarkably frank about his own inadequacies, real or imagined. What a pleasure it must be to work with him. She hesitated before walking through the open door to which he had led her, stopped by a stone mask balanced atop a spear-like metal rod that looked as if it couldn't support the weight. Symmetrically divided between the human and the bestial, half of the mask's "face" depicted a mustachioed, bearded man; the other half was an animal with muzzle, whiskers and a single painted tooth: A carnivore. The surface and lines of the sculpture were smooth, angular and modern, but again, the content was just a re-creation of a recurrent primitive theme. She didn't recognize the artist's name. "Man: half human, half beast," she murmured to herself as relief restored her breath again. She turned to Kronan. "This one is a modernized version of a stone-age piece that was found in El Juyo, Spain," she said. "Which have we become today, do you think? Man or beast?" She flashed a smile over her shoulder.

Kronan looked startled, and his lips barely moved as he invited her to enter the room with a gentlemanly gesture. His pulse quickening, he answered her jest literally. "Wild or tame? Civilized and rational or savage and instinctual? Religion calls the dichotomy 'God and the Devil.' Psychology calls it the Ego and the Id." *And I call it me*, he thought. "I don't know," he said, "perhaps a few people *may* be totally human. It would seem by the brutality we see in the world that many are worse than beasts, but this motif has not fascinated man for centuries without reason. Most of us, I'm sure, are cursed with both attributes, aren't we? It is, after all, *the* curse of being human, isn't it? Man, eternally torn between the divine and the diabolical?" *But the strong don't give in to the animal urges. Only the weak among us do.* He felt drained of energy from an overwhelming wash of guilt.

Tara didn't answer. She entered the room in silence. "Oh!" She stopped just beyond on the threshold. "This room isn't finished yet. What's going to be in here?"

Kronan sat dejectedly on one of the several wooden seats in the room, wishing that Blair would arrive. "Considerably late" would soon be "No show." This art was so alien to him, and this young woman was so actively interested in it that it wasn't fair to give her such an uninformed tour. "Well, it's mostly finished," he said, trying to ignore his steadily deepening depression. "The visual and sound systems haven't yet been installed. They'll simulate the passage of sun and clouds over the surface of the canvases, and they'll also broadcast the sound we hear when we put a conch shell to our ear, they tell me. I don't know how that sound can be simulated, but," his voice trailed off, "this is a meditation room. A religious room, they tell me. It's inspired by that small, modern museum in Houston with all those black canvases—I can't remember the artist—but this is technologically modernized by all sorts of multi-media gadgetry and is symbolically Medievalized by the presence of church pews, so they tell me . . ." his voice vanished into an eerie silence.

Tara studied the octagonal space in which she stood.

Now she saw that all eight walls were not painted, but already hung with huge, vertical rectangles. All of the canvases appeared to be exact duplicates of each other, but on closer scrutiny, each one displayed different tonalities of color. The cumulative impression one received was that of black, but when you looked long enough, hints of purple and green and blue could be discerned. There was nothing else in the room except what did look like wooden church pews covered with faded calligraphy. Or graffiti? One had been placed in front of each canvas. And a long piece of iron or something spanned the room across its center, an I-beam of sorts that looked to be left over from recent construction work. She tried to imagine what the room would look like when it was finished, with the sound of a conch shell, the visual passage of sun and clouds and the absence of the leftover construction piece. A "meditation" room?

Kronan was sitting quietly on a pew. He seemed lost. Some quality in his hunched posture made her feel instantly sorry for the man. He had said he didn't understand this kind of art; it must be stressful, then, to oversee a museum containing it. She wished Blair would arrive to shed some light on these dark canvases. She sat down on the seat next to Kronan. Perhaps they should rest; he was, after all, an older man, and he had already walked with her for almost an hour.

"I really don't know what to think of this," she confessed. "What's the reason behind creating a 'meditation' room in a museum, anyway?"

"Once I would have asked that question, but today, it doesn't surprise me. It even seems a logical extension of the direction museums have been going for some time because, I'm afraid, they are encroaching upon the traditional role of religion. It's almost as if people think that by looking at art, they can infuse a modern equivalent of religious meaning into their lives. There's been such a boom in the numbers of museumgoers in the past many decades that it has to go deeper than the fact that more people are aware of and can afford high culture. I, for one, don't think they're coming to look at the *art* as much as coming to look for *God*. If so, then a meditation room in a museum seems consistent, doesn't it?"

Tara sat observing Kronan silently. He rested his chin in his hands, now, his elbows on his knees; he was completely absorbed in his own pondering. Perhaps the room served a function, after all.

A flash of red and white in the doorway astonished them both: red boots, white lynx coat, red hat, *very* red cheeks, and red lips, laughing.

"Caught you meditating, did I?" Blair posed on the threshold with a big smile on her face and a small package in her hand. Breathless and radiant, her eyes sparkling with mischief, she hugged Tara and handed the package to Kronan. "Advance copy of *Art World*. Cover story!" Then her eyes darkened slightly with a wistful hint of ennui. Why was she losing the edge so quickly after sex this time? Her high usually lasted for hours. She noticed Kronan's resemblance to William again.

"I'm sorry, I'm sorry and I'm sorry," she murmured. "But," she pushed herself back into her habitual buoyancy, "I'm not *too* sorry to have missed the tour up till now. The fun part of the exhibit is the last part anyway. That's where we present *only* artists who make current news. Come on," she whirled out the door. "This room is too heavy with spirit for me. Let's have some fun! Then I'll take you both to lunch!"

Kronan begged off. "Pick me up at my office when you're through here. Your 'fun' art will ruin my appetite. You know how I feel about the last part of this exhibit. By placing the works of artists who make 'current news' in a museum, you legitimize their art before enough time has passed to assess it. In my view, they still belong in galleries, not museums."

"Okay, you go back to your own safe turf. Tara and I will do it alone."

Blair started a running commentary about what they would see as she led Tara on to another space. "Most American moderns, thank heaven, aren't dragged down by all the weighty mental baggage of the old European masters with their philosophies and manifestos. They're more concerned with the *act* of creating, so I find their art much more exciting. It's really an aesthetic conduit to the inner spirit of the artist for mystics who don't buy formal religion, formal philosophies, formal politics or anything: a *direct* conduit to the artist's own subconscious realm."

"Is that why you like it? Because of its unexpected surprises?" Tara asked.

"Indeed I do. My friend Flo—Leon's agent—says that art today is just a hyped-up commodity, but she's wrong. This is my favorite section of the new wing: a sanctuary and a playroom at the same time, church and carnival, both. Even though it's twentieth century, the Meditation Room gives me the creeps. It's too ponderous. Not here! The works done directly on that wall over there will be painted over after the museum's opening to signify the transience of life, so get a good look now. Next year, they won't be here. Well," she waved her hand around the room. "what do you think?"

I think my mind is unhinged, Tara thought. She walked slowly around the huge room. Why should the emotional content of an artist's inner life be of any interest to anyone other than the artist himself, his loved ones and perhaps his psychiatrist? Well, it must be of considerable interest; the paintings are *here*, aren't they? And some of it was wonderfully decorative. Certain canvases reminded her of textiles or ceramic tiles. One gigantic canvas swirled with both metallic and muddy colors and seemed to be held together with something sticky, like rubber of some sort. *Balloons?* Another one, all gold and white and black and blue, with sprinkles of other colors here and there, glittered on the surface with . . . ground glass?

Blair watched Tara intently. She was so caught up in it all! She seemed to have forgotten Blair's presence in the room. Her round, gray eyes were so direct, looking at everything intently, wanting only to understand, seeing as if through a child's eyes.

Tara stared dumbly at a large wood rectangle dripping globs of orange paint. She turned to Blair. "You have so much power," she marveled. "By displaying contemporary artists, you become an instant arbiter of cultural standards. People in the future will use the art you choose as evidence of who we are, what our lives are like, what we value and what we feel is worth preserving. It seems like an enormous responsibility."

Blair smiled indulgently. Tara was taking all this too seriously. "Patrons of the arts have always set the cultural standards, only now we don't have the power to dictate. Commissioned artisans of the past are now independent "artists." So it's the *artists* who now decide what will be next on the agenda. *We* can't even predict what they'll do."

A fluid abstract piece that looked like a sculptural line drawing drew Tara's attention. Curve upon curve upon curve of bluish metal became a fat crayon line cutting through space to form—what? The nameplate carried a woman's name. How could she have passed through so much of the museum and not see even one of Leon's pieces?

At the edge of her vision, she noticed a balcony hanging out over a small courtyard. As she looked at the bronze sculpture at its center, she was flooded by a torrent of relief. "Oh, *this* must be Leon's!" she cried in utter joy. "Oh, Blair, this is Leon's! Isn't it? I can't see the nameplate from here, but it just has to be. It's so reminiscent of a nude he did when he was fifteen: *Spring Flower*, it was called. This is much more stylized, but—" Of course Leon's mother would find this a dramatic change from his youthful work, she thought. But the bronze nude, glorying in herself among nature's glories of vines and flowers, still projected the human spirit! The bronze vines it held in its hands reached for the sun; the spirit of the female reached for her own sun god. It wasn't as romantic or detailed as *Spring Flower*, but it was still Leon! A suit of armor beamed out at the figure from a corner, as if accepting its role as a silent guardian of the nude's vulnerability.

"*Leon's?*" Blair joined Tara on the balcony. "No Tara, of course, that's not Leon's. It's a stylized but derivative rendition of a female American sculptor who worked at the same time that modernist work was beginning in Europe but who was academically trained in Italy. This copycat shows more of the modern edge, but the piece is still trite. You can see that, basically, this sculptor—I can't put my finger on his name—was solidly traditional and decorative, too. The work is here only because my mother insisted. It doesn't belong with this other art at all. You know, Tara, Leon would never do anything so sentimental."

Blair was smiling at her with an expression hovering between surprise and tolerance. "How could the same artist who created *Eternity*, with all *its* heroic power, create something as trivial as this?" Blair asked her.

Tara fought for words. "*Eternity?* I don't think I saw it. Did I?"

Blair took Tara's arm and began to march her back through the rooms.

"Well, I assume you saw it, since you were sitting right next to it when I came in. But you may have missed his name, I guess. Leon won't permit nameplates or labels, and he won't even actually sign his name to his work. He just engraves his initials into the surface in some obscure place. On *Eternity*, the initials are on one end of the piece. She waved a hand at the huge canvas covered with colored glass fragments as they retraced their steps. That painting, *City Lights* by Adria Cass, Leon had a lot to do with. I recently learned that, in fact, he co-created it. You ought to ask him about it some time." She led Tara back down the hall and into the meditation room. "Now, *there* is one of his most famous pieces. It still belongs to me. It's so important in Leon's oeuvre that I've only loaned it. We have four more works still to be donated outright that will flank each of the side exit doors and one already in place at the entrance. You certainly couldn't have missed seeing *that*. Leon is one of the best-known sculptors we have today, so he'll be honored with important positions in the museum. "Besides," Blair squeezed Tara's arm, "Perry and I, personally, have a whole lot invested in him." She floated down onto a seat like an exotic red butterfly.

Tara looked in bewilderment around the octagonal room. The dark scenery, the canvases, the pews— She felt like a fool, but she had to ask. "*Where* . . . is it?" she stammered.

Blair looked up at her incredulously. This child really was a complete throwback of some kind. "Tara! My sweet, are you blind?" She walked to the center of the room and kicked the I-beam with her red boot. "Good heavens, you have to step over it to get anywhere in the environment!" She walked alongside the slab to its end. "See? Here are his initials. 'L.S.' Wait until I tell Leon you sat right next to his work and didn't even know it! But then, you and Kronan were so deep in meditation—" Blair laughed with a good-natured toss of her head, put her arm around Tara's waist and strolled her around the room so she could see the piece from all angles.

Tara walked. I must be walking, she thought; my feet are moving one after the other and I'm not falling down. And I'm seeing; I must be seeing because I'm not tripping over anything. She moved in concert with Blair, staring at what might be a tragic "ruin": a remnant of a once magnificent building, part of the skeleton that had once lifted a city's skyline to the height of its aspirations, fallen now, as if struck by a disaster, fallen stricken and dead across the room like a tree felled by a streak of lightning torn loose from a storm.

A silent scream tore through her body. *This* is Leon's "heroic" artwork!

She tied the sash of her coat tightly around her waist and began to pull on her gloves, watching herself perform as if from afar. You're doing fine, her observer-self said; you're even smiling. Now say a few words in departure. Look at your watch; show Blair the time. You didn't realize— You'd love lunch but you just remembered— You appreciate her taking the time to show you the art— Please thank Kronan, how generous he was— She watched from afar as her own hand reached out for Blair's. She felt Blair's dewy cheek against hers as Blair kissed the air and bid her goodbye. She must be talking still; Blair was nodding her blonde head in understanding. Now, she must be walking again; she could hear the click of her own heels against the marble flooring in the hallway.

As she moved her body carefully down the stairs, she heard Blair's footsteps racing after her. "Tara!" Blair was calling from the top of the staircase. "Please bring that smashing fox cape Leon gave you to Palm Beach. I want your picture taken with us in a sleigh. Look! There's another major piece by Leon right in front of you. The 'megalomaniac's doormat,' I call it. You can find his initials on that end tile over there."

Tara descended each granite step as if it were made of ice. At the bottom, she stopped, paralyzed, before the "doormat": tiles pushed together like children's building blocks that possessed no further function of building. She could walk over it or around it; it was her choice, but an annoying one because it was demanded; the "thing" was most definitely *in her way*. The whole idea seemed malicious, somehow. And it was Leon's! From the ceiling, the brightly painted metal wires pointed down at her with long, sharp fingers of accusation. "How stupid could you be?" they clinked together in collective agreement. There was no air in the lobby. She hurried over Leon's metal tiles and out the revolving door to the street. A cold blast of air slapped her in the face; she turned up the street toward the park.

    The sculpture that had taken the place of the park bench was empty now. She slumped down onto the huge, rectangular mass and stared back without comprehension down the street to the new wing. Stunned into immobility, she sat that way for a very long time, one gloved hand clutching the end of the "bench" as if in fear that if she let go, she would fall off the slab altogether. Under the leather of her fingertips, engraved deeply into the bronze mass on which she sat, were the initials, "L. S." When she finally managed to stand up, she saw them.

At the sound of the key in the door, Kostas didn't need to look at the clock again. He had made the family wait dinner for nearly an hour after the restaurant was closed and cleaned for the night, but when Tara still had not arrived home, they had all eaten a quick silent meal around the kitchen table. Now everyone else was upstairs in bed, asleep. Kostas alone had remained awake by the large kitchen fireplace, watching the clock, watching the fire, and watching wood shavings fall regularly from the cut of his knife as he whittled a circular shape into a bracelet for Kally's Christmas stocking. He listened to the footsteps coming up the first set of stairs; the steps were even and unhurried; there was no danger, then. He didn't breathe a sigh of relief; he hadn't the energy left; the waiting had drained him of, first, the anger that she hadn't called to let them know she would be so late, and then of the fear that something had happened to prevent her calling. Now all he could do was listen to the sweet sound of her even, unhurried steps. His firstborn was late, but she was alive and well.

She was not well. His immediate sight of her told him that. He got up from his chair and headed for the fireplace. "I was just about to make myself some popcorn," he said carefully. "Will you join me?" He watched Tara's head bob up and down; he watched her sit down carefully at the kitchen table as if she were a stranger.

"Do you remember when you were a little girl, how you used to love popcorn at the movies?" Tara's head bobbed again. "And how you used to spend all your allowance on Cracker Jack just to get the prize? Do they still make Cracker Jack, I wonder?"

No answer.

Kostas poured corn kernels from a cloth bag into a well-used fireplace popper and extended the wire pan section over the low flames. Within a minute the pop-popping sounds produced fluffy, white blossoms. He riveted his attention to his task. "You know," he said, "there's such an argument about whether the white ones make better popcorn than the yellow ones. But anybody with any taste knows that white kernels make the best."

Tara had walked to his chair and picked up the unfinished bracelet. She said nothing.

"It's a Christmas present for Kally." Kostas emptied the popcorn into a serving bowl and dropped some butter into another pan to melt over the fire. "After I'm through with the first finish, I'm going to make 'Ks' back and forth around the entire thing with brass nails." He poured the butter into the popcorn and began to divide the snack into two small baskets. "The brass and the walnut wood should make a good combination, don't you think?"

He watched Tara's head bob up and down again.

"You know, you're an archaeologist. I read that some people in your profession were rummaging around down in Mexico, and they say they found little fossils of popcorn dating back to the Stone Age. Did you know that?"

Tara's head moved back and forth.

Kostas handed her a bowl of popcorn and watched her return to her chair. "You don't find any 'old maids' in *my* popcorn. It's those electric poppers that leave unpopped kernels in the bottom of the pan." He sat down in his own chair and picked up his whittling. "Where have you been, Tara?"

"Walking."

"Where?"

"Around."

"Do you know what time it is?"

A shake of the head.

"Have you eaten?"

No response.

Kostas's knife made slow scrapes at the wood. Both baskets of popcorn sat untouched.

"*Tara*! *Where are you? My 'Charis'?*"

Then she was where she had belonged from the first moment: on his lap, her head buried in his big chest, her tears drenching his shirt, her slender body shaking with sobs that found their trembling echo in the warm and loving center of his heart.

Kostas held his favorite child in his arms for as long as she would need to stay, hoping that whatever had caused her hurt, he would never again have reason to hold her this way, that she would never again need him this much.

"Lost, Papa. I'm lost." he heard her whisper.

TWENTY-TWO

"I REALLY DON'T WANT TO BEAT HELL out of you, you know, but if you're going to become the skin for this other guy over here, I'm going to have to do it."

Leon raised his hammer, laughing at his reluctance. He really didn't want to beat this beautiful, burnished sheet of copper. Mesmerized, he studied the material, his hammer still in the air. Reds and golds swirled and melded together like molten lava in the depths of the metal's composition, surging to the surface as one flow, to be cooled instantly and trapped into a flat surface that contained their fire without diminishing their flame. Copper. It pulsed with color and light. Yet it sent softer signals, too; sensuous surfaces could be wrought, delicate tracings could be etched, intricate patterns could be cut. He just wished he didn't have to beat hell out of it to get it to respond. He felt too happy to beat hell out of anything these days.

He used to feel invigorated after the physical effort that made his art, as if some driving force in him had been used up and left him lighter somehow. But during the past several weeks, he had lost some inner reservoir of energy. Leon didn't know nor did he care to know that what he had lost was his anger. All he knew was that lately he couldn't gear up his energy level for the physical labor it took to make his work, and that he resisted making the effort to put forth that exertion every night. Unlike clay, metals and iron required tools and acts of aggression: hammers, fire and muscle power coerced them into shape. Some of his contemporaries merely assembled their materials, but Leon pummeled, cut, welded and corroded with acids; he wrestled his materials into shapes and textures, against their will. And he always won. By the time he was through with them, they were entirely transformed because they had yielded (entirely) to *his* will. For more than ten years now, he had loved that battle. The most prestigious institutions and the most prominent people in the country had paid millions of dollars for the results of his battles with inert matter. Telling himself he was going for a beer, he walked over to the refrigerator to postpone the first strike.

This would be the first time he had ever worked with copper, and for some reason he couldn't identify, he wanted to do this piece alone; he had unexpectedly called his two regular helpers this afternoon and announced that as of today they were being given a two week paid vacation, an early Christmas bonus he told them. But the real reason had something to do with his wanting to approach this enchanting metal in private. All his previous work had used homelier metals, and the harsh pounding and cutting sounds, along with loud rock music accompanying the transformation process, matched the crude battle taking place. But even when he'd worked with stainless steel, he and his workers had beat the life out of it and corroded its surface. His was not decorative art.

Yet yesterday, when he went looking for materials for a commissioned work for a corporate client in California, this sheet of copper had called out to him. He also didn't know why he had decided to beat the copper into curves instead of into his usual hard, straight edges. Or why he planned to beat its own color and light into an even greater glow. He only knew that he wanted to make these sheets of metal breathe, and he wanted to do the deed solo, in peaceful quietude. He also knew that when the piece was finished, he would have it treated so it couldn't corrode; it would shine forever. It would be like a new planet that, when installed in its setting near the corporate mountain lake poised high over the Pacific ocean, would look as if it had fallen from the atmosphere, a golden astro-bauble dropped from a distant, glittering galaxy as a gift to meager earth.

He set down his beer and lifted the hammer again. The first blow would be struck tonight. It might as well be now—

"Hello, Leon."

"Tara!" He held the hammer aloft in shock. Happy shock. Putting down his tools and taking off his gloves, he grinned and went quickly to the door where she had materialized. He gathered her into his arms. "What are you doing here? It's—" he looked at the clock on the wall, "two AM. Shouldn't you be in bed?" His eyes warmed as he pulled her into the huge warehouse that was his studio. "Or did you come here to take *me* to bed? How did you get here?"

"Papa brought me in a taxi."

Leon headed for the door. "Well, have him come in!"

"He's already gone. When we saw your light, we knew you were here, so I made him leave."

At last he noticed her numb facial expression and her swollen eyes. He wrapped his arms around her again. "What's wrong? Is something wrong? Tell me! Darling! What is it?"

Tara stared at him as if he were a stranger. "Are you aware that I've come to your studio uninvited?"

"Oh," he grinned. "So you have. Well, then, welcome to my studio."

"Don't you remember that you asked me to wait to see your work until the opening of the Harrington's new wing?"

The corners of Leon's grin slipped downward until his mouth was reshaped into a grim set of concern. "Yes, of course I remember, but if something's wrong, I want you to find me wherever I am."

Tara began to pace. The place was cluttered with metal, iron, wire, blowtorches, hammers, vises . . . Her father had convinced her that she should talk to Leon right away about his work. Until she had more information, he said, she risked forming emotional conclusions that might not be valid or fair. If she cared for Leon, she couldn't let that happen. She must try to withhold her judgment until she learned *why* he created the kind of art he did.

Various photos and newspaper clippings were tacked haphazardly along one wall of the two-story space. One tear-sheet displayed a photo of Leon helping a young sneering model, clad in a bathing suit, down from the I-beam that Tara now knew was entitled *Eternity*. Why Perry Gothard had called it "heroic" eluded her beyond caring; it was that description of Leon's work that had misled her from the beginning. Other models, all wearing swimwear, were lined up along the piece; they were obviously using it as a kind of ramp for a fashion show. Among the other memorabilia, she saw a framed photograph of the ruins of the Temple of Athena at Delphi. Under the photo, a text read: "I shall define beauty to be a harmony of all the parts, in whatsoever subject it appears, fitted together with such proportion and connection that nothing could be added, diminished or altered, but for the worse. Leon Batista Alberti, Italy, 1480." Beneath it, in the same handwriting that appeared on the margins of Dimitrios's essay, was the inscription: "To *my* Leon with love, Mother." Tara whirled to face him.

Leon was watching her silently, waiting.

Tara found her throat so tight she could barely speak at all. "I saw that piece called *Eternity* at the Harrington today," she whispered, "and I know the handwriting of the inscription on the Athena Temple is the same as the scribbling on the margins of the *L'Ancienne* article."

"I see."

"What you said about your mother's notes was simple fraud against both her and me. Why you lied about that I can't imagine, but at this moment, I'm more interested in discovering whether or not you've committed fraud against yourself. When we first met in Greece, you talked of Classical and Renaissance art. At Dorina's studio, you talked of what I now know is your own in-your-face abstract art. Because it sells, you said. Where is your heart?"

"My heart is with you. I told you that." He picked up his beer and began to sip at it.

"But *my* heart is with *this*." She pointed to the photo of the temple at Delphi. "You can't love us all equally! Either you love this art and me or you love your brand of art and *not* me. Don't you see?"

"That's true, Tara. I don't love any of the art I make. I love only you."

"Then why do you *make* these things?"

"They sell."

"Oh, Leon. *Shoes* sell! Why do you make this art?"

"I make it precisely because it *doesn't* mean anything to me, because I *don't* love it."

The more Tara wanted to scream, the lower she dropped her voice. "Why do you *not* make art that you *do* love?"

"Because it doesn't sell!" Leon burst out laughing. "Don't you *see*?" He felt something coming alive inside him again. It was the anger. It was all back; he could work now. He picked up his hammer and began to beat the hell out of the sheet of copper, words, laughter and movement all coming out at once. "And even more important than the fact that the work I love—correction, that I *did* love—doesn't sell, even more important is the fact that it *isn't real*. The kind of art you love, that Nicky loves, that Dorina loves, that my mother loves, that I *used* to love . . . isn't *real*. It has no place, no meaning and no relevance here on this earth. It's too good, it's too pure, it's too beautiful and too rational, it's not possible . . . here."

Tara grabbed his arm to stop him. "Leon. You don't mean 'it's not *possible*,' you mean 'it's not *perfect*,' And if not 'here on this earth', then where, Leon?"

He shook his head and went back to hammering.

"If not here, where *is* it possible?" she demanded.

"It isn't possible anywhere. The ideal is just a childish, romantic illusion. It sounds good in theory, but practically speaking—"

"Is *happiness* possible?"

A sharp pain stabbed at his temples. He slammed his hammer on the workbench and closed his eyes, waiting long moments for it to pass. Then, taking her hand, he pulled her down gently to sit with him on the floor. His eyes were steady. "I didn't think so until you," he said.

"Leon, I wouldn't feel so betrayed about the work you do now if I hadn't seen your early work, or if I hadn't seen the sketch you made of me in Dorina's studio, or if I hadn't seen every detail of your apartment, or if I hadn't slept with you, really *been* with you. Everybody has the right to exchange the hours of their life for whatever they choose in return. But *you*! You could never have created *Spring Flower*, even as a boy, if you weren't at heart a deeply affirmative human being. I know it! There's got to be a part of you still that doesn't believe the things you say now. I saw the expression on your face in Athen's National Museum, when you looked at *Poseidon* and at all the other Greek figures. I didn't believe just your words, I saw in your eyes that your affinity for them was intense and genuine. And your deep knowledge of the ancient world: one has to learn information like that *on purpose*. I mean, it isn't the sort of trivia one picks up on network TV! What happened to make you reject your ideals, your hopes, your dreams, what you loved so much?"

"When I was sixteen, I fell in love with a girl who modeled for me, and she turned out to be the school whore."

"No good, Leon. No matter how horrible that must have been, that alone couldn't have driven you from doing work like *Spring Flower* and compelled you to make these stillborn lumps of metal. The fact that your work is abstract disappoints me, but some of the abstract sculpture and painting I saw at the museum at least had harmony of design. It was *alive*, at least in composition, if not in content. You're just reshaping inert matter into other inert matter. One can't ignore it just because it's too large. One has to walk around it or over it. It's always there, *in the way*."

Leon laughed. It was an ugly laugh, his lips pulled back in a grimace so menacing that Tara sprang to her feet and stared down, aghast, at him. He reached for his beer and drained it, then went to the refrigerator for another. "You're wrong," he said. "One *could* ignore it. And one should! But no one ever has. It's a fair trade. My art is a joke to me and a commodity to them. But *they* are the fools, not I. *They've* climbed ladders to see it, *they've* walked around it so as not to muddy it with their shoes, *they've* stood in the cold while I burned it at a 'public corroding ceremony.' They don't want art, they want theatricality: something to write about, something to prattle about at cocktail parties. I give it to them. One critic, for years, called me the 'last *Enfant Terrible* of Art.' He didn't give a pig's eye about what I made. He loved me because I was a brat who gave him his headlines, his reputation. But what have they all given me in return? Their independent judgment. And why is that? Because what once were called standards by which to judge no longer exist, proof positive that most of the last century defined art as just what an artist *does*. And who's an artist, you might ask? Why, anyone who *says* he's an artist and can get a few other influential people to believe him. It's all a big joke! Why shouldn't I cash in on such a society? Some people still think art means something. Some brainwashed fools even really think that a heap of horseshit means something *if* it's varnished and shoveled into a gallery or a museum. But at least I'm honest with myself. It's all just a big, sad mercenary joke!"

"On whom, Leon?" Tara walked over to the magazine picture of *Eternity*. "You chose your apartment—your home!—so you could be inspired by your favorite buildings, and then you recreate an *I-beam*, isolating that single, structural element from the whole that you worship, and you call *that Eternity*. Is that humorous?"

"Yes, because it's a metaphorical work of irony about the truth that everybody evades every day. Our lives are over all too soon, have no real meaning, and in the end, all that will last of each of us *are* the parts, the separate elements, the nuts and the bolts."

"Oh, Leon! What about the *idea* behind a building? What about the human mind who envisioned all of the parts together and then created such a thrilling whole like the Empire State or Chrysler buildings that you want to see it every day of your life? If human life is meaningless, how can you value *me*? That's like saying you value, that you *love,* only my bones because, in the end, that's all of *me* that will last.

Never mind." She slumped back down to the floor. "I'm not angry with *you* after all, I see. Or even hurt. It's my own fault for letting myself get involved with you too quickly. And you're right. I was never interested in Greek artifacts for themselves. I was in love with the Greek spirit. With any heroic spirit. Greece is the home of my soul. America is my political home, but my deepest experience of my own personal spirit lies in Greece. Not in any mystical sense, of course. I don't believe that the spirits of the men who created ancient Greece are still around. But they were such giants. I love to be where they were when they were alive. I feel a rush of inner energy just walking up the same steps, looking out over the same sea, trying to feel as they felt about the world and humanity: the vast possibility of it all, the glorious wonder of it all. I feel that exaltation about only one other thing: love. I know that art and sex are the most sacred things in the world to me, because somehow they're the quintessence of life. That's why I can't accept the fact that I may love a man whose art offends me. Don't you see? Maybe there's a basic mistake we're both making, but in different ways. You think the ideal isn't possible, so you abandon the struggle to make it real and satirize it instead. I think the ideal *is* possible, but since it isn't here ready-made for me, I bury myself in a dead civilization that did believe it was possible. But both of us seem to be working on the premise that the ideal isn't approachable in the here and now."

Leon dropped to the floor and knelt beside her. Cupping her face in his hands, he kissed her, soft and long. She answered his kiss. It was a truce, a moment of rest between them.

"One more thing, Leon. You say that life is meaningless, but *I* believe it's life that is sacred. I talk about art and sex because they're the most intense life experiences I know, so I feel that they must be sacred too. They let us experience the values we've chosen for our lives in one, exquisite moment, not of pleasure, exactly, but of *oneness* with all of existence and with our own personal relationship to it. Art lets us feel oneness with reality, and sex lets us feel oneness with another living being. Art says: 'this is Life.' Sex says: 'this is Living.' It's as if both experiences purge my whole being of any pettiness and leave me with just the essence of my soul and my mind and my body, all unified. I wouldn't want to live without either."

"I love you, Tara. And I know you love me, at least to some degree, or you wouldn't be here."

"But I can't divorce you from your art, Leon. A person's art is his soul revealed."

"Maybe once, Tara. But not in today's world. If my art means so little to me, why should it matter to you? If you love *me*, that's all that matters."

"I love *part* of you, Leon. How can I separate you from your work? I need time. Too much is happening too fast. I have to slow it all down."

"You have all the time in the world. I was wrong to lie to you about the notes, and I was a coward not to show you my work myself. My only excuse is that I knew how confusing it would be for you, coming from your sheltered world. I didn't plan on falling in love with you, you know. In the beginning, in Greece, it started out... well, never mind how it started out, but once I came to know you, Tara, once I came to know you, I realized that my childhood vision of a woman was possible! I knew I could never let you go, no matter how I had to keep you, even if it was with lies. I'm sorry."

"What if you learned that your childhood vision of the *world* was possible too? What would you do then?" Tara smiled at last. The lines of tension around Leon's eyes and mouth disappeared; he looked ten years younger.

"Maybe we can help each other," she said. "But, now, we both need time to think. When I got to the museum this morning, there was a message to call Dimitrios. It seems I have to return to Athens for a couple of weeks. He's arranging a quick meeting in Crete with the team for our next project. It has to be held now because of some schedule problem with the private benefactor who helps finance our more exotic ventures, and he has to be in on the preliminary discussions about possible sites."

She raised a hand to stop his protest. "It's not unusual. I'll be back and forth many times during the two years it's going to take me to mount this exhibit for three museums. Maybe the timing is good. It will give us a chance to think separately. Then when I return, we can think together. I'll be back just in time for the Gothards' 'Palm Beach party.'"

Leon pulled her into his arms. "Don't go," he whispered. "Stay with me."

She stood up quickly for fear she would grant his wish. "I wonder," she said, smiling tenderly at him. "If you hadn't given up on the world and taken off your 'rose-colored' glasses, what your art would have become?"

"Come home with me now." His face was in her hair, his hand pressed her thigh. "If we got through tonight together, we can get through anything."

Tara pushed Leon's hand away, gently. She could see the cab driver snatching glances at them in his rear view mirror. "We didn't 'get through' anything, yet. We just proved that we can communicate enough to—" She turned to him. "Blair said I should ask you about a painting you had something to do with making, co-creating it or something. It's by a female painter. I think her name is Cass? Did you paint at one time too?"

"No, I've never painted. That was just a joke." Leon looked out the window. They were crossing over the Brooklyn Bridge back to Manhattan. He felt so light, so free. She had seen his art and she didn't like it, but she did love him; she had answered his kiss. The cab whisked over the bridge like a hydrofoil. Off to the left, he could see the Statue of Liberty standing solitary and still as they sped by, her bright torch held aloft and shining as if ready and waiting to light the dawn. Damn Blair!

"How a joke?"

"It was years ago." The past was like another life. And it *had* been a joke.

"Adria Cass and I are old friends, and she actually believes that some mystical hand guides her painter's hand and that by giving up human intention—you know, reason—whatever objects she creates become vehicles for cosmic connection. Anyway, one night, *years* ago, we got wrecked—"

"What's 'wrecked'?"

"God, you *have* been buried, Tara. It means high, drugged. Anyway, we got wrecked and decided to experiment with a new kind of paint. We bought a bunch of the stuff. Then—it sounds so childish, now—we went back to Adrias's studio, spread a canvas on the floor and rolled in the paint to just let cosmic energy direct our bodies into non-preconceived patterns. Adria named the painting 'Screwing'." Leon forced another laugh, though he knew it was no use. Tara had shrunk away from him, inch by inch, until she sat huddled in the corner of the car seat. "It was a long time ago, Tara! I'm not like that any more! It was just a joke!"

Her eyes flashed with the dangerous spark of a trapped animal. She was so outraged that she didn't trust herself to speak.

He turned on her, the anger inside him taking life again, his voice rising. "I *told* you that my past is *past*, I can't change it now. What I was then is only a memory. What I am now is yours."

"Leon, when did this past of yours miraculously end?" Her voice was a faint whisper.

"When I met you. Is that what you want to hear? Yes! I slept around for years: with Adria, with Blair, with so many I can't remember them all. But not since you, and never again."

"Leon, we met in August. It's December. That's *four months*." She felt ill. She felt dirty. "Art and sex—sex and art. You've degraded them both. Once I saw the one, I should have guessed the other. It's always been my problem, seeing the best in everything and moving too fast. It's my own fault."

The cab stopped for a red light. Before Leon could realize what was happening, the seat next to him was empty. The door was open, as she had left it, her footsteps already swallowed by the darkness into which she had fled.

TWENTY-THREE

"DOING HOMEWORK SO EARLY in the morning?"
"Yeah, sort of."
"Mind if I join you?"
"Guess not."

Nicky set the carved wood oval he was carrying down on the floor with a clank and, crouching beside it, began to polish its surface with fine sandpaper.

Kally continued to stare at the street from her window-seat. She probably wouldn't see the limousine tonight. The Gothards and their friends seldom came to the restaurant on Fridays or Sundays anymore; now that the place had been written up in *New York Magazine*, they showed up only sporadically, usually mid-week. Kally wondered what rich people did on weekends. Most people she knew went out only on weekends. Of course to people like the Gothards, coming to her father's plain restaurant would hardly be considered "going out." It must be like slumming for them. Why did they come, anyway? Could it really be because the food was good? Well, even she had to admit that her father and her mother were great cooks.

Nicky spoke without looking up from his polishing. "Papa let me off work tonight so I could go up to Massachusetts with Dorina this morning, to a museum that used to be the estate of a famous nineteenth-century sculptor. She has to examine some of the paintings he collected. She's picking me up in her van in half an hour. Leon's coming too. Dorina let me invite him. She likes Leon, I think, in spite of his art. I like him too."

"Tara doesn't like him any more. She didn't even see him before she left for Greece yesterday, and I heard her crying in her room the night before that."

"She saw his work. Papa told me. Listen, would you like to come with us today? It would give you a chance to get away from here for a while, Kally. It's beautiful in the mountains. I know you're still mad at Papa for firing you and keeping you from seeing the Gothards and their friends again."

"No. I don't want to come. You'd think I was chasing Leon, even though Tara doesn't want him anymore."

"No I wouldn't. And I'm sorry I slapped you the other night. No matter what you may have done wrong, I had no right to do that. Papa never hit you, even when you were little. I'm really sorry. I know it's no excuse, but I was just very upset about the discussion on art. I know I'm at a very sort of dangerous place with my own."

"You're *so* narrow. All you think about is your art."

"Well, what do you think about?"

"Being rich. Like the Gothards. I want to be *that* rich. Before Tara sent them here to eat, I only saw pictures of people like that in the newspapers. And the minute I did start to get to know them, Papa ruined it. Who knows how being with people like that could help me get a good job, or meet a really rich boy. Connections. That's what's important to get someplace. It's not what you know, it's who you know. If I were you, I'd use Leon to get some connections in the art world."

"Leon's already told me he'll bring his dealer to the studio to see my paintings. He wants her to see my sculpture, too, because he says abstract pieces sell better. Especially to corporations. That's why I'm hurrying to finish this piece at home. I don't want Dorina to know yet that Leon said he'd help me."

"And when did Leon make this generous offer?"

"Just a couple of days go. He called me. That's when I decided to ask Dorina if I could invite him today. Anyway, even though he's abstract, Leon was trained in drawing and realism. It'll be interesting to see what he thinks about sculpture from the nineteenth century." Nicky stopped sanding and looked up at his sister. She was gazing out the window again. She was chewing on her pencil, and that sly look of hers was creeping into her eyes. He hated that smug expression. She was so pretty! Why did she have to spoil her nice looks with that negative attitude of hers? "Why did you ask me *when* Leon offered to help?" he demanded.

Kally breathed on the windowpane and then traced a heart with her pencil eraser. "Just because. It's no coincidence that he called you right *after* Tara saw his art."

"What's that got to do with anything? He only saw my stuff for the first time a week ago. What do you mean, Kally?"

Kally wiped the heart off the window with the palm of her hand and turned around, still with the sly look in her eyes. "Just that Tara obviously didn't *like* his abstract art, if that's what made her cry in her room. And Leon called you the very next day to tell you he'd help with your art, especially your abstract art."

Nicky picked up his wood piece. "You really have a conniving mind, did you know that?"

"Yup. I know it."

He walked out the door without a word. Kally shrugged and turned back to the window.

✻ ✻ ✻

As they drove up a long dirt road that went deep into the Berkshires, Leon felt they were entering one of Dorina's paintings. The three of them had been silent for some time, and part of him wondered what he was doing on this trip.

Another part of him knew. He had phoned Nicky with only one thought: to keep a channel of communication open to Tara. That was all. But the moment he heard Nicky's voice, he knew he'd called because he needed something more. It had to do with sitting here with Nicky and Dorina in her old van in the middle of these mountains.

Nicky leaned back in his seat, staring at the ceiling. Leon suddenly felt protective of the young man. He realized he had been exactly Nicky's age when he'd decided what kind of art he would make. The choice had been obvious to him; but for Nicky, it was clearly torture. In his own way, Nicky could follow Leon's path or he could follow Dorina's. But he couldn't pursue both with conviction. No artist can park himself in both camps, he thought.

When they reached the sprawling estate, Dorina left them alone; she had work to do inside the main museum-residence. Nicky, still brooding, walked silently beside Leon to what had been the sculpture studio. A friendly guide began to tell them about the artist's life and work, about which Leon knew nothing except that he had done the *Lincoln Memorial* in D.C.

Bored, he wandered around by himself, casually scanning the large number of plaster casts. Part of his brain observed that the dead sculptor's work seemed particularly fresh and "American" in a strange way he had never noticed in this type of stuff before. Actually, except for the obvious, he had hardly noticed American nineteenth-century sculpture at all. It was art from another, more innocent time; it pertained not at all to modern life. Still, there was a certain quality of modernity to it all. What was it Dimitrios had said about contemporizing the Greek ideal?

Some of the figures were draped and others wore one sort of armor or another, but all of the apparel was sculpted to define the nude forms rather than to hide them. They were all, in essence, nudes. The craftsmanship was certainly from another age; hardly anyone worked with this technical ability now. Except, if he were honest, Dorina in her painting. Leon had not seen pure painting skills such as hers in another contemporary artist. But, of course, he didn't keep up on contemporary realist work in general, so what would he know? But most of what he'd glimpsed was commercial and shallow, without either talent or technique. Looking at the sculptor's drawings that were hung here and there on the walls of the studio, he also decided that the superb draftsmanship in Dorina's drawing was just as good. And to be fair, what Dorina said in her studio about the loss of drawing abilities in today's artists, even when representational, was certainly true.

He found himself in an anteroom off the main work area; in it was something large covered with a huge canvas wrap. The guide and Nicky followed him in. "This *Andromeda* figure was never completely finished," the young woman offered. "He was still working its surface when he died." She pulled off the canvas and they saw a marble female nude, nearly life-size. There was no drapery and no armor. The figure was completely nude, lying back and arched over the shape of a rock.

Leon reeled. This female form was fully mature and fully developed, but the composition was virtually the same as *The Promise,* his youthful sculpture of the budding Valerie, with one leg extending down the rock and the head lying back, the body totally open and vulnerable. "Exercised and educated both," Dimitrios had said. Who was this clearly intelligent, independent, feminine figure? She couldn't be Italian or French. She couldn't be from the nineteenth century or the *quatrocento* or from antiquity. She was a quintessential twenty-first century American female nude. And the guide was telling them that this particular work had been sculpted in the early twentieth. "Sovereign," Tara had declared.

"It was a personal piece, just for his own pleasure. He was eighty-one when he died in 1931, and he was still working on the surface polishing."

"*It was The Promise, realized fully.* It needed no more polishing. The white marble was sensuously pure and smooth and translucent. Finished. The sculptor simply hadn't wanted to stop creating it, to stop touching it, to stop loving it. At eighty-one!

"It's warm in here," Leon said tightly. "I think I'll take a walk in the woods." He made his way to the nearest door, anxiety rising in his viscera. His hands—his *hands*—began to shake uncontrollably as he crashed through branches and low brush like a frightened animal.

Pausing near a huge sycamore tree he held on to steady himself. His cries of "No! No! No!" were like a hammer on his brain. It was the same "No!" that had split his mind open when he saw Dorina's art for the first time. Then he ran on.

Bursting into a clearing, he slumped onto a stone bench and then suddenly pitched forward face down into the snow. He couldn't stop it this time. The dam was breaking.

He'd felt the first fissure the day he met Tara, and he had cried through the first real crack in his armor the night he made love with her in the Athens workroom. He had beaten back the mounting, turbulent pressure trying to break through in Dorina's studio, and a gathering torrent three nights ago when Tara fled from the cab on the way home from his studio. Each drop of love he had permitted himself to feel for her had been one drop too many for his internal dam to hold.

He remained prone, moaning convulsively, his fists pressed into his burning temples, his body shaking in a last resistance against the creative force he had denied, had drowned, had turned into anger, into the rage it took to make his art. It was breaking in him at last.

When Dorina found him, he was still lying on the ground. She dropped quickly to her knees beside him and, cradling his head in her arms, lifted his face out of the snow. How long had he been lying here? How long had he been crying here? She could only guess. But it didn't matter. Her heart went out to him.

"It's all right," she offered gently. "Let it *all* out." She pulled him up to lean against her.

"No, no, no . . ."

"Leon, it's okay. What's wrong?" Dorina coaxed softly.

"No." Leon began to settle down as he lay his head on her shoulder.

"You're safe now. What happened in there?"

"*It's too beautiful.*" Again a sound of deep hurting welled into Leon's moans. Dorina felt his pain as if it were her own, and felt she knew what it was about. She had suspected it from the moment she saw his sketch of Tara.

"He felt his love in his hands." Leon was able to say at last as his head slumped, hopeless and limp.

Dorina had sounded out the depth of Leon's vulnerability and decided to take a risk. Maybe she could reach him: "Leon, you're one of *us*. I knew it the moment I saw your sketch. You've never belonged to them in your heart. You're one of *us*. *Listen* to me! I'm not the only artist working in the established Western art traditions." Her words tumbled out in a torrent. She knew this could be her one and only chance with him. She had to tell him all of what he needed to hear while his defenses were down. "Listen! We're not alone! There are other *ateliers* like mine. There are several in the Midwest, where *I* studied, some on the East Coast. There are a few writers, many poets, and a couple of composers, whom I personally know, doing really marvelous work in New York, Minnesota, Arizona, California, lots of places really. I can't say any of us are making big names for ourselves, but we *do* exist, Leon. We aren't many, but we're *real*. You can see some of the work yourself at A IS A GALLERY. I'll take you there to see it. We *need* you. The future needs you. And *you* need *us*, Leon.

Forget your fame! It will take time, but you can do it. You could be the greatest of us all."

He was on his feet, his hair wet, his face red, his eyes wild.

Dorina stood up quickly and grabbed his shoulders. "Leon! What you believe in, deep in your heart, *is possible*. Believe me!"

She had gone too far.

"Believe you and be *like* you? You *admit* you're an unknown. A *nothing*! Believe Tara and hide myself away, blind myself to the world I live in like she does? Or carry the mantle of that sculptor in there and pretend that I live in his time, not my own? *No*! It isn't possible! I won't let you ruin my career as you're trying to ruin Nicky's. No. No. *No!*"

Dorina sat cautiously on the stone bench and put her head precariously in her hands, unable to answer Leon's impassioned rebuke and holding tight reins on her own emotions; inside she was howling like a banshee ready for war.

Leon was gone.

She sat alone in the clearing with the outline of his body in the snow. It looked like the kind of chalk drawing the police make to mark the spot where a victim has died. Where the outline of his head should have been, a jagged circle of brown and withered leaves lay exposed through the tear-melted snow.

TWENTY-FOUR

NICKY STRUGGLED WITH the cork. A bottle of wine could be replaced but, he glanced at the broken glass in the wastebasket, how would he explain the goblet to Dorina? If only he'd thought ahead and brought wine and glasses from the restaurant. It had never occurred to him that Leon would offer Mr. Van Varen a drink while he looked at the work. He gave up and handed the bottle to Leon. His fingers were too nervous to do anything this afternoon. A respected critic, here, to see *his* work.

Van accepted the wine and nosed it approvingly. He felt fifteen years younger today. This was like the old days, visiting an artist's studio at the invitation of the artist, not a dealer. And Leon had been right. This place, anachronistic as it might seem, was a working *atelier*. Who would have dreamed of its existence in this nondescript little building on bustling Broadway, only two doors up from Zabars? Independent of the artist, too. She obviously didn't feel the need for the security of an "artistic" enclave.

"Are you the only apprentice here?" he asked Nicky.

Nicky took a gulp of wine. "Yup, that's me. My teacher, Dorina, has tried out three others since I've been with her, but," he searched for words, "she decided they weren't *atelier* material."

"And what does this teacher of yours say '*atelier* material' *is*?" Van smiled at Nicky. How long had it been since he'd met a young artist who showed no signs of cockiness?

"Well, Dorina, along with several other artists, have been reviving the *atelier* system of teaching. You know, where a master selects students and students select the master they'll study under. Dorina wouldn't use the term 'master,' of course, but she sure does insist that her students display a lot of . . . stamina. She says the art academies in the nineteenth century all but ruined painting, because once you have 'official' schools you have deterioration of quality and stagnation of creativity. Plus, she says modernism all but ruined the *craft* of picturemaking because most contemporary artists, today, anyway, have virtually no knowledge of draftsmanship. Dorina will only accept students who have the staying power to learn the traditional skills of painting, and they need a very long apprenticeship. The first year I was here I spent three hours a day just drawing in charcoal from plaster casts of antique statues. Only after that would Dorina let me pick up a brush, and then for a couple more years, I could only paint in black and white, still working only from casts. I started studying with her when I was ten and never painted even simple subjects from real life in color until I was fourteen. It was grueling!" Nicky shrugged apologetically. "Dorina's very set in her ways."

Leon laughed. "*That*, Van, old boy, is the understatement of the century! This teacher's a dinosaur."

Van held out his glass for more wine; it was a fine Margaux from an excellent year. The lad is so young, he thought, undoubtedly he didn't know what precious wine he'd chosen from the rack; this great red, obviously, was his teacher's taste, and she clearly bought early and knowledgeably and laid her wines down. Fascinating. "Don't call me 'old boy,'" he retorted. "The fact that you brought me to see Nicky's work should remind you that you're not so young and up-and-coming yourself anymore. You're establishment. Besides, some of what Nicky says is true. The biggest reason the early modernists had so much pictorial power is because they *all* were trained in traditional skills."

"Hey Van," Leon jumped in. "Skip the talk and look at the work, okay?"

"I can look and talk at the same time." He hadn't neglected to scrutinize the work; he'd seen all he needed to see, and, in fact, the freshness of Nicky and the whole place intrigued him. In this crude culture, what *artist* lined her cupboards with lace? Nevertheless, you swim with the tide or you sink. The only way to rescue this boy was to speak honestly to him. What this child had to sell, no one of importance was buying. Too bad, really. A century ago the kid would have been hailed as a real "comer." His paintings were brilliantly executed, too brilliantly, perhaps; every intention was realized to perfection. Van had seldom witnessed such joyful exuberance in any art made, certainly, in his own lifetime. And it wasn't 'Pollyanna'; it was mature and sincere. But it was too beautiful and too benevolent. No caustic edges anywhere to resonate the perils of today's all too volatile world, entirely out of step with the times. Yet, it clearly wasn't a throwback either, no sense of any stubborn nostalgic revivalism to enshrine the innocence of the past. There was nothing to write about here.

"You've really accomplished your very complex goals, Nicky," he offered gently. "But your work is a very personal and anti-social vision of the world. And in a world with highly impersonal yet very social attitudes, I truly don't know what I could say to others about it to catch their very distracted attention. Maybe if you had a movement behind you, a group, I could talk about a new direction, even backward, but only you and your teacher? I'm afraid it's just not possible in today's market."

Leon interrupted him impatiently. "What about the abstract pieces, Van?"

"Oh, they're very appealing, very decorative. Look, everything here could have a limited audience. It's just that I can't find a story to make news, or even mention in a general culture piece."

Nicky ignored the burning sensation behind his eyes. "How is my abstract work decorative and Leon's not?" he asked.

"Good question and easy to answer! Why didn't you tell me *Van* was invited to this sneak preview?" Flo Halldon burst into the studio without knocking. Van looked chagrined. "These abstract pieces are too small. If they were enlarged by about twenty times, I might be able to sell them." Stopping to look hard at Nicky, she said, "You're cute, too. And young. That helps." Then she swept quickly around the room, viewing the paintings and drawings as she whirled by. "Bold enough color and light. Powerful visual effects. Dramatic. Dynamic. If only they'd left out the subject matter. Drawings too classical."

How little they know, Van sighed. "That is *not* why Leon's work is popular, my dear Flo. Leon couldn't possibly have lasted this long if his work was merely large decorative art. Leon's work is a forceful and accurate metaphor for today's society. It displays a repressed power, a stopping of all motion, including *e-motion*—even molecular—deadening all false hopes of earthly joy. It blatantly refutes not only traditional values but *all* values. Period. It's anti-beauty. It's anti-meaning. It's anti-everything that animates life. It's large because he means to confront us, and having confronted us, the work just sits there and stares at us. 'This is all there is,' it says. 'Don't dream of anything more than this. This is it. And this is *you*'."

Leon said nothing.

"Don't 'my dear' me, Van. So you're the critic. So what? I never pretended to know a lot about art. But I do know about merchandising: Leon's name is money in the bank. His stuff is sold before it's made, and the battle's getting bloody out there. I can't sell anything I can't market better than the next guy. She turned to Nicky. "You know, that's just the real world these days. Your paintings are swell and your abstracts are real pretty, but it's war out there." She turned to Leon. "Except for corporate clients, I don't think I could launch *you* today." She kissed the air around Leon and Van. "Look, I have to run. Thanks Leon. Good luck, young man." She stopped herself in mid-flight halfway out the door. "Oh, Van! If you can come up with some hook to hang a story on, let me know. I'd love to take the kid on if he's a friend of Leon's, but my mind's just not focused these days—"

She was gone, leaving behind a stunned silence. Leon thought he would kill her the next time he saw her.

Nicky stared, bright-eyed, at the closed door.

"Dealers." Van snorted. "She's all torn up inside. She can't take the heat. Why doesn't she go back to selling tee shirts? She's as burned out as half the artists pounding the pavement."

Nicky poured wine into his glass, up to the rim, and gulped it down like water.

"Don't let her get to you, Nicky," Leon tried. "She's that way with everybody. That's the art world. Like everybody else, she's in the business of surviving."

"Dorina says our business as artists is to show why surviving is worthwhile."

Van felt sorry for the boy. Flo needn't have been so lacking in tact. "Look, Leon. Why don't you try the Malinow gallery? Jacques is foreign-born and older. He might be drawn to the romanticism of this work. Flo's never handled anything representational. This might be too original and daring for a traditional gallery like Jacques's—the work is so *committed*—but you could give it a try."

"Am I interrupting?"

Nicky nearly backed out the window. "Dorina!"

"Nicky. Hello Leon." Dorina looked at Van, waiting to be introduced.

Van smiled and extended a hand. So this was Dorina, of the hard opinions and the soft lace. "I'm Robert Van Varen. Leon invited me here to view Nicky's work."

Dorina remained standing without removing her hat and coat. "I see. And have you viewed it?"

Leon and Nicky exchanged glances. Nicky had assured Leon that Dorina did restoration work every Wednesday and wouldn't be in the studio at all today. What was she doing here? Both knew enough to keep silent.

"Yes, and yours, as well. It's all very interesting. This *atelier* . . . everything." Van felt distinctly unwelcome, even though the woman was as courteous as could be.

"I am familiar with your name, Mr. Van Varen. Are you here to view Nicky's work or *review* it?"

"Well, sure, I'd *like* to review it, but to be honest with you, this work is not really about what's going on in the art community right now." He smiled carefully. "Nicky's work, being romantic and realistic at the same time, is rather . . . well, it's an unpopular viewpoint these days. Your own technical abilities are flawless, by the way."

Leon's head snapped up. It was one thing to be rejected because your work was no good; it was something else to be rejected because your work was *too good*. This whole idea was backfiring fast.

Dorina hung her coat on a rack and tossed her hat to the petit-point settee. "Then if your 'viewing' is finished here, you will please leave." She didn't look at Leon. "Since you invited Mr. Van Varen, you may leave with him, Leon."

"*I* invited them, Dorina." Nicky glanced at the wastebasket. Now he wouldn't even be able to try to replace the wine glass. Dorina regarded Leon. "Is that so? But this isn't your studio, Nicky. It's mine." She turned to him. "How many of Mr. Van Varen's reviews have you read, Nicky?"

"Well, none, really, I guess. You always said that his magazine was—"

"Well, let me recall some of Mr. Van Varen's articles for you." She locked eyes with Van. "One reviewed a darkened room full of TV screens oscillating rapidly but showing no image. Another gave notice to 'sound sculpture' that was a room amplified with traffic sounds. Let's see: a canvas painted over with human excrement and framed in monkey bones; paint thrown into the propeller of a plane running in reverse and splashed back onto a gigantic canvas; a slab of yellow foam rubber pasted over with torn-in-half theatre posters; 'drawings' made from a blindfolded 'artist' who scribbled on paper to the motion of a subway, thus creating a new 'artwork' between each stop and—one of the most newsworthy—a circle of fireworks that exploded at random, scattering the onlookers and causing the fire department to be called, but the event had been planned that way from the beginning. Well, I can't remember them all. I must confess I didn't read them all. Only the ones that are making art history."

Van returned Dorina's glare. She was such a tiny woman, but what spunk! "You forgot the fortune cookies containing 'minimal novels'." He smiled, amused. "News is news."

"And why do you think that *our* work is *not* news?"

"The public has come to expect something that will shock them, jolt them into feeling sensations. Their threshold for sensorium is very high these days."

"*Epater le Bourgeois*? That's pretty out of date, wouldn't you say? I'd say the public is shockproof by now." Dorina started to ready her paints and brushes.

"Shock the bourgeoisie!" She moved her easel into light from the window. She laughed. It felt wonderful, to say the thoughts she had harbored for so long. She had asked him to leave and he had chosen to stay, so she went on. "I have always loved that slogan. Most of the artists who want to do the 'shocking' are middle-class themselves. Modernism is reputed to express irony. Well, the most ironic twist of all is that the very class they seek to escape has embraced the works of these so-called avant-garde artists. Their 'art' is *retail,* the darling of interior designers and the fashion industry. The middle classes *love* modern art. Now that, I agree, is 'irony'."

"You sound bitter, Ms. Swing."

"I am. But only because you don't give us equal time."

"What do you mean, equal time?" Van looked at her with genuine confusion.

"I mean that the *philosophical* base of most so-called 'modern' art has always been the same. You know as well as I that many serious artists in the twentieth century sought to give primitivism and mysticism a modern face, and they ransacked the whole of art history to do it. Fine. Artistic freedom and all that. Exploring the dark and the absurd may be what some artists need to go through, but the best of those types always emerge from the cave back into the light. It's the debt we owe to maturity. But if you and your cronies were fair, you would also write about art whose makers never entered the cave of anxiety, irrationalism and fake reality to begin with, those who shed light on the real world: the humanistic light of reason and beauty. It's time to grow up, boys."

Nicky bit the rim of his glass. Dorina was getting very agitated. She'd always advised him to avoid discussions of art unless there was something to be gained. The studio should be a peaceful oasis, she said. Today, it was Dorina who was bringing unrest to her oasis; he blanched, remembering his own lack of responsibility in bringing a critic here without permission.

Van refused to take offense. How long had it been since anyone thought he was worth the effort of an argument? He watched Dorina paint as she talked. He was utterly enchanted. With the painting and with her. What a powerhouse she was! What conviction! At her age! She had to be at least forty-five!

"Look carefully at our work, Mr. Van Varen, before you say we're not news." Dorina's words tumbled out like an avalanche, words held in check for too long, words full of invisibility, loneliness and pain. "*We* are attempting to *advance* the work of the Greek and Renaissance artists by showing you the *contemporary embodiment* of universal ideals, fully in light of the knowledge we've learned about man and the universe today, in light of science and the progress of what has been achieved in our own era. We do not bastardize or repeat the past. We *improve* upon it, creating positive modern images that point the way to a better future, at the same time trying to resonate a sense of grace and beauty that never needed to be abandoned. We are pro-beauty, pro-human, pro-individualism, pro-reason, pro-world: pro, pro, pro. Your kind, artists and critics alike, have never been *for* anything except your own 'elite' positions."

Silence. No rebuttal. So Dorina continued. Nothing could stop her now.

"Now you choose to support and review the flotsam and jetsam that has taken modernism's place: the glut of so-called postmodernist art that has become nothing more than cheap gimmicks, blatant commercialism and, especially, bald socio-political propaganda, the Will to Power. Well, do it if you must, but why shut out opposing views? Why not expose your readers to the light as well as the dark, to beauty as well as ugliness, to harmony as well as dissonance—"

She stopped painting and walked slowly to the window. Pressing her forehead against it, tears streamed down her face unchecked. What a fool she was. What a stupid, stupid fool. She could not stop crying now, anymore than she could stop talking before. "Don't ever permit any hostile element into your studio," she had always warned Nicky. She had broken her own rule. She had not only permitted Leon to enter her studio, but her life. She had permitted herself to hope for him . . . and for his art. Now, because of him, she had ranted and raved in front of the enemy.

She turned to Leon. "All right. Now, we've done it to each other." Walking carefully to the door, she opened it.

"Go away, all of you. Please."

Van stood helplessly by the door. What had happened here?

Nicky ran to her.

"You too, Nicky. Go. Please."

Leon was the first to walk out.

Crossing Central Park at 72nd street, he flopped down on his "bench," which, as usual, was occupied. Two bag ladies sat together at the opposite end. One hugged a sack containing her belongings close to her; the other rocked a shopping cart stuffed with household goods back and forth like a baby carriage; both wore sneakers and several overcoats. The slab of iron was uncomfortable as hell, and that suited him just fine; it served its purpose and added to his bad mood. He had made the "bench" five years ago as a joke, what else? No one called the piece officially by that name, of course. Too much money had been paid for it, and investments had kept the last three-quarters of a century of art going; anybody who mattered knew that. So he had entitled the work *Solidarity* to make it ring with respectability to the know-nothings. But everyone "*in* the know" remembered the old bum who had become a permanent fixture on the real bench at that location for years. So Leon had known before the fact that the public would continue using his sculpture as a bench. *That* was the point. The joke was on the City, for buying what amounted to another bench for $400,000.

Leon had laughed all the way to the bank. But today, he found nothing funny. And it wasn't just the disaster at Dorina's studio. It was also Tara's absence causing his loss of humor. She had been gone for four days. He hadn't worked in four days. He had opened his studio each evening, walked around the still-flat sheets of copper, glanced over the drawings for the work, drank a beer and left. He could see, now, that the intricate sphere he had envisioned came too close to decorative art; it had no aggressive power. It was too beautiful. He had been too happy when he designed it.

Sullenly, he pondered the outdoor sculpture placed in front of a few of the apartment houses across the street on Fifth Avenue, one block either way from where he sat: metal lumps, arcs, verticals—solid constructions of abstract form or simple line drawings in space. He thought of other outdoor art he knew well, installed at important buildings and sites here and there around the city: the crushed and corroded auto parts welded together on a hospital lawn, a red spiral of painted steel coiled like a spring over fifty feet of concrete before the entrance to a bank. But what else could inhabit America's modern public spaces? What sort of monumental art would Tara wish to see? What would heroic sculpture actually look like in today's context? Statues of generals on horseback were hardly appropriate for men who walked on the moon. What kind of idealized art could speak to people today? Could any? Interesting question.

Did Dorina Swing have the answer? What was it about the woman that brought out the worst in him? So remarkable of her to know that, deep down, seeing the work of that nineteenth-century sculptor would hurt him where he had once hurt the most. Perceptive and cruel. And in return, his inviting people like Flo and Van into her studio had been a monstrous insult to her. And for what had he hurt Dorina? He and she detonated like pure hypergolics whenever they came near each other. Why bother? His idea hadn't even worked; neither Van nor Flo was going to help Nicky anyway.

No doubt about it. He'd been behaving uncharacteristically ever since Tara left him. He'd even scouted out A IS A GALLERY with the thought of taking Van there. "A IS A," he found to his amusement, stood for Aristotle's theory of existence but was also a tribute to the Italian Renaissance, where *Artists* were also *Artisans*. He'd even bought one of Nicky's paintings there, strictly in the hope of impressing Tara. What a jerk he'd been! Anyway, he couldn't get to Tara through Nicky's art in any way whatsoever because *nobody* could succeed at championing art like Nicky's and Dorina's in any big way. Not in *this* culture, where beauty kneels before the almighty buck. What a joke! Wait.

Just a damn minute—

He stood and stared down at his own work.

This is what Tara hates. This joke. This nothing. It's not the man she hates, but the art, *any* art that dehumanizes or trivializes. If nothing else, his own work expertly rode the dragon of baldly expressing twentieth-century cynicism, as Van had so succinctly noted.

And yet, right now, his personal contribution to the last century's perpetual temper tantrum, didn't seem to mean anything to him any longer. Not even as a joke. So this inability to do anything in his studio every night wasn't just a temporary thing? Whatever had driven him seemed truly to be over. He felt empty. He felt finished anyway.

Then what he had told Tara was true! His art really didn't mean anything to him? On *any* level?

He let the idea roll around in his brain, as he walked round and round the "bench," starring at it with fresh interest. Then he threw his head back and began to laugh. Hell! Yes! Oh, the hilarity of it all! He *did* have one last joke in him, one so bad it was brilliant. One that would rock the art world. And one that would prove to Tara in a way that would leave absolutely no doubt about his love for her over allegiance to his work.

Leon jogged to the nearest phone booth and dialed information. "Manhattan. Residence. *Alexandros, Basilious Alexandros.*"

TWENTY-FIVE

AS THE PLANE BROKE THROUGH a cloud cover into a morning of luminous blue, Tara rested her head against the seat with the intention of letting herself think seriously about Leon for the first time in ten days. When they weren't presiding over meetings or scouting sites, Dimitrios had kept her so busy with research in the archives of the Heraklion Museum that she'd had no time or energy for anything else. Now Crete lay behind them, and after a couple of days back in Athens, she'd be off to New York again. Dimitrios, at work beside her, gave his concentration to the piles of paper in front of him. Strewing his handwritten notes over both their eating trays, he had plunged immediately into creating a preliminary blueprint for their next expedition. Complications loomed: three separate countries, private and public money, six archaeologists, one geologist, and a larger team of divers than ever before assembled; the sheer gymnastics of the venture would overwhelm anyone less bold than Dimitrios. Yet, he seized each problem that raised its head with the thrill and skill of a snake handler; she had never seen him so excited about a project.

There was reason for excitement. Postponing thoughts of Leon yet again, she pulled papers from her briefcase and nudged Dimitrios playfully to make room on her own tray.

"If we can verify the details of the social and religious practices of the Minoans, history will be made. Right?" she asked. "I mean, I'm not exaggerating this thing, am I?"

Dimitrios nodded indulgently. "History will be made."

"*No one* has yet discovered royal burial grounds on Crete. Right?"

"Right. Don't forget that even those large and impressively constructed tombs discovered near Knossos were ransacked of their contents. So we can speculate, but it's impossible to determine for sure whether or not they were created for royalty."

A flight attendant arrived with the bar cart, but Dimitrios threw up his hands with a diffident smile. No room on their trays for a peanut let alone a drink. "*But!*" he continued to Tara, his mind vaulting ahead in anticipation, "I'm sure the underwater city cited by Homer that *we* shall excavate with the help of that state-of-the-art American equipment is untouched by looters. Pristine! If we unearth a palace as important as Knossos, or even one like the lesser sites at Amalia or Phoestos, *intact*? Yes! History will be made." He winked. "By *us*!"

"But this project won't even *begin* in physical excavation for two or three years. We won't 'unearth' any answers soon."

"Right! But so what? Maybe we'll find a few gods along the way to garner your attention," he teased.

Tara glanced at him and shook her head affectionately. It didn't matter to him if the project spanned the rest of his lifetime. He loved his work. "I guess you're right," she said thoughtfully. "It's what keeps me going. I think that deep down I chose archaeology as a profession because ancient Greece is so intriguing as the seminal time of heroic gods and godlike heroes. I've been told recently that I'm a hero worshiper. It's true. I love heroes. And there aren't any anymore."

Dimitrios looked up, and then quickly returned to his papers. So something *had* happened in New York; he was sure of it now. Except for her work, she simply hadn't mentioned New York at all. He'd known all along why she loved ancient Greece; the surprise was that *she* was beginning to understand her attraction to her work. Don't let me be too late, he prayed to no one. Don't let me lose her before I can make my case to her.

"Well," he said cautiously, "heroes are a step in the right direction. Do you think I'll live long enough to see you advance to loving just an ordinary man?"

"Any man I love would not be 'ordinary'."

"Well said. And no ordinary man would require *you* as the guardian of his love." He drew more papers from his attaché. This kind of talk edged too close to his purpose for comfort. He had chosen his time and place, and this wasn't it.

Tara turned her attention out the window. And, at last, to Leon. Whatever Leon might be, the term 'ordinary' did not apply. She must summon the courage to fit all of the puzzling pieces into a coherent picture.

A man fleeing from his true loves. That much was certain. Why couldn't he have hung onto his vision of what he wanted? He hadn't just given up on his dreams; he'd spent his entire adult life attacking them, as if driven to destroy them. He'd told her he had changed as a man because of her, and she believed him. But if that were true, he really hadn't changed at all, just reverted back to what he once had been. Could the same reverse metamorphosis occur with his art? She shuddered. Those huge, dead monsters he made. Frozen.

Frozen.

She felt light and heavy at the same time as her brain grappled with the identification that what Leon had done as an adolescent was to arrest all emotion, all feeling . . . all life. He had been such a romantic boy that nothing less than the total, brutal repression of all the childhood ideals he had loved would permit his sentient survival. It must have been the only way he could withstand the shock and pain of discovering that dreams do not necessarily come true. He was angry, not at the world, as he said, but at himself for what he perceived to be his own stupidity.

And she had run out on him!

Just when he had dared to surface again, to open his heart and extend his hand in trust again, to lift his eyes to the possibilities again. In the studio, he had taken her face in his hands so tenderly. He had confessed that he believed for the first time since he was young that happiness was possible . . . with her. He had begun to believe again, because of his love for her.

She felt sick. She squeezed her eyes tight to prevent tears. She'd been concerned only with her own confusion, her own suffering. What private hell was he enduring now?

Dimitrios was stuffing papers back into his case. Passengers stood and crowded into the aisle. The plane had landed; she hadn't even noticed.

"Hurry." Dimitrios shot her a roguish smile. "We haven't much time to make our connecting flight."

"Connecting flight?" Tara struggled to pull herself together. "Aren't we in Athens?"

"Yes, but we're continuing on." His smile broadened.

"What do you mean? Where?"

"I'm taking you on a long weekend to Istanbul. We both deserve it. I wanted to surprise you. Our reservations are confirmed, so all we have to do is arrive." He looked at her closely, and laughed. "Well, I didn't intend to surprise you *that* much. You look as if you're in shock!"

She felt dizzy. "Dimitrios, I can't." she stammered. "I have to finish these reports and get back to New York—"

He led the way. "No, you don't. I say you need a little vacation bonus. Work can wait. We've done a month's worth of work already this trip, and you've never been to Istanbul." He grinned at her over his shoulder; he looked positively jubilant.

Tara clamped her sunglasses over her eyes. Why

couldn't he have thought of this some other time? *Any* other time? But how could she disappoint him?

Dimitrios slipped the tote from her shoulder and swung it over his own. He curled his arm through hers, fairly skipping them through the terminal. "So," he said beaming at her. "Istanbul, here we come."

TWENTY-SIX

THE PHONE RANG. Adria's voice was frantic. "Leon! Somebody's buying up your work! All over the place! I just got off the phone with a friend who's on the Arts Council. She was calling to tell me that the city's considering selling that Central Park piece of yours. Flo's offering to buy it on behalf of some fellow who she says is systematically buying up everything of yours he can lay his hands on. Do you know about this?"

"Yeah, I know. Flo called me before the first sale almost two weeks ago. Evidently the guy's buying fast. Says he wants to put all my stuff in one place."

Where? A museum just for you, or what?"

"Don't know. Neither does Flo. She's never met the guy—they do all their business over the phone—but she loves him because he wires cash in advance."

"What do you mean, you don't know? Somebody's buying up all of your work, and you don't know who or why?"

Leon laughed. "I mean I don't know, and I don't care."

"Well, if you don't care what happens to it, I do! For God's sake, Leon, you have to think about your place in history! This is precisely why we're lobbying to get federal laws passed to protect artists' rights to their works after they're sold. And Flo's making a fortune! What are you getting?"

"Not a damn thing, Adria. And I don't want any rights to my work after it's sold. It becomes the property of the person who bought it. If I design a building, should I have a say in whom the owner sells it to next? Forget it."

Forget it?" Adria's voice was incredulous. "Are you mad? This isn't buildings, you idiot. This is *art!*"

Leon winced as the phone slammed down in his ear.

✳ ✳ ✳

On the third floor, inside the room designated for the public hearing, TV cameras bullied their way through a throng of protesters that spilled out into the hallway as cameramen jockeyed their positions in order to film every angle of what had become a media event for the evening news programs on New York's local channels. The huge turnout was triple what the Parks Commission had expected. There were always clumps of activists hanging around and disrupting hearings on matters of the city's parks, pushing one cause or another, but this group had all the earmarks of careful organization. Gina Lopez had held her post as Parks Commissioner for only thirteen months. Today, she felt her most insecure.

The red-haired woman was approaching the microphone again. Of the two recognizable contingents inside the meeting room, she wasn't sure where this young woman belonged. One group was certainly representative of the art world; their dress was casual but studied. The other discernible group was made up of men in expensive suits and women wearing fur coats. But it hardly mattered whom she represented because everyone in the room seemed in vehement agreement that *Solidarity* should stay where it was.

"It's not the artist's fault if your department could never keep people from sitting on his work as if it were a bench," Denise Sommers was testifying. "You should have protected it against the public from the beginning. It's a work of art, after all. If government institutions don't protect public art in its time, then the art is lost chronologically. Art is history! And it's your job, just as much as any museum's, to guard that history for posterity. If your department buys a work of art *for* the public, it's your responsibility to protect it *from* the public, not just sell it to get rid of the problem."

A member of the Board spoke up. "But surely we all know that many artworks in the park are used by the public. Children climb all over the *Alice in Wonderland* piece every summer. They've been doing it for years."

Denny smiled patronizingly. "But that piece isn't really serious art, is it?"

Commissioner Lopez spoke: "The point is, as far as *this* work is concerned, we've tried everything from signs to fences, and we can't move the piece to another location because the artist stipulated in his contract that it be placed in that exact spot and never be moved. And now we have a chance to sell it at a very attractive profit and have it replaced by another work of art at no cost at all to the taxpayers. The Parks Commission will then have a half-million dollars with which to commission other works of art, so without losing anything except what turned out to be a bench, we can support other artists to make other things for other parts of the park. That's the real advantage of this opportunity, which I'm attempting to explain here today: more arts commissions, more work for artists."

Adria marched to the stage. Lopez rightly guessed (because of all the air kisses surrounding the woman) that this queen-size quarterback was behind the entire grandstand public play, complete with TV coverage, no less. "What I see is this." Adria beamed a vivacious smile into the red lights of the TV cameras. "If the contract says it can never be moved, then you can't sell it, can you? Because by selling it, you'd be moving it."

"We've determined that that would be a very narrow reading of the law," the attorney for the Commission responded impatiently. "We've determined that, although we don't have the right to relocate it, we do have the right to sell it without violating the intent of the artist's contract."

The Commissioner began to address the new work that was being donated to the city to replace *Solidarity*: "The proposed piece was done by the only living son of the very famous Fontana brothers who, of course, did all of the 'pointing up' and rough marble sculpture for those pre-eminent sculptors who created our most treasured public monuments all over the country in the late nineteenth and early twentieth centuries."

"This is a *marble* piece?" Adria's supercilious smile intensified. "The weather will destroy it. That's reason enough right there to leave well enough alone."

"No it won't. Mateo Fontana, who sculpted the original work twenty years ago, is still at work, and he's agreed to design a sort of house for the piece, a smaller version reminiscent of the one that surrounds the *Lincoln Memorial* in D.C. Why don't I just let him show you what he has in mind? And this will be donated, mind you, by the same man who is buying the ben— Sorry, buying *Solidarity*." The Commissioner sat down, removed her glasses, and busied herself with her handkerchief again.

The crowd stared as a short man with only a few gray hairs left clinging to his scalp walked proudly onto the platform, carrying some drawings under one arm. Holding the sketches up one by one for both audience and cameras to view, he explained his plan and how it would not only protect the figure standing within it but also how it would be lined all along its interior with one continuous marble bench. This, he stated lucidly, would be part of the architecture and not the art, so the public could sit and rest, since that's what they seemed to like to do at that spot anyway, and contemplate the marble figure at their leisure.

A young male protester raised his hand politely from the crowd. The elderly sculptor acknowledged him.

"Excuse me, I don't mean to be rude, but I'm not familiar

with your name. Could you tell us what you've been doing for the past twenty years in the art world since you sculpted the original work we're discussing?"

The proud stance of Mateo Fontana wilted just a little. "Well, my kind of art, and my father's, went out of style for a while, so... I've been very busy. My shop still employs three sculptors, and we're quite successful."

"Well, what is it you actually *do*?"

"We work for the most well-known interior designers in New York. Our works, our plaster castings, have been mounted in some of the most prestigious townhouses in the city. And we still, sometimes, do a marble copy of some famous work from antiquity."

Adria's face burned red. Leon's art being sold and replaced by an outdated, traditional figure in marble, sculpted by a craftsman who supplies *decorators*? "Why isn't Leon Skillman here to defend his work?" she demanded. "I called him to inform him of this hearing, but did *you* invite him to come and speak for himself about what happens to his work?"

"Of course Mr. Skillman has been consulted." Lopez breathed a sigh of relief. Thank God the lawyer had warned her she'd better call the artist personally. "Mr. Skillman, as I would have told you all in good time, was in fact a little quiet when I first told him what we had in mind, selling his work, that is. But when I told him what is going to replace it he, in fact, burst out laughing over the phone he was so pleased at the news."

Denise and Adria spoke as one. "Well, what *is* going to replace it?"

The Commissioner looked around the room baffled. "Well, what do you mean? What do you think it's been doing standing here on the stage all afternoon? Do you think we'd hold a hearing and not let the public *see* what is going to grace Central Park as well as bring $500,000 to our budget? It just arrived from Greece yesterday, all the way from

Stagirus. It's right over there beside the flag. Didn't you see it?" Lopez fidgeted with her glasses again. What on earth did they think it was doing there on the stage, if not to be seen? Why the nuisance of having to explain anything to these hostile people in the first place?

Adria, Denny, and the entire crowd, including TV cameramen, swung their attention to the flagpole situated at the end of the platform where the speakers sat. Next to the flag stood an over-life-size figure of an older but dignified man with a full beard and one hand raised, as if asking for silence and attention. His flowing marble robes fell gracefully about his body, and even though the figure stood still, he seemed about to move forward with great thought; his eyes were intent in an intelligent face, and his lips were parted as if he were about to speak. The abstract design of the sculpture was powerful and commanding, it's lines fluid but urgent and demanding. It had stood, waiting, during the whole meeting. Yet no one had noticed it.

"Let us see, too!" "Come on, move over!" The few dozen people who, because of the big turnout, had been forced to stand out in the hallway and listen patiently to the proceedings over a loudspeaker, began pushing their way into the room to get a look at what was going on. Peering over the shoulders of the crowd in the hearing room, they joined the collective stupor as everyone stood struck dumb in recognition and shocked outrage at what was intended to replace the work of one of the most famous contemporary artists of the time.

Denny and Adria cried out together:

"*Aristotle!*"

TWENTY-SEVEN

"I CAN'T DO THIS, DIMITRIOS! What if they find me out? It's blasphemy to them!"

"They won't find out. You're wearing pants, you're tall and your hair is short. Here, wrap this scarf up around your neck and up over your chin the way they do. Put on your gloves. I want you to see a prayer session close up. Just let me do the talking to get us in, do as I do and don't speak."

Approaching the mosque, they passed men ritualistically washing their feet at a public fountain. Inside, in their stocking feet, they sat quietly on sumptuous oriental rugs while the Turkish males prostrated themselves on the floor; then, turning their faces to the walls, the worshipers kneeled and began rocking back and forth on their heels, chanting softly. Tara absorbed it all in silent amazement: the domed architecture of the building seemed to reverberate with the sounds of the hypnotic ritual, making the whole experience appear as if the mosque were a microcosm of some secluded otherworldly world, a place where one felt anaesthetized by all the repetitive sensory stimuli as well as removed from daily demands. In the background, she could hear the amplified wailing from the minarets that called the faithful to prayer five times a day as it rang out over the city, commanding and eerie. Surreptitiously, she glanced back at the women's section where she would have been forced to go if her gender were known. She felt saddened for these women, still regarded as inferior, interchangeable chattel. Dull superstition clouded the eyes of the devout, whatever their sex.

But outside, modern Turkish women raced around the city in western attire, with heads unveiled, and held jobs that required independence and know-how. And other remnants from the lavish Ottoman Empire spoke not of the brutality of that regime, but of its devotion to beauty, to design, to exactitude. Istanbul was a city of contrasts: primitivism versus progress, fundamentalism versus feminism, beauty versus brutality. Even geographically, one part of the city lay in Europe, the other in Asia.

"I can't drink any more tea!"

"You must. Otherwise you'll offend them."

"At every stall?"

The Grand Bazaar was, indeed, grand. They had finally learned to hurry past hundreds of hawking merchants until they found certain booths where they thought they might actually buy something. Dimitrios was already overloaded with purchases, including her most treasured one, an antique prayer rug. Now Tara sat on a small, squat stool, sipping her fifteenth glass of sugared tea and surrounded by dozens of hand-painted plates. Although the asking price for the plates wasn't high to begin with, the mustachioed young salesman gave her his total attention and drank tea with her as they bargained the price. She marveled at his persistence and stifled a laugh. "He must drink gallons of this stuff by the end of a day," she giggled to Dimitrios. "He must be a camel!"

On the way out of the Bazaar, knowing that whatever they had paid was too much, a young boy chased after them, waving long brass shishkabob skewers in the air. "One American dollar each!" he cried.

Dimitrios hailed a taxi.

"Okay! Special price. Ten dollars for a dozen."

"Wait!" The boy rushed to the taxi window. "Last price! Five dollars the bunch! Three dollars!"

The cab pulled away from the curb. "Okay! I give you free!"

Dimitrios couldn't stop laughing. Tara, tears running down her cheeks from laughter, piled packages on his lap.

"Free?" she gasped.

"Too much!" they agreed.

Just having fun seemed to have become an end in itself.

Their hotel, built a century ago to receive passengers from the Orient Express, now reflected a refurbished grandeur as sumptuous and exotic as the famous train. In her room, Tara studied the prayer rug and laid it atop various other oriental rugs that overlapped each other Muslim style. The walls and ceiling of the bedroom were as completely covered as the floor; blooming with flowers and vines entwined together to form intricate patterns on mosaic tile, every surface of every perimeter of the jewel-like chamber intermeshed with so much ornamentation that one moved, mesmerized, through a palpable peace. The room was a miniature of one of the several mosques they had visited; familiarly called "The Blue Mosque," it was their aesthetic favorite.

She left the rug on the floor—she couldn't bear to pack it away in her suitcase just yet—and set herself to wrapping eight ceramic plates into her carry-on luggage. Each plate was a cherished memory of the astounding attention to ornament she had encountered in this remarkable culture. How had Dimitrios known that this exotic environment would wipe out all her other preoccupations? She had obeyed her own orders with surprising ease once she and Dimitrios were alone in this city. On the plane here, three days ago, she had stated those orders firmly to herself: "Postpone work, postpone Leon, postpone New York. Just have a good time and refresh your mind."

Since the moment of their arrival, Dimitrios had choreographed their activities with the same imagination he gave his work, and she had danced willingly to his direction. Istanbul was captivating. And the long weekend, like a single drop of arrested time, had eclipsed the rest of the world. Dimitrios had delighted in introducing her to every new adventure and, she noticed, they had never once talked shop.

Yesterday, even though it was cold, Dimitrios had bundled her up in blankets borrowed from the hotel and taken them on a privately hired boat for a cruise down the Bosporous. Later, they had remained silent on a quick trek through Istanbul's archaeological museum, too polite to observe aloud that most of Turkey's greatest treasures were from the ancient Greek settlements of Asia Minor. They had danced to Turkish music and drunk exotically flavored vodkas. Dimitrios had bought her a bracelet worked intricately in both silver and gold, a delicate recreation of one she had admired at Topkapi palace. At first, she had refused the gift because it was so soon after her birthday, but he persisted by saying that she would deny him the pleasure of enjoying it from time to time when she wore it.

She clasped the cuff to a wrist now, and passed her hand before the mirror. The gold of the bracelet echoed the russet-colored velvet of her caftan, the silver, the sparkle of her gray eyes. She smiled at what she saw: relaxed, she was ready to fly back to "the real world" tomorrow morning.

And she was ready for dinner. Dimitrios had suggested they dine quietly in the living room that adjoined their two bedrooms. Looking out over the Bosporous at night, the opulence of the intimate, blue and gold-gilded parlor outshone any modern restaurant in town. She opened the *portieres* to the suite.

Dimitrios, wearing a short black lounging jacket with burgundy foulard and gray slacks, was standing, deep in thought by the window. A round table in the alcove dripped brocade and glittered with crystal. Tara felt instantly transported to that original train of a hundred years ago, speeding along to frontiers new and unknown. This sitting room had been designed to reproduce the train's royal dining car. Dimitrios's bedroom was a reproduction of a room in Versailles, the train's departure point. Joining him in the dining car, she curled an arm through his and followed his gaze with her own. Dozens of lights from otherwise invisible boats swung back and forth across the water below; their dining room seemed to slip smoothly past while the lights remained still, dotting the route to mark their journey. She smiled up at him. "Thank you, Dimitrios."

He pressed his lips to the palm of her hand; he seemed very serious. "I want you to call me 'Dimitri,' Tara." He moved to the bar to open wine.

Live music from the combo they had danced to only the night before was piped in from the hotel's restaurant through speakers built into the bar. For a moment, Tara actually thought she heard the clicking of train wheels on a track. *Dimitri*. Would it seem strange the first time she called him that? Two waiters in white jackets appeared silently to serve their dinner and disappeared just as silently. There was no need for conversation; the surroundings, the sounds and the sights from the window were enough. *Dimitri*. Could she get used to that now?

"Well." Dimitrios lifted his glass to her, to the room, to the weekend. "Are you ready to return to your heroes?"

"Yes." She touched his glass with hers, "but I'll never forget this interlude. It's been like a—" She looked out the window, confused; she had been about to say, *honeymoon*. "like a wonderful 'vacation bonus,' as you called it."

"And what would your hero be like in person, Tara? If you met him at a party, let's say?"

She laughed easily. "Why he'd be just like you, I guess. I've always dreamed of finding someone just like—"

Before he lowered his head, too stricken to speak, Tara saw the collision of joy and suffering in his eyes. She stared blindly at the top of his bowed head; she looked carefully around the room. The train had stopped. They had reached their destination: the frontier to the new and unknown. The room stood still. Her hand rose, imperceptibly, to touch her mouth; on it was the remembrance of a kiss.

Dimitrios raised his head. His eyes were clear again. "Forgive me."

She thought he was smiling, but his expression was more radiant than a smile: it was some inner fusion of pain and happiness that was washing his face with this serene glow. She looked into his dark eyes, seeing nothing and seeing everything.

"Forgive me"—his voice was steady, deliberate—"but I was only leading up to a well-rehearsed speech: I didn't expect you to wipe out the whole first half of it with that response." His eyes were steady, unguarded. "Now I'll amend my speech by asking you a direct question: *Why not me*, Tara? Aside from the fact that I don't mirror your ideal physical image, why not *me* instead of someone *like* me?" His hands were steady, palms up.

The private dining room hung suspended now, above the lights on the Bosporous, the way the one in New York had hung over the lights of the city on the night of her birthday.

"Tara, I've tried to tell you in so many other ways for so long, but you have never heard me. Will you listen to my words?" Tara sat perfectly still. She was listening.

"I'm telling you these things tonight because I want you to think about them while you're away from me. I want you to know that I love you."

She stared at his hands on the table. She was seeing: she was diving with her hand in his hand, beneath the surface of the sea. She could see smiling eyes—they were brown—through his mask. His arm was tight around her waist as they hung on the anchor line together that day. She was hearing: she heard the smack of tennis balls as they played together at his place in Sounion weekend after weekend. She heard their laughter as they cooked together in his kitchen for a group of friends or colleagues.

"But the fact that I love you isn't the most important thing I want to tell you. I thought I'd loved you for as long as I've known you but that's not quite true. When you were younger, I was excited by the brilliant student. Later, I was proud of the outstanding protégé, but only in the last few years, as you have realized yourself fully as a woman, have I actually fallen romantically in love with you. That's why your earlier affairs didn't hurt me, and why I cannot bear your affair with Leon Skillman. I know you believe you love him. I saw you at Thanksgiving."

Tara began to interrupt, but he held up a gentle hand. "But I also saw the way you were with me the next night. That's what gave me the courage to gamble on this weekend with you. I didn't bring you back to Greece just to make this confession. The meetings on Crete were required. But I did bring you here, to Istanbul, hoping that perhaps you could see *us* with fresh eyes."

Us? She was remembering: she was his hostess, greeting guests at a party in his home. She was on his arm at an international gathering of archaeologists in Rome. They were drinking champagne together in Central Park; dancers were floating across an outdoor stage; she wore the gown he had designed for her that felt so light, like a nightgown.

"And it's only since I returned from New York that I have understood it all completely myself. It's new to me too, and I don't have time now to let you know any other way except to tell you. When we left Dorina Swing's studio, the day I bought two of her drawings, she stopped me after you had walked out the door ahead of me—she is a very unusual and direct woman—and said to me: "If it doesn't work out with Tara and you, will you consider an alternative choice?" I was shocked. Her openness and forthrightness overwhelmed me. I told her that whichever woman I ever pursued, that woman would never be an 'alternative choice.'"

Tara was feeling: the Poseidon gold armlet, her birthday gift from him. The night he gave it to her in New York, it had made her feel "owned" somehow. The earrings: scales to weigh men's souls. *Her* soul. The conch shell ring: a private symbol of sharing the sea's mysteries. The Turkish bracelet she wore tonight, his tribute to this weekend. Dozens of meanings, thousands of dollars. From her employer? From a friend? It had all seemed so natural.

"That's when I knew I couldn't go on hoping you would just somehow feel what I feel. It's not complicated, but I want you to understand, completely, what I want and what I need. And what I think *you* want and need. I *love* you. There's nothing you can do about that. But my loving you is not a primary need to me. What I need is for *you* to love *me*. At home, when I studied Dorina's female and male nudes carefully, I saw much more than our observations in the studio. Even though Dorina meant for her nudes to stand alone as single units in order to express human identity, *I* saw them together. I saw *sexual* identity. I saw that woman carries within her a primary sexual desire: to love. Man, in perfect counterpart, wants primarily to *be* loved. You know I don't mean that woman is in any regard inferior or subordinate to man. We're equal. But we're different. So it follows that our romantic needs are different too. It was studying those nudes that made me realize *why* you've always been such a hero worshiper. You need to love someone you can admire and—"

Tara rose from her chair and backed away into the heavily draped alcove. Her voice seemed to come from a distance. "You've always been my teacher, my mentor, like a parent. That's why I look up to you."

"Not for years. We have been colleagues."

"Yes, but I've always admired you with such *awe*."

"As I've admired *you* with awe."

Yes, she had worshiped him for as long as she could remember. For how many years? Did it matter? His brilliant intellect had blinded her so that she had taken the rest for granted. But she had lived the most precious moments of her life with him. And all the time she had been looking for someone else. How could she have been so dense? Her knees weakened suddenly and she clutched the draperies behind her for support, the same sinking feeling she'd had in her father's hallway after Dimitrios had . . . kissed her. She'd attributed it to the champagne.

He moved from the table to stand very close before her. "It dovetails perfectly, don't you see?"

She stared at his mouth, remembering the brief taste of his kiss, suddenly wanting it again, wanting it long and deep this time, long enough and deep enough to wipe out the rest of her will.

Dimitrios continued carefully, afraid he was frightening her but determined to make her understand at all cost. "As perfect as a man's and a woman's bodies merge in physical celebration of love, so do their minds merge in psychic celebration, a twin celebration of common values. We have human identity. That comes first, of course. But we also have a sexual identity that cannot and should not be denied. Woman wishes to surrender, to let go, but only to a strength equal to her own. Man needs to possess, but a man of self esteem only wishes to possess a strength equal to *his* own, a strength that is given freely in tribute to the love offered to him by the woman he wants *because* she is equal to him. I love you, Tara, not only because of what you've become as a person but also because you're the only woman I have ever met by whom I wish to be loved."

Images flooded her mind: her gods, her athletes, her heroes, and the human spirits whose souls they embodied.

They flowed through her, now, like the hot, molten bronze that cast the figures she so loved. Then they left her, *cire perdue*, with a great aching weight. She felt a desperate need to lie down. "I've left Leon," she said.

"Oh. That's not good. I don't want you to run away from him and come to me as a second choice. I want you to come to me because it's me and me alone you want."

Why couldn't she think? It was the wall. It was the draperies. They kept moving behind her. Closing her eyes and grasping the fabric with both hands, she began to whisper the only name that could give her the strength to stand up: "Dimitri."

Then his hands caught her from her sagging slide and his mouth covered hers.

She drank his kisses until she was drunk from the hot metal pouring through her again, remolding her will, recasting her image to his will.

When they were on his bed together, Dimitrios stopped them both. He didn't remember carrying her to the bedroom. He didn't remember undressing her. Calm! He drew his hand slowly, tenderly over her naked body, hoping to quiet her, and himself. This was not right.

His hand memorized each curve and crevice of her body, cherishing places he had known only in his dreams. She was all he had ever wanted.

"Dimitri!" She called his name dangerously, knowing the power of that name, the power of *her* saying it. "I do love you. I feel it. I just didn't know it. Dimitri!"

He clasped her to him. "This is not fair to you! I wanted you to go slowly."

"Dimitri. Your name. It's so natural, like everything else."

He covered her mouth again with his own in a moan of protest to stop the sound he had waited so long to hear.

"Dimitri. Now."

He held her tighter to stop her from moving against him with her demands, to stop himself from moving to answer those demands. His voice was no more than a groan. "I want you more than I've ever wanted anything in my life. I love you more than my life. But I cannot have you this way. I want you forever, not for one night."

"You said you love me."

"Yes, but do you love me? You can't know that now, like this."

"I do!"

Pushing himself up from the bed, he stood, knowing that this was the supreme achievement of his life.

Her arms reached up to him.

He covered her quivering body gently, reverently, with a blanket and forced himself to breathe calmly while he dabbed helplessly at her tears with one corner of the sheet.

"Shhhh." His legs were shaking badly, but he stood still over her. "When you can say those words in the cold light of morning, I will believe you. Not now, Tara. My dearest one! Try to understand! I want you for more than one night. I want you for all the nights of my life. This is my fault. Forgive me."

Sobbing in angry frustration, she turned away from him.

Dimitrios looked at the clock beside Tara's bed. It was five AM. For two hours, there had been no sound from his room, where he had left her. She had finally stopped crying. Longing pinned him to her sheets. Awake all night in her bed, he had lain in her sweet smells with the memory of her body in his hands. How could he possibly have guessed how she would respond to his words? He had ruined everything. He had only meant to lead her, to give her a choice. But somewhere deep inside her, she had known on some level more than either of them could have imagined, and typical of Tara, her impulses had hurled her far ahead of both of them. And now he would lie alone forever, wanting her.

Sobs racked his body, and he turned his face to the pillow to stifle them. She was right to have sent him away. He had to believe that when she could think clearly, she would not hate him quite so much. At least now she could go back to New York knowing how he felt, back to whatever had transpired between her and Leon, and think things out. That much he had saved for her. But at what cost? He stared up at the vaulted ceiling of her bedroom, its tiles painted with flowers and vines that enclosed the space like a secluded arbor. He knew the price of his blunder would be paid out in endless nights of self-torture like this, dreaming of her, wanting her more by far now than on any of the nights he had longed for her before. Because now he had touched her.

The curtains parted.

She wore nothing but the gold and silver bracelet he had given her. It looked heavy on her arm. She went to the window and drew back the curtains there. A cool, gray dawn had begun to lift the city into another day. Her body was a soft pale outline emerging from a far-away gray mist.

"It's cold," she said evenly. "It's light. And it's morning."

She stood over the bed and pulled the bedclothes away from him. Her eyes traced his entire body with the same tenderness with which his hands had touched hers hours ago. He lay resolutely still. When her eyes met his, they smiled.

"*Kokonas.* You *are* beautiful," she said simply.

For the instant it took him to make the decision, Dimitrios closed his eyes. Then he extended his inviting hand.

"No. Here." she whispered. Kneeling, she accepted his hand but pulled him to the floor with her, onto the prayer rug that still lay on top of the other oriental rugs that surrounded them like a colorful bed of wildflowers. "They say this is a sacred rug. I know of only one way to make it holy."

"Tara."

He kissed each part of her body he had dreamed of,

had touched for the first time only hours ago, pressing his mouth into each secret spot as if he were taking a permanent imprint of its touch, its smell, his lips hot and searing, flaring anew their earlier passion but firing it with even more intensity now, with complete abandon.

Tara cried "Dimitri!" It was a demand. He answered it.

And she felt her body rise again and again to surpass his desire, his love, until she lost all sense of her own existence and became willingly, wonderfully, wildly part of his.

The morning began to gather and intensify its light, washing their private canopied sky with all of its shimmering colors, spreading its rays over their tiny universe like a blessing. Their hands clasped tightly together to contain the tremors of a new and glorious sunrise.

TWENTY-EIGHT

BALTIMORE! She was supposed to be in New York! The wind cut across Tara's face as the ship made its way from the pier at Baltimore's inner harbor. The rain was no less brutal, soaking through her windbreaker and chilling her blood. The thought of a dive in this weather, and at night, even wearing a wetsuit and armed with underwater spotlights, chilled her very brain. She fought against the resistance she felt that this was asking too much. If anyone less than Uncle Basilious had asked such a favor of her she would have flatly refused, especially since she had just endured the long trip back from Athens, the short hop down here and faced another flight tomorrow afternoon to Palm Beach. Aside from her exhaustion, this dive barely gave her the twelve hours she needed before it was safe to fly again, and she didn't feel like pushing that envelope at all. Uncle Basilious knew her work and travel contexts, so this must be an incredibly important mission. He'd insisted he needed her opinion both as a diver and as an archaeologist and that, because of time pressures from his client, the "look-see" couldn't wait until she got back from Florida; it had to be tonight. Now he stood with her on the deck of one of his freighters, his eyes squinting out to an unseen horizon through a biting downpour. He seemed worried.

"It's not too far," he shouted above the din of waves assaulting the hull of the ship. "I just hope it's positioned right. That's what I need to know. I'm told that the depth isn't as important as the position. I'm sorry the weather's so lousy."

Tara nodded and closed her eyes, not out of fatigue alone, but out of the need to give herself over emotionally, for a few precious moments, to an inner stillness that had become a new and vital source of strength for her. The weight of Dimitri's bracelet beneath the sleeve of her jacket encircled her wrist like an embrace, acting as a reverse reminder of the weightlessness she felt inside. For the first time in her life, she felt complete and in touch, her whole being centered and utterly at peace—because the center of her whole being had found the center of his: "Dimitri." *Dimitri*. His hands. His mouth. She could let herself go completely with him. Everything she had ever experienced of love was, with him, experienced to a higher power. And more: feelings she had never had before, a whole new level of tender love and passionate lovemaking.

Unwilling to let her go away from him yet, he had impulsively insisted on taking her south from Istanbul to Pamukkale for a brief but important visit to one of his "holy" places. He "collected" them, she had learned, places and structures that were holy for him.

"What do you mean,'holy'?" Tara had asked in disbelief. "You're not religious." They'd been driving a rented car from the airport at the ancient port of Smirna to this remote place she'd never heard of. About Dimitrios, she knew all. About Dimitri, she was learning, there were endless paths to explore.

He drove up the side of a hill to go around a flock of sheep blocking the dirt road. The old shepherd who was driving the animals raised his staff and sang out thanks— or a curse, who knew?—in his musical language. Dimitrios waved back, smiling broadly. Tara had never seen him so free and easy. Ever since coming to Turkey, he seemed younger to her, more adventurous and more energetic. It was as if their love had transformed him. Or maybe she was the one transformed.

"Oh, I don't mean 'holy' in the institutional sense," Dimitrios explained breezily, "but in the philosophical sense. 'Holy' as in *whole* or *complete*, the total experience of perfect union between existence and consciousness. You know, the feeling of oneness with yourself and the world. It has nothing whatever to do with the supernatural. In fact," he delighted in his cleverness, it's "wholly" *natural*. Anyway," he continued, "Delphi is such a place for me, always has been since I was a boy. And the Acropolis. And Sounion, of course." He took her hand and pressed his lips to her palm. "*You* are such a place."

Tara let her hand linger on his cheek for a long moment. "And the Blue Mosque we love so much in Istanbul? 'Wholly,' too?"

"Definitely! But Pamukkale is *sui generis*," Dimitrios went on seriously, "because, historically, it never held any formal religious connotations at all. Even in antiquity, it was sacred strictly because of its curative waters."

They turned down a narrow entrance road approaching the site, and Tara looked around her. Hundreds of sarcophagi and mausolea covered every foot of available land. "Sorry to disappoint you," she said with a grimace, "but this place gives me the creeps."

He laid his hand over hers. "Trust me," he winked. "Even though Romans by the droves came to take the medicinal waters of Pamukkale's hot mineral springs, they didn't all make it, you know. In spite of the miracle of the waters, many died. So here they all are, buried with their jewelry, as was the custom of the day."

Tara sighed, understanding now that this sea of destroyed funerary monuments had been broken down over the centuries by graverobbers as well as time.

"Oh!" Suddenly she saw it. As usual, she should have trusted him. "Oh, my dear love!"

And once fully inside the boundaries of the ancient city, she instantly felt the place as Dimitrios meant for her to. Huge, soft-shouldered, pure white cliffs, frozen formations of calcareous water, rose up hundreds of feet high from the plain. At the top of each, opaque streams of fresh water gushed over glistening surfaces, cascading down into the great basins they had carved, that overflowed, in turn, to repeat the pattern again and again. Like some shimmering fantasy planet from a science fiction movie, the entire surface of the earth appeared to be a series of enormous, pearl terraces linked together by countless interconnecting cliffs, each dripping huge opalescent stalactites. In every direction, a balmy winterland of scintillating white forms rose and fell from mountains to valleys, all sonorous from the rushing and dripping of water, all bathed in a gentle, rising mist as the hot water evaporated from what looked like solid, diamond-crusted snow into the cool, dry afternoon air.

They drank the liquid "cure" from each other's cupped hands and splashed through knee-high pools of deliciously warm water, bare feet sliding sensually over the smooth, porcelain-like floor of each basin. Yes, this was *hieron*, even today, a sacred city so pure that centuries worth of time only seemed to enhance its powers of redemption. Tara felt cleansed and purified. Sharing her feelings of awe with Dimitri only intensified this rare experience of deep connection with the glory that was the physical world.

Dimitrios had checked them into a modest motel, and that evening, while the other few guests were dining inside, he wrapped them both in huge bath towels and led her to a meandering hot spring that spread its sparkling warm water throughout the rambling courtyard of the horseshoe-shaped building. Subtle underwater lights cast a dim incandescence into the shimmering water, and low-hanging trees gave an intimacy to the pool's perimeter, while its center was left free and open to apparently endless space. Tara could not believe her eyes. Dimitrios hid their towels behind a rock, and they slipped quickly and silently into the water.

Against the black, star-studded sky and a backdrop of huge, blue-white mountains built of the same water, the floor of the shallow pool was strewn with ruins from the ancient city: marble columns, steles and capitals lay underwater like stark white, sacred bones. Most of the place was surrounded by the remaining walls of an eleventh-century Byzantine castle, but by moving carefully over the slabs of marble, she and Dimitrios were able to swim very near the edge of the open side of a cliff to look over the rim and watch, spellbound, as a waterfall spilled majestically down seventy or eighty feet into another, waiting pool.

Bubbles broke soundlessly on the surface of the water where they swam; it was as if they were gliding through warm champagne. Coming to rest on one of the marble capitals, remains of a Roman temple that once stood at the pool's edge, she and Dimitri sat together and brushed away the bubbles clinging to their nude bodies, propelling them off one another in long sweeps that sent brilliant flurries of phosphorescent lightbursts through the water. Tara wore only the gold and silver bracelet Dimitrios had given her. She floated to his lap, legs and arms both entwining about him, and they sat together that way for some time, staring into a sky glittering with so many stars that there seemed no room left for the dark space of night. Kissing softly and murmuring little words of love into each other's ears, they indulged themselves in the fathomless depths of the universe without and within.

At last, cheeks resting against each other, they simply gazed silently into the endless night.

"Oh, Dimitri!" Tara caught her breath. "A falling star!"

"A comet," he corrected quietly.

Then as if the celestial arrow had pierced the very heart of her being, Tara felt consumed by an intensity of desire she had never before experienced. Ardent and urgent.

His hand found her first, but within seconds, gasping for breath, she wanted it all.

Dimitrios gave her all of what she wanted.

They were become one, sharing in the flesh the love they bore each other and sharing in the soul every value that made them each who they had become, the primordial energy of nature merging in one physical act of spiritual love with the scattered remains of human achievement that lay beneath them. As their passion churned the water around them, their warm bath glittered with pulsing phosphorescent brilliance, as if all the stars from the dark night sky had fallen into the water surrounding them.

It was a supreme moment of their being.

For many long moments after the burning star within her had been extinguished by the hotter blaze of his, Tara and Dimitrios held each other tenderly, knowing that they had experienced the essence of creation.

Finally, Tara had uttered one word, one thought, one name. Looking deep into the soft velvet brown that were his loving eyes and feeling his strong presence protecting her even as it had on the day she had found her athlete, she marveled to herself at the new path to the future that he had forged for them both. And she named the holiest of all possessions in life for her: "Dimitri."

Now, here in the blinding wind and rain of a raging Chesapeake Bay, the gold and silver cuff on her arm liquefied again to warm her from the heat that the familiar form of his name would forever forward bring to her senses, and it spread again like molten metal through her body in remembrance of its giver.

How could she possibly get through the next few days?

Tomorrow, in Palm Beach, she would wear Leon's fur

cape and arrive at Blair's party in a sleigh drawn by horses over real snow for TV cameras and the newspapers, as she had promised Blair she would. She would see Leon.

Dimitrios had told her she must do this. He had also told her that she must give Leon a chance to win her back, that she must go to the Gothards' party and acquaint herself fully with Leon's world and his friends. Even after all the bliss they had shared only a handful of hours ago, Dimitrios resolutely refused to accept her declarations of love as final until she had seen Leon again. They had sexually celebrated their new feelings for each other prematurely, he said, and he would await her final decision until another morning when she could confirm her passions after a separation from him and with complete knowledge of her choices. He had said these things to her as directly and as simply as he had said, "I love you." A small smile crept onto Tara's mouth, lifting its corners into an unspoken salute. Dimitrios was always fearless before the truth.

Uncle Basilious touched her shoulder lightly. "Better change into your gear. We're almost there. One of the men will guide you down." He put an arm around her. "Will you be all right, Tara? I mean with the weather and all?"

"Just have a big ouzo waiting for me when I come up!" she said jokingly. "Now, what am I looking for?"

"Nothing recognizable, really. Just junk metal. But with the environmental laws the way they are, my client couldn't get rid of the stuff on land."

"Why not compact it the way they do cars?"

"Too solid. Iron, steel, things like that."

"What exactly *is* it?"

Basilious shrugged. "Junk! But my client doesn't want the stuff *ever* found, not even by future divers like you. That's why I need your opinion. We've dumped the stuff just over a natural shelf. As I said, it's not too deep, and all ship's pilots know about the rocky area and avoid it because during tide changes they could suffer a bad scrape, so they always navigate a couple of miles south to begin their entry into the harbor."

"Why not just dump the cargo in the middle of the ocean? Then it would go so deep you wouldn't have to worry?"

"No time. It was a fast job. The client decided he'd rather hide the stuff."

Tara peered through the curtain of rain at her adopted uncle. "Why are we doing this in the dark? Is this legal?" she asked suspiciously.

"Never asked. We're only doing this 'look-see' at night because there's a time crunch and you're an expert in this kind of thing. Couldn't do it in New York's busy waters, of course, but we openly dump the stuff in this unused little bay during the day and nobody's stopped us. One of my harbor pilot friends down here told me about the spot, so it must be okay."

Tara started below, wishing she really could have a nip after this dive. Her whole body shivered from the cold as she undressed in the captain's cabin. She changed quickly into her bathing suit and then added the heavy wetsuit, wrapping Dimitri's bracelet in her sweater before she returned topside. One of the crew was already geared up and waiting for her in the dinghy. Carrying her fins, snorkel and mask, she climbed down the long steel ladder and joined him. He was already wearing his tank and mask and helped her into hers. The pilot steadied his ship as best he could, while Basilious let out the line that secured the dinghy to the main vessel.

About fifty feet out, the dinghy flinging wildly about in the storm, Tara's diving companion signaled her overboard. Tipping herself backward off the side of the boat, she caught her breath as the freezing water slipped between her skin and the wetsuit. But by the time her diving buddy joined her with their lights, the temperature had equalized and she felt more comfortable than she had up on the deck pelted by the rain. Once they were down twenty feet or so, though she knew the waves still raged above them, the water became calm enough to swim the rest of the way without too much effort.

Her partner led the way. The lights were good; she could see him clearly ahead of her as they descended.

Suddenly, he disappeared. But in the next instant, she spotted his light below her again; they had passed over the rim of the ledge; it was straight down now. Following the light as if it were a lifeline, she wished that they had tied a real line between them just in case; it was so black down here.

Slowly, they settled onto the floor of the bay amid what certainly did look like a junkyard. Huge hulks of iron and steel surrounded them, at least thirty or forty, Tara guessed. And Basilious said there were more to come? She swam carefully over and among the hunks of metal. Some had landed alone and stuck up from the mud like gravestones, while others had fallen on top of each other to form piles of tangled forms. She had explored many shipwrecks over the years, but this dive gave her a particularly eerie feeling, because it was an intentional disaster.

What an untimely contrast to Pamukkale, where she and Dimitrios had swum in ecstasy over the magnificent marble ruins of antiquity.

She signaled her partner that she was finished. The site was good. Basilious had chosen well. Nothing around of interest to excite professional divers, and the general region was heavily trafficked by steamships, which would discourage any casual sport diving. Since the ships were aware of the rocky ledge and their navigation routes automatically set to circumvent it, a future shipwreck would be unlikely. She thought of her bracelet and warm sweater waiting for her at the surface; even with the wetsuit, she was by now frozen to the bone.

She started her ascent, but her guide waved his light, signaling her back to one section of the site. He must have seen something that she had missed? With an agitated sigh, she swam to his side to see what had caught his attention.

The triangular piece was all pitted and corroded, but otherwise she could see no distinguishing characteristics that gave it greater interest than anything else. Her guide beckoned her closer and focused his light close to the surface of the metal. Glancing at her watch and fighting off a growing annoyance that this man was prolonging their time below, she swam to the light. Basilious had sent this man along with her, which meant he must trust his judgment. She thought, marginally, that she could discern something on the metal, but she still couldn't make any sense out of it. She shook her head to indicate that she didn't understand. He moved quickly to another piece. This one was rectangular in shape and had a rough, pebbly sort of surface. Losing all patience, now, Tara braced her legs against another iron hunk to steady herself. Grabbing the edges of the rectangle, she pushed her face as close as she could get to the metal, pressing her mask right up against the place he had lit up for her. She recognized the same sort of scratching on the surface that the first piece had. It looked like hieroglyphics of some sort, like a symbol signature. Like *initials*.

She looked again, even though she didn't have to. She had seen these initials before. She had suffered anguish over them. "L. S." She traced the initials now, with a cautious finger, while her whole body began to tremble uncontrollably.

She snapped her head up to look at her guide and shined her own light directly into his face. Behind his diving mask, she could see his green eyes smiling at her. Leon!

The turmoil she felt inside was no less violent than the storm raging above. After surfacing and when their dinghy reached the ship, Tara sprang aboard like a seething wildcat, ignoring Leon's shouted attempts at explanation and screaming her anger at Basilious as she demanded he follow her to his cabin.

Her body racked furiously from both cold and outrage. Ripping off the cap of her dive suit, she slammed the deadbolt into the door behind them, locking it. "You risked my life for *this*? This insanity? Are *you* crazy, too?" It was a monumental achievement to keep herself from tearing apart the cabin. She felt like smashing everything in sight. "How could Leon have conceived such a thing? How could you have helped him do it? How? *Why*?"

Leon was banging on the door from the outside, begging Tara to listen to him. "Don't you get it? I'm quitting! Within a few weeks there won't be a trace of my work anywhere, and when I'm finished with that, I'll be finished financially, too. What more do you want from me? Tara! Talk to me!"

Panicked by her unprecedented show of temper, Basilious backed away from his dearest niece. "But you *love* him," he stammered. "Kostas said you did! Your own father told me how much you hated Leon's art, so when Leon asked me to buy it all up and dump it, we all thought you'd be *happy*. Tara! What a sacrifice! What more can you ask from a man to prove his love? Through me, he's anonymously buying back all of his own work just to destroy it for love of *you*. It's also some sort of joke on the art community that I don't understand. Leon bought my *Aristotle* from the town of Stagirus and had it shipped over here. He's putting my statue in the same spot where one of his own works used to be."

"Aristotle!" Tara exploded. "If I hear one more word about that goddamned statue, I'll break it to bits and you along with it! Is *that* why you agreed to do this stupid thing? And risked my life in the process?"

Basilious dropped his head, shaking it from side to side in shocked despair, tears streaming down his wrinkled old face. "How could you think such a thing?" he choked. "We all love you. We all did what we thought you would want."

Tara began to pull off her wetsuit. "Take me back! she ordered numbly. "And keep Leon out of my sight."

But when Basilious opened the cabin door, Leon burst in.

"Get out of here!" Tara screamed. "You could have killed us both! And for *what*? Get *out* of here!"

"For *what*?" Leon grabbed her wrists and pinned her arms to her sides as she flung out to strike him. "For what else? *I love you*! Don't you understand? *Nothing* else matters to me. *Nothing*!" He shook her roughly, as if to shake her into understanding. "Tara!"

She was struggling to tear herself from his grip with such violence that he feared she would hurt herself, but he continued blindly on: "I would never have let anything happen to you down there. Both Basilious and your father know how I feel about you. They know that I would forfeit my own life in a second to save yours. And they also know how stubborn you are. Given my past and the way we parted, I couldn't just *tell* you that I'm giving up the art that you hate. I had to *show* you. I had to prove by my actions in a way you couldn't ignore. *No one* could possibly love a woman more than I love you!"

Tara stopped fighting him and looked up in stunned shock at his last words.

Then sobbing beyond caring, she crumpled listlessly into his arms.

TWENTY-NINE

"Now WHY WON'T YOU talk to me? You said last night that you would."

Tara looked out the window of the small jet to avoid Leon's pleading eyes. "I also told you last night that I need time to absorb what you've done," she whispered back. "You can't continue to overwhelm me by carrying last night's escapade into a public place. I know we must talk, but it's just going to have to wait until after the party. Then we can have an open-ended discussion with no interruptions and no one to hear." She smiled tightly, "and with no emotional outbursts from either of us," she added. "You must see we can't *possibly* discuss it here."

After her breakdown, she had finally convinced both a frantic Leon and tearful Basilious to leave her alone for the long five hour trip back to New York; she was so exhausted both emotionally and physically that she actually slept for a few hours. Basilious had called her father on ship-to-shore radio, and Kostas had been waiting at the pier with a taxi when they arrived back to New York. Wrapping her in the birthday blanket that her grandmother had made, he had held her gently but securely in his arms during the car ride home. From time to time, she had felt his warm tears of culpability falling softly into her wet hair, but he had blessed her with the silence she so badly needed.

Now, she and Leon sat together in the Gothards' plane. The other passengers were Blair and Perry, Robert Van

Varen, the middle-aged art critic and his young girlfriend, Denise Sommers, Leon's agent Flo, and—Tara masked the revulsion she felt—Adria Cass, his painter "friend"; Kronan Hagen and his wife, Sydelle, were in the rear seats. Only the steward, who had just served them drinks, sat alone.

Leon seemed dangerously fragile now. Maybe he really *had* changed? And what would that mean to her now that Dimitri was romantically in her life? She thought of the day last summer in the islands when she and Dimitri had first met Leon, and of all that had transpired since that fateful day. Each of their paths was altered, now. Where they were all headed? Who knew? *Crosspoint*, she thought silently. All three of us.

She tried to focus on the plane's decor to distract herself. The peach and gray interior of the Gothards' streamlined jet was more sumptuous than most homes. She mused that Blair displayed magnificent taste in every realm but art and husbands. But these distractions were useless given her inner upset. Loving Dimitri the way she was sure she did, how could she still be in such conflict over Leon? She knew it was right that she had come; she had to see this through to its end. She swallowed her martini in three gulps and signaled the steward for another.

She liked Blair, she realized, and had continued to like her from the first evening they met on her boat in Greece. There was something vulnerable about the woman that made Tara feel protective. Strange to feel protective of an older woman as beautiful and wealthy and sophisticated as Blair, but some elusive quality about her reminded Tara of a little girl, eagerly awaiting surprises around every corner.

She closed her eyes and felt the drinks begin to calm her nerves so she could focus her mind enough to summon the strength she needed. She had been so *sure* of her feelings on the plane back from Greece. Now? Everything seemed upside down.

Leon studied the length of Tara's closed eyelashes, the skin of her cheek, the curve of her mouth. He was totally confounded. She seemed so remote from him, yet he was certain about the source of the fire he'd felt from her even when she was so outraged at him right after the dive; she wouldn't have reacted so ballistically if she still didn't care for him. Well, he consoled himself, coming to the party with him had to be a good sign. He would just have to trust her. The deeper implications of his sacrifice will sink in and make sense to her soon. She couldn't possibly remain unmoved by his enormous declaration of love. No one could! And tonight she would see him in the context of the best of his world. She would see the genuine prominence he enjoyed, even though the art that had brought him that prominence meant nothing to him anymore. She would see for herself what celebrity he was leaving behind for her.

Tara opened her eyes and gazed out the window again. She just couldn't look at Leon and see his suffering. He needn't have been so grandiose! But maybe it was better for him this way. He *was* changing—it had to be!—but this gleeful destruction of his work was very disturbing, and it complicated things immensely. Dumping his art in the ocean where it never could be found! There was something vengeful about it, and it was more than a guilt trip.

He touched her arm tentatively. "I have a surprise for you when we get back to New York," he ventured. "I now have a work of art in my apartment." Wait till she saw that he had bought one of Nicky's paintings!

Tara permitted no show of interest. What now? She pulled work from her briefcase. Knowing how hard he was trying, knowing how much she meant to him, knowing that, on some level, she must still care for him, she was more confused than ever. Everything was a blur.

THIRTY

IF THE GOTHARDS' OCEAN YACHT and private plane were like movie sets, their Palm Beach home was an entire back lot. The jet had landed in West Palm, where they had been picked up by limousines and driven to the grand mansion. One facade of the Georgian revival residence was oriented to beach and ocean, the other to lake, gardens and pool. Spanning the two fronts of the palatial home, a living room nearly the size of a football field had been built under the ocean boulevard to connect the two sections. Tara's bedroom was on the lakeside, one of twenty-six that opened onto its own private terrace or patio. If it wasn't a movie, it was a beautiful dream.

Denise Sommers joined Tara at the top of the staircase leading to the ocean entrance. "Disgusting, isn't it?" she scoffed. "As if a thousand feet on the ocean isn't enough, they have to have an equal amount of lake frontage. Greed. That's what runs in their veins."

Tara started. The young woman standing beside her was lovely to look at. Gowned in an antique Victorian lace dress a shade lighter than her copper-colored hair, she seemed a vision of graciousness, and the name "Denise" was poetic and just right for her. But the moment she opened her mouth, the feminine vision vanished, and Tara understood why everyone called her "Denny." So Blair not only had a lizard for a husband, she also seemed to have at least one profoundly unappreciative friend. If the girl was offended by the Gothards' lifestyle, why had she accepted this invitation as their houseguest?

At the foot of the stairs, she had an even more unexpected encounter. Adria Cass, ready for the photo op she'd been anticipating, paced the foyer clad in what appeared to be farmer's overalls, silver Western boots with rhinestone spurs, a shaggy gold jacket and a purple, friz-styled wig. Tara turned back up the stairs as if she had forgotten something; she had nearly burst out laughing. Moving directly into Leon as she turned, she remembered in a flash that he had once been intimate with that creature. Gravely, she took his arm and let him lead her back down the stairs, where they all caught their breath in collective approval as Blair emerged from a side door, floating into the room like a scintillating Christmas bauble that would outshine all of the other ornaments on the foyer's immense tree. Her white satin gown fell in perfect folds to the tips of her topaz-studded sandals and was topped by a topaz and diamond collar that shot golden sunbeams to the tips of her lightly suntanned shoulders. Her smile sparkled as brilliantly as the gems; her brown eyes reflected their glow. Blair Gothard looked the consummate hostess.

"Oh Adria," Blair hugged her guest. "You're going to upstage us all, aren't you?"

"Yup. Court jester to the gentry." Adria laughed. "Who's gonna sit next to me in the sleigh? Denny?"

Blair examined the diamond "B" on a gold fingernail. Her mother would never forgive her if a government bureaucrat were to appear in the newspapers with her, and that's who Denny was. "No, the lead sleigh only holds six, and I want boy-girl, boy-girl. You don't mind, do you Denny, dear?" She rushed on, "Van, be a darling and take Denny and Sydelle into the bar for a drink. Kronan will sit next to you, Adria. Hurry everyone, the snow's down and the other guests will begin to arrive any time now."

Leon helped Tara into her fur. "You look incredible," he

whispered. "In that Grecian gown and those museum pieces, you're right off a classical frieze!"

And you, Tara thought silently, adjusting her fur hat in a hall mirror but seeing only his tuxedo-clad frame, his sculptured features and his penetrating green eyes. You still *look* just like my athlete, just like a . . . god. But who are you now?

Kronan Hagen opened the French doors and stepped out onto a patio at the very moment the sun made its final descent and was extinguished. He could barely see the line of limousines that curved like a dark snake along the driveway, or the many visiting yachts dotting the sea. The only sounds he could hear were the occasional, contented snorts of the horses still hitched to their sleighs, resting now on the last of Blair's four dozen truckloads of snow. Margaret Harrington Crane's home sat regally in the midst of it all, a multi-faceted iceberg set in pearl-white and mounted between ocean and lake, a rare jewel.

He would always think of this home as Margaret's. She had given the estate to Blair and Perry as a wedding gift twenty-five years ago, but Blair hadn't altered an inch of it. The furniture, the art, and most of the staff all remained as Margaret had installed them. All exquisite. Like Margaret herself. Kronan was glad Margaret had decided to attend the party tonight. Her quiet elegance shone like a steady star above the rest of the guests, a reassuring sight to him in a crowd of so many glittering people with whom he had nothing in common.

Over the years, he had become quite an outstanding fundraiser. The key, as it would be tonight, was to have all of the donors offer their gifts in the presence of others, which encouraged them to give much more than they would ever give in private. Kronan sighed heavily and turned back to the house. Here, Blair was turning the event into a charade, for the gifts tonight would not be based on the beauty of sacrifice, which might bring each person closer to God, but on status and showing off in front of others stricken with the same social disease.

How little people really know of one another, he thought, compulsively visiting yet again his ever-recurring theme. We can interact with others for years on end and never even glimpse the interior life of anyone, especially their secret agonies. Hesitating for a moment to collect himself before crossing the entrance, he silently thanked God that no one could glimpse his own agonizing guilt. Then, for one searing instant, he felt that if he crossed this threshold now, he would be taking the first step toward Hell, that to raise money for the art in the new wing (for the likes of Adria Cass!) would be an evil act only compounding his previous transgressions. He must not do this! Insane to think this way. Of course he must.

Anxiety ridden and desperate for comfort, Kronan forced his feet in the direction of his good friend and true hostess, who was standing with some of the house guests at one end of the long room. Margaret kissed him, it seemed, with as much gratitude for his presence as he felt for hers. She was nearly as tall as he was, and her silver-blonde hair, as it brushed his cheek, smelled faintly of jasmine. She opened a gold case, and taking a cigarette for herself, offered one to Kronan and lit them both with a gold lighter from her evening purse, blowing smoke impatiently into the air. "What are we doing here, Kronan, dear? We're too old for this sort of party. Blair's new art wing! I'm glad my husband isn't alive to see it. I wonder how the public, all of these people here tonight included, would react if they weren't assured before the fact that such objects *were* art. Why couldn't Blair have stayed with her horses?"

"You just don't understand contemporary art, Margaret," Van chastised her. "You don't even try. You've never deigned to considered the proposition that a work of art by merit of its own inner coherence may, by way of metaphor, express truths and experiences and ideas that aren't expressible through any other means."

"That's a modern thought," Tara said. Her voice was more strident than she'd intended.

Leon took her empty glass and headed for the bar to refill it. He would not abide talk of art this night.

"So? It's only logical for modern ideas to be visually translated into a modern type of art," Perry bantered idly. He was completely absorbed in a wordless flirtation with Denny. She had come with Van, but she was obviously available and delicious. And demanded tasting as soon as possible, he decided. He picked a green, spun-sugar apple that looked like a piece of Venetian glass from a bowl and handed it to her. "Try one. The chef learned the technique from a glass blower in Murano."

Denny bit into the apple, her face breaking into delight as the sugar broke into sweetness inside her mouth. "It tastes wonderful," she said. "But," she held the apple to her nose, "it smells bad. It smells of *money*."

Perry and Van smiled at her audacity and looked expectantly in Margaret's direction.

"Money *should* smell, dear girl." Margaret offered Denny a cigarette and lit it with her gold lighter. "My father always said that money should smell from the sweat, mental or physical, that went into making it."

"Well," Denny retorted, "if you believe so much in the work ethic, what do *you* do?"

Margaret raised both eyebrows in amusement and stubbed out her cigarette in a lavishly hand-etched ashtray. "Oh," she said simply, "I garden, I guess. And what do you do?"

"I'm New York's Second Deputy for the Arts Council," Denny beamed. "I'm also the *working* daughter of Senator Theron Sommers."

"Well then," Margaret lit another cigarette, "*you* and your father should be delighted with *my* daughter's new wing. It's the sort of thing that government types usually support. But, a serious question: since you folks have to choose among it all on a daily basis, how do you tell the difference between the genuine and the fake?"

Denny smiled. "The same way I tell the difference between anything real or fake, *dear lady*. If it's made with somebody's hands, it's real. If it's made from the exploitation of those who work with their hands, then it's fake. If it distributes its wealth, then it's real. If it hoards it, it's fake."

Margaret smiled back thinly. "Well, since I garden, that makes me real, because I work with my hands. But since I keep my earnings, where does that put me in your scheme of things?"

Denny examined Margaret's perfectly groomed hands and the rings that adorned them. "Are you trying to suggest that *you* plant all the pretty little posies with your own pretty little hands?"

"Don't worry, Mother." Perry slipped an arm through Denny's and began to steer her away from what would soon become a very uncomfortable encounter; his mother-in-law wouldn't long remain tolerant of Denny's potshots. "We patrons still have the telling power, not the government. We may not produce the art, but since our money still finances those who *do* produce, *we're* the ones who are answerable to history."

"Not *we*, darling boy. *You*."

Van watched Denny and Perry whisper their way to a side room containing Blair's famous "coke" bar. He knew he would lose her to Perry now, he just knew it.

Perry accepted a tiny silver spoon engraved with the ornate initials of his wife from a butler and handed it to Denny. "Souvenir," he bowed. "It was Blair's idea. Guests who want to shovel *this* kind of snow tonight either have to buy a spoon for a thousand dollars or else buy each line through a hundred-dollar bill."

"I want another spoon," Denny demanded, her eyes

brightening.

"You're an expensive date. Come on." He steered her in another direction. "I have something better upstairs."

"Ah," Denny breathed. "The big H? What do we do? Snort or smoke or shoot?"

Perry headed toward a staircase. "Your choice, babe. I snort. My wife smokes, chasing the dragon with silver foil instead of a silver spoon. If you want to shoot, you have to bring your own toys." He assessed the age of his target again. "On the other hand, if you just want prescription drugs like my daughter at Vassar, you can do them instead, he teased. I hear from Michelle that inventive mixing can do a perfectly fine job of deranging your senses."

"I'm past Ritalin and Oxy-Contin. Who wants to play with poor man's shit when the real stuff is handy? And why should I fool with boys when I can go over the top and back again with an experienced guide? I told you I like older men."

Blair glimpsed the departing pair on her way across the room to greet new arrivals but never missed a beat. Yet, some of the glow faded from her eyes. Did he have to take her *there*? And so soon? He was, after all, the host.

The stairwell, enclosed in a cylinder of glass, spiraled up to the master bedroom and plunged downward to its floor of clear glass, revealing waves crashing on the beach forty feet below. Denny reeled and grabbed Perry's hand. "I'm dizzy, and we haven't even started yet," she giggled. "I was just at a party in LA where a man-in-the-moon sign dropped from the ceiling and snorted little, twinkling lights up its nose," she continued, staring down until the vertigo made her feel like swooning, which she pretended to do.

Perry carried her into the circular bedroom, slid her onto the circular, rotating bed and pressed the button that opened the skylight dome to the circular motion of the stars. "Cool girl!" He went to a cupboard to get the stuff. "Have you ever inhaled toad venom? Or Climax? Too bad my mother-in-law's here, which is why all we can offer is conventional stuff tonight. At our last party we sprayed Climax from the building's sprinkler system onto over the dance floor, which sent the dancers into an ecstatic frenzy. Instead of putting out a fire, we started one. It was almost as good as Rush."

"What's 'Rush'?" Denny watched the stars swirl slowly by above them.

"I'll show you later." He began to unfasten the dozens of tiny, satin-covered buttons on the bodice of her antique lace gown, one at a time.

Leon hesitated from habit as he passed by the coke bar. Better not even think of it. Knowing instinctively that she would disapprove, he had never suggested doing drugs with Tara. He found her and Margaret standing alone before a large oil portrait of a young Blair. Good. He knew that these two would be drawn to each other. Margaret had always liked Leon for some reason, even though he knew she didn't like his art. He was sure she would never undercut him to Tara.

"Blair's father died shortly after her coming-out party," Margaret was explaining. "I was always so happy he made it to that day because in his eyes Blair was brighter than the sun." Indicating the portrait, she pointed to the small, diamond butterflies that caught the overskirt of Blair's shell-pink ball gown in a dozen places to reveal layers of vericolored pastel petticoats beneath. "Jonathan designed those butterflies so that when the evening was over, Blair could hook them all together and wear them as a belt. She wears it to this day. Apart from horses, she loved butterflies best. At midnight, for that ball, instead of the usual balloons, we released ten thousand Brazilian butterflies that hung in gossamer nets from the ceiling. They weren't harmed, of course. And—see here in the painting?—we hung crystal chandeliers from the wisteria trees in my gardens and let the horses roam at will. It was a lovely party. We always thought Blair would go into horse breeding seriously. She took her degree in equestrian studies, you know. But her interest in art—Perry's influence, I think—seems to have eradicated all other interests. Given her background, it's still hard for me to believe Blair's art preferences. The younger generation, I suppose. But when I think of her expertise with horses! She could have become one of the finest breeders in the country. Oh well," Margaret mashed a cigarette in her already overflowing ashtray, "as long as one has purpose in life. That's all that matters. You know she built the new wing over my outdoor gardens in New York." Margaret waved a butler over. "I always insist on clean ashtrays," she mused. "I don't want to know how much I smoke."

Leon handed fresh glasses of champagne to each of them. "Margaret keeps very quiet about it, but her 'gardening' really means that she's one of the foremost horticulture experts in the country. She supervised the White House gardens and she's just finished a private botanical and bird sanctuary on one of the barrier islands off the coast of Florida."

Tara laughed in amazement. "Then you *do* work?"

"Of course I work! One doesn't have to work because one needs the money. One works from love of purpose. Harringtons have always worked. What's ailing this crowd is that everybody's avoiding work, avoiding purpose, avoiding responsibility. It's pathetic." She put an arm around Tara's shoulder and waved at the room. "Look at them. Your ancient Athens bent every effort to discover the meaning of life. Modern America bends every effort to prove there is no meaning to discover. No effort, no risk. That's what they're fleeing from: effort and risk. Look at them all. It's enough to make you cry."

Tara looked. Leon looked too. He saw attractive, successful women and wealthy, successful men enjoying themselves. He saw Florida, California, Texas, Washington D.C.,

Chicago and New York represented like the separate spokes of one giant wheel that turned the country. He saw the arts, business, politics, the press. He saw the power and the energy that moved the world. He glanced over at Tara, who was staring at the same people. She looked dismayed.

Tara saw shallow smiles, ostentatious jewels, anxious eyes. She heard conversations that were too rapid, laughter that was too quick.

Nettled by her expression, Leon looked again, trying to see these people as Tara must be seeing them. Hell! Everyone looked fine and dandy! Several people noticed him and waved. He took Tara by the arm and asked Margaret to excuse them. She wasn't a good choice for Tara after all. He must introduce her to friends who had come to have a blast of an evening. They needed to be with happy people tonight.

"I think I see what you meant by making art for the public in its own time," Tara whispered to him. "Somehow I can't imagine any of the people in this room getting excited over my artifacts or Nicky's seascapes or Dorina's nudes."

Blair glided across the room and came between them. Linking an arm with each of them, she piloted them toward a corner. "You two are *so* gorgeous together. Everybody wants to meet you, Tara, to see who's finally snared our Leon."

Flo Halldon and a tall man in a tuxedo, western boots and western hat were dominating the group where Blair led them. The man gestured continuously with one hand, drawing attention to both his Rolex and the college all-star football ring he wore on the same finger as his wedding band. His other hand, with one thumb tucked into a diamond belt buckle that was shaped into the State of Texas, held a bottle of Red Stripe. His wife, standing beside him in a lavishly beaded evening gown, also drank beer from a bottle, but she had wrapped the base of her bottle in a paper napkin. "Well, my real estate business let me become an art collector, but what's money for but diversion from work?" the tall man was saying. "In real estate, everything's the bottom line. It's all numbers and lawyers. In the art world," he grabbed Flo's hand and shook it, "it's all done on a handshake."

Tiffany Tate, the silver blond star of TV's latest soap opera, sounded as if she had a cold. She twirled a little silver spoon in one hand. "Don't you have any other diversions from work except art?" she asked flirtatiously.

"Of course I do, darlin'. I play poker, I watch sports, I play tennis, I go to fantastic restaurants, I chase girls. I'm just your average all-American boy, don'tcha know?"

"Binky's also a generous patron of the arts," Flo cut in. "He's just built a mini-park for one of Leon's future pieces in a luxury shopping center he developed in North Florida, and he's also commissioned another work for a corporate headquarters he's building in California. Adria Cass's largest canvas yet has just been installed in the lobby of an office building he just finished outside Austin."

At Leon's approach, Tiffany turned her attention on him as if she'd switched on a searchlight. "Leon, honey, how *are* you? And *why* weren't you at my party in Malibu? We missed you. Oh!" She noticed Tara, her mouth remaining in the tiny round rosebud that had shaped her "Oh." She touched one of Tara's earrings with her spoon and lifted Tara's hand to better see the armlet and ring. "*Where* did you find *these*? They look right out of a museum!"

Leon laughed and introduced Tara. "They *are* out of a museum, Tiffy. Tara's an archaeologist with one of Athens's most important ones. She's got the collection for borrowing."

"Actually," Tara spoke to the actress with words meant for Leon, "these aren't museum pieces. Even I don't have privileges like that. They are *recreations* of museum pieces, though, crafted with the same techniques as in antiquity, and with the same twenty-two carat gold."

"Twenty-two carat! Where did you *get* them?"

Tara spoke deliberately. "They are all gifts."

Tiffany wrinkled her nose at Leon. "You never gave me anything so . . . historical."

Leon said nothing.

The glow in Blair's eyes reappeared. She linked arms with Tara and Leon again to lead them to another group. "Come on, you two. I'm not finished showing you off." And you're not finished with me either, darling Leon, she thought, charged by the challenge ahead. Tara's jewelry had to be from Dimitrios. Who else? Jewels like that meant there was, after all, more than a business relationship there. So gorgeous Leon might not be so unavailable after all.

"Wait a minute." Flo stopped them. "Tara *Niforous*? You must be related to my newest star baby, Nicolas Niforous. No?"

Tara shot a glance at Leon. "Why, yes I am. Nicky is my brother. What do you mean your new 'star'?"

"You can thank this chap here for the introduction. He invited me to Nicky's studio to see the work, and now I'm going to represent him. Your baby brother is going to be *my* newest baby star."

Tara turned in shock to Leon. What else had he done while she was away? She felt a warm smile spread over her face.

Leon smiled back and shrugged as if he had known. Why in hell hadn't Flo told him she was going to represent Nicky? When had all this happened? "It was going to be a surprise," he lied. "I told you I had art on my walls. Well, it's one of Nicky's paintings. I'm glad I bought it before Flo added on her astronomical commission."

"Oh, it's not his *paintings* I'm going to sell, lovey. I have no market for them. But now with the huge gap left by that foreigner buying up all of your work, I have a new windfall market for his sculpture."

Leon tried to keep pace without showing his ignorance. "It's a great idea, Flo. But how are you going to replace my big stuff with Nicky's small pieces?"

"I'm not selling his small pieces, silly. Of course they couldn't fill the sites left by the sales of your art. But while your work is being ensconced in a one-man museum, I'm grooming your protégé by using his abstract works as models, which we're going to reproduce in fiberglass twenty times larger. I've got this boat manufacturer up in Maine who's going to do all the big construction," she turned to Tara, "but, of course, your brother's name will go on every piece, and he'll be the star. His small models will go in the reception rooms of companies or the presidents' offices or somesuch. It's really a unique idea. I'm rather proud of myself, in fact. And your brother! He's so cute and so young! He'll be in real media demand."

Tara turned and walked away. Nicky's abstract pieces, huge and made of fiberglass? She couldn't imagine it. Did Nicky really want this? Or had Leon talked her brother into the idea? What about Nicky's beautiful paintings? She let Blair lead her once again through group after group of introductions. *Go slowly*, she told herself. She felt a rekindled fury at Leon, but checked herself; she knew she didn't have enough facts to conclude anything yet.

Blair, with Tara back in tow again, focused her attention on Leon like a cat on her prey, while continuing to show off her archaeologist to guests. Leon's mind raced as he nodded and shook hands in greeting. Was this good or bad? He observed the uncharacteristic stiffness of Tara's movements and handshakes. Bad.

"I should have opened a branch here in Palm Beach years ago," Flo's voice trailed after them as she retrained her attention on the Texan and his crowd. "Now Carlo Napolitano has beat me to it. He ships *truckloads* of art from here to the Midwest after the holiday seasons. People come here for vacations and have the time to browse."

"Tara, meet Leyla Berke." Blair's voice was bright. Something was definitely wrong between Tara and Leon; she could feel a palpable tension between them now. "Leyla is the most soughtafter psychic reader in Washington. A third of the Senate consults with her on a regular basis—" She steered Tara through several other knots of conversation.

"A professor must either believe he knows everything or believe he cannot know anything," Van was lecturing a group of face-lifted, middle-aged women from California, whose low cleavages proudly boasted their youthfully firm, silicon-implanted breasts. "That's why I became a critic. The great thing about art is that nobody's right and nobody's wrong—" Depressed at Denny's disappearance, he kept his back to the staircase where she and Perry had last been seen.

"The same thing was said of many religions in the declining Roman Empire," a serious young man with a small diamond earring pierced into the tip of his tongue was saying to Kronan Hagen. "They said religions were 'all considered by the people as equally true, by the philosophers as equally false and by the magistrates as equally useful—'"

"This is our special guest, Tara Niforous, an archaeologist from Athens. Of course you know Leon."

"My new design on the cover of *Flair*? I call it a 'subway' bracelet. It has sliding gold panels to hide the diamonds—"

"What do you mean, '*what do they mean*'? A collection of empty boxes in an *art gallery* is obviously a metaphor for the enigma of existence—"

"An archaeologist? Well, you must come out to Santa Fe and dig on our back forty. I'm sure the Indians buried something wonderful there at one time or another. We have millions of rocks—"

"Museums provide the most crucial experience of our

day: Direct contact with hand-produced objects. The real thing! There's a great resurgence in all hand-crafted objects because, in a society full of secondary images from the Internet, television, movies and magazines, the public is hungry for direct experiences."

Leon bolted for the coke table. He was beginning to see these people through Tara's eyes! He was beginning to see other things clearly as well. The "gifts" were obviously from Dimitrios. Who else? And what did that mean? Had Tara once had an affair with her boss? He realized he had acquired another raging headache. Tara would detest the idea of her brother being made into an art star by blowing up fiberglass versions of his abstract sculpture. He was sure of it! There was no need to hang around for the "open-ended" conversation she'd said she wanted at the end of the party. He had messed it up good this time. What had he been thinking of? What was this ridiculous power she had over him anyway? From the beginning: Crying, lying, begging, dreaming. Everything he was doing and feeling was abnormal, had been ever since he met her. To hell with her. To hell with everything! Hey! He needed a line. He plunked ten hundred-dollar bills down on the table and received his silver spoon.

Tara watched Leon vanish from her side. Stoically, she held herself together. She had to get through this evening, if only for Blair's sake now. Blair was leading her toward the group where Adria Cass was holding court. But how could these pretentious people be Blair's friends? Perry's, maybe, but not Blair's. Blair seemed so free of games.

"*Psychic automatism?*" Adria was in the middle of her perennial monologue. "Pure, visual free association. My brush wanders at will. I have no preconception of what it will do. And when you see the results, *your* mind, reason, takes a little mini-vacation and lets your senses have such an intense experience that you mentally leave matter behind and receive a mystical experience. Get it? You've heard of Jung's collective unconscious? Well, my paintings lead you to a connection with something beyond *all* forms of consciousness. To *oblivion*!" She interrupted herself, "Oh, this is Tara from Athens." And continued: "As Dubuffet said . . ."

Tara and Blair moved on to a bored man wearing mirrored sunglasses, ragged jeans and running shoes, who had mesmerized half a dozen women in formal gowns. " . . . neuroses and perversions. It's no accident that we hold the annual MTV Music Video Awards at the Metropolitan Opera House, turning that tradition musical shrine into a mini-circus."

Blair smiled with satisfaction at Tara. "Isn't everyone just fascinating? These people are no intellectual lightweights, as you can see. You archaeologists aren't the only ones interested in serious subjects. Is there anyone else you'd like to meet? I can't introduce you to everyone. They're several hundred people here." And it's time for me to catch up with Leon, Blair thought with a tingle of anticipation. She shot a sharp glance at the stairwell where Perry had disappeared with the Sommers girl. She would have to do something absolutely vile with Leon to pay Perry back. For all his normal philandering distractions, this one was unprecedented by her husband. Oh God! He just passed his fiftieth birthday. Lord help us!

Tara caught a glimpse of Margaret Harrington standing in an alcove, alone except for a waiter with whom she seemed to be enjoying a conversation. "I think I'll visit with your mother a bit more, Blair. Thank you for the tour of your guests."

"They all love you, you know. You're like an exotic species to us ordinary folks—" Blair was off. It was nearly time for the gift giving and then, thank God, dinner, where she could sit down, for a change. Her necklace was too heavy, her shoes were too tight, and her panty hose were squeezing her to bits. Then, automatically squelching all her many discomforts, she continued on her breezy tour, and along the way, picked up Leon, who was loitering by the coke bar, and wore him as her brightest, lightest jewel for the rest of the evening. Tara had vanished.

Tara didn't expect the knock on the door. The clock by her bedside read one AM. She had been lying awake in bed, thinking. She'd pleaded travel lag to Blair's mother, who had sent dinner to her room on a tray. No one else had noticed her departure, apparently not even Leon. The last she had seen him, Blair was whisking him away from the drug bar just as he was spooning cocaine into cute little lines for Tiffany Tate's cute little Hollywood nose.

Only when she saw Blair and Leon together, laughing and kissing other guests, did she remember that he had slept with her, too. When he'd blurted it out in the cab that night, she had been so repelled by the Adria Cass story that she hadn't registered the rest of what he said. She registered it tonight. What kind of people were these? She lay still and stared at the door. She could hear no sound. Good. He had gone away. He was probably "wrecked," to use his word, and she knew she couldn't cope with that at any time, let alone tonight.

Over the past several hours, she had begun to realize that she had come to this party through misplaced friendship for Blair and false hope for Leon. It was all beginning to fall into place: Leon's art and his friends. It seemed probable that, no matter what positive directions he might now be exploring, he still belonged here, that he never had belonged with her, after all. *She* certainly didn't belong here. But, as Dimitrios had said, she must sort *everything* out clearly in her own mind, and Leon was, at best, misbehaving all over the place.

Who could have imagined he would do this crazy thing of destroying his art to prove his for love of her? She couldn't just dismiss such a colossal gesture. On the other hand, how could she approve of Leon's helping Nicky into the commercial arena? Even if Nicky had already been confused— On the *other* hand, she, herself, had asked Leon to help Nicky, so she was just as much to blame. But fiberglass made by a boat company? Things not even made by Nicky's own hand?

The knock came again, louder, and more insistent. He meant to wake her, then. Blair had given them adjoining rooms, separated by a bathroom, and the knocks were at the bathroom door. What now? She got up, pulled on a robe and went to the door.

"I'm in bed, Leon. Please go away."

"We have to talk."

"What could there be to say at this hour that makes any sense, Leon? Go to bed."

"There's *everything* to say. I'm clean. I haven't had anything at all. And I didn't do anything with Blair. But Tara, I've learned a lot tonight. Please open the door. I need to tell you a few important things now."

"Like what?"

"I didn't know about Nicky. You've got to believe that. I took Flo to see his work—Van, too—but I meant to help him, and to try to get back in your good graces."

"Did you really buy one of Nicky's paintings?"

"Yes. Well, I like Nicky. I really do. But this business about manufacturing his pieces by an outside company? Even I'm against that, and always would have been. Tara, please open the door."

He was still in his tux, his tie off and his shirt open to reveal a small, nervous pulse at his throat. His eyes were clear.

"Is the auction over?"

"Yes. It was really very funny. One woman from Newport Beach donated a forty-carat diamond engagement ring from her fourth husband to please her fifth. Then a Houston guy donated a prize Hereford bull, and someone from

New York donated his deed to a landmark townhouse on the Eastside—Blair didn't allow any checks, only real property. There was a title to a 1929 Ford Model A, two Rolls-Royce Silver Ghost titles, one Harry Winston Art Deco emerald and ruby brooch, lots of assorted Tiffany stuff, quite a few Rolex, Patek Phillip and Blancpain watches, even a small castle in Ireland and an eleventh-century chateau in Gascony. But the best gift of all was Margaret's. She was just passing by and—it was obviously a spur of the moment gesture—she suddenly reached into her evening bag and announced that she had a gift after all." Leon burst out laughing in spite of himself. "Well, she tossed her eighteen-carat gold cigarette lighter into the pile of jewelry and deeds and stuff, and then she said that when they all came to their senses, they could use it to burn the art in the new wing."

It was Tara's turn to smile. She could just imagine Blair's mother "donating" her cigarette lighter. The awkwardness between them was broken.

"What can we say to each other now, Leon?" Tara asked wearily. "You must know, aside from all our other problems, that I don't belong here, that I'm not like any of your friends, not even Blair, who I thought had some core sincerity. Margaret's the only person I enjoyed at all tonight, and Kronan, of course. But really, I'm totally out of place here. I finally caught on to the fact that Blair invited me because I would provide some freak appeal for her party. Archaeologists in America, apparently, aren't a common commodity. But *you* should have known better."

"I know. I'm sorry." He sat on the edge of the bathtub and looked straight into her eyes as if before a tribunal. "I woke you up to apologize. Seems that's all I'm doing lately, apologizing. But I also want to tell you that because of *your* presence, something happened to me tonight, something important. I've been to hundreds of parties just like this one. But seeing you here, watching you move like a goddess among the others shocked me into a fresh perspective. You were like a rare flower standing out in a dull weed field: your quiet grace, your serious eyes, your judicious comments, your understated elegance."

"Leon, the jewelry I wore tonight are all gifts from Dimitrios."

"I figured that. It rocked me at first—you and he are so unalike—but then I realized it must have been when you were young and impressionable. Anyway, it doesn't matter. Who am I to cast stones?"

"Leon—"

"Tara! From the time you came to New York I wanted to bring you around to accepting the world I move in. Now, forget about my art, I don't even want this environment for myself anymore. After the auction and dinner, I nearly went to bed with Blair just to spite you. I knew you'd blame me for Nicky's going commercial. But after I'd managed to stay away from drugs the whole evening even though I stood in front of that coke bar for twenty minutes, I also managed not to run away from the truth by going to bed with someone I don't love. I went for a long walk on the beach instead. I was remembering what you told me about art and sex, what they are for you."

"I said 'sacred'."

"Tara, I swear to you I have not slept with anyone but you since Athens— He blanched, remembering that if not for his impotence, this would be a lie, so he quickly moved on to his real truth: What I learned tonight was that doing that now is actually impossible for me. Earlier this evening, I wanted to hate you, but I only ended up hating myself. I don't know how it happened, or when. But the truth, the *truth* in the middle of all the stupid lies, is that I really belong to you. Even if I never intended to in the beginning. Please forgive me for my past! And please give me a chance to try and change Nicky's mind."

"Leon, there's something else—"

"Wait, please! This is so important. About the other thing that's sacred to you: art. On the beach tonight, I realized that although I started out to renounce my art just to show you how much I love you, the funny thing is... now I really don't *want* to make it anymore. I haven't been able to find the energy for my work ever since I met you. And now I know why. You were right. I can't love both you and love the art I made. I... I can't even *touch* my work anymore. And after tonight I don't want to be a part of that world on any terms. Or with those people. I was independently wealthy. Now, by the time I'm finished buying up my stuff, I won't have much. I don't know what I'll do, but I do know it will have nothing at all to do with art. I really *have* changed, all because of you. I've tried to trick you into loving me, and I've tried to flatter you into loving me. But I know better now. I don't know what *you* want, but I know that no matter how I try not to, I want only you. So *you* set the terms. I'll be whatever I must be to have you. Please Tara," his voice was low, his eyes dry; only the pulse at the base of his throat revealed the great price of his words, "can't we start over? Won't you give me a fresh chance to deserve you? You're the only woman I want."

Tara thought that if she breathed, Leon's fragile composure might shatter beyond repair. "Why quit the whole world of art?" she suggested carefully. "Why not quit just the part you no longer care about? Why not go back to the work you started to do, like *Spring Flower?*"

Leon couldn't even smile at her naïveté; he was too drained. "It would be like starting over, and," he leaned his head back against the marble wall, "and I have nothing to say."

"Leon, if you want me badly enough to give up your work, don't you want *yourself* badly enough to go back to the kind of work you used to do, for your own sake? There must be people out there who are different from the people here, tonight. There just has to be a market for Nicky's other work, and Dorina's, and yours, if you decide to go back to your original direction."

"No. I don't want to have anything to do with any kind of art at all anymore. I just want you to love me. You're all I need, all I want."

Tara grabbed the doorframe for support, her admiration for him rising irresistibly in response to such open, unguarded honesty. She had made mistakes, too. She had fallen for Leon too quickly. She had encouraged him; she had behaved as if they could have a future together. What she said was, "Not true. You need art. You need to express—"

Leon laughed the laugh of a child, innocent and clear and joyous at its own sound. "I can enjoy other artist's art. I know you're probably thinking that buying Nicky's work was just another trick to bring you back to me. Well," his voice held pride at truth telling, "at first, that was true, I already told you. I thought if you came back from Athens and saw that I was trying to help him, you'd forgive me my . . . other things. It never occurred to me that Flo would get this diabolical idea about his abstract pieces. I swear it! But the funny thing about Nicky's painting is that after living with it for a while, I truly love it! Every time I walk into my living room, I feel the sunlight—his flowers are sunlight, you know—and the hope in that picture. It makes me want to lie down in it and dream like I used to when I was a boy."

"Leon, you can't give up your art!" Her face was as white as the marble doorframe.

He pulled her to him and buried his face in her breasts; his arms were clamps around her hips. "All right! I love you. I need you! If it's art you require, then I'll do it. I'll go back and start over. I'll become a student and learn all over again. Not for my sake, but if you ask me to do it for you, I'll try. I don't know if I can. It would be going back to the beginning. But if that's what you demand from me in order to give me another chance with you, *I will try.* Even that."

Tara moved a hand tenderly over his hair. He was suspended between two worlds, between what he once was and what he could become, and he saw her as the bridge to connect them. Should she let herself be that bridge? Did she love Leon? Was it possible to love two men at the same time but in different ways? She knew that Leon's biggest battle was still ahead. She decided: He had to fight it alone.

Prying his hands from around her, she walked reluctantly back to her room and returned with the blue fox cape. "It's all too confusing, even in my own mind, to talk about anything more tonight, Leon. I never lied to you. I thought you were all I had ever dreamed of in a man. What I didn't know until this past week," she searched carefully for the right words, "is how close I have always felt to Dimitrios. You said that he and I are unalike, but that's not really true. And the ironic part of it is that if you hadn't come into my life, Leon, I might never have realized how much I . . . *care* for Dimitrios. It was only when I stopped trusting you and I left you that I could see *him* clearly."

She saw a wild refusal come into Leon's eyes. "Dimitrios?" he whispered incredulously. "*Now?*"

Hurting for him, she nodded her head helplessly. She saw the terrible pain invade his eyes. Very gently, she handed him the coat. "I think we shouldn't see each other for a while, Leon. We both need time to assimilate all that's happened. We're upset and confused right now, and really, given my feelings for both Dimitrios and you— I mean, I feel differently about each of you, but I truly don't know what to make of all this right now." She paused at the door. "Don't blame yourself about Nicky. What's happening to him is partly my fault. I asked you to help him." Her voice had become a whisper. Part of her wanted to rush to him, to hold him against the pain she was inflicting upon him.

"I'm still on your side, Leon. Your best side. The side of you that I'll always love," was all she said.

At some point, Leon slipped noiselessly to the cold marble floor, still staring at the closed door.

THIRTY-ONE

PERRY FOUND HIS WIFE sitting in the living room, alone.

There had been no one to let him into the townhouse and he'd had to use his key, something he wasn't sure he'd ever done before. He had also hung his own coat in the closet. Another unusual event. And now here was Blair, sitting alone in the living room. Not drinking. Not reading. Not playing the piano. Not doing anything. Just sitting. She wasn't even listening to music.

He went to the bar. No ice in the bucket. He poured Belvedere into a glass and dropped a couple of ice cubes into it from the freezer. Then he turned to his wife, cautiously. Something was very wrong.

"What's happened? Where are Mike and Mary? What are you doing, sitting here all alone?"

Blair didn't look at him. She sat with her hands clenched together on her knees. She was examining her hands; her nails were painted red again, their normal color. Her voice sounded meek. "I let everybody off for the night."

"What do you mean, everybody? William too? We were having dinner guests tonight as I recall, and he was to collect some of them. Right?" No answer. " Blair?" Perry's patience was beginning to break. "Where is our staff? Where are our cocktails? What are you doing sitting here like some lost soul?"

Blair looked at her husband with an honest plea in her

eyes, fastening her hands together even tighter to hold down her panic, one that had been growing in intensity all afternoon. This evening, she had decided to address it. "Perry, what do you love?"

"Blair!" Perry exploded onto the sofa beside her, anger replacing any apprehension he may have felt. "Answer me!"

She examined her hands again. She had never imagined fingers could grow so tight to one another. "I let everybody off tonight, and I canceled the dinner so I could be alone in the house. Do you know, Perry, that I have never been alone in my own home? And it's very odd. I know I want to be here, alone, but I don't know what to *do* here."

"Blair!" Perry rose to the phone. "You must be ill. I am going to call Mary down here and then I'm going to call a doctor. Which doctor would you like? For your head or your body?"

"It won't do any good to call the staff. I told you I let them off."

"So you let them off. I am going to call them back on. They *live* here!"

"Not tonight. I've put them up in a hotel."

"*You've what?*" Perry stood rooted to the spot, the phone in his hand. "Blair, you *are* ill."

Blair peered up at him again. This time he could see the confusion. The fear?

"No. Well, maybe. Perry, please answer me. What do you love?"

"What kind of question is that? I love everything I do, otherwise I wouldn't do it. I love you and the children and my parents. I love cute young females, and I love having ice in the bucket when I arrive home. Blair, this is very unlike you, you know."

"Yes, I know. But I asked you because I don't think I know what I love. Ever since we got back from Palm Beach— I don't know . . . I mean, of course I love you and the children and my mother, but those are automatic loves.

What I mean, I think, is what have I *chosen* to love? Take Tara, for example: she loves her work. She chose it *because* she loves it."

"Blair! We've only been home from the party for three days. This is ridiculous. You let the staff off and canceled a dinner party so you could think about what you *love*? Look, it's only natural to feel a letdown after such a big event, especially when you've still got the museum opening to pull off. But try to remember why you *had* that party and why you took on the colossal project of *building* the new wing. Because you love *art*." She was finally focusing on him. He went on: "Look, you love clothes. You spent two hundred grand on clothes last year, not counting furs. You love decorating. God knows you've traveled the world over for a fourteenth-century urn here and an eighteenth-century armoire there. Come on! Put on your famous smile, and we'll go out to dinner. How about Mama Rosa's? Some people we know are bound to be there and we can have a good old lasagna to make you feel better."

"No, I don't love decorating. It's just something one does. I mean, homes have to be furnished. And I don't love clothes. I mean *love*. And I don't love art. It's a toy, like everything else. And the new wing? What did *I* do on my own but give and raise money? The architect, chosen by my mother, designed the building. Kronan, much as he hated the task, filled it with art. Oh, Perry, most of the people at the party were *nouveau riche*. They're so lucky. They've all made their money in professions they chose. They could do or be anything. They could love anything or anyone they chose."

"And you can't? You're just being morose."

"No. We're expected to be what we are because we're born *who* we are. I never actually thought about what schools to attend. I just knew which ones were for me because of my family. I married you because—don't look stricken, my pet, we're perfect for each other and I know that. But . . . why *did* I marry you, after all? It seemed so inevitable at the time that it was almost automatic, but I didn't select you as a real conscious choice. Don't you see what I'm trying to say? What do I love that I *choose* to love? When a person loves, they love some *thing*. Why *that* thing out of all the other things available? People without wealth are forced to choose because they have to. Each generation is moving from one economic and lifestyle expectation to another. But we never move. We just are and do and love whatever has been established for us, in some sort of unspoken way."

"That's absurd. People like us do all sorts of things, including work. Decorators. Designers. Editors."

"Yes, but only in certain categories. Even our children, who will work not because they need to but because it's expected in today's chic circles, are straightjacketed in their choices. What would everyone say if Michelle decides to run a little clothing boutique like Flo used to do? Then she would be considered a mere *merchant*. It would never be accepted." She paused. "Listen, I've wanted to sleep with Kronan Hagen for years. He always brushes me off. Not because he loves his wife or some tripe like that, but because he loves God. And God says 'No.' Today I had lunch with him, and, for the first time, I tried to figure out *why* I've always wanted to sleep with him. I don't love him. I don't even like him. I don't dislike him either. Don't you see? I don't have any reason to sleep with him any more than I had any reason to marry you. It's just there to be done. I feel like a fish that's swept along with the current, mouth open, just swallowing everything that happens by me. And our friends are just the same. One says to another: why don't you become an editor for our publishing firm? Not because you know anything about literature, but because you have a lot of well-known friends, and by having you with us we'll be able to publish their memoirs, which have built-in sales appeal because of *who* they are. And another says, why not decorate? You have such flair, and all your friends would be a built-in clientele for you. It's all an interconnected game of influence and brand names. So these people gobble up a career the same way I gobble up the art world. Because of my background, it was always floating near me, ready to be swallowed."

"Blair," Perry set his empty glass down on the bar," you *are* being morose. All of us are precisely who we want to be, love whom we want to love, and do what we want to do. Right now, I want to go to Mama Rosa's. You may join me if you wish. What you need is to laugh and have a good time."

"Yes, but don't you see? I've never even thought about what to do for a good time. I don't even know how to cook. Oh, please do try to see, Perry. So few of us ever *choose*, really."

"Goodnight, Blair. Have the staff back by morning."

Blair stopped herself on the way to the bar. No, she would not. The panic—No, she mustn't call it that; it was boredom. It was restlessness, and it would pass if only she could calm down. But not with anything that impaired her ability to think. Or to feel. No substitutes tonight. No alcohol, no drugs. No socializing or making love to Perry simply because there was nothing else to do. No! No non-stop distraction tonight. Besides, she was still angry with Perry. Not because he'd gone to bed with the Sommers girl, that was to be expected, but because he'd taken her to the master bedroom. Perry and she had always abided by an unspoken agreement that none of their flings would ever take place in their own bed; it was, in some indirect way, in honor of their children. Not only had he broken that agreement, but he had also neglected his duties as host for most of the party. By the time he'd come back downstairs he was so out of touch he was useless; it was clear by his limp body movements and the lingering scent of bitter almond trailing after him that they'd done heroin. No, she didn't want to be with Perry tonight. And certainly not with Leon. She was furious with him too. Leon had refused sex with her. Refused! She had never been rejected before in her whole life! She sank back down on the couch.

Thank goodness that party was over. Aside from the spectacular donations she'd received, the whole affair was, in her mind, a disaster. Even her mother had lost her manners. Blair had never known her to behave distastefully before. But she knew why. Blair wasn't the only one angry with Perry. She had watched her mother seethe beneath her composure when Perry and Denny left the party for the bedroom. First the girl had tried to insult Margaret in her own home and then blatantly teased her daughter's husband into bed before everyone's eyes. No one else had cared, of course, and everyone else had a wonderful time, but her mother had not enjoyed a moment of it. And Blair hadn't enjoyed a minute of the party either. Beyond Perry's revolting behavior, Tara Niforous's presence also had something to do with her lack of enjoyment. Blair regretted she had ever invited her. Tara had been a perfect guest, lovely and charming, but something about her reserve came off as a silent reproach to everyone else there.

Rising, Blair tossed her head defiantly. She felt angry at the whole world tonight. She wanted to be alone. She *was* alone. And she would *do* something, alone. But what?

She went to the kitchen and opened the refrigerator. She would try to prepare her own dinner tonight. That would be a good start.

She closed the refrigerator door. There must be *one* thing out of all she loved that she had *chosen* to love. She tossed her head again as if to throw off the unnerving restlessness crackling inside her. She should go riding tomorrow.

Lickland! Of course! She had chosen *him*!

She raced upstairs to her bedroom and flung riding clothes from closet to bed, grateful for action. She would go and ride him *now*.

William didn't answer. Why? Because she'd let him off

for the night, that's why. Blair laughed aloud at herself. Perry was right. She had been morose.

The cab driver was on the young side. Not especially attractive, but that didn't matter; he'd been willing enough to drive her to New Jersey after she had pressed a hundred dollar bill into his hand.

"What else do you do, driver?" Blair felt suddenly back in a good mood. Most cab drivers loved to talk and, aside from the third-world imports, many young ones still seemed to drive part-time while pursuing a career in something else. Maybe it wasn't so lucky to be middle-class after all.

The young man observed her in the rear view mirror. "My name's Dean Fulton. I'm an actor."

Aren't we all, Blair thought.

The countryside was dark. There were few cars on the road. The winding back roads of New Jersey were even emptier than the interstate.

"Say, if it's not too personal, can I ask you why you're going out to Far Hills all alone at this time of night?"

"I'm going out to say hello to a horse that I love. And then I'm going to ride him in the morning."

"Well, you must love him a lot. It's getting late."

"I do," Blair said. I *do*, she thought. I'll feel it when I see him. I know I will.

The stables were dark, but her actor-cab driver aimed the high beams on the door until she found the switch for the floodlights. She sailed in to the barn, the wind of purpose setting her course.

He *was* beautiful. She led Lickland out of his stall and patted one hand approvingly over a muscular flank. His black coat quivered under her touch. Blair moved her hand slowly over the rest of his strong body waiting for the feeling, waiting for the inner charge of pleasure, waiting for the thrill of owning him, of appreciating him, of loving him. She ran the stallion out into the ring. The cab driver followed her with a saddle, but by the time he reached the horse, Bill Daniher was ambling toward them from the carriage house where he lived with his wife. Bill had cared for two generations of Gothard horses.

"Oh, it's you, Miss Blair. And what brings you out here, may I ask, at this time of night?" he asked without curiosity. "You aren't going to ride him, now, are you Miss Blair?"

"Hello Bill. Yes, I'm going to ride him now. Just a little around the ring and then a nice long trailride in the morning. I've missed him so."

Bill Daniher saddled Lickland and then leaned against the riding rail, not saying a word. To his knowledge Blair Gothard had never missed anyone or anything. She had never shown affection for any of her horses and, even though she declared him her favorite, had ridden this stallion only seldomly. But when she did ride him, she rode him hard. Bill had always thought it was for thrills. He watched her circle the ring, slipping gracefully from gait to gait, her back straight, her hands relaxed.

Dean Fulton gazed with admiration at Blair. She was luscious; her long blonde hair, flowing down her back, contrasted intriguingly with the coarse tweed of her jacket. What a wild woman, coming out here like this so late at night just to ride a horse. Well, rich people could do what they liked.

Blair leaned down and stroked the horse's neck. "Come on, big boy," she whispered, "give it to me. Give me the feeling."

The animal responded willingly enough to every pressure of her knees, to every subtle movement of her wrist, the way every man she had ever known responded to her in bed. But where was the feeling? A burst of anger shoved her heels deep into the horse's flank. *Where was the feeling?*

She dug her spurs viciously into the horse's side again and again until his pace tripled. She strained forward with him as if their collective speed would wipe out her growing inner panic. *Not* panic, merely restlessness. *Not* inner fear, merely restlessness. Lickland let out an anguished cry and stumbled—

She brought the horse sharply to a standstill, staring down at his head in utter shock, panting as hard as he was panting, confused as completely as he was.

Bill came running as she dismounted and, grabbing the reins from her hand as if to rescue the horse, led a staggering Lickland back toward his stall. *This* he had never witnessed in his life.

Blair, shaking uncontrollably but no longer out of breath, noted with a small triumph the steadiness of her voice and the length of time Bill remained standing perfectly still before turning back to her, certain he could not have heard the command correctly.

"Shoot him," she repeated.

"I'm sorry, Ma'am, what did you say?"

"I said, Bill Daniher, to shoot him."

"*Shoot* him?" He shook his head as if to throw off a sudden sleep. "Shoot *Lickland*?"

Blair inclined her head in the direction of the cab driver. "Well, I don't mean for you to shoot Mr. Fulton, here."

Bill moved automatically closer to the horse as if to protect him. The woman didn't seem drunk or drugged. But she had ridden the horse cruelly. "I don't understand the order, Miss Blair," he said warily. "Is it a joke or something?"

Blair's face hardened. No it wasn't a joke, goddamn him. Goddamn them all! If she loved this horse, and she watched him die, *then* she would feel it. If she sacrificed this one thing that she really loved, she would at last feel *something*. Maybe then.

"No, of course, it isn't a joke. Just do as I say. He doesn't please me anymore."

"Are you crazy?" Bill's cry was shrill. "This is the finest stud in the state. He's worth a quarter of a million dollars!"

"Bill Daniher, who owns this animal?" Blair's eyes flamed dangerously, daring him to disobey.

"Well, you do, of course, Ma'am, but I mean . . . I just can't! You can't possibly mean—"

"If you don't, I will. I know where the gun is, although I'm sure I'm not as adept at using it as you are."

Daniher stood staring at her for a long time. If she actually shot the poor beast, Lickland might suffer senselessly. *If* she shot him. He looked harder at Blair's face. *Would* she? He glanced at the cab driver; the young man was staring dumbly at Blair. Daniher looked back at her in disgust and dissolving disbelief.

She would.

The trainer walked to the barn, came back with a handgun and, without another word, put a bullet into the horse's temple. He returned, his face expressionless, to the carriage house and vomited, and wept.

Blair stared, her eyes wide and dry, down at the giant hulk that had been Lickland. Bill's shot had been so clean there was virtually no blood at all. The horse looked asleep.

She waited for the pain to start, the tears. If not pleasure, then, at least pain.

The cab driver rubbed his eyes. "You *are* wild, lady, he said softly.

Blair burst out laughing as a rushing breath of relief spread through her like a fresh cold wind. Her shaking stopped. It was over.

There was no pain. There would be no tears. Her innermost fears had died along with the horse. It was done! She had killed the thing she loved most in the world. But she had also killed her fear that her life, that *she*, was meaningless. A line had been crossed. She would never feel restless again.

THIRTY-TWO

THE UPPER WEST SIDE NEIGHBORHOOD was improving as she got closer to the Columbia University area, but it was still pretty lousy. Garbage cans spilled over, and old cars lined the streets, some of them stripped of tires. The buildings crouched together cracked and crumbling; only their seamed proximity to each other appeared to hold them up. Down a short set of stairs leading to the basement of a dingy, smelly brownstone Tara finally found the sign: A IS A GALLERY. Nicky's and Dorina's paintings were here? Frowning, she pushed open the door.

The four days since her return from Palm Beach had been depressing. She worried about Leon: would he make it back to himself *by* himself? And she worried about her brother: would he really go commercial? She knew she couldn't interfere with either man, and Nicky *was* a man now. The only good thing was that she'd finally convinced the powers that be at the Met of the importance not only of the exhibit's specific presentation but also of its placement in the museum at large. Work was winding down for the holidays, so she had used the extra time to educate herself about New York's contemporary art scene by visiting dozens of art galleries, both uptown and down. In most of them, a peek inside was all it took to kill her interest; even when representational, most of the work was blatantly commercial in both form and content, and poor in quality. In quite a few, however, the painting and sculpture on display were competent if not inspired, and in a select few, the work was truly excellent. But even at its best, the work was largely derivative and banal. Or just plain saccharine, exactly as Leon had said: "pretty pictures." And when it did project ideational content, most of it was, as Leon had also said: "activist." What was missing in virtually all of it was a commitment to beauty and an elevation of spirit that resonated positive contemporary life in a sincerely positive way. She hoped she would find these attributes here. With whom were Dorina and Nicky keeping company?

Oh! Wondrous company! Her mood lifted instantly upon entering the large gutted basement of the townhouse, with steps at its far end rising up to a platform that opened out onto a backyard of equal size. The paintings and sculpture—superb, lush images!—commanded her attention to such a degree that she didn't know where to begin. What a breath of fresh air this place was.

She went first to a large painting that dominated one wall of the small gallery. Signed by a Richard Samson, it was titled *Love Asleep*. A framed poem with the same title hung next to the canvas. Ecphrasis? A poem written to the painting? Or was the painting inspired by the poem? She decided to read the poem first:

LOVE ASLEEP

> His shoulder bare, her flaming hair
> spread like sunset's hues
> across his chest to warm him where
> his life beats silent, still
> in restful sleep, so unaware
> and yet of her aware, taking care
> especially in these tranquil hours
> that none should alarm nor
> one should dare
> disturb her gentle face in sleep.

> Entwined together, now they share
> the night, vulnerable and fair.
>
> What moments these, what blissful ease
> threads like trust imbued
> beneath their breasts a quiet peace;
> the sky a coverlet, soft
> and dark and deep, comfort keeps,
> and when the breezes flee, they never flee
> completely from these fragile hours,
> when none should alarm
> nor one should see
> their sweet embrace in sleep.
>
> Entwined together, now they seize
> their right to dreams and memories.

So unapologetically romantic! Anachronistic? Or a conscious desire to use diction and syntax from another era in order to focus on past, more innocent sentiments and bring them into the harsh "now" of today? Tara turned to the painting, which depicted a man and a woman floating—no, lying nude together in an embrace and sleeping, with the woman's head resting on the man's shoulder, on what appeared to be some color field that formed an indescribable couch of space. No anachronisms, here. Timeless, no matter what the vocabulary. The richly modeled forms were sensuous and lyrical, the colors subtle, and the lighting at once dramatic and seductive. Passion and peace. Power and vulnerability. Visually and conceptually. Romantic and ... troubling. She had slept in the arms of two different men this month. Which one did she want to sleep with forever? She loved Dimitri, of that she was sure. But if Leon was *really* changing in a deep and complete way?

A young salesman appeared at her side. "The poem came

first," he said. "Everybody asks. The painter, from New Hampshire, read the poem in a journal published by the owners of this gallery and was inspired to translate it into his own medium. A woman wrote the poem and a man made the painting."

Tara's interest piqued. "How many subscribers to this journal?"

"Oh, about nineteen hundred, now. It's really growing." The young man handed her a brochure.

Such a tiny number, she thought sadly, turning to another painting. And this little operation was the only outlet for Nicky's work? Yet, modest though it might be, the quality of the work was very, very high. She had seen nothing else to match it anywhere. *Invitation to the Dance*, the title card read. A female nude reclined on a fox fur thrown over a petit point racamier—the one in Dorina's studio! The female gazed directly at the viewer, and she held a lavender rose in one hand, offering it to . . . ? The entire painting was an invitation: the nude offering the flower, the champagne bottle sparkling through a faceted crystal ice-bucket, waiting with two glasses on the oriental rug-covered floor. Gorgeous painting! Dorina really was a powerhouse: a nude and a still life combined. Luxury and love combined: '*Luxe, calme et volupté*', one of the great traditions of Western-heritage art. Tara's attention kept returning to the nude's face: soft hint of a smile, proud but feminine tilt to the head, and eyes of such intelligence that one could not mistake the value she placed on her gifts, above all the gift of her own person. A dog (symbol of fidelity) and an open book (intellectualism) lay at her feet.

Tara searched her memory for female nudes throughout the history of Western art; this was unlike anything she had ever seen. Neither Venus Celestial nor Venus Vulgaris, this was *woman*, now, here on earth, thoroughly contemporary and 'real,' and just as thoroughly romantic and ideal. And it *was*, a word Leon had told Dorina could *not* apply to her work, 'relevant.' Tara thought of some of the other nudes she had seen a couple of days ago in a posh Madison Avenue gallery, where human figures were depicted in bald realism: bulges, bloated bellies, elbows, knees, male stubble and female pubic hair in stark detail. Dorina's female nude was body, but it was also mind and soul. Just like her drawings that Dimitrios so loved. And Dorina, truly a remarkable woman, was in love with him? Tara couldn't tolerate the thought. She moved on.

Only a few works of sculpture were displayed. The craftsmanship was superb in all of them, and they were each arresting in their own way, but Tara couldn't help wondering what kind of power the sculptor who had created *Spring Flower* could imbue into his mature work, if he should decide to make it. Could he ever believe again in the idealized nude? Could Leon recapture the vision of his youth? *Would* he? Given all she now knew about him, would it make the telling difference to her if he did? Why her reluctance to give him up?

Tara leafed through some loosely bound manuscripts lying on a table in the center of the room, and called the young man.

"These are unpublished works," he explained. "We represent two playwrights and three novelists, who write in the Romantic Realism School but haven't been successful in selling their work to big publishers."

"Romantic Realism?"

"Well, it's not exactly in fashion or even a well-known term, actually," the clerk hesitated, "but that's what we call it. It's Romanticism in the nineteenth-century sense, narratives rooted in serious ideas and style rising from passionately held values. But it's realism because the settings and characters, instead of being exotic, historical or fantasy, are real-life contemporary." He sighed. "It's difficult because most people confuse Romanticism with popular *Romance* fluff." He picked up a musical score and opened it for her.

"Our composers write in the Romantic school as well, melodic and harmonic works, and that's pretty difficult to sell as original work to either the mainstream or academic music people today—you find it mostly in movie music—so we sell copies to small chamber groups around the country who are looking for contemporary works that expand traditional forms."

"Neo-Romanticism?" Tara laughed; this fellow was so serious, while the place was so joyous! "Artists born too late?"

The clerk snapped his head up in astonishment. "Certainly not! We think this is the art of the *future*."

Tara was peering out French doors leading to the garden in the back of the building.

"We give concerts out there during the summer," the salesclerk commented.

"Looks as if you offer a little bit of everything here." Tara sent him a soft smile.

"Well, that's not exactly by choice. The arts are still dominated by . . . other viewpoints at the moment, so there's not much press coverage or buying activity for art that portrays reality as generous and man as noble. The owners of this place mean to provide a choice for that part of the public, no matter how small that part might be, who are starved for art that's positive and uplifting."

Outside again, Tara wandered the squalid streets, no longer noticing the squalor. Surprise! It wasn't just visual artists but writers, poets and composers, too! Something was stirring, and only a foment of *ideas* could cause that. Could there actually be some philosophical weathervane pointing the way? The owners of the gallery were certainly sure of their direction, and that took commitment and courage.

Ironically, the whole thing smacked of an underground movement (in a basement, yet) totally unknown but totally committed and undeterred by their obscurity. What if it came above ground? If *Leon* returned to this kind of art, his name alone could carry the others into the spotlight. Wasn't there anything she could give him during this difficult period to give him support without giving herself along with it?

THIRTY-THREE

LEON THREW HIS HALF-EMPTY BOTTLE of beer at the sheet of copper. It felt good to throw things again, to be energetic again. The bottle made the desired dent. Since college, Leon had always drunk beer while working, but now he was downing it only as a chaser, after several slugs of scotch. Back to work on the copper piece, he'd been sipping and slugging for almost a week now, the exact amount of time he'd been back from Palm Beach. The original design for the spherical copper sculpture still remained pinned to the wall as a daily reminder of the sentimental trap into which he'd nearly fallen. He appraised the metal's transformation now with satisfaction: no sphere, the copper sheets had been reshaped into a huge, off-kilter, blown-out, box-kite form. When installed by the lake at the California corporate headquarters, the piece would be balanced in such a way as to make it appear deliriously *off* balance on one precarious point of a tilted granite pyramid. The design was ingenious, because viewed from any angle it would make *observers* feel dangerously off balance as well; in fact, they would feel as if *they* were keeling over instead of the piece. That, after all, was the joke, was it not? He watched now, also with satisfaction, as dribbles of beer mixed with muriatic acid and slithered down the sides of the metal construction to leave behind burned-out tracks that scarred the copper's once-gleaming surface. He analyzed the work closely. It was great! But was it finished? He had crimped and cut some of the hard edges into jagged warnings: "Don't come too close." Much of the surface, far from being beaten into a greater glow, he had beaten until it was ... well, beaten. Then he had corroded it with acids until it was lusterless as well.

He opened another bottle of beer and leaned against a wall, still regarding the work. He felt it was the most powerful thing he had ever created. It stood beaten and battered now, like a once-beautiful object, a once-promising idea that had suffered trauma and time. But it still stood. Alive. Leon chuckled indulgently to himself. What was it he had said this piece would be? A "shining *astro-bauble* dropped from a far-off and glittering galaxy as a gift to meager earth?" He shook his head in wonder at the temporary insanity that had caused him to envision such an insipid image. He threw the second bottle of beer at the sculpture, denting it precisely where it called for another dent, and picked up a blowtorch. A few charred holes would add the final touch, impact marks from meteorite hailstones dropping from space to destroy any glimmer of beauty. Then—Oh yeah, so bad it was "beautiful," the final, final insult!—he would splotch the whole hellish thing all over with gobs of paint a là Adria style, something he'd never done before: guck his work up with paint. Now, that *would* finish it, especially when salt-sea air, humidity and heat began to cause the peeling process. And *this* joke would cause some fresh headlines, too; he'd never used paint before.

He wielded the torch expertly, a sense of renewed abandon guiding his hand. It felt good to play with fire again. He felt like a kid just released from the disciplines of military school, free to become a troublemaker again. Tara was well out of his life, and for good this time. To think he'd wanted to give up his *work* for her, actually dumping millions of dollars worth of it into the ocean. Insane! Well, he could get it all back. *He* knew where it was. It would be some feat; hauling it out would be a hell of a lot harder than dumping it in. But with Basilious's help, he could do it. He pulled a smug grin. One great thing about his kind of art was that if it got damaged during any of the dumping or retrieving processes, he could always say that that was the plan: he had "transformed" his old art into new art; retrieved from the sea, it would be a modern archaeological "discovery." Then Flo could sell it all over again. Or maybe he *would* donate the lot of it, as his phantom buyer had insinuated, and get some city to build a space for it. That had been done before, even by biggies like—who was it, up in Toronto? You give the work and they give *you* the venue. What the hell. Hey! That's what he'd do.

He should have seen all along that it was Tara who had pushed him into behaving like a madman. Sex and art as sacred! If all of her other nutty ideas hadn't penetrated his brain, that proclamation should have tipped him off that she wasn't quite normal in the head. No wonder she'd spent years with that fossil Dimitrios in their musty, old museum. She was like Dimitrios after all. They were a perfect match, like a pair of worn-out slippers.

Leon wiped the sweat from his face with a shirtsleeve and took another slug of scotch. He was over Tara. It was like being over a nightmare. Throwing the blue fox cape into the lake in Palm Beach had ended it. He had watched the mound of fur sink slowly downward, a matted, dying animal pulled into a watery grave. When it disappeared completely, leaving not even a ripple as a remainder of its existence, he had awakened feeling clear-headed and like himself for the first time in months.

He might have felt even better if he'd been able to make up to Blair as well that night, but the sun was already creeping over the lake by the time he had returned to the house, and Blair was gone by the time he awoke that afternoon. Poor Blair. He should have slept with her. She was so lonely anyway; she always kept herself non-stop busy to avoid knowing how lonely she was. And for what had he refused her? For Tara to refuse *him*! He'd called Blair to apologize every day since his return, but the butler said she was at her horse farm for a few days' rest and didn't want to be disturbed. Poor Blair. She was probably "resting" by riding her horses to death to get over that party: first Perry's vanishing act with what's her name, the redheaded Arts Council girl, then her mother throwing the cigarette lighter on all the goods, and then his own refusal to sleep with her. All in all, a real tough evening for Blair. She always ended up with her horses when she was upset about something. He'd seen her ride many times; it wasn't a pretty sight. But he'd make it up to her the moment she returned to New York.

 Maybe he should call Adria. She'd looked spectacular at the party, especially that purple wig. He stood back and scrutinized his work. It was finished. What he would tackle next, he hadn't the foggiest idea. But this would take care of the corporate headquarters in California. Now, what he needed was a good lay. No, a good homecooked meal and *then* a good lay. Adria's homemade pasta and clam sauce. Perfect.

 Skirting the edge of Brooklyn in a cab, he could see the Statue of Liberty patiently holding her beacon aloft in the distance. He turned his head away.

"Garlic. Garlic. And more garlic. That's the secret. You can't have too much of it." Adria handed him another bulb for mincing. "And good olive oil. You can't cheat on the quality of the oil. That's why you like my clam sauce best. Fresh tomatoes and fresh clams. If you hadn't gone to Randazio's in Sheepshead Bay for them, I couldn't have the privilege of concocting this meal for you at two o'clock in the morning." Adria gave him a playful look. "What is it, Baby? Pregnant or something? What's Flo doing with your *art*?"

 "She's re-selling it, Adria, like I said. And I'm getting

back my old appetites. *All* of my old appetites." He took a long swig of wine. Adria's breasts swung heavily back and forth beneath her flannel nightgown as she pressed garlic into the simmering oil.

Leon shucked clams at the kitchen table. "So what's hot?" he asked idly. "What's next for you serious folks?"

"Don't you mean what's *way cool*? See how out of touch you've become?" Adria reached over and dribbled some white wine into her sauce.

"Well, modern mythology continues its medieval revival path," she said, splashing the remaining wine into her glass and motioning for Leon to get another bottle from the refrigerator. "And demonology, too. But we're deep into inner demons, now: psychic aberrations instead of aliens, that inspire horrors and atrocities only the *human* mind can conceive. Add to that our obsession with regurgitating and revising a whole lot of history—look at all the war movies!—not only to make it politically correct for our warrior state but to justify our escalating desire for sensational gore, lately bringing it all up to date by exploiting all sorts of religious fanaticism and fears. Plus continuing to explore our bodily functions, of course, especially the degrading and thoroughly messy acts of shit and sex. Potty humor is out but self-loathing is still in, so along with 'reality' perversities, we're also continuing to explore the shame we all have over our animal bodies, including our disgusting fluids. Look around you! If you didn't spend half your time on vacation and the other half filling corporate commissions, and *then* complicating your life by packing your head with rocks from that Greek archaeologist for months, you'd know that these preoccupations have been in full swing for a long time now."

Adria smiled indulgently at Leon's quizzical expression. "Don't worry, Babydoll. I *like* your sexy mess. You've just been so downtime lately that I've forgotten the taste of it. Anyway," she chatted blithely on, "by continuing to modernize primitivism, medievalism and mysticism, all living creatures are now being held sacred again as interdependent organisms. Even the earth itself is unquestionably considered so. All living creatures except humans, that is, because now *we* are vile oppressors of the sacred and must sacrifice our needs to those of nonhuman or subhuman life." She turned fully to him, raising one eyebrow and looking smug, as she loved to do. "And politically, my Babydoll, *my* 'radical' generation's hippie-flowerchild ideas are mainstream by now, so we're moving solidly into an epoch that is profoundly anti-individualistic, all under the facade of global peace, which can never happen without global socialism, of course, which can't come about until after global military control levels the playing ground, which complements of the one and only three-faced God, it's doing big time right now." She laughed at Leon's puzzled expression. "Never mind, you're not supposed to understand. But don't *you* worry, Babydoll. Your work's already there, 'there' being wherever that damned foreigner decides to build you a one-man museum. I don't know how you let Flo do such a thing, pulling your work up by the roots all over the country. Anyway, postmodern artists like us, savvy activists or 'useful idiots', doesn't matter which, help pave the way for the new world anarchy that's expanding exponentially now. And anarchy's the first step to global *order*. Get it? Nihilism is over! The basic values of Western civilization have finally been met and destroyed."

Leon hadn't the vaguest idea what she was talking about and couldn't care less; she always tied art with mysticism and politics like this. But the word "sacred" was popping up too often, from the mouths of diametrically opposed women. "Very few American artists have ever been truly philosophical the way you are, Adria," he mumbled. "We may be angry, but most of us have never been thinkers. Now even the angriest of us are tired. It takes energy to live on the cutting edge."

"That's my point, Leon! *Everybody's* tired of the demands

of reason and a 'civilized' society. Look at the continuing trend in commercial *memoir:* It's a titillating mindbender to know that your neighbor could be a rapist, your child a murderer, your favorite politician or priest a pedophile. And just think of all the other aberrations we're uncovering in the depths of our own unworthy souls."

Adria's son, Jason, stumbled sleepily into the kitchen. Leon could sense a headache coming. Oh, hell, let it come. These weren't just headaches from too much booze or too little sleep, these were *brain* aches. Only since Tara came into his life. He wished he'd never met her! "So what are *you* going to do next?" he asked Adria, slugging more wine in an effort to dull the growing pain locating itself, this time, in his forehead.

"Oh, Leon. You're getting too old to be so naïve. Our audience is set. Once we were the darlings of the avant-garde and the press. Then we were the darlings of the socialites and the dealers. Now we're the darlings of the real estate developers and the corporations. *We* are now *safe.* We're established. We're in museums."

Her face flushed from the steaming pasta, Adria tested a strand of linguini by throwing it onto a wall to see if it stuck. Then she emptied the pot into a colander. "Let's eat." She tossed the pasta with the clam sauce and motioned for Leon to pull the bread from the oven. Jason opened a bottle of red wine. His mother said he had to be twelve before he could have a whole glass. Next year.

"By my Karma, Skillman." Impulsively, Adria leaned over and deposited a wet kiss on Leon's mouth. "Welcome back. Tonight reminds me of the old days when you first quit college and came to the Rails. I haven't seen you want to discuss art seriously like this for years. What's up?"

"Everything that *used* to be up," Leon teased, fishing through his pasta for whole clams. "I'm not over the hill yet, you know."

"Good! You know, you've always been rather ignorant

about art ideas. You just make your art. You've been one of us by instinct rather than on purpose."

Leon drained his glass and, his hand shaking, managed to pour another one without spilling. "*You've always been one of us*," Dorina had said.

Adria turned to her son. "And you, my sweetie, will not be happy tomorrow morning when I have to haul you out of bed for school unless I send you back to your pillow. Scoop that sauce onto your bread and head off, now. Kiss Leon goodnight."

Leon wiped sauce off his cheek. Adria never managed to put napkins on the table. He dunked his own bread into the remaining sauce in his bowl and downed it with the last of his wine, eyeing Adria's pendulous breasts as she herded Jason off to bed. It was like the old days. This is where he belonged. Sex and art. Food and drink. All consumable. Eat life before it eats you. He grabbed Adria's nightgown as she reached in front of him to clear away dishes. The gown ripped open and a huge breast fell out; he caught it in his mouth as they tumbled to the kitchen floor along with the dishes Adria had been holding. Straddling the bed of broken china, he buried his hands deep in her flesh and felt his own pants being torn off. He was ready for real life with a real woman who wanted him for what he was not for what he could be.

Adria was shrieking with delight, smearing clam sauce from a broken plate onto her thighs, on her breasts, and then on him. Leon licked the sauce off her breasts, ignoring the fact that it was turning to bile in his mouth. He dug his tongue into Adria's mouth, ignoring the rising hint of vomit from his stomach, then raced to the bathroom just in time, his forehead drenched in sweat. *Tara*! *God damn her*!

He couldn't stop throwing up. His shoulders shook violently and his teeth began to chatter, but he still couldn't stop the vomiting. Adria was at the bathroom door to help.

He slammed it shut in her face. "It must have been mixing the drinks. I'll be all right."

He hung his face over the sink and splashed cold water again and again over his burning eyes. He sucked on a tube of toothpaste to freshen the foul taste in his mouth. He took off his shirt and wrapped a towel around his shoulders. It was over. He was all right now.

He peered at his ashen face in the mirror, seeing more than he wanted to, then quickly turned away and sank slowly to the bathroom floor. So what? So he'd thrown Tara's fur into the lake the same way he'd thrown *The Promise* into the river. And he had come to Adria for sex in the same way he'd gone to every willing female he could find after breaking with Valerie. It was the same scenario, but turned against him now. This time, he was the whore.

So he was not all right. He had seen a flash of it in the mirror, in his own eyes. He was sick. But not in his body . . . in his soul.

He drifted into an exhausted sleep, not noticing when Adria covered him with a blanket. Dreading a nightmare, he slipped gratefully into imageless oblivion.

※ ※ ※

Helene Skillman's knuckles were white on the steering wheel. If only Leonard were with her. She'd called his office, but he'd left early to do some last minute shopping. It was still only four-thirty, but it was nearly dark. In another half-hour, evening would set in, and then she'd never find Leon. Outdoor evergreens sparkled with colorful Christmas lights in front of the homes she passed. Helene didn't notice them. She wanted to drive faster, but she still wasn't sure where she was going.

After Leon's call, she'd raced to her car, only to sit paralyzed in the driveway for five minutes until she could figure out where he might possibly be. "Mother, help me," was all he had said. She had never heard such quiet desperation in anyone's voice. "Leon! Where are you?" she had whispered into the phone. "At the river."

"What river? Leon?"

No answer. Not even the click of his cellular phone being turned off. He must have just dropped it.

There was no river near their home. Could he mean the river near the high school? Some intuition told her if her son was in enough trouble to call her for help, it had to have something to do with his art. The river near the high school was where he had sculpted *Spring Flower* and ... the other one. The one he had thrown in the river. Helene racked her memory. The river was a long one. Even if she were searching the right river, how would she find the place where Leon had taken her only once, fifteen years ago?

That had been in the spring. Now snow covered the ground. She drove to the school and then to the nearest point where she could follow the river's path downstream. Nothing looked familiar. She crossed a steel bridge. Had it been here then? She looked back at the bridge through her rear view mirror. No, he wouldn't—

The river was active here, unfrozen except for some spots where rocks collected together to form icy islands midstream. It didn't look deep, she observed with relief, not deep enough to ... She fought back a wave of panic. Why hadn't he told her where he was? If only Leonard were here! At a fork in the road the paved surface angled away from the river and a dirt road followed its path instead. Had there been a dirt road? The spot had been right next to the water, she remembered, because Leon had placed his figure at the edge of the stream for her to see it there. It was getting dark. He could have meant the Hudson River for all she knew; his Brooklyn studio was near there.

Suddenly she swerved. Of all the stupid places! Someone had left a car parked almost in the middle of the road. She braked hard, her heart in her throat. It was a gray sportscar. Leon's!

She turned her own car so the headlights shone on the water, but she could see nothing. Grabbing a flashlight from the trunk, she began to walk down the road, her boots slipping in the half-frozen mud, shining the light here and there across the span of the river. There was only empty space and silence.

Finally the road came to a dead end. She walked on, through low brush, keeping close to the water's edge.

"Leon!"

He was in the middle of the river, standing in water up to his waist and then ducking his whole body under. Swimming? No, stumbling about on his knees. She felt the freezing wetness inside her boots. When he surfaced, she shined her light into his eyes. Even in the half dark of evening, she could see that his whole face was blue.

"Oh Mother. I'm so glad you came." His eyes were wild, but his tone was steady. "Can *you* think where it might be?"

"Leon, come out of the water."

"No, I've got to find it. I'm sure it was right around here somewhere. There was a clearing. I was never here in the winter, but I'm sure I must be getting close. I haven't been here since high school. It may still be in decent condition, you never know. I've searched the whole river from where I left the car."

Helene looked back up the distance she had walked, at least half a mile. Had he had been in the water that whole way? Ducking under every other minute?

She knew the answer, but she asked anyway. "Leon, what are you trying to find?"

The blue porcelain of his face cracked then. "Oh, Mother. I'm trying to find *myself*. You called my marble nude *The*

Promise. Don't you remember? But it wasn't just the promise of the young female figure you were thinking of, was it? It was *my* promise too. Wasn't it, Mother?

Helene choked out the words. "Yes, sweetheart. Please come out of the water. We can look for it in the spring."

Leon ducked under the black water again. She could only imagine his torn hands scratching the bottom of the riverbed in their futile search. She waded chest-deep into the icy water. She knew she had to get him out before he fell unconscious from hypothermia.

When he came up again, he looked at her in horror. "Mother! Get out of here. It's freezing."

"You come with me."

"No, I have to find it. I want to give it to Tara. It was Tara I was dreaming of when I made it. Now she's left me—"

Then Helene understood.

"And," he struggled for words, his lips so stiff he could barely talk, "and, I still love her so!"

"Leon, we'll both perish in here. Please! You have to come out!"

He ducked under the surface again and when he came up, his face had passed from blue to purple. "Do you recognize anything around here?" he asked.

She shook her head. She was shaking all over.

"Don't you understand, Mother? If I can just give my vision to her, even though it's a past vision, she would have to love me, at least a little."

He was still sobbing as she led him out of the water.

THIRTY-FOUR

KALLY LET HERSELF LUXURIATE against the plush leather seat and gazed past the chauffeur's cap at the giant trees lining the two-lane highway, as if it were a royal road leading to a palace. It was the first time she had been out of the city since last summer when her father had taken the family by bus to Atlantic City. The thought of him sent a spasm of guilt through her euphoria, but she quickly shrugged it off. Nothing was going to ruin this day for her. Nothing.

She pushed a CD into the player and was surprised to hear Rap music. She giggled. She'd imagined that rich people listened only to classical music, or opera. Well, Mr. Gothard was anything but stuffy, so the music seemed right, somehow. He'd been very sympathetic when she told him about her problems at home. How she'd found the nerve to send a note into her own father's restaurant with the Gothards' chauffeur she still didn't know. She was just driven to do it. It had all started when her parents and Tara had received engraved invitations to attend the opening of the new wing at the Harrington. She wanted to be there too. To see the gowns, the jewels, the people! She'd read about the opening in *Vanity Fair* last month. There had even been a picture of Mrs. Gothard in the gown she was going to wear: hand-painted swirls and blotches on silk, by Adria Cass, one of the artists who was going to be exhibited in the new wing. Well now, *Mr.* Gothard was *her* ticket to that party. He was the only person she had ever met in her whole life who could help her out of the surroundings she hated so much. He'd come right out of the restaurant and sat with her for a few minutes in the back of the limousine. When he found out she wanted to quit school and get a job so she could support herself and leave home, he had agreed immediately to see her. Today! Today, he was giving his time to actually see what he might do to help her. And once he helped her, maybe she could be as rich as Nicky might get with his new art. Nicky thought he was so smart! It would serve him right if she turned out to be just as successful as he would be. *His* friend, Leon Skillman, was helping him, and *her* friend, Perry Gothard, would help her.

It was a little odd, though, that he wanted her to come all the way to his horse farm in New Jersey for the meeting. Could it be that he wanted to hide from his wife and be romantic with her? But then she remembered he said he was playing tennis in a tournament at his club this afternoon and would be meeting her after the game. Of course he couldn't take time from a business day in the city to worry about her little problems. Well, anyone could have a job interview in an office. That's how average people do things. Rich people do things any way they want.

She thought of the bracelet her father had made her for Christmas, so homemade looking. She would never wear it. Couldn't he have bought her one? She thought of Thanksgiving dinner with her family, so loud with everybody talking at once, dishes being pushed across the table and people even drinking out of each other's wine glasses like peasants, laughing and talking with their mouths full. Kally had been taught that *she* must do none of those things, and yet there was her own mother dancing with a pot of vegetables and sipping wine from any relative's glass who passed her by, laughing with her stainless steel tooth right out in plain view. Kally rubbed the polished mahogany of the limousine's bar. Not any more. Her family's stupid holidays, their whole world, was very far from the world she wanted.

She turned her mind to the interview ahead. What could she offer in the way of skills? She played piano well. Everybody in her family had loved her music at the Thanksgiving party, even Leon's father, and he was certainly one of Mr. Gothard's kind. She didn't know exactly what kind of business Mr. Gothard was in, but businesses probably didn't need musicians. Maybe she could just begin as a receptionist. Mr. Gothard had whispered to her one night while she was still waitressing that she was pretty enough to be a model. She spoke Greek fluently. And good Greek, too. Her father had made sure of that. Even though he didn't speak educated Greek himself, she and Nicky learned it all properly. Maybe she could be a translator. Anything! Just to be with these exciting people. She knew Mr. Gothard was going to be her ticket out of her cramped world. He probably thought of her like a daughter. Maybe he even *had* a daughter her age.

"Mr. Gothard!"

Suddenly he was before her. She'd noticed that the car had swung off the highway onto a country lane and passed several horses in a big pasture, but now they had arrived at the end of the long driveway and there was Mr. Gothard coming to open her door. The chauffeur must have called him to let him know they were here. She had seen him pick up the car phone a little while ago.

In the flash before he opened the door, she noticed that Mr. Gothard looked freshly showered and was dressed in casual pants and a sweater. He'd said he would see her right after his game, and no one could look like that after a game. Then she remembered he'd said a tournament; he probably had to go back and play some more and was squeezing her in between games. Her heart went out to him in gratitude. As he guided her into the house, it was like walking straight into a movie, everything was so beautiful.

She realized he was talking to her, something about the heat being out in the house and only one room being warm enough to sit in. Kally felt like giggling. Who would think that rich people had trouble with their furnaces? It didn't seem cold to her at all. She waltzed through the living room, the sight of flowing draperies, gold urns and antique furniture wiping away all other thoughts.

When he opened the door to the room they were going to interview in, all she could focus on was the huge, antique day bed, like a big sofa but much wider and backed with pillows. The only other furniture was a desk with a chair and a tall, standing closet-type thing in the corner. She felt a pang of nervousness when she realized there was no other place for the two of them to sit but together on the bed . . . sofa, she corrected herself. What if there *was* plenty of heat in the house and this was just a clever way of getting her to a room with a bed in it? She sat carefully on the edge, striving to appear confident and ready for the interview. "Mr. Gothard," she started—

"Call me Perry." He smiled as he slid onto the bed-sofa next to her. He leaned back on both elbows, and as Kally noticed the tightness of his pants, she thought he had not struck a very business-like pose. If he'd been one of the boys at school, she would have thought he was trying to draw her attention to "that part" of his body. But rich people are different, she reminded herself quickly. He's just being casual to make me feel okay.

She began again. "Well, Perry, it's like I told you. My father is so old-fashioned that I think I'll go crazy if I stay in that place one more day, let alone my whole senior year in high school. I was thinking if I took a job now, I could get my own studio apartment and finish school on a correspondence program and then maybe work my way through college, or . . ." she faltered, "maybe not even go to college at all if the job was good, or maybe go into modeling, the way you—"

Perry laughed and began to twirl a lock of her hair absently in his fingers. "Too much parents, have you? What would you say if I told you I saw so little of my parents that one time my mother went into the hospital for three weeks with a nervous breakdown and I never even noticed she was gone?" This was partially true, but truth didn't matter; he just needed to relax the girl with conversation that would open up her sympathies for him. His mother *had* suffered a breakdown one summer, because of her philandering husband in general but specifically because his father had given Perry a razor and a package of condoms for his thirteenth birthday. His mother had been so horrified that it just kicked off years of resentment.

Kally offered an understanding smile to Perry, but a little nervously. When he first took her hair in his hand, she had been afraid that he might be becoming romantic, but now she saw he was just trying to be sensitive and let her know that all kids have troubles. Even rich kids. Besides, she reminded herself, he had played with her hair in front of his wife too. No. He was just being nice. She went on to detail her complaints against her family, and it seemed like no time at all before she heard a knock at the door and looked up to see a butler entering the room with a bottle of champagne in an ice bucket and two glasses on a tray. The butler was in shirtsleeves with only a light vest to keep him warm.

Then an elegant, slim glass of cut crystal filled with bubbling, golden liquid was being offered to her and the rest of her thought slipped away. What an existence! Champagne during an interview. Her nervousness gave way to excitement. Not too much, though, she warned herself. She had never had much to drink in the way of alcoholic beverages before, only the small glass of Greek wine or Ouzo that her father permitted on special occasions. This was a tall glass and she delighted in the tingles that reached her nose each time she raised it to drink. Her first champagne!

"What kind of business are you in, exactly, Mr. Goth—" she blushed, "Perry?"

"Well," he leaned back easily on the bed. Afternoon interludes had been a common practice with him for years, and this little Greek girl was perfect; like young wine from any country, she was meant to be drunk while still young. But, as any wine aficionado knew, you had to open the bottle gently and ease the cork out without rushing. "I sit on a lot of Boards. You think it's boring to live with your family? Well, in my set, everybody's family. From the time we go to our first school, through college and beyond, we see the same faces. We do business with some of the faces, marry one of them, socialize with others, sit on Boards with a few of them, but they're all the same people for your whole life."

Perry refilled both their glasses and Kally thought he shouldn't drink before playing tennis again but, sensing a warm glow surrounding them both, she didn't want to interrupt him. "That's why," he was saying, "we love doing unexpected, exotic things and enjoy spending time with different people, people not of our set. Special people, from another way of living. Like you." He smiled. His smile made her feel very welcome in this place that had seemed so foreign to her less than an hour ago. These people had needs, too.

Perry got up, flipped on the radio, swooped her off the bed and, circling her with only one arm so they could keep their glasses, he danced her across the small room. She started to resist but a fuzzy little feeling in her head blurred the thought. Perry must have more time between games than she thought. And he *had* said she was "special" and that he enjoyed meeting other kinds of people different from his own set. She certainly couldn't say no to a dance, considering all he was going to do for her.

As he nuzzled his face into her neck, she smelled a sticky sweetness from his cologne and then she started as she felt a particular hardness pressing against her. Instinctively, she pulled away, but felt herself being drawn tighter into his embrace, and the hardness growing. "Don't worry. I won't hurt you," he said in her ear and she felt his mouth open to explore her earlobe with his tongue. Panic told her to pull away, but a delicious hot stirring between her own legs kept them from helping her to run. "DANGER!" But the warning signal in her brain flashed through too fast to be noticed, and with each new fear, there was a new heat to dissolve it. And with each new wave of panic there was the soft wetness of his mouth covering hers and probing it in a way not even the most experienced of boys at school had ever attempted. She felt a dizzy feeling and, remembering the champagne, realized that the glass was no longer in her hand. Perry must have taken it and set it down.

It crossed her mind that she could *stop this now* and *run into the bathroom* to get hold of herself, but then she felt him guide her hand between his legs and, at the same time, slip his own hand under her skirt. And then nothing crossed her mind again because she had no mind at all, only a body and feelings of want mixed with fear and pleasure mixed with pain all forging together into one motion back on the bed until she felt him drive into her so deeply that she thought she would die right then and there.

Suddenly, it was over.

Perry rolled off her and lay on his back. He was breathing very hard, and she wondered for a minute if he was ill. Then, as he calmed, she waited for him to look at her, to tell her it was all right, to let her know that he cared for her. He didn't open his eyes.

She looked with horror at bloodstains on the gilded coverlet. Why wouldn't Perry look at her? It was as if he had forgotten she was there, as if he got what he was after. No! She pushed the thought away with another. This must be the adult world. What it's like to give a man so much pleasure that he needed to recover before showing her any love, and he must love her, otherwise why would he have chosen her? He could have any woman in the world. She fought against panic and lay her head tentatively on his shoulder. She had felt the heat of his passion, but now she needed warmth from him. And affection.

She felt his hand patting her thigh. His voice was low and far away. "I always think I want erotica until I get a sweet, untouched piece. And you *are* sweet, my kitten. Why must you all turn eventually into cats? Why must the wine age, only to sour?" His voice trailed off and he sort of snored, as if he were all ready to fall asleep.

Kally didn't dare move her head. What did he mean? The tone was affectionate but the words were funny. What did he mean by "piece" and "turning into a cat" and "wine?" Was she supposed to do something else, now? For one moment she felt like bursting into tears. If he loved her, why didn't he hold her? Why wouldn't he open his eyes? What if this was all? What if he was through with her now? But that couldn't be! He had said he would help her.

"Have some more champagne," he said rousing himself, and she watched him walk off *without looking at her* to the bathroom. "Oh," he turned—he didn't see her!—"take anything you want from the closet over there, in the bottom drawer. Just choose whatever you want, kitten. There's another bathroom through that door, and William will take you back whenever you want."

"But . . . what about my job?" she asked tentatively.

"Oh, anything you want. Go to the . . ." he thought a minute. "You speak Greek?" She nodded. "Okay, go to the travel agency. They'll have something part-time for you. William will tell you where."

The bathroom door closed behind him and she heard the shower being turned on. She felt abandoned. This was not the way she ever imagined making love would be like.

There was no *love*! But she also never had imagined that it would be with such a rich, successful, older man. He was so busy. She should be proud that he'd singled her out of all others for this afternoon. She hadn't even had a chance to ask him about an invitation to the museum, but, well, soon she would see him again. She could ask him later.

Feeling better, she poured herself more champagne and went into the other bathroom to clean herself up. The first job made her feel dirty and she still had a good deal of pain down there, but once the messy task was over and she sipped some more of her drink, she began to feel better again. As she combed her hair, she noticed in the mirror that her cheeks were very pink. She didn't look at her eyes.

Perry was still in the shower when she came out. Curious, she went to the closet and opened the door. A TV was in the top part, and in the drawer he had indicated, she found herself staring at an open box containing several bracelets, necklaces and earrings.

For one second a shudder of revulsion shook her body. It crossed her mind that of all the things that had happened to her today, this was the last chance she had to stop the spiral. She must think. Now. She must listen to this last of all the little warnings that had crossed her mind this day. *Now.* A job didn't mean anything. An invitation didn't mean anything, really.

A gold mesh scarf caught her eye, just a small one, to tie around her neck—it crossed her mind that this wasn't right, none of it was right—gold so fine it looked like silk.

Don't take it. Don't take it! This is Cross—. She felt the coolness of the mesh in her hand and forced the sound of her father's voice out of her mind as it named the sum of her day.

THIRTY-FIVE

NICKY STUFFED PAPERS into his knapsack and tucked the bag behind a file cabinet. He'd be back tomorrow; he still had six more days. It had been a crash course: Introduction to Philosophy 101. But who else in the world had the luxury of four librarians (one with a Master's degree and two with Ph.Ds) answering his every beck and call? All year long, he worked for them, but during these past days of Christmas vacation, he felt they existed solely to work for him. They answered his ill-formulated questions on art history and helped him hunt up everything from definition derivations buried in obscure ancient documents on up to magazine articles written last month.

Who would have thought that ideas could be so much *fun*? It wasn't exactly as if he'd neglected his intellectual development up until now, but he realized that he'd thought about many issues in a "kind-of-sort-of" way, passively and implicitly assimilating concepts, not actively and explicitly understanding them, and never critically judging them. By now, he'd acquired a jumble of notes that would take months to organize and longer to integrate; this was only a small beginning. But his mind had emerged clear and directed. His decision was made.

He'd come to the conclusion that while an architect could endlessly explore mass, shape, volume and space (and scale!) and really make something of it, abstraction as a visual art would restrict his imagination because the form itself was too limited. To enter the world of abstract design deeply enough to stretch himself to his greatest capacity, he felt sure he would end up becoming an architect, not an artist. With that he had found his starting point. So he would stay with representation, but now he hungered to make art that really meant something.

He went over the fundamental issues again in his mind: free will versus determinism, knowable universe versus unknowable— Nicky thrilled inwardly. He wanted to be *in* on it! Mr. Van Varen was right; they needed a movement. It wasn't enough for the artists at A IS A to go quietly about their business, to create obscurely, to sell cheaply. It wasn't just he who stood at a personal "crosspoint" in his artistic career; it was all of art: Art, the physical manifestation of ideas, revealing the philosophical and spiritual battles of mankind as surely as weapons and sunken ships revealed the physical and territorial battles. He couldn't wait to talk with Dorina.

"I was hoping you'd decide to follow me. I should have known you'd set out to lead me." Dorina hugged Nicky warmly. "You've made me prouder than any artistic mentor has a right to be."

Nicky wriggled out of her arms and, picking up a brush, went back to work on his canvas. The last of the seascape trilogy was nearly finished. If all went as planned, he would finish it before it was time to leave town.

Dorina went to the hotplate to make tea and changed her mind. "Nope! I think we'll celebrate with this very old bottle of red wine, instead." She lifted a bottle carefully from the wine rack. "When will you tell your father? I don't think he's going to be entirely happy with this decision."

"Tonight at dinner, after I see Uncle Basilious— Oh!" he interrupted himself. "There was a message on the answering machine from Mr. Van Varen when I came in. What does *he* want? I put the number on the pad."

"I know what he wants." Dorina frowned. "He's called and left that message every day for a week."

"Do you think he's changed his mind and wants to write about us?"

"No, I think he wants to make amends."

Nicky stopped painting and accepted both the glass of wine and the silent toast that went with it. Embarrassed, he grinned back into Dorina's shining eyes. She didn't say a word, just lifted her glass to him and kissed the rim before drinking.

"Why? Even you said it wasn't his fault, what happened that day."

Dorina picked up her own brush, savoring both the wine and these precious last moments with the child, the young man, she had tutored so carefully for so long. "Since I was a little girl, I've been cursed with 20/20 vision into people. My father used to say I had an x-ray machine inside my brain somewhere that permitted me to see immediately to the character center of a person. I say it's a curse because this inner mindsight has seldom brought me pleasure. Robert Van Varen is a rudderless man. He sails with whatever current is strongest at the moment." Dorina sipped reflectively on her wine. "Something about me and this *atelier* fascinates him. He doesn't have the vaguest idea what happened here that day, but because he likes this place for some reason he never bothered to identify, his attraction makes him feel funny or guilty or something. But that's about as deep as he can go. Don't even dream that he's fascinated with our work. He's fascinated with the art world, not with art itself. He has no center of his own either artistically or personally, no inner base that anchors him to himself."

"But he's powerful."

"Only because of longevity and connections. He has no explorer's spirit. He wouldn't touch shore on us unless he knew we were safe harbor. And safe, we most definitely are *not*." She laughed ruefully. "Who would have imagined that the day would arrive when art imbued with beauty and projecting universal, life-affirming values would be radical, while 'art' that is unintelligible, offensive or politically tribalized would be 'safe harbor'? In any event, we're not militant enough to be safe."

"Okay." Nicky poured them more wine carefully, so as not to disturb any sediment; he'd learned about more than art from this remarkable woman. Blanching all of a sudden, he realized that in some way he loved Dorina. Today was like old times in the studio, only better. He loved to see Dorina happy, and he loved the fact that, today, it was he who had made her feel this way. He never, *ever* wanted to see her cry again. He looked around the room, realizing how much he would miss this place. He had worked here since he was ten years old. Now, about to leave it, he saw it freshly, as a whole, with something akin to the inner "mindsight" she had herself described. Dorina's oasis and Dorina: inseparable. He had never thought of her as a woman before, except that one time at Thanksgiving when she had let down her hair when dancing with Dimitrios. Nicky had seen a wondrous light come into Dorina's eyes whenever she looked at *that* man. She had not been cursed by her mindsight then; she'd loved what she'd seen, that was obvious. But maybe she was cursed after all, because even though Dimitrios had loved her work, he didn't return her romantic interest.

"Why didn't you ever get married?" Nicky had asked the question silently, inside his own head. It was only when she answered him that he realized he had spoken it aloud.

Dorina continued to paint, seemingly unsurprised by his unprecedented curiosity into her private life. "Because I never found a man I wanted who also wanted me," she answered simply. "I don't settle." She glanced at her protégé to read his reaction. "Don't worry. Romantic loneliness is not the worst thing in the world. It's a lot better than romantic compromise. For me, anyway. Besides," she nodded her head toward Nicky's paintings, "I have children. I'm much more fulfilled being an artistic mother."

"You could have had both."

"True. But then I couldn't have chosen my children. It's better for me this way." She raised her glass again to Nicky, toasting them both this time. "Don't feel sorry for me, Nicky. I'm living exactly the life I choose to live. And today, your decision rewards me beyond any momentary misgivings. It's rare for a visual artist to seriously explore philosophy as you intend to do. Oh, they all spout some watered-down version of one trendy philosophy or another, but few ever grasp the scope of wider issues. Heaven knows we never needed philosopher kings, but the time may just be ripe for artist-philosophers."

They looked up, startled. No one *ever* knocked unannounced at the studio door; even the Super knew he had to call before seeing Dorina. Nicky went to the door and unlocked it. Robert Van Varen walked cautiously into the room.

"I apologize for interrupting you," he said tentatively. Dorina didn't turn around; her brush never missed a stroke. Van continued speaking to her back. "I finally realized you were never going to return my phone calls. I know I shouldn't be barging in like this, but all I wanted to do was apologize to you. I don't know what happened here that day, but I know it had to do with my being here. So, anyway, whatever it was, I'm sorry."

"Why are you sorry?" Dorina still didn't turn around.

"I'm sorry because there are now over ninety-thousand so-called 'artists' living and working in New York City, all competing for attention and hardly any of them deserving it. And I'm here because you and your little group really are unique. I went over to A IS A GALLERY and had a look at the work. You've achieved high art through superb craft, you've integrated form and content, and your work proposes a positive viewpoint that quite simply is not being done these days. Well, I just wanted to say that I'm sorry you dislike me so. I've never been thrown out of anyone's studio before, and it makes me feel rather unsettled. I know it's not me personally whom you're against, but the art world of today that I represent. I'm merely a man of my times. I'm not going to change at this late date, and I'm still not going to write about you, because you're a woman either too late or too early, I don't know which—"

Van interrupted himself. Something pinned to the bulletin board had caught his eye. A drawing. A sketch. He turned back to Dorina. "Isn't that a sketch of the young woman who goes with Leon Skillman? I met her recently at a party in Palm Beach."

Nicky answered. "Yes, that's my sister, Tara."

Van studied the sketch closely. "Who made this? Neither one of you. Neither of your hands is here. This is one of the most remarkable sketches I think I've ever seen: so spontaneous, every line so bold, yet so detailed."

A lilting note of triumph crept into Dorina's voice. "Leon Skillman made that drawing, Mr. Van Varen."

It was actually comical. She knew it would be: the way Van spun around on his heels, nearly losing his physical balance in the same way he was now losing his professional sureness. He couldn't even speak, just stood there like the dumb mouthpiece he had become: a man with no values of his own. Justice had been served. He wasn't an idiot. He knew masterful art when he saw it. He just didn't look at it anymore.

"But I didn't know Leon was capable of this," he stammered, his words as unsteady as his footsteps. "Why then—"

Dorina opened the door to usher him out. "Because *your* art world won't give equal time to art like that. Leon Skillman is an artistic genius. He could have been one of the few great sculptors who ever existed. But as you yourself say: today's art world doesn't want to hear about our art, let alone what his *might* have been. Good afternoon, Mr. Van Varen. Now please don't come here again."

"But," Van stuttered, "I did want to set things straight."

"We have. Good afternoon, Mr. Van Varen." She closed the door.

Nicky couldn't help grinning back at her. She was smiling so widely that it was completely contagious. It was finished. Her oasis was tranquil once more.

Dorina picked up a brush and returned to her easel. "He'll be back."

Nicky dropped his grin in shock. "Why do you say that?"

"Because he's never left here yet of his own free will, no matter what I've said to threaten or insult him."

"Maybe he just likes to be insulted. Some people do, you know."

"Well, I don't think he's one of them. I think he's fascinated by anyone who has the guts to do it, though." She winked at Nicky, mischief broadening her smile again. "And now, my young philosopher, let's get back to work. Remember, as some wise man said: 'One picture is worth a thousand words'."

"What? You honor your family with your presence at dinner for a change? We thought you had decided to *live* at that library of yours."

Nicky, glad for his father's good-mood bantering, sat down at the table. Yes, he wanted to share this dinner with his family tonight for many reasons. Since Tara's preliminary work at the museum was finished for now, she was leaving soon for a couple of months in Greece. And he would be leaving soon, too. He had finalized it all with Dorina, and once the proper strings were pulled to get him a transfer and mid-year registration—

"What I learned at the library these past days made me realize that I *ought* to live in a library to understand all that

I need to for my art to progress, Papa. Dorina has taught me how to paint, and you (the compliment was contained in Nicky's tone of voice) have taught me how to think. But now I see that I also just have to get plain knowledge."

Kostas heaped moussaka onto Nicky's plate. "What is all this fancy smancy talk? Start your dinner before it gets cold." He tiptoed to the refrigerator with a gleam in his eyes that promised a secret about to be revealed. "Tonight we have a special treat." He pulled a bottle out of the refrigerator with a flourish. "Champagne! Tara will be gone from us tomorrow night for the real holiday, and so we celebrate the New Year's Eve a day early. Tonight! With champagne!"

The word jolted Kally out of her habitual funk. She sat up in anticipation. *Champagne.* Then, awash with the memories of her first champagne, she turned sullen again. Mr. Goth—Perry—had kept his word. She now had a Saturday and after-school job at a travel agency, typing itineraries into the computer and answering the telephone. She hated it. All she did was pine away to visit the places she typed on other people's travel plans. She had not seen Perry again since that afternoon in the country. She had waited for him to call, to send a message with his driver, to contact her somehow. But she had heard nothing. At first she had worn the gold mesh scarf with pride (only away from home, of course) showing it off to her friends and hinting of a secret romance, but now the prize (or the price) of her initiation into the world of sex and money lay untouched in the back of a drawer. The sound of the cork popping as her father opened the bottle could have been a gunshot for all she cared.

Kostas had pulled the bottle from the refrigerator with too many flourishes, and Tara wiped bubbles of foam from the table where it had gushed over. Kostas didn't mind a bit. "It doesn't matter. We have plenty. *Two* bottles I bought!" He stood at the head of the table, bursting with pride at his wife and children. "To *my* family," he growled, his eyes bright, "to every one of us, I toast the New Year to our health and happiness. We are together tonight, and together we will always be, no matter..." He glanced at Tara, "*where we each may be.*" He clinked glasses with Marguerita and with each child separately, in the Greek fashion, to add the sense of sound to sight, taste, smell and touch, and then drank deeply, draining his glass in one grand swallow. "Drink, drink," he commanded his family. "There is plenty. Happy New Year to us all."

Tara sipped her champagne, shaking her head in warm amusement at her father. At his rate, two bottles would last two minutes.

Nicky cleared his throat. It was now or never. Uncle Basilious had warned him to tell his father right away and get it over with. He was glad Tara was still here. If need be, she would back him up.

"Papa," he cleared his throat again and clinked his glass against his father's, as if about to pronounce the best news in the world, "Tara isn't the only one going away for a while."

"What do you mean, Nicholas?" Kostas's growl deepened with suspicion.

"Just that, if all goes well, I'll be leaving New York too, except for summers, when I can come back and work—" He rushed on before anyone could say anything. "I've talked it over with Dorina, and I've decided that I want to leave City College and go to a university in Minnesota where I can major in philosophy. But don't worry! Dorina's old art teacher still has his *atelier*, just like hers, so I can continue my painting with a teacher just as good as Dorina." Nicky gulped air. He had to get it all out before his father exploded. "So I can continue my art training, and I've talked to Uncle Basilious this afternoon at his office and he's agreed to lend me the money to go to this school, and he says I can pay him back after I graduate and that he won't even charge me any interest."

"*Uncle Basilious?*" Kostas exploded. "If *my son* wants to go to another college, *I* will pay for the education of my own son! What do you mean going to your Uncle Basilious before you come to your papa with your decisions?" Kostas opened the second bottle of champagne furiously and filled everyone's glasses, hurt rising to his eyes.

Nicky sat up straight and looked directly at his father, seeing the hurt, knowing there was nothing he could do about it. His father could never afford to send him to this school, and they both knew it. "Because it's just that, Papa," he said firmly, "It's *my decision*." He watched, and then thrilled as hurt made way for pride and respect in his father's eyes. He had succeeded! He walked around the table and put his arms around his mother, who was crying. "I'll be back for holidays, Mama."

"Where is Minnesota?" was all Marguerita could sob. The entire family broke into laughter.

"Nicky! Get a map for your Mama! If it is your decision to go to Minnesota, you can at least show your Mama where you will be while you expand and progress this experience and knowledge of yours! No, never mind. We can show her later. Now that that's settled, *I* have a New Year's surprise for you and Kally." Kostas beamed another secret around the room. He loved surprises . . . to give them, that is. "Tara, you know, has been sent an invitation to the opening party of the museum that is owned by *my customers*, Mr. and Mrs. Gothard." He lifted his chest, "Your mama and I have also received an invitation to this fancy party. That is what happens when you do business with fancy people. My customers have invited *me* to their party! Now," he bowed toward Kally as if he had just announced that she were to be made a princess, "Tara does not want to go to this party because she wants to spend New Year's Day with Dimitrios in Greece. So," he drew the news out as long as he could to taste the delicious words better, "we have two invitations, enough for four people to go to this fancy affair. Now! Your mama and me, we have talked this over and we have decided that tomorrow we will buy all of us the right things to wear except, Tara tells me, that Nicky and I can rent suits for a party like this. And *you* my little Kallisti, may have a new dress of your own choosing. I don't care about the cost for it. And your mama may also have a new dress. Tara has pointed to pictures in a magazine the kind of things we must buy so we look right."

Kally stared at her father, speechless. How *could* she? The one thing she would have given her life to do, to see, to be part of. But how could she go, now? What would Perry think? Say to her?

"Now, there is only one other thing I want to tell you about." Kostas was subdued now. "Your mama and me, we know we are simple people and we do not know about such things." He poured himself more champagne. These words did not taste so good. "So," he spoke gently to Kally, so gently that Tara thought she had never loved her father so much as she did at this moment. "So! My children, if you two would want go to this party alone, without your mama and me, it is *right* that you should go alone. You are American and you will know what to say and how to act. This is your decision, and," he straightened his shoulders to bear the blow, "whatever you decide will be right."

Nicky sprang up from the table and, standing beside his sister, extended his hand to her as if she were, in fact, a princess. "Would you do me the favor of accompanying me to the gala opening of the Harrington Museum on New Year's Day, Miss Niforous? I should be proud to have such a beautiful young woman as you on my arm. We shall have to endure the photographers because of your beauteous presence, but I pray you will attend in spite of the fuss." He lowered his voice, knowing how much this moment must mean to her, "I would be proud to escort you to this affair, where you can be with *your* kind of people."

Kally stared tongue-tied at her father, two images colliding in her mind: a gold mesh scarf and a brass-studded wood bracelet. She stared at her mother: Marguerita's stainless steel tooth shone almost as brightly as her smile, her mother's stainless steel tooth because her parents would not spend money on a better one, but a new dress for *her,* and piano lessons, and perfect English and perfect Greek. She stared at her sister, who had offered her own precious invitation. She stared at her brother, still standing by her side, holding her hand in his, knowing how much she didn't deserve this gift from her father because he knew how much she had always hated Papa for being himself.

Kostas poured the last of the champagne into everyone's glasses. "It's all right, my little Kallisti, *my little perfect one,* to go to this party without your mama and papa. You are a big girl, now, with an important future. We don't want to embarrass you."

"No!" The violence of her voice matched the violence of her action. Throwing off Nicky's hand, she raced around the table, tears streaming down her cheeks, and dove into her father's arms. "No, Papa!" she choked into his big chest. Was it the generosity of her big sister? Was it the generosity of Nicky's hand (the same one that had slapped her) taking hers, now, in understanding? Was it the generosity of both her parents in offering not to embarrass her? Was it Perry's ignoring her after he got what he wanted? Or was it the first baby step of growing up, making real to herself the truth of what life was really about?

She looked up finally into Kostas's bright blue eyes, exactly as bright and as blue as hers, and offered him a smile of forgiveness for crimes he had never committed. She looked hopefully at Nicky, seeking forgiveness for herself in *his* eyes;

she found it. She walked slowly over to the Christmas tree, and opening a box, took out her father's present and slipped it onto a wrist.

"If we go to the museum opening—"

She had made a mistake, a big one, but her father had always taught her that mistakes were all right *if* you learned from them. Well, she had learned something very important from her mistake, and no one in her family ever had to know about her foolishness. She would hold her head up high when she saw Perry Gothard at the party because mistakes were nothing to be ashamed of. She could cancel one bad crosspoint with another good crosspoint. Now!

"If we go to the museum opening," she repeated, tears vanishing but eyes shining and her voice even now, "we *all* go! Thank you, Papa, for . . . everything."

Kostas kissed Kally's forehead, while patting her hair with great affection. He looked around the table and, embracing them all with the widest of grins, raised his glass.

THIRTY-SIX

KOSTAS LUMBERED DOWN the stairs, muttering to himself, the smells of roasted meats and puddings trailing behind. Can't they read? The sign says: "Closed for New Year's Weekend." Can't they leave me alone with my family for one single night and not keep knocking and knocking and knocking like that? And if I don't open the door after five minutes, don't they know I don't want to open the—

"Leon! My boy!" Kostas's arm closed quickly around the hunched shoulders because he had immediately noticed the haunted eyes, and he drew Leon protectively into the hallway. "Come in! Come upstairs! The restaurant is closed for a couple of days. We are celebrating the New Years early tonight, and we finished dinner already, but you will have dessert and coffee with us."

Leon followed obediently as Kostas led the way to the family apartment. Halfway up the stairs, Kostas turned back to Leon and whispered confidentially: "You know she's going back for a little while? What can we do? We all want her here in America like you do, forever. Ah! Who can predict what a child will do? Anyway, my boy," he patted Leon's shoulder, "you are always welcome to this house and our family, with or without my daughter. Can I help you with that? It looks heavy."

Leon shifted the bulky object he was carrying from one

arm to the other. "No Kostas, but thank you for your kind words." And no, he didn't know Tara was leaving for Greece again. They had not spoken since Palm Beach, but they had parted on good terms; why would she leave without telling him? Well, regardless, he had to do what he had to do. He trudged purposefully up the stairs behind Kostas.

"So! Look who has come to share our New Year's celebration! Nicky, get Leon a glass of wine, or . . ." he looked soberly at Leon, "something a little stronger, maybe? Ouzo? What? Ouzo or wine?"

"Just coffee, thank you." On some peripheral level, Leon registered the huge Christmas tree laden with handmade Greek ornaments, the unwrapped boxes spilling gifts, and a table heavily laden with food. All of this he subconsciously observed without full recognition to remind some forgotten part of his brain of certain events and relationships in life that he had chosen to deny. All he could consciously focus on was Tara's shocked expression. He could read her mind: "You just arrive here? Without even a phone call first? Without an intervening word since Palm Beach?"

"Hello Leon." was all she said.

Marguerita hurried over with coffee. She, too, had noticed the bruised circles of blue under Leon's dull green eyes.

Kally handed him a plate of pastry and a napkin. He touched her bracelet. Obviously handmade, the walnut circle was painstakingly studded with brass nails forming reverse "Ks" around its circumference. "It's lovely, Kally." He pushed the words forward with effort. It hurt him even to talk. "I'm sure I know who made it for you."

Kally removed the bracelet and handed it to him with a shy smile at her father. "It's better than if Tiffany's made it, that's absolute."

Nicky beamed at his sister with new pride in his eyes and grabbed a small wood box from under the tree. "Papa made this, too." He grinned at Kostas and offered the box to Leon for inspection. "See? It's for holding playing cards.

I guess Papa figures if I never make a living with my art, I can always play poker."

Leon was feeling acutely the discomfort his unexpected visit had brought to this private family celebration. Every person in the room had sneaked at least one curious glance at the blanket-wrapped object he had set on the couch beside him. But there was nothing he could do to dispel their discomfort. It had taken him days to gather the strength to come here, and even if he had known they were celebrating the New Year early, he would have still come tonight; if he'd waited any longer, he knew he would have lost the courage to come at all.

"Are you really going to let Flo enlarge your pieces in fiberglass, Nicky?" he asked. "If you're going to give her enough product to sell, you'll have to devote yourself to the abstract sculpture. You won't have time for your painting." Nicky's future was part of why he'd come. His mother agreed with him that he bore an enormous responsibility toward Nicky now.

"I've decided," Nicky shot a warm glance at his father, "to stick with my painting. But you might as well know that Dorina will never let *you* set foot in her studio ever again. She blames you for everything. I think it's just her way of not blaming me."

Leon finished his coffee, feeling slightly revived by Nicky's answer. "These are hard decisions that only you can make, Nicky." He glanced tentatively at Tara. "Even if you make the wrong decision, let it be yours. Then if you ever regret the path you've chosen, you'll have no one to blame but yourself."

"That's what Dorina said. And Papa, too."

"Yes, they would." Leon succeeded at a tired smile. "But even though you've already decided, *I'd* like to offer you some information just because I owe it to you." He could feel Tara's eyes boring holes into him. He wasn't worried; he wouldn't disappoint her.

"I'd like you to know, Nicky, that when I was just about your age, I had the same decision to make, and I am profoundly sorry that I followed the path I did. It may be right for others, but it was never right for me. Not my *real* me. My work has never made me happy, not even while I was making it. And when I look honestly at my admirers, I'm not even proud of my celebrity status. I wasted my talent and I wasted myself. To have the talent you have, to have the vision you project in your painting— Well, if it makes any difference to you, I think you've made the right decision. And I can tell you from first-hand experience that if you went the other way and it turned out to be wrong, the price for that kind of mistake would be unbearable." He nodded toward Tara. "Your sister knows just how unbearable that price is for me. And she also knows that I'm quitting and leaving the art world forever as the final payment for my own mistakes."

Leon turned from Nicky's astonished eyes to Tara's pained ones. He could see she was hurting for him. Picking up his package, he offered it formally to her. "I'm sorry for interrupting your family holiday. I just want to give this to you. Please accept it, Tara."

"What is it?" Her gray eyes narrowed in confusion.

Kostas jumped up and anxiously herded both her and Leon to the door of the apartment. "Go downstairs to the restaurant, you two. Go to the kitchen. It's still warm in there from the grilling, and the fire is still going. Go down there and be alone—do us a favor!—it's time for us to watch our TV programs, so you are only in the way up here. Here," he handed Tara two glasses and the bottle of Ouzo, "now out of our way for a little while, okay?"

Kostas burst back into the room. "So what are you all staring at? Marguerita, get me more dessert! Nicky, get me some wine. Kally, turn on the TV!"

Everyone scurried to do his bidding. Everyone wondered what was in the package. Everyone sat down to discover what on earth they might find on television. They had never turned on the set during a holiday celebration in their lives.

Tara stoked the fire slowly to gain time for her emotions to settle. Whatever his purpose now, Leon's speech to Nicky had softened her heart. He looked as if he'd been through a war. Who was really here tonight? The man or the boy? Was he struggling, or scheming?

Leon gestured for her to open the package.

The first thing that hit her when she pulled back the blanket was the fragrance. Nestled beneath the first layer of wool, a gardenia was pinned to a note. The gardenia that had lain atop the blue fox had also been accompanied by a note: "Will you come and live with me? I love you." It seemed a long time ago, her thirty-third birthday. It was only a month ago. She looked up at Leon now with the scent of all gardenias fresh in her senses. How happy they had been together in the Athens nightclub when he had showered her with a dozen of them. *That* seemed a lifetime ago. Too much had happened to even imagine in what direction he was headed now. She opened the card. "To Tara, in salute to the courage it took for you to become in the summer of your womanhood what you promised in the spring. I will always love you. Leon."

She unwrapped the rest of the blanket, not needing to imagine its contents now. *Spring Flower* rose exultantly before her to greet the morning of her womanhood. Tears rose to Tara's eyes. To bid farewell to the twilight of their love? To accept his gift as a symbol of the love between them that never fully was, but could have been?

Leon's eyes were dry. Too dry. She understood now, looking at him closely, that all his own tears were over and done with; his decisions, too, whatever they were, had been made. Just as hers had been made; she would have called him tomorrow, before she left for Greece. But his were default decisions; his green eyes, always so ready for laughter, were empty. He had given up his battle. This gift was his farewell. She felt admiration for him stir inside her for the courage it had taken to admit his unhappiness to Nicky and the depth of his feelings for her to give her this precious gift, the very best of his work.

"You mustn't give this to me," she said softly. "It belongs to your mother."

"No, it never belonged to her, I just left it behind in my childhood home. And my mother agrees that it should be yours. This is in return for what you've given me, or for what you've given back to me: my vision of what a woman can be."

"Does this mean you might also try to recapture your vision of the world and go back to making this kind of art?"

"No, I was right about giving up art, as well as giving up my old friends. Since I got back from Palm Beach I did try to return to my old life, but I don't seem to be able to do it anymore. Oh, my anger at you returned to me long enough to complete one last commission, and the self-pity returned to me long enough to even try to . . ." Leon looked away, "be with Adria."

Tara froze. If she had ever cared for him at all, she would have to hear it.

"But I couldn't do it."

Leon saw hope lighting her face and killed it. "I can't do any of it anymore. And it's far too late to start over now." He sensed resistance trembling in the depths of her gray eyes, like the distant thunder of a storm yet to come. "Please." He hadn't the energy to hear what she might be thinking. "You've done enough to change me as a man, don't waste your time trying to salvage the artist too. Don't you see, I can't go back, and there's no way to go forward. To what? I'm just quitting, that's all. I'm announcing it at the Harrington Opening on New Year's day." He laughed suddenly, wildly, but his eyes remained dull. "Actually, it will be quite fitting. Blair is planning a rather morbid media fanfare tomorrow night on New Year's Eve as a way of agreeing to remove the last piece of my work in her museum. So soon, it *all* will be over."

"I never changed you, even as a man, Leon. Don't you know that? If I've done anything at all, it's just to *exist* so you could remember and connect with yourself when you were a boy."

Leon interrupted. "I tried to find *The Promise*. That's the piece I wanted to give you. I tried to rescue it from the river where I threw it away, just like you rescue your bronze and marble gods from the sea. I wasn't as successful as you are. I couldn't find my goddess. And I nearly died trying."

Tara stared at him, horrified. A river, at this time of year? No wonder he looked this way. She dropped to her knees beside him. "Oh Leon! Don't you see that my bronze was from another age? The creator of that figure has been dead for over two thousand years. But you're alive! You can create another *Promise*. You can fulfill your own promise. The man and the artist in you are the same person. All artists are inseparable from their work. That's what makes you artists! As you create your art, you create yourselves in the same process. If you truly believe again that your ideal woman is possible in real life, then you have to believe that a world in which such a woman could naturally and harmoniously exist is possible. Wait here!" She left the room abruptly.

Leon watched the fire die down. What did it matter if it went out? Why was she trying to keep anything burning? What difference did it make? He was through. The gift was given, the debt paid. It was enough. He got up to leave.

"Here! Look!" She was back in the room, fueling the fire, her eyes blazing with purpose. "Look, Leon. I did this 'crosspoint' exercise only one day after coming to New York. It's about you. There are some things here I think you should see."

Tara smiled. Unfolding it, she spread the piece of paper

before him on the kitchen table. "*Crosspoint* is Papa's word for marking those times in our lives when choice or lack of choice can determine the direction upon which our future, successive crosspoints will depend. It's a lifetime process, of course, because life is made up of thousands of crosspoints. Most people miss most of them, don't even know they've come to one when they're standing right on it. They believe that fate or environment or heredity or circumstance or luck or the stars or Divine Will control their destiny. But Papa has always drilled it into *our* heads that our own personal destiny is just that, our own. Our own choice. This isn't original with Papa, of course. It's a very Greek idea: think of Aristotle's *Eudaimonia*, for example, that happiness is not a transient state of pleasure but a *process* of rising to one's own capacity."

Was he listening? He couldn't give up his art again. It would be like giving up the remnants of his soul.

"Leon," she pleaded, "won't you understand? Because we have free will, human beings are their own creators. Just like with your art. As you create the content of your art according to an inner vision, so every human being—each of us individually—can create the content of a personal soul, a personal art, according to an inner vision, according to chosen values."

He was staring past her into the fire. Tara grabbed the paper from the table and thrust it into his hands. "Look! You heard Nicky say he's at a crosspoint with his art. Well, *I* was at a crosspoint with you from the very beginning only I didn't know it, fully, until right now. I've always led a consciously designed life except for one area: my love life." Was he hearing her at all?

"Leon! I always loved, *love,* your style, your intrinsic energy, your confidence of choice. Look at your car, your clothes, your apartment. Nothing about you is weak or passive. Even when you're wrong you're decisive. Your very essence is strong and *good,* Leon!"

She was shaking him, as if to wake him out of a coma. "Leon! Don't give up! Don't quit! Give me *Spring Flower* as a tribute to us both, your vision and my accomplishment, but not as a tombstone to the promise she embodies. You weren't wrong! We can always be friends because of this. And you'll have other friends, too, if you'll just give yourself a chance. You have them already if you'll accept them. Not just me, but Nicky and my whole family. They love you. And Dorina, too. Oh, yes! Nicky's wrong, she *will* forgive you because she's glimpsed the best in you. She could never resist that. You're not alone, Leon! And you don't just have friends, you have your *art* if you'll make it."

The wild-animal look came into his eyes again, the same look she had seen in Palm Beach when she had told him about Dimitri.

"Oh, Leon."

Then, her heart broke silently with shame for him, because she understood fully, now, for the first time that he was shutting down for fear of confronting something deeper.

"Leon, did you get my Christmas presents to you? I left them with your doorman a couple of days ago."

"You gave *me* a present?" He lifted his eyes cautiously.

Tara nodded. How odd, she thought. She'd borrowed *Spring Flower* from Helene Skillman well over a week ago to make one of her holiday gifts for Leon. How could any of them have dreamed then that she would possess the actual sculpture now? "Didn't they give the package to you?"

Leon shook his head. "I've been staying with my mother since Christmas. Do you want to tell me what it is?"

"No. I'd rather you see it fresh. Leon, listen! Robert Van Varen told Nicky at the studio that he might be able to write about 'their' kind of art if a movement were behind it. *You* could be that movement! Even if you feel you can't create in the ideal anymore, you could champion it. That would be enough for Van Varen and the art crowd. They have to write about whatever you do because your name is so big. And it would let you connect with the part of yourself that you tried to destroy. It's all still buried somewhere inside you. You must know that. You've got one foot on the path to your real self. Can't you step onto that path with the other foot, too? As an artist? Go back to when you were sixteen, to the way you *felt* before you were hurt by . . . so many things. Then you thought only your mother shared your visions. But now you have all of us! Oh, Leon, believe it. Try!"

He looked back at her as though she were a stranger, yet somehow known to him. Curious.

"Oh, Leon! There are so many crosspoints in life. We all have so many chances. We can change our direction at any time. It's *never* too late as long as we're still alive. Give *Spring Flower* to me if you want to, but don't give up on all that made her creation possible. Don't give up on yourself."

"Tara?"

"Yes?" she whispered.

"If I had continued, and become all I could have as an artist and as a man, both, would you have chosen me instead of Dimitrios?"

His eyes were alert now. He wanted to hear *this* truth, whatever it was.

Then she looked inward to her own heart and understood it all: her endless search for the ideal not at the bottom of the sea but in *real life,* and the whys of her love for both men. She loved Dimitrios completely. He was no second choice. She had been looking for "Dimitri" ever since she met Dimitrios, because he was the very man who had set her mature standard for the search that led her back to him. But Dimitrios, who *had* achieved his best versus Leon *if* he had fulfilled *his* best potential? Dimitrios, the protector of her values versus Leon as the *creative source* of her own ideals?

She looked up helplessly into his clear, green eyes once more. She could see by the gentle warmth she found there that he already knew the answer. But she had to say it. Because it was the truth.

"Yes," she whispered, still shocked by the question, yet certain of her answer. "Yes. I would have chosen you."

They kissed then, for all that could have been, for all they still would always mean to each other, for all he could ever still mean to himself. But Tara knew that even she could not kiss into life his failed spirit, his dying soul.

It was all she could do for him. It was a kiss "goodbye."

They sat silently for many long moments together, Tara kneeling in front of him with her forehead pressed into his hands which lay still and listless in his lap, and Leon leaning, exhausted, back into her father's big chair. After a while, Leon fell asleep. Tara understood. His mission for tonight was accomplished.

A lock of sand-colored hair fell over Leon's forehead as he slept, peacefully at last, after his long losing struggle. Tara resisted pushing it back from his face and kissing his forehead as a mother would do to a child. What a terrible loss. What a tragic waste.

She spent the night with him there, fueling the fire and sitting on the floor staring emptily into its flames until she, too, dozed off just before dawn.

When Leon awoke from the sound of muffled footsteps coming from the apartment above them, he found Tara curled up on the floor by his feet, sound asleep. Her head rested on one arm, and her breathing was as even and tranquil and trusting as that of a young girl. Leon moved quietly from Kostas's big rocker, and removing the blanket from himself, gently placed it over her. He ached with the desire to lift her into his arms, to love and cherish her for all her life. But he had no right.

Hearing the door close, Tara sat up and leaned back

against the chair in despair. She noticed that the fire had died and turned to cold ashes in the big fireplace, like the cold lump she felt in her heart, where hope for Leon had burned out and died.

THIRTY-SEVEN

IT TOOK SIX men to lift *Eternity* into the gigantic fiber glass "bath tub." Thank goodness for Flo, Blair thought. The boat manufacturing company had cut down and squared off a sailboat hull; it had been installed in the Meditation room of the museum only yesterday. The camera crew stood by as the workmen positioned the hose, which would bring the acid solution from the tank truck down on the street up to the fiberglass container and "bathe" Leon's art.

Her eyes flitted dangerously around the room. She felt like her old self again, afire with anticipation for . . . what? That was the fun of it! She didn't have a clue as to what would spring up next to turn her on. No, she felt better than her old self: the restlessness was gone. And recklessness had taken its place. After years of continuously upping the ante for thrills, Lickland's death had finally set her free. Sex had never been so decadent as it was with the cab driver that night; they had nearly wrecked his taxi in the process, but so what? She'd paid to have it fixed.

So it's true after all: if you have enough money, everything in life is fixable.

And Bill Daniher had quit, leaving the farm the next morning, so all she had to do was tell Perry that the Irishman had done the deed while drunk. Violence and sex turned into secrets and power: what an elixir! Who would it be tonight after *this* act of destruction? Annihilating a work of *art,* something she had never done before. She eyed Leon. No, too drained.

No wonder. He'd been a busy boy lately. When Flo had approached her, she'd flatly refused to sell the one piece of Leon's work that she still owned personally. The rest, except for this last major piece, she and Perry had donated outright to the museum and, *without telling her,* Kronan had sold them to Flo, flexing an independence Blair never dreamed he possessed. She glared hard at Kronan. What he had done was within his capacity, but—look at him!—sitting hunched over between Flo and Adria on one of the "meditation" benches with his head bowed, probably praying she wouldn't fire him. That she wouldn't do. But, maybe she just would pay him back for his unprecedented gall. In a worse way. By finally soiling his puritanical soul? Maybe later tonight. Yes. She had thought about sex with him and had flirted with him for twenty years. She *would* make it happen. Tonight. Then he could drag that cross around with him, too, while promoting art that he hated or feared. If he couldn't have fun with the new wing he should have quit long ago. Madonna-whipped weakling! Never refusing her advances outright, of course, yet always resisting in his ever-charming way. Well, not anymore, not after his inane act of selling art without consulting *anyone.* She would come back later and seriously seduce him in the early hours of this New Year, when she was flamed from heavy partying and he was exhausted, vulnerable and alone in his office, as she would direct him to be. She was his employer. If it came down to that, his love of the old wing would likely keep him from refusing a direct advance.

Her sexual agenda set, Blair refocused her attention on *Eternity.* Splendid! After all, what was eternity but the ceaseless transformation of matter and energy? She'd thought of the "metaphorical" act when Leon, trying to convince her to sell the piece, confided his secret: No museum. He was disposing of his repurchased art, making his last work of art the *disappearance* of all his art. It was then that she'd trumped him by demanding the destruction of this last piece as a media event. His art would be gone, as he wished, but *she* would then have on film the slow death of Leon's career, capped by his retirement announcement tomorrow at the official opening of the new wing.

Suddenly her attention was diverted by Adria, who as the moment drew near, had begun to bound here and there like an overgrown puppy, following close upon the heels of the workmen so as not to miss a thing.

Leon, Perry and Van stood woodenly on the far side of the room, together yet apart. Van noticed that Leon looked pretty beat. Perry seemed merely bored, but Van knew he was impatient to begin the rounds of New Year's Eve partying because he'd recently embraced the several-year-old fad of New York's male socialites and had begun to bed very young, very blond Slavic girls, who were arriving daily to "fall in love" with some American billionaire. Blair, who usually was blasé about her husband's philandering, had surprised Van by brusquely refusing his own request to bring Denise Sommers to the "Happening," so it appeared that in spite of the fact that Perry had already tired of the Senator's daughter and was moving on, she still felt stung by his public embarrassment of her in Florida. What crazy rules these people had! But lately he'd begun to wonder why he continued seeing Denny himself. She had turned out to be, after all, her own favorite slogan: "Public property."

Wearily, he pulled a pad and pen from his jacket pocket. Showtime was imminent now. Leon and the metallurgists had worked out the mechanics and given him the details: Because Leon had used manganese structural bronze, they'd increased the ratio of nitric acid to water up to seventy-percent, a solution so powerful it was sure to do the job. Once the acid hit the bronze, the chemical reaction in the tank would produce—what was it? Nitrogen oxide? No, he checked his notes: *tri*oxide. Well, whatever it was, it was a red toxin, which would be sucked up in an instant by the museum's anti-pollution system, but which also provided a nice element of drama and risk to the event; after all, the contraption could malfunction. Unconsciously, he edged his way closer to the door.

Blair's eyes sparkled impishly at her guests. What a way to kick off New Year's Eve! "We won't see much in the beginning," her voice was bright and shiny,"but the camera crew will remain throughout the night, along with the guys who'll replenish the acid. Kronan, *you* will stay on to supervise."

To her delight, Kronan's head shot up in astonishment.

Paralyzed by her unanticipated order, Kronan stared blankly up at Blair. Dressed as she was in a crimson long-sleeved, rather Gothic-inspired velvet gown, with its hood framing her fine features and secured to her blond hair by a diamond clip shaped like a half-moon, all he could think of was that his employer looked like some beautiful yet bewitching Medieval alchemist, presiding over her simmering cauldron and conjuring up her magic potions: *"For a charm of powerful trouble, Like a hell-broth boil and bubble . . ."* Blair, one of the witches or Lady Macbeth herself? Did it matter?

He lowered his head again, shamed and crushed to the core by this never-ending comic tragedy in which he was forced to play a part. He'd thought that by selling what he could of Skillman's nasty jokes he could hasten the end of this theatrical game, but Blair had become maniacal over the subject. Why he could not fathom; he knew she cared nothing about anything, that *everything* was a game to her. "Please, God," he prayed. "Tell me this is Your Will." This can't be right! No matter how I distrust the art here, something in my heart keeps revolting against this whole enterprise. Why create if only to destroy? And isn't this meditation room supposed to be a spiritual space? How can I oversee such destruction?"

The chemical engineer signaled to Blair. "Ready."
Blair received nods from the cameramen.
"Leon?"
"Do it," he said.

Clear liquid began to pour out from the hose. One of the men moved it carefully over the top of what looked to him like a construction piece of some sort—like an I-beam—and as the liquid began to accumulate in the bottom of the fiberglass container, thousands of little bubbles began to break on the surface from its interaction with the metal, and an acrid reddish haze began to rise from the tub and spiral its way to the ceiling vents that drew it immediately out of the room.

Blair watched the curl of red, mesmerized by the beauty of its dance of death.

Adria marched resolutely to Leon. "Are you sure of this? I see that you intend to transfigure one work of art into another. Clever media ploy, Leon. But are you sure you'll end up with what you want? That stuff looks potent."

A strange light appeared in Leon's sunken eyes. "Oh, yes Adria, I'm sure. Within an hour, the color will darken and pockmarks will begin to appear. By midnight, it will look like a giant chunk of gray Swiss cheese." And, by tomorrow, he thought silently, it will collapse of its own weight and leave behind a tub full of rust, if that. In its own sick, creeping-slowly-to-death way, it was a perfect farewell.

Adria looked back uncertainly at the bubbling bathtub but didn't question further; Leon was a pro. She began to wonder how fiberglass would look framed in something else. Or unframed but covered with . . . feces and human hair? Like a fetish. A technological *fiberglass fetish*. The medium could be shaped a million ways. But a fetish of a really relevant technological God would have to be electronic in some way, computerized or . . . Maybe she could use encaustic, instead, and go the inner way to give the scientifically created fiberglass a seductive outer, wax skin, evoking eerie bodily sensations and emotions to give it a more organic, spiritual quality.

Flo riveted her attention on the fiberglass container. That damned little Greek boy! She could have made a mint with that cute little face and fiberglass. Well, she'd just have to find another kid to make the models. The boat manufacturer and the fiberglass were still marketable ideas.

Wha . . . ? Van stopped taking notes, feeling suddenly glued to the door for some inexplicable reason, overwhelmed by a morbid reluctance to seriously write about this bubbling acid that was destroying a hunk of metal. Art? Art criticism? Art history? The image of Leon's masterful sketch of Tara Niforous seemed to Van as if it trembled on the surface of the liquid for one second and then vanished from sight. *"Because your art world won't give equal time to art like that."* Dorina's voice was a shock wave through his brain. He stared at Blair. She was nuts doing this! Look at her! Her smile was as plastic as the fiberglass. And *he* was just as nuts to be here! Before walking, unnoticed by the others, out the door, he took in the scene with fresh eyes and found himself cracking up inside with laughter as a modernized Pirandello headline flashed across his brain. There they were: diversion-seeking Blair, ultra-religious Kronan, mystical Adria, money-grubbing Flo, sex-absorbed Perry and cynical Leon: *Six Characters in Search of a Cartoon Artist.* If *that* didn't capture the guts of this story! Forget it! Given the twisted state of the arts and the culture in general, the cartoon bit would no longer make it as either shocking or funny. It was all too real. This kind of art farce was not even unusual anymore. *Everybody* had turned into a caricature by now, from Hollywood to D.C. to New York, from TV News "commentators" to radio talk show hosts to the man and woman next door! And he? Forget it! He could *not* write about this particular "transformation," even ironically. Not after seeing Leon's sketch.

Beaming with bravado, Blair delicately slid her bejeweled

hands into red velvet gloves, and slipping her arms into invisible panels sewn into her skirt, lifted the train of her gown up over her shoulders like a cloak and motioned to the group. "Come on. Time to 'party'."

As her chosen ones filed out of the room, she turned to Kronan and barked her order at him: "You can catch a nap on your office couch. Just check in once in a while." She crooked an arm through Leon's. "Happy?"

Leon regarded his work and the simmering liquid that would eat it slowly away into . . . eternity. He laughed a tired laugh, thinking of Tara on her way to another man. This was his final payment to her; by tomorrow *all* of the work that she hated would be gone. "Yes, Blair, I'm happy." He supposed it was true.

Returning to his office, Kronan walked pensively across the lobby of the new wing. Leon's steel tile "doormat" had already been dismantled and granite flooring laid down in its place. At least he'd saved visitors from having to confront that particular offense. Yet . . . he glanced furtively back up the stairs, sensing a fearful complicity in an immense travesty that he still couldn't fully identify. He reminded himself that the art here was better than that displayed by many other institutions. Blair hadn't gone so far as to include piles of coathangers, or feces stuck onto religious paintings, or vats of cow's tongues and testicles floating in semen and blood, sensational "art" the likes of which were being exhibited, now, even in respected places the world over, including New York's own Brooklyn Museum, who even sent out press releases for one show that claimed "the contents of this exhibition may cause shock, vomiting, confusion, panic, euphoria and anxiety." He had hardly believed it when he read it, and the horror of it stuck with him. Such exhibits often caused brouhaha, but the exhibited "art" remained and, in the process, was legitimated.

Still, from its inception three years ago to its completion

tomorrow, this project had always made him feel anxious, as if he were being pulled ineluctably into some abyss of madness that, like quicksand, looked safe on the surface but was inescapable once caught in its death grip. He had felt apprehensive every step of the way, dragging his feet toward the inevitable, suspecting intuitively that this was not a museum so much as it was a house of the deliberately insane. Goethe had warned about this, he thought, fraught with worry for his own salvation: "There is an empty spot in the brain . . . just as the eye too contains a blind spot. If man pays attention to this place, he becomes absorbed in it, pursued more cruelly than specters of night's empty space if he does not tear himself from its grasp . . ." Blair had called this macabre event a "happening, an art form in itself." Well, "Happenings" had been *happening* in the art world for forty-odd years; they were media moments, amusing or obscene, and they were no serious harm to anyone. But destroying something that was already a metaphor for nihilism? Even Adria Cass had seemed worried about the "transformation."

He stopped in his tracks. Now, that was interesting, considering how she made her own art. To Adria, both were art: the original and the transformed. She even boasted that her art was made without intention; it just "happened" too. Like that painting of hers where she and Leon had—

She had called it "Screwing." Could it really be? Lust as art? Most of the earlier modernist artworks that he didn't understand, he had come to accept because they had for one reason or another passed the test of time. But contemporary works like animal lust converted to a painting displayed in a museum? Kronan hurried back up the stairs and entered the gallery where Adria's *City Lights* hung in the most prominent spot. The broken glass she had thrown onto the wet paint glistened on the surface of the canvas he had always thought of as a psychotic war. But war is part of life, isn't it? he argued to himself. Tribulations are but God's method of testing our love for Him. But, lust as *art*? He had *participated* in the enshrining of this absurdity. He had helped Blair to house these "creations." Now he was helping to destroy them.

He cracked open the door to the meditation room, half hoping in his high state of agitation that this entire evening was merely a hallucination from which he might emerge sane and clear-headed. The bronze hulk was being hosed down with acid again, while several cameramen trained their lenses on the action. Such a harmless-looking liquid it was. It looked just like water. Yet it was corrosive enough to— Kronan shut the door quickly.

Crossing the street to his office, the dread thought occurred to him again. Corrosive enough to . . . If it could destroy bronze, it could destroy anything. Certainly canvas and paint and, maybe not the glass. No, the glass on the painting would just fall undamaged to the floor. That's why they had constructed the container out of fiberglass, because the acid wouldn't react with plastic or glass. But the rest of that evil thing—It wouldn't take much. He thought of the devastating damage done years ago to Rembrandt's "Danäe" by some lunatic in the Hermitage museum. Just a few splashes would probably be enough for this.

Back in his office, he lay down on the couch, his mind racing. After a couple of sleepless hours, he arose and began to pace. Feeling feverish, he splashed cold water over his face in his private bathroom. The same bathroom where on occasion over the years— "Only a few times, Lord," he said the words aloud, not knowing whether he was confessing or praying or just giving voice to the desperate pleading that overflowed his heart. "Only when the devil found his way to me again."

"But the devil is *living* in the new wing, Lord," he raved on, suddenly certain that for the first time in twelve years, he was being heard. God was listening at last. "He's hiding in that painting, laughing at you and mocking me. That painting is lust, Lord. She even admitted it. Now I understand why you provided me with this event. You were telling me to cleanse the place by annihilating that blasphemous work, to cleanse my own lustful act by destroying hers. You were showing me the way to exorcise the devil from me by exorcising what I've helped take hold there. I see it so clearly now."

Certain and glad of his mission, he grabbed a large ceramic coffee mug from a cupboard. The handle of the cup would keep his hands dry.

On his way back across the street he changed his mind. Re-entering the original mansion, he passed through several rooms filled with art that glorified life, crossed the courtyard where Margaret's birds twittered high above in the trees, and walked rapidly to the new wing by way of the overhead bridge. Yes, he thought, as he felt the architect's anticipation flow into his purpose. Yes! I will avenge you all. Beauty and love and nature and nobility of spirit. And I shall avenge myself in the process. Now and forever.

The men were all resting and chatting on various benches as he approached the bubbling container. One of the technicians jumped up to stop him as he dipped his mug into the fuming liquid. "I'm in authority, here," he stated quietly. The man backed warily away. "Your hands," he warned.

"I'll be careful." Kronan closed the door behind him. He had never felt so powerful. So *right*. All the years of penance with no answer from God. It would all be over through this one act of destroying the devil of lust with his own hands.

He stood before Adria's painting and heard the sound of laughter. His own. Adria was correct. She didn't move her artist's hand. *The devil was her astral dictator.* And this was his portrait. Never on his knees in church had he felt such spiritual joy.

He stepped back and flung liquid into the devil's face. The erosion began instantaneously as the acid ate its way through the paint into the canvas. The wreckage was immediate. But was it enough? Parts of the canvas still hung like rags on the wall. He remembered seeing twists of faded knitting fragments arranged randomly as works of sculpture on a prominent art gallery's floor in London. Could these tattered pieces be perceived as just another "transformed" work of art? He couldn't leave that to chance; he had to demolish it all. Back in the meditation room, he scooped up another cupful of acid, careful, even in his growing euphoria, not to get his hands wet. The men watched him without curiosity now.

The second splash was more successful; there was very little canvas left, and hundreds of bits of glass had fallen like so many odd shaped marbles onto the floor. One more should do it.

On the last trip back from the meditation room, his cup refilled for the *coup de grace*, an image caught his eye.

Oh beauty. Oh love. Oh woman. He stepped out onto the parapet overlooking Margaret's pocket garden. The bronze female figure lifting her arms, lifting her breasts, lifting her spirit. Suddenly Kronan felt the elation begin to ooze out of his body like a slow leak, as he realized that, like Leon's, this work of art was made of bronze. But this work was holy! It immortalized God's greatest gift to man: woman. If woman was holy, not to be defiled by man, would God have let bronze be used as the medium for this work if that metal itself was not also holy? Bronze, used throughout the ages for great works of art. It would last for eternity. Eternity? Could it be that Leon's work, even though a mystery to Kronan, was the sculptor's private tribute to God's eternal creations? If that were true, then Leon's work would be holy too. So the destruction of *it* would have to be the work of the devil.

Working through *Blair*, who had ordered the work destroyed. So, the devil was in Blair. She was destroying *art*. And he was helping. Perhaps it wasn't the face of the devil he had obliterated in Adria's painting. Perhaps it was the face of God but in a different form that he couldn't understand, as he didn't understand the bronze of Leon's piece. As he didn't understand the one same God invoked by so many and loyal to none. Oh, blasphemy!

Kronan raised his eyes in anguish to the flowers that flourished and flowed through the living branches of Margaret's garden. God's creations, too. "Help me, Lord," he cried aloud.

His eyes traveled down the living vines to the bronze vines caught in the sweet hands of the youthful figure who inhabited this eternal Garden of Eden, a garden that would never be soiled by the knowledge of nakedness and never spoiled by original sin. "Forgive me, Lord," he whispered.

He gazed back at the female, all innocent, all beautiful. How could loving such a creature ever be a sin? To make that a sin was a sin itself. Another blasphemy! Who was he to judge the God over whose forgiveness he had agonized for twelve years, waiting for Him to answer?

Suddenly, from across the room, Blair Gothard's image flowed toward him like a specter. But she was real! She was coming to join him on the balcony, her crimson gown swirling up and around her like a huge cape, her hooded face smiling seductively at him. Blair! The red devil coming to get him!

Panic-stricken, Kronan looked down at the coffee mug in his hand, filled with—it looked like water. Quickly, before she could reach him, he put the cup to his lips and drank.

Blair's screams rang through the empty gallery rooms like a fire alarm gone wild as she backed off the balcony and turned to flee from the sight of Kronan's ghastly demise.

But the image that now confronted her was the ragged remains of Adria's painting, dripping in clotted shreds down the wall to the floor, where bits of glass lay scattered around in pools of coagulating multi-hued blood. She turned toward the Meditation Room to call for help but was struck dumb by her realization of the hideous, cancerous scene taking place in there.

Swiftly and silently, Blair Gothard collapsed to the ground, the names "Lickland" and "Mother" the last her trembling lips could form before stillness embraced her in its restful sleep.

Alerted by what sounded like a shrill siren of some sort, one of the workmen opened the door of the Meditation Room to peer out into the adjacent gallery, but all was quiet now. He could see nothing unusual except a large mound of red cloth piled on the floor in the middle of the room that he didn't remember noticing when he'd arrived earlier in the evening. Assuming that another crazy contemporary work of "sculpture" like the one he was "transforming" inside had been installed for the museum's Gala Opening tomorrow, he closed the door without further interest and returned to his task. Never would he have imagined that beneath the mass of soft red velvet lay the alive but catatonic form of a woman who had finally gone too far.

THIRTY-EIGHT

WHIRRR. HUMMM. WHOOSH.
In the hush of the early wee hours, the Boeing airbus lifted smoothly off the runway into a darkened sky.

As the plane ascended, New York, like one shimmering monument to the heroic human spirit, appeared to rise with it, the sculptural contour of its skyline defined by lights, the cold blackness of night hovering close to the island as if seeking warmth from its ever-symbolic glow. The plane banked sharply, offering a fleeting glimpse of a single torch shining, patient and steadfast, in water as black as the night from over the tip of one dipped wing. The gesture could have been a salute.

Tara watched, mesmerized, as New York began to shrink into an elegant miniature of itself. The sight was so exquisite that, in this moment of suspended time, it was impossible to imagine anything evil or anyone suffering anywhere on the whole planet, let alone in this defiantly shining citadel. Peace seemed to rein over the night that would soon become dawn to the ever-renewing promise of a new year, especially over the eternally scintillating, now-celebrating city of New York, Tara thought, leaning her head back against the seat in calm contentment.

Peace. And promise. Even to New York, a city that no matter how battered physically would never be beaten in spirit. Perhaps even to one as tortured as Leon Skillman. How she wished it could be so.

Skillman. How odd. She had never given Leon's last name a second thought before, but at this moment, the combination bore down on her with oppressive irony, destroying her otherwise mellow mood. What a crime. She understood too well that Leon could regain his skill only after regaining himself as a man. How inexpressibly sad. She had failed to help him only because he'd willed himself to fail. She also understood that giving up his current art was easy for Leon, and that without the courage to confront *all* of his past honestly, he'd continue to lose his vision. It was worse than a crime, because his might have been an artistic talent to stand alongside the names of Phidias and Praxitiles, Donatello and Verrochio.

She understood all of this. Yet she still fought against guilt. Could he have made it back to himself if she'd stayed with him? She pulled down the window shade. No. That kind of recovery would have been based on a flimsy scaffold. He had to build his own foundation. He had refused. And in the strangest twist of circumstances, it had been Leon who had brought her and Dimitrios together. And now he was left with nothing, as if determined to be lost to everyone who might have loved him, including himself.

Tara raised the shade again and gazed, unseeing, into the void. When she arrived in Athens, it would be morning, cold and light. Turning at a hand on her shoulder, she accepted a glass of champagne from the flight attendant and sipped it reflectively. "Happy New Year from the Captain," the stewardess said.

Well, a New Year is always an obvious opportunity for a new beginning, Tara thought. And Leon was right on one point: she'd buried herself in the past rather than fight for her values here and now. America was suffering both a moral and spiritual crisis. She would never have understood the depth of this ideological struggle without having met Leon and Dorina and their diametrically opposing viewpoints. But now that she was acutely aware of what was at stake artistically, she couldn't resist a role for herself. She had experience as a writer. Instead of *L'Ancienne*, as she returned part-time to New York to finish the exhibition tour, she would also champion the artists at A IS A GALLERY and elsewhere in the country. She would write about the future from her unique position as an archaeologist intimately acquainted with the past. She would attempt to reawaken America to its classical heritage: instead of mining the past, she would now try to help forge the future.

She loved Dimitrios with a love that was deeper and wider than she'd known was possible, but that must not deter her from giving up archaeology. He was realistic; her new plans would not upset him; they would work out the details together. If he wanted marriage from her, she would marry him. They loved each other; the rest was all logistics.

The flight attendant set a tray on her table and Tara looked up, startled. "I'm sorry. Did I awaken you?" The young woman smiled apologetically.

"No," Tara smiled back. "My mind was just wandering."

"Is Athens your home? Or New York?"

Tara began to laugh as she opened her napkin. What a timely question!

"Both," she answered with conviction. "Both are home to me."

THIRTY-NINE

"TO THE FIRST DAY of the year and the last day of a career." It was a great line to finish off his speech this afternoon. The press would love it. Hey! What the hell! He'd fed them headlines for years. Leon rolled out of bed and stripped off the navy blue sheets; he'd slept later than planned.

Stupid, putting those sheets on the bed last night just because he'd slept on them with Tara her first night in New York. Extra stupid, because they had brought fresh images of her, of when they were happy together; he could still see her wandering about the apartment that first night, wearing one of these sheets tied around her like a toga. And dancing. Late last night he'd remembered the penny whistle. First, he'd pushed the guilt away. Then he threw the whistle away. He'd paid for it a million times over. Thank god she would never know how it all had started. And how could *he* have suspected, in the beginning, that he would love her so completely in the end? Or that he would lose her? *Tara.* Her name was a silent ache.

As he threw the sheets into a corner, a magazine fell to the floor. Only then did he remember that he'd finally read the "other" man's article last night, when he was sure he was drunk enough not to care. He stepped into the shower and let hot water rain over his body, seeking solace in its healing pleasure. He dried himself and set out his tux and accessories. As he tossed the copy of *L'Ancienne* on top of the sheets—he would throw them all out together—it opened to a page where a red line circled a paragraph in Dimitrios's article. Tara's red line; his mother's were blue. Clear-headed, now, he read the passage as he dressed. "Man free, unafraid and unashamed. Man and woman with feet firmly on this earth. Note that the '*Winged* Victory' is from a late period. The temple on the original Acropolis was built to the '*Wingless* Victory.' Victory on earth."

Right. Dimitrios would write that, and Tara would highlight it. Oh, yes. He'd consorted with a bunch of these diehards lately, including Dorina and Nicky and all those other artists whose work he'd seen at A IS A GALLERY. How many? Several dozen of them altogether. Right. Tara even wanted *him* to join them! R-i-g-h-t. He remembered her pleading with him during their last night together. He'd heard her all right, every naïve word: "*You have friends, if you'll accept them. Not just me, but Nicky and my whole family. They love you. Dorina, too. Oh, yes, she'll forgive you because she's glimpsed the best in you, and she could never resist that. You're not alone, Leon.*"

Right. He had so many friends. Blair and Perry and Adria and Flo and Van, Tiffany Tate and the California crowd, Binky Jones and the Texas crowd. Everybody loved him, it seemed. Even Kostas had told him he was always welcome in his house: "With or without my daughter," he had said. Right. He sure was a popular guy. And he sure was a treat to look at. Hell! A good night's sleep was all he'd needed for weeks. He looked like himself again, standing before the full-length mirror, resplendent in formal clothes. It sure was time to retire, at the top, with no evidence of the past to haunt him and no demands of the future to tempt him.

Entering the living room, he stopped short and stared dumbly at the wall above his couch. R-i-g-h-t. *That* part of last night he had totally forgotten about this morning. He didn't even recall hanging them, Tara's Christmas gifts. He must have been drunker than he'd thought. They hung crooked on either side of Nicky's oil painting of yellow flowers. He shouldn't have hung any of them, ever, though all three pieces looked perfectly happy strung together along the wall. She had left the package with his doorman as she'd said; it was waiting for him when he got back to his apartment. He'd opened her note first: "Greece discovered the concept of liberty. America gave the concept physical form. Mind and body, now free. What needs freeing next? Think about liberating the spirit during your retirement. Love, Tara." *Love.*

In the package were two framed photographs. She had formed a collage of two photos in each one and then photographed the collages. In the first, her bronze athlete stood before the Parthenon, stood *like* the Parthenon: tall, straight, independent. In the second, *Spring Flower* rose next to the Empire State Building, rose *like* the Empire State Building: aspiring, confident, beautiful. Centered between the two black and white photos, Nicky's vibrant yellow flowers sprouted every which way with exuberant abandon into a sunlit bed, inviting a young boy to lie down and dream.

Leon looked out the window. The real Empire State Building sparkled in the sunlight. New Year's Day. The first day of the year, the last day of a career. A headache planted itself behind his eyes. Not again! He looked back at *Spring Flower* and he thought once more of *The Promise*, still lying somewhere at the bottom of the river.

He looked out the window again. The Chrysler Building's gleaming silver arcs showered the city with sun drops, scattering light like confetti. He looked back at *Spring Flower.* "*Go back to when you were sixteen,*" Tara had urged, "*to the way you felt before you were hurt by . . . so many things.*" Leon squeezed his eyes together, trying to press the pain out of his head; it was getting worse. He looked at Nicky's flowers. *That* was how he had felt at sixteen, dreaming and making love with his first love in those flowers. He felt it now. Don't feel it now! It hurt worse than a headache to feel those things again. To feel hope. "*It's not just a dream,*" Tara had promised. "*I'm here. It's all here if you'll just have the courage to look. It may not be perfect, but it is possible.*"

Dorina's words rang through his headache, searing his brain worse than the pain. "*You're one of us.*"

Adria's words echoing in laughter: "*You've always been one of us.*"

Tara's words: "*You can't love us both!*"

Right. Leon went to the kitchen, opened a fresh bottle of Krug and drank straight from the bottle. He didn't love anything. He had never been "one of" anybody or anything. His work had never been part of any theory; he was no intellectual. He had no theories, no philosophy; he just did what he did. And what he did was over.

The intercom rang. "Dorina Swing to see you," the doorman announced.

What in hell could *she* want? He set the bottle on a counter and went to the door.

"I know I should have called first," Dorina said hurriedly, "but I was afraid that either you would refuse to see me or I'd lose my nerve and never come at all." She stood in the hallway. Leon didn't invite her in.

"What do you want?" he asked.

She handed him what looked like a scroll of some sort. "I just came to give you this—it's yours—and to thank you for speaking to Nicky. I think your honesty sealed his decision to reject the Halldon Gallery's offer and go on painting with complete confidence. Fame and wealth are hard things for a nineteen-year-old to pass up, especially in favor of a lifetime of devotion to art that will almost certainly bring obscurity."

Leon unrolled the paper and found himself staring at the sketch he'd made of Tara. It was so *her*. It hurt him to look at it. "Would you like to come in?" he asked.

"No, thank you, I—" She was looking past him. "Isn't

that Nicky's daffodil picture?"

Leon ushered her into the living room. "Yes. I bought it at A IS A."

She stood pensively before the painting. "I'm going to miss him terribly," she said quietly. "Oh!" She was looking at one of the photos hanging next to it. Then she looked up at Leon with an expression of such profound sadness that her eyes could not hide it. "*Spring Flower*?"

"Yes."

Dorina dropped her gaze to the sketch that Leon still held open in his hands. Then she stared back at the photo. She turned to Leon. "Do your hands remember how to sculpt, too?"

"I don't know."

"What are you afraid of, Leon?" She blanched. "I'm sorry! I had no right to ask that." She headed for the door. "I'll leave. Here, your doorman asked me to bring this up to you. Someone evidently dropped it off." She handed him a large square package wrapped in gift paper. In the hallway again, she turned back to him and smiled. "Leon. Because of what you did for Nicky, my door will always be open to you. Happy New Year, Leon." Then she was gone.

Leon walked back to the photo of *Spring Flower* and stood before it. Then he looked down again at the sketch in his hand. Tara.

FORTY

TARA.
Dimitrios checked his watch for the tenth time in ten minutes. The TV monitor before him still blinked numbers that confirmed her plane would be on time. But had *he* been on time? Tara had not communicated with him since their return from Turkey two weeks—two centuries—ago. He'd told her not to contact him. "When you come off that plane, I'll know," he had said to her. "In the cold light of morning." He hadn't slept through a night since.

A woman standing at a check-in counter was breast-feeding her infant. The man next to her, presumably the child's father, devoured a souvlaki sandwich wrapped in waxed paper. It was the Greek way, he thought: If you are hungry, eat. If you are thirsty, drink. If you are human, think. American rock music blared from the loud speakers, but blessedly, the airport at this season was free from too many tourists. Foreigners came to Greece for the Easter holidays, not for New Year's Day.

The new terminal, twenty-five kilometers outside Athens, related in no manner to any ancient Greek heritage. Dimitrios had hurried in and out of this ultra modern airport only a few times since it was built, this was the first he'd ever had a spare moment to really look at it. And at the people in it. Yes, a certain pride was reflected in the stance of every Greek citizen, including the family he observed behaving so naturally at the ticket counter, but if he were to be ruthlessly truthful, it was only reflected pride, the pride of past glory. Yes, a kind of joy beamed from every Greek eye, but it, too, was a legacy, an ancient understanding in the appreciation of the "now" in each passing moment. Yes, there was individuality, but— No. He sat down at last. What was the use of depressing himself with negative observations? Modern Greece rose only marginally above the level of a third-world country. Whatever survived, in substance, of its ancient achievements now resided not in Greece, but in America, a brilliant but increasingly irresponsible offspring. It was understandable that Tara had chosen to make her life in Athens, the home of her philosophical idols. Because there was no possibility of a renewal of the ancient spirit in modern Greece, it was easy to bury oneself in a preservation of its past. In America, one would have to live with the chronic frustration of hope. Greece and America, Dimitrios thought, forever locked together, willingly or not, by a bond stronger than blood: philosophical fiber. America carried the torch, now, but Greece had set the flame.

A flower woman passed by with a basket full of star jasmine. He bought one perfect blossom and held it to his nose, breathing in deeper scents: the fragrance of her sheets, the sweet smells beneath her breasts. He glanced at the monitor again. His answer was moments away. Was she still his? Had she ever really been? Even for those few stolen days? He had driven from his house to Sounion at daybreak. The rock was there, waiting: "To the woman I shall love, I pledge the man I will have become." Would Tara ever read that vow?

He had asked her to give Leon Skillman a final chance, because he could accept nothing but her complete love. Had that been wise? What had happened between them? He thought of the day Leon had entered their lives, the day Tara had unearthed her athlete. How long ago? August. Five months ago. Was it possible? If Tara came home to him now, he would, in a certain way, have Leon Skillman to thank. Leon had given Dimitrios's own cowardice corporeal form. He had acted like a catalyst—Dimitrios's mind reeled. *Catalyst* or contender? Whatever else Leon had done, he had forced Dimitrios to finally stand vulnerable as a man before Tara and declare his love.

Now he was the only one of the three of them who didn't know the outcome. What would he discover in her eyes when she arrived?

"It's cold. It's light. And it's morning."

She stood in front of him. He hadn't even heard the arrival announcement.

Smiling, she took the flower from his hand and lifted it to her mouth to taste its perfume. It was the Greek way: if you are hungry, eat; if you are thirsty, drink; if you are in love, love. Dimitrios rose to greet her and drank the perfume from her breath as her lips met his.

"I love you, Dimitri. Only you."

He was nineteen. The columns of the Temple of Poseidon rose into endless blue before him, rising like his dreams. The sea—Homer's sea, his sea, Tara's sea—sang its hymn to all heroes, its soaring strains crashing against the rocks in violent salute, rising in joyous crescendo, culminating in separate chords and isolated melodies played out over a lifetime, all joining now—every note of his life—in harmony until he was left only with the sweet echo of the words he had waited more than two decades to hear: "I love you, Dimitri. Only you."

They stood quietly, looking into each other's eyes.

"Come." Dimitrios extended his hand.

"Where?"

"Sounion, to the temple."

"Why?"

"I have something to give you."

FORTY-ONE

TARA! HE'D NEVER had a headache in his life until he met her. He'd had nothing else since. He drank more champagne and paced the apartment. Against his will, an image was growing in his mind, *in his hands*. He couldn't let it complete itself.

It was a female nude, much, much more than life-size. She stands at the edge of the vast corporate lake set into a mountaintop in California, looking out over the Pacific Ocean, in the very spot his beaten and burned-out copper cube would have been installed. The female nude holds nothing in her hands. She stands on a curved shape of solid ground holding onto nothing but herself. Her hands lift slightly from her sides, her chin lifts proudly, and her eyes look up, as if to the promise of a sunrise. She is naked and alone, exposed to all that the heavens might rain on her, yet she stands "sovereign" (Tara's words), "free, unafraid and unashamed, both feet firmly on this earth" (Dimitrios's words). She is not carved of stone or cast in bronze, but executed in the ancient technique of copper *repoussé*, like his beloved Statue of Liberty.

The crash of the champagne bottle against glass left his reflected image cracked and jagged in the full-length mirror. In a rage, he tore off his clothes and stood naked before his broken image.

Who was he? How had he arrived at this day? In his tuxedo, he was the successful, famous, fawned-over celebrity artist about to retire in a frenzy of media fanfare. Naked, he was a tortured, broken remnant of a man. Leon's headache raged on in perfect concert with his tumultuous thoughts. Tara had decided that the inside didn't mirror the outside. In the workroom where they had loved for the first time—so long ago!—he had flipped the Socrates answer to her quote challenge strictly for the purpose of impressing her. For him, his keen classical memory had been no more than intellectual gamesmanship used as sex play; for her the significance of the words to which she alluded was that of spiritual essence: "... give me beauty in the inward soul; and may the outward and inward man be at one."

He was so utterly unhappy. Admit it! He had never experienced one moment's joy as an adult except with Tara. And in the end he had created neither the art nor the man she could love. Art and sex: he had lost her by betraying both of her most sacred values.

Fleetingly, he saw a threatening expression flash into his reflected image that he didn't want to see. He had glimpsed this furtive expression in his eyes before: first in Palm Beach and again at Adria's. With supreme effort, he now confronted it. He kept looking.

Stop.

A word came to his mind: "CROSSPOINT."

Kostas's generous smile bid him welcome to the thought. And Tara's words: *"There are so many opportunities in life. We all have so many chances. We can change our direction at any time. It's never too late as long as we're still alive."*

Then he saw clearly, for the first time, his own guilt. It wasn't *Tara's* most sacred values he had betrayed.

He started to turn away from the mirror. No, keep looking. Do it. Now!

He felt it rising in him then, like an actual physical force. It filled his chest and stung his eyes as if it were pushing its presence slowly but steadily into his consciousness. It was amazing, the simplicity and inevitability of it all, once he opened the passage for the truth to reach him.

But could he bear what he now saw? He shook his head slowly from side to side in denial, knowing at the same time that it was too late to deny anything.

It was more than even his own values that he had betrayed. It was his very nature. The very thing that made him human: His soul.

He had thrown his vision to the bottom of a river in order to accept the false notion that ideals are not practical in real life. Now he understood: One didn't need to *be* a hero or a goddess, only to strive for the hero or the goddess within oneself. Our visions of the ideal inspire us with the values toward which we journey. And the journey is all.

He walked slowly back to the kitchen and picked up the package Dorina had brought up to him, guessing, now, who must have left it for him. Gingerly, he carried the box to the dining room table. He couldn't bring himself to open it; he didn't deserve the contents now.

He had created from his own defiled soul the distorted shapes and dead spirits of his past art. He had played God as a cynical jokester and given the world only the contorted shapes of Hell. Someday, he might be able to think of that work with indifference, but at this moment the mere thought of it next to what he *could* have done brought unspeakable horror to his mind.

He unwrapped the paper and found two boxes, one on top of the other. The first was the one he himself had closed fifteen years ago. Inside lay the handmade tools with which he had sculpted *Spring Flower*.

"My dearest Leon," the card read. "*The Promise* can be found because it is in *you*. Happy New Year. Love, Mother."

He stared at the gift that his dear mother had placed

beside his dinner plate when he was nine-years old.

Could he? If he gave physical form to the image he now saw in his mind, the corporation would have to accept it. His contract gave him *carte blanche*. Van and the other critics would have to review it; his name was too prominent to ignore. Could he? Was it too late? He'd have a great deal of technical relearning to do if he were to project this new vision. It had been so many years.

But Dorina had said that her door was open to him. Did that mean she might help him with such a monumental task? And could he live up to her expectations? Or to his own?

If he could, might it bring *Tara* back to him someday? She had said she would be his friend. If he began to make art she could love, could he make himself into the man she could love? Perhaps Dimitrios deserved Tara now, but life was long and Tara and he were young.

No. Even if what he dreamed of with her could happen, he must not do it for her. She would be the first to warn that he must never do it for anyone other than himself.

He picked up a tool he had not held for more than a dozen years. Could he? *Did* his hands remember?

He looked into the living room at *Spring Flower* in the photo with the Empire State Building. He looked back out the window at the real Empire State Building, its skeleton constructed of many I-beams—beams just like the one he had turned into a joke called *Eternity*—here an inspired edifice, a skyscraper that reached for, that "scraped" the sky outside his window, a structure that had become a symbolic monument to the *idea* of reaching. Reaching for heights, reaching for truth, reaching for beauty, achieving it, and reaching higher still, floor on top of floor, as if standing time after time on its own shoulders to see new vistas and higher goals.

He opened the second box. The smell of clay sent him

reeling, like touching again the flesh of a lover you thought you had lost. The form of the female nude appeared again at the edge of his mind, her copper skin glowing in the dawn of a rising sun. She stood free on a ledge bordering the water.

※ ※ ※

Tara. My Athena, Dimitrios thought, leaning back contentedly against a column and watching her silently. His childhood dream come true. A modern-day Praxitiles, if there were such an artist, should immortalize her as a work of sculpture.

She stood at the edge of the bluff and looked out over Homer's wine dark sea and up into the sunrise of a New Year. Her eyes were set for distance, seeking vistas only she could behold. Lifting her hands sensuously away from her hips to catch the breeze, her simple wool dress flowed softly out from behind her like sculpted drapery, while clinging closely to the front of her body like wet silk, not hiding but defining its elegant contours: a draped nude from antiquity, exquisitely contemporary. Alive. A rose-colored mist drifted up from the temperate water below and swirled into the crisp air around her, making it appear as if, down from Olympia, she had just alighted momentarily on this sacred spot to signify a victory. Her own victory. It was as if the temple were hers, as Dimitrios had always meant it to be.

No, not Athena, he mused. Nor "Tara," anymore, either. Her victory was better than both. She was *Kantara*, Goddess of the Human Spirit, aiding her heroes not in battle but in achievement. Her symbol? The tiny scales of gold to weigh men's souls. What a glorious counterpart to the Goddess of Wisdom: a Goddess of Excellence, born not from the head of her father god but from her own mind. Her heroes no longer waited for her at the bottom of the ocean as treasures in bronze, nor any longer were they sought on land in the flesh of a single man. She had finally learned that her heroes were within her; they were her essence. She could celebrate herself in ecstasy with her lover to be sure. But now she understood that she was, as every woman must be in advance of choosing another to match her, her own true heroine. Her gods had been the outward manifestation of the goddess within her. That's part of what he had been trying to tell her in Istanbul, why he admired and loved her so completely. But because she had made the crucial mistake of confusing her personal identity with her sexual being, she had gone astray on her quest, searching for the ideal in another that already resided within her. Now, at last, she belonged to herself. She would possess dreams, but dreams would never again possess her. Today—it was apparent in her feminine but proud stance, in the soft but secure serenity of her mouth—she had reached the vanishing point merging womanhood and personhood, blending the two into one whole. Dimitrios smiled.

Tara felt the wind sweeping her hair smoothly away from her face, caressing her cheeks with a healing touch as if it were a blessing, an outward manifestation of her new composure felt deep within. Reveling in the distance she had come, up from Poseidon's sea to his temple, a plateau of self-actualization, she breathed in the pure air of the future. The whole world was open and inviting to her now. She looked out to the far horizon, up to the rising sun, and felt herself rising with it—rising, rising to all that is possible.

※ ※ ※

Leon's hands began to work the clay. They remembered. It had always been in his hands: his talent, his visions, his dreams. He felt the life in the clay that would soon become his maquette, his small sketch of the over-life-size sculpture he envisioned.

The first day of the year and the *first* day of a career.

Tara. How he loved her! How he always would. But it didn't matter that he no longer held her in his arms or in his bed. She, the ideal, was back in his *mind*.

He could!

Yes, it would be Tara, because he wanted to immortalize every spark of her courage, every line of her body, every breath of her soul. But it would be more: In some strange way it would also be a female mirror image of himself, of his own conquest at this very moment, as he now stood molding the figure, knowing here and now that he could do it, that he could put into action his thoughts born anew.

He would call her "*Victory*." In Tara's *L'Ancienne* article, she had talked about male Greek gods as "Apollos." So the females had been thought of as "Victories," because so many of them were: Nike, the messenger from the gods who, touching her foot upon the prow of a navy vessel as the "*Nike of Samothrace*" or descending from Olympia on a cluster of clouds as the "*Nike of Paionios*," blesses and grants the victory.

His admiration for all things Classical came streaming back into his consciousness, into his hands. Not self-loathing, but self-love. Not shame, but pride. Not worship of irrationality, but allegiance to reason. Not Adria, but Dorina. And always, Tara.

Beneath his hands, the figure began to emerge and take on a life of its own. He gave free reign again to the young hands of his boyhood that had always seemed to presage the shape he would sculpt before his mind could catch up.

He saw one of his hands turn one of hers, *Victory's*, open just slightly, toward the future, to give and to receive both. He brushed a fingernail across her eyes to widen them with the wonder of what she saw before her as she gazed up into the sunrise of a new day. He lifted a hip slightly, just enough to thrust the opposite shoulder forward and give drama and energy to her torso, so she appeared not moving but able to move. He lifted one heel to raise it away from the other, steady her foot and create a stance full of stability, but poised for motion, dramatizing that fragile yet empowered moment between thought and action.

He saw his hands begin to add a softly swirling drapery around the nude body of his *Victory*, not to cover her form but to accentuate it, as if the fabric, like her hair, were being swept away from her body ever so gently by a faint wind. And then, to his own stunned amazement, he watched as he added the brilliant touch: wings dropping to the ground!

Yes. This would be a *Wingless Victory*, a contemporary version of the one Dimitrios had described from the original Parthenon. Victory on earth! A victory possible in the real life of every man and woman as the supreme triumph of the self, of rising to one's highest capacities by one's rational choices, of becoming one's own best self by one's own will. An inner victory.

Beneath his heroine's feet, on the curved base that was the world, he scribed the outline of America, so that this single figure would be understood to be a symbol for a whole nation standing on the brink of an aesthetic and philosophic sea change—as the Greeks had once done—with a new opportunity and renewed commitment to fulfill its original promise.

To the joy of it all!

The window framed Leon's lithe athletic nude body: a living, breathing, contemporary version of the ancient bronze that Tara had rescued and brought back to the world, as she had brought *him* back to the world. The circle was complete.

Leon looked inward to the future, believing in himself at last.

BVG